ELIZABETH SIMS STARTER PACK

GET FREE STUFF TO READ!

Sign up for my no-spam newschat and get three exclusive pieces of my work:
a novelette, a brief on writing convincing characters, and a personal essay about
being a Midwestern writer,
all for free, as a thank-you.
Details are at the end of this book.

BOOKS BY ELIZABETH SIMS

You've Got a Book in You:
A Stress-Free Guide to Writing the Book of Your Dreams

The Rita Farmer Mysteries

The Actress

The Extra

On Location

The Lillian Byrd Crime Series

Holy Hell

Damn Straight

Lucky Stiff

Easy Street

Left Field

Tight Race

Other fiction

Crimes in a Second Language

I am Calico Jones: Four Short Stories

Go-Go Day: Four Literary Tales with a Dash of **DARK**

PRAISE

"At last, a main character I can truly relate to! I loved how Bambi acknowledges her criminal, irresponsible past self and doesn't make excuses. Everything in this book feels authentic, from the wintry Michigan landscape, to the people Bambi meets in Detroit, to Bambi's own wit, her flaws, her heart. I also loved how she works with old connections, knowing she can't go it alone."

—Certified Reviewer

Down to the D

Bambi Pentecost Crime Novel #1

Elizabeth Sims

Spruce Park Press

CONTENTS

CHAPTER 1

SO FROTHY AND FLIMSY

I almost drop the last vial because my arms are super tired from the repetitive movements. But I cap it, snug it into the corner spot, then wave my hand in a cross shape over the rack. "I bless thee in the name of the father, the son, and the holy mother, amen." Holy mother is wrong, for sure, but I never got around to looking up the right way to say the sign of the cross. Close enough.

"What are you doing? What did you just do?" This would be my boss, Jimmy, coming up from behind. He walks quietly in his foam-pillow sneakers, cruising all around the warehouse in patterns only he knows, like a giant Roomba.

"Blessing the holy water."

He stares at me like I told him I made a pipe bomb and was planning to send it to the Pope.

"That's wrong. Only priests can bless things, *especially* holy water."

"It's just that, you know, Jimmy, it says on the label it's been blessed, which is how come they're buying it at a markup. And it's not even from the reverential headwaters of Tahquamenon Falls, though we could certainly go and capture water from there so the label would be true as far as that. You're the closest thing to a priest around here, because you're at least mildly Catholic, but I haven't seen you even try to bless this water. So I've taken it upon myself."

1

"Your blessing isn't real!" Jimmy pushes up his glasses, and I push up mine. He goes on, "It's worse than not real, it's like …" Jimmy can't explain what he means, but I get the point: like I'm somehow contaminating the water, making it the reverse of holy.

"A blessing from me is better than nothing," I tell him defensively. And it doesn't increase the cost of your raw materials."

Jimmy's business is selling wholesale Catholic items to gift shops and churches. A strange ethical mix lived inside Jimmy. It was OK to sell non-blessed items as blessed, but now it's not OK for a non-priest to say a blessing over them. I guess the line must be drawn somewhere. I'm but a lowly part-time employee, working four or five mornings per week.

You'd be surprised how many Catholic gift shops there are in the North country. Jimmy pays regular visits to the shops in the Upper Peninsula, hauling wholesale orders in his van, but we sell a lot of the goods online as well. Those orders go all over the place. It's easy to sell stuff online. All you have to do is write up a description that digs at people's wants and worries.

A troubled heart can find peace through this cherished medallion of St. Joseph. Beautifully enameled in red and gold, this medallion is designed to be worn next to the heart, where the quality will be a constant reminder of the love and work ethic of the father of Jesus. Bring St. Joseph into your life and see what happens!

Pricing is less important, if you've got an alluring description. Mostly Jimmy wrote the descriptions, but I tried my hand at a few (such as above), which Jimmy said were halfway decent. Plus I took pictures, which he didn't have enough of before. The labor pool in Balsam Ridge, Michigan is pretty skimpy.

Jimmy goes to church every Sunday, doesn't swear, and donates his t-shirts to charity just before they get completely ratty.

We carry about two hundred different shelf-keeping units, which means items, of dashboard Christs and Marys, rosaries, prayer cards, candles, and thousands of vials of holy water "from the crystal pure reverential headwaters of Tahquamenon Falls and blessed by humble parish priests of the North Country." Each vial holds two ounces, which I fill with tap water plus a dash of rubbing alcohol, so they're less likely to freeze while en route anywhere in the winter. I pack them into shipping racks, which hold 144 bottles each. One rack goes for $199. A store can sell each vial for anything they can get for it, say between $5 and $10. If you sell all 144 for $7.50 each, you get $1,080, which gives you a whopping profit. The warehouse is just this steel building on the outskirts of town. Concrete floor, steel shelving. Not too big, so the heaters are able to keep the temperature in the high 60s in the winter.

"How long have you been doing this?" Jimmy wants to know.

"Blessing stuff? Oh, I don't know. A few weeks." I'd started on the job four months ago, in mid-September. Now we're past New Year's and the whole Upper Peninsula is frozen solid, therefore all anybody can think of is the spring thaw, grim months away. I boost myself onto the worktable.

Jimmy's business casual outfit this day is a Metallica t-shirt and knee-length jorts. When the temperatures are this cold, near zero today, he pulls on an insulated onesie before going outside.

"Impersonating a priest is a mortal sin, Bambi."

"Would you please try to call me BB?"

"I could fire you for this. Probably *should* fire you." He looks around as if nervous that God is watching us through binoculars.

I know Jimmy won't fire me, because he gets too many jollies out of watching me work and imagining having sex with me. He isn't a bad guy, on the whole. Listen to me judging somebody else's character. Jimmy never put the moves on me, and surprisingly stuck up for me when one of the delivery guys tried to take liberties.

"I wasn't trying to convince the water I'm a priest," I go. "But fine. I won't do it anymore. I'll finish these orders before I clock out, OK?" About ten orders are lined up on the computer screen.

Jimmy turns sharply and walks away, which is his way of saying, "I'm still mad, but carry on!"

Of *course* I'll continue to bless the holy water. Just gotta do it a little more quiet-like.

You'd think post-Christmas business would be slow, but actually as soon as New Year's hits, the religious-supplies business is a good one to be in. Why? Because people make New Year's resolutions like exercising and quitting smoking. Those are hard resolutions to keep, so you need extra help in the form of holy items. You put a Mary figurine next to your running shoes, for instance, and it's like she's cheering for you to put them on and go out. And if you don't, she's maybe sad, so the guilt becomes a motivator. Guilt never works for me, though, just speaking for myself.

Sometimes Jimmy and I eat our lunches together, but I'm not feeling it at the moment. I catch him peering at me from across the warehouse as I tape up and stack the outgoing boxes. He always made the post-office run late in the day after the UPS guy came.

At noon my shift is done. I get my purse and lunch box, and take off in my taxi towards St. Ignace. The highway was plowed two days ago after the last blizzard. My ruby red Lincoln Continental, which I'd scored cheap at an auction in Marquette last year, is handling great. Six years old, it is now. The transmission was shot when I bought it, but my brother, Bing, rebuilt it and only asked me to pay for parts. He's a professional mechanic. Then he fitted it with a moderate lift kit, and finally installed the biggest and best winter tires I could afford. It's been a fabulous car. But for the long wheelbase, I could go off-road in it no trouble. Gas mileage is lousy, but I can cram four big guys and their bags into it.

I pull over at the waterfront and switch on the mini propane heater I keep in the passenger footwell. Those things are made for deer blinds and ice shanties, did you know that? They run on the little one-pound propane canisters you can buy anywhere, and it's a catalytic burner, which therefore somehow you don't die if you're in a compact space with one.

I eat my peanut-butter-and-banana sandwich in comfort while listening to the radio and gazing out at the white winter ice stacking itself in huge shards against the shoreline, ahead of a strangely penetrating northeast wind. The cold today, two below zero, is the kind of cold that makes the hairs inside your nose crinkle. It can get much colder here, but two below is enough. The trees are black against the white sky. When you walk the shoreline when that ice is pushing in, you hear the creaking which sometimes turns slightly musical, like somebody rubbing a screwdriver on an empty oil drum. I pour hot tea from my steel bottle. A peanut-butter-and-banana sandwich along with some nice black tea will keep you going for hours.

I wish Jimmy would call me BB. I want everybody to call me BB, because I super hate my first name. Bambi. So frothy and flimsy. As you may know, it's short for bambino or bambina. Baby. And of course we have the famous Bambi movie of Disney. So hokey. BB sounds like I might have an interesting past. Which I do, boy howdy.

Why did my mother name me Bambi? I found out when I was eleven, having gotten caught shoplifting three lipsticks from the drugstore. When I stupidly tried to lie my way out of it, my mom sat down on the back stairs and cried into her apron. I stood staring at her. She looked up at me and said, "I named you Bambi because you were so tiny and innocent, and I thought you would always stay that way. I just felt that. But see what you've become. A thieving slut. Nothing but a thieving little slut. Bambi. Bambi. I should have named you Jezebel." Her thin shoulders shook, and she seemed to fold in on herself, like an Italian movie star in a tragic scene.

"Jezebel," I repeated to my reflection in the bathroom mirror that night. "Jezebel." I thought it was a pretty good name. Jazzy, bell, jagged, cool. Totally better than Bambi. I was lumpy and homely and needed glasses, but nobody knew that yet because the school did eye tests in seventh grade and I was only in fifth.

Our last name is Pentecost, which is serious and different. I looked it up one time, and it seems it was given to people who were born around Pentecost in someplace like England. Pentecost is a complicated zone of days from olden Hebrew times. Our family didn't go to church, though. I learned who the Biblical

Jezebel was via a schoolteacher who spewed random facts when he discussed books with us.

In spite of that little tiff with Jimmy, I feel pretty good about my life at this point. I'm three years out of jail, almost out of debt, and fully out of Detroit. Back home in the north. My one-bedroom apartment in Balsam Ridge is free of roaches and bedbugs, has decent food in the cupboard, and that is pah-lenty for now. I'm supporting myself. Lots of pieces of my life still need work. But food in the bitchin' cupboard.

Balsam Ridge is roughly halfway between St. Ignace and Sault Ste. Marie, the two big cities in the eastern Upper Peninsula. Big cities, I say in an ironic way, as everybody knows the combined population of both places wouldn't fill up the main ballpark in Detroit. There are rural people around here who've never been to either town, though, because they consider St. Ignace and the Soo to be as confusing and dangerous as the Casbah. Which I saw in an old movie and would hesitate to visit.

People call the Upper Peninsula the UP for short. You say each letter, not 'up.' This gives rise to the silly term 'yoopers,' meaning people who live here. I don't know why I hate that word so much.

It's always extra bright in the winter if the sun's behind only thin clouds, which it is today. After finishing my lunch, I flip down my sunglasses and set off for the Kewadin casino to see if anybody wants a ride to the airfield or the Soo. This is the slackest time of year for my business, because of the shortage of tourists coming and going to Mackinac Island and everyplace else. When I'm not fooling around with religious trinkets, I run a one-woman taxi and tour service called Jaunty Taxi. Figuring that it's nicer to call a taxi trip a jaunt, I used that word, plus then the 'y' at the end makes it sound like even a little more fun. I try to project a sense of jauntiness when I drive and talk to customers. I ordered a couple of those magnetic panels to put on each side, with *Jaunty Taxi* and my phone number on them. Next ones I get, I'll put my website on too. It's just basic at this point.

People sometimes ask me why I don't drive for the phone-app services. The answer is, I prefer to run my own show, plus when I do tours such as to the falls or the locks, I can easily set and advertise my own prices.

As I'm nearing the casino my phone rings, and it being a Detroit area code, I almost ignore it, as I'd been getting so many spam calls. But I pick up, because whatever, and it's a guy named Ethan.

CHAPTER 2

NOW OR NEVER

"I was Gordy's AA sponsor," Ethan says. "Do you remember me? We met once or twice, you and I."

"Oh! Yeah. What happened?"

He stops for a minute, as if wondering why I would say that. But not being born yesterday, I know instantly there must be trouble behind some guy calling me about Gordy, who never reaches out to me unless he's in trouble. And if he's in whatever condition that he can't even call me himself, but has to get somebody else to do it, I'd say there must be trouble of a bad kind.

This being totally apart from the fact that if you're calling *me* for help, you are scraping the bottom of your sorry barrel.

"He's in jail," says Ethan.

"For what now?"

"Murder."

"Wait, what?" I wrench the car into the casino lot and throw it into park. *"What?"*

Gordy and I got married almost 20 years ago, produced our daughter Laura immediately, then split up when we both got busted in Detroit for drug possession. Solicitation was in there for me as well. So now you know. Laura was four.

She went into the foster system until she was fourteen, when Gordy retrieved her by getting somewhat clean and convincing a judge. I was nowhere to be found.

Is it any wonder I turned out to be a hooker? I mean, what would you expect of someone named Bambi? A hooker or a porn star. I never had the bazongas to go far in porn, though, well, there are a few audition tapes out there.

Ethan says, "He came home to his house last night and found a dead girl, evidently."

"What girl?!"

"Not you guys' daughter," Ethan says hurriedly. "His girlfriend."

"Are you talking about that Sandy person?"

"Sandy O'Rourke. Yeah."

"I thought they broke up."

"I don't know."

"So she's dead? In his house? Did he kill her? Holy mother."

"Bambi, I don't know. It looks bad."

"What do you mean?"

Ethan sighs. "From what I've heard, Sandy was found *in* Gordy's house, stabbed, like more than once, blood everywhere, and Gordy can't prove he wasn't there. And they have fingerprints, I guess, and maybe other incriminating stuff."

You know how when you get shocking news, normal life changes? It changes instantly. Like I was staring out my windshield, but I didn't know what I was looking at. There could be a sudden Irish ballet show in front of my eyes and I wouldn't know it. I think your vision somewhat shuts down because of how much else is going on in your brain.

Last I knew, Gordy was renting a crumbling mansion in Boston-Edison. I love calling it a crumbling mansion. Boston-Edison's one of the old historic districts of Detroit, which used to be rundown, but now lots of the grand houses are renovated and nice. Gordy's landlord evidently wasn't interested in selling or fixing up the place, though, and the rent was some insanely low amount like $800 a month for a six-bedroom house. Granted, it had a leaky roof, moldy plaster, and probably rats and roaches, but still. Gordy was reportedly making good money working as a sysadmin, whatever that is, for some financial company. I kept expecting him to move into a nice apartment or even buy a house for himself.

"Well, who reported it?" I ask. "I mean, if he—"

"I don't know, Bambi. I can't imagine Gordy murdering anybody. He's such a gentle soul."

If I'd still been drinking my tea, I would have spewed it all over the dashboard. Gordy's soul was about as gentle as a threshing machine.

"Do you have any idea who did it, if not him?"

"No clue at all. We didn't really hang in the same social group."

"Well, Ethan, what does Gordy want me to do?"

"I don't know. He just wanted me to call you."

Wisps of snow chase each other around the parking lot.

Gordy being in jail carries so many ramifications. "Have you talked to Laura?"

"No, no. I don't think she knows. I guess this is gonna be in the news, maybe already is. But I don't—"

"Uh-oh. OK. Do you know if he has a lawyer?"

"I hope so. I gotta go."

"Wait. Where is he?" But Ethan is gone.

Before hitting Laura's number, I sit for a minute. Apart from the shock, I have to be honest, I'm feeling a strange sense of happiness. Gordy was an absolute pig to me during our short marriage, and although both of us were drug-addled idiots, he was worse.

I finger the left side of my jaw, the place where the bone is thicker because of the fracture and subsequent surgery. He never apologized for that punch. Nor any of the others. We'd argued about something, probably a bill that didn't get paid. I flipped a slice of pizza at him, and he reached over and knocked me out of my chair. If I hadn't hit the carpet, I would have had a worse concussion. I believe he kicked me as well, but being that I was unconscious, all I had were the bruises as evidence. I do remember Laura screaming just before the pizza slice went airborne. She was about three at that point.

No, I didn't file a complaint. Neither of us wanted police coming and nosing around our cruddy apartment and maybe taking Laura away, although that did happen only a year later. Both of us were drinking and drugging, and I have to confess to some petty theft in there as well. Maybe a little more than petty.

So I'm sitting here feeling happy that Gordy is accused of murder. If he goes away to prison forever, I'll never have to deal with him again. Never argue about something involving Laura. Never have to stress about him trying to control her life, and mine, for that matter. Never have to say no to sending him a hundred dollars because he was short on rent because he lent money to a friend. Right. Never get another call from Ethan.

It is not a nice happiness.

I left him behind, along with Laura, to fend for themselves in the Detroit that had well and thoroughly shredded me.

Laura will turn 18 on April 1, which I'm anticipating with elation. College student, living on campus, working part-time, fairly well launched. No worries about Gordy keeping his commitments to her. While I admit Gordy got his act together better than I did, he was still half-assed about almost everything: can't handle money, always broke, can't figure out how to do basic stuff such as cook or change a flat.

Would he have killed this Sandy person? Stabbed her, that's what Ethan said? Why? Why not? Yeah, why the heck not?

I phone Laura. In the blighted desert of our marriage, she's been like this little drinking fountain of goodness. Pure and ice-cold. An interesting kid.

As I'm trying to think what message I'll leave her, she picks up.

"What." Her annoyed tone never changes when it comes to me. She wouldn't call me Mom. We'd been in touch in recent years, bits and pieces of phone calls, short visits. I took the initiative on these things, despite knowing there would never be a way to fix all the damage I'd done.

I tell Laura what Ethan told me, and am not surprised by her reaction. After a bunch of Oh my Gods and some quivering I can't believe its, she pulls herself more or less together and says flatly, "There's no way he could have done that. No way, Bam. There's just—no way. He's been clean and sober, he's been a *good dad.*"

She thinks she's being factual with the clean and sober part, and I can't prove otherwise. But *good dad* with emphasis was over the top, I felt. She'd started idolizing the guy when he got her away from the last foster family. He didn't hit her and fed her junk food for dinner. What kid wouldn't love a dad like that? But he was no more reliably sober than he was a cardiologist. He'd grown good at hiding it, I was sure.

"Frankly, Bam," she says in her clear, clean voice, "I could think it of *you.*"

"What!" That hurts, but she's already said worse to me before. Much worse.

"And Sandy!" says Laura. "She was a nice person! Now she's dead? Are you sure?"

"You knew her?"

"Oh, my God!" Laura shouts again. "Someone—just showed me their phone—they heard me talking—it's on the news already."

"OK, honey, try to—"

"We have to help him!"

"Listen for a second. If he didn't do it, do you have any idea who *did* it? Or could have done it? Somebody they knew, like?"

"No! I don't know. Bam, we have to *do* something. I know you hate him. But you have to—"

"I don't hate him. Come on, Laura, eh?"

"OK, OK." I hear her taking a deep breath. Then she says, "You've let me down over and over in my life, Bam."

"I know it. I'm sorry, honey."

"You've said that a thousand times. It doesn't make anything better. It doesn't change all those years I had to spend with strangers. Trying to work out my life. Trying to grow up amidst strangers. Needing my first bra. Getting my first period."

"No, it doesn't change anything you went through. All that stuff was beyond sucking."

She doesn't say anything. When you agree with people, it sometimes brings them up short. Besides, she'd laid all this on me before, several times. Although her words cut my heart, I have no right to feel sorry for myself.

"For whatever it's worth, honey, I love you."

"Hard for me to believe that."

"I'm entitled to nothing from you. I know I was a terrible mom."

"You weren't even a mom."

Man, she was sticking it to me. I defend myself slightly. "Well, I was, a little bit."

"Ugh. You pushed me out from your vagina. What else did you do for me? We never did the things moms and daughters are supposed to do! All I wanted was to cuddle up with you on the couch and eat popcorn and watch scary movies!"

When she was too young to be able to say how she felt about me, she'd just stare at me and cry. But now at age 17 she's as articulate as a redneck preacher. It feels like she's laying the groundwork for something. A quick thinker, Laura.

I appreciate that she likes scary movies instead of rom-coms, which are so boring.

I say nothing about the money I've been sending to her dad for her benefit, nor the greeting cards I've written to her over the years. I'd been gifted a multi-pack of Gwen Frostic notepapers and thought they were pretty, so I used them to write little greetings and hellos to Laura. Sometimes I'd enclose some bit of money, a five or a ten if I had it. Gwen Frostic was a Michigander who grew up with a disability where she couldn't walk right. She was a badass woman who figured out how to support herself by drawing birds and plants, printing them on nice papers, and selling them. I thought the drawings were beautiful. Delicate and quiet-like. Gwen built up a significant business. I never knew whether Laura even opened the notecards. She never mentioned them.

The cumulative nice things I did for Laura could never possibly outweigh the hippopotamus of the bad. I accepted that long ago. Still, I hoped that one day she at least wouldn't despise me. The grievances would somehow recede, and we could do things like go shopping or hang out with ginger ales and a bucket of hot wings. Watch a scary movie with popcorn.

She says, "If you love me, you'll help Dad."

So. There was the bargain. Right plain. *Show me your love. How much do you love me?*

I've never played detective before, but what the hey. "Let me see what I can find out," I tell her. "Just go home today and try to clear your mind. Maybe something will come to you."

"Now or never, Bam." The connection goes dead.

Staring into the icy whiteness, I picture my child. Her face is so thoughtful, her body strong and solid, having made it through puberty quite successfully. She liked to dress square, as I would call it. Jeans and sweaters, skirts that actually cover her butt. No jewelry, which I find odd. Just a little lip gloss, pink. She liked things plain.

Laura still acted a kid, always ready to take stairs two at a time, throw back her head and laugh hard at some little joke, grasping out with her hand as if to keep from falling over. I don't know how she kept that enthusiasm for life while in the foster system. She once told me she didn't have it as bad as some other kids she knew. Still, that's grim. That's grim.

CHAPTER 3

I WATER MY PHILODENDRON

I pick up a fare at the casino and get him to the Sault Ste. Marie airport in time for his 3:15 to Thunder Bay. Wait around for a few minutes to see if anybody getting off the inbound needs a ride, but they don't.

Back at my apartment in Balsam Ridge, I water my philodendron, the upkeep of which is a sign of a responsible homeowner, then grab my laundry and haul it down to the row of Speed Queens in the basement. As I sort my clothes on the chipped enamel table some tenant left behind, I give some more thought to the Gordy situation.

I don't like to beat around the bush with anybody, and recently I'd tapered off doing it with myself.

Well, Bambi girl, you're on the brink of a decision here, right?

I so, so don't want to do this.

Why not leave it open-ended for now?

That's a thought.

Gordy going off to prison would bring more simplicity to my life. Fine. But if I didn't at least pretend to help him, I'd lose a real good chance to gain traction with Laura.

Nothing's ever simple.

I toss my clothes into the machines, one light load, one dark, one towels and bedsheets. Throw in some soap powder and resentfully insert six quarters each in the hungry coin slides. I love the smell of powdered Tide. I shove in the coin slides, my money disappears, and the machines start their hissing and clunking.

All those quarters every week, plus 75 cents per load for the dryers. I double up on the dryers, though, so my weekly outlay amounts to six dollars. People compare everything to how much a latte costs. I wouldn't drink a latte for free. The word just bugs me. Lattay.

But so if you multiply $6 times 52 weeks in a year, you get $312. Now that's serious money. Plus sometimes I wash my blankets and whatever else extra loads.

My old street pals would call me stupid for paying. But today's machines won't work if you put slugs in, and if you simply break open the coin chamber, the landlord will put a camera in the laundry room. The greater point is, I'm trying not to be a cheater anymore.

My own house would have a washer and a dryer, which I would buy on special at the Home Depot in Petoskey. You can get good deals on floor models. They'd pay for themselves in a few years.

I've always been good at numbers.

But you can't always fall back on numbers.

I'm very interested in having my own house. Not a rental.

For the entire wash and dry cycles, I sit in that cold basement under the dual low-watt bulbs the landlord saw fit to bestow upon us. I didn't bring a book or my phone because I have to work this out. I did shove my small notebook and a pen in my back pocket.

I keep going over the same basic question I started with, which was should I get involved in Gordy's life to the extent that this seemed? I write that down.

This wasn't wash day, I forgot to mention. I do my wash on Saturday mornings, because everybody else in the building, like 30 people, sleeps in, either from Friday-night hangovers or regular exhaustion from work. But this is Wednesday.

I didn't even realize why I got my wash going at first, but there it was: some piece of my brain knew what I was going to do before I did.

When I was using, I hardly thought about Laura. That is, thinking about her was so painful I blocked her out. There was a period of time when I even tried to tell myself she was dead, so I didn't have to feel guilty about not being in her life. That was low.

If it was a matter of splitting the difference, if Laura didn't exist, I wouldn't bother helping Gordy at all.

But so here I am now, thinking of my ex's troubles totally selfishly: how can this situation help me? I write that down. I keep writing.

Do I crave Laura's esteem that bad?

Yes, I do.

Any idea of how to exonerate someone from a murder charge?

No.

Fake it 'til I make it?

I've lived most of my life by that motto, not that I'm proud.

Start where?

One thing about being a repeat criminal is you get to know the police. A few of them rather well. It can go that way.

Back upstairs I turn on lamps, because after 5:30 in mid-January, black night is coming on. I fold up my stuff and put it away, then call a guy.

"Alvarez."

"Ted, hi. It's Bambi Pentecost. I'm going by BB these days."

"Bambi. Huh." Long pause. "Been a while, huh?"

"Yeah, about two years."

"Huh." His voice goes chilly. "Wasn't sure I'd ever hear from you again."

"It'd be better for you if you didn't, believe me. Look, I've got a problem."

"Back on the junk again?"

One more thing. I was a narcotics informant for a while. After the second time I was busted for possession, I agreed to be what they call a CI, confidential informant. Ted Alvarez, a detective in the narcotics division of the Detroit Police Department, was my contact. They give you a lighter rap, or maybe let you off entirely, if you agree to give them information about the other druggies, hopefully dealers. They love to get dealers, naturally. So on top of everything else, I was a rat. I know that's a lot to absorb.

"No, Ted, actually, I've stayed off it." Primarily, I liked downers in those old days, so benzos, Vicodin. Besides the vodka. A little cocaine if I needed to pull myself together for something important. "Two and a half years semi clean, one year really clean. I'm back in Balsam Ridge, in the UP. I have a job and a driver's license. And an apartment."

"Impressive."

"Listen, this is about Gordy."

"Of course it is," he says bitingly.

"Are you familiar with what happened yesterday?"

"Not very. He's in custody. I'm not involved with the case, but I did take note of a white-on-white murder." So he already figures Gordy did it.

"I'm just gonna put all my cards out. Gordy's and my daughter thinks he's innocent, plus so does his AA buddy, so—"

"You want me to go unlock his cell and turn away for a minute?"

"Don't be a butthead, Ted. I didn't think you'd be a butthead." My language used to be extremely raw, but I was trying to clean that up too. So I called him a butthead instead of a different term. "I'm just wondering if you can find anything out, you know, like what kind of evidence there is. If there's anything unusual, you know? I don't know. Like is he the only suspect?"

"You know it's against the rules for me to tell you anything."

"That's why I'm calling you on your personal cell. After five." I don't say, dude, like the rules have ever been a big deal for you? Trying to be polite here. "Plus are you still in narcotics?"

"Yeah."

"I myself am questioning this thing, Ted, honestly. Gordy and I have a bad past, to say the least, but he was supposed to've been broken up from that Sandy person, and b) I just can't think of him murdering anybody."

"Even though he broke your face with his fist?"

"That happened when he was drunk. I was drunk. He got clean, eventually, more or less, you know that. He took care of Laura for a while. Our daughter."

"I'm not even in homicide, so—"

"You don't want to help me here?"

"Frankly, no, Bambi."

"In that case, I have just one word to say to you at this point, and that word would be Darlene."

Silence.

I was banking on the fact he still cared about his marriage.

A coffee-slurp sound breaks the silence, but still he doesn't speak.

After a moment he swallows and says, "You would talk to her about us?"

"If I felt I had to."

"I'd deny everything."

"You could. But I think I'd be pretty convincing." He has a tattoo of a squirrel on his butt, for one thing. You can ask, but I really have no idea.

"Ted," I go, "how much skin off your nose is it for you to just give me a little bit of information?" I have too much dignity to offer him a blow job per interesting fact. To be clear, I'd sworn off hooking, which included even informal use of my body to gain a deal.

He sighs. "You know about Vic Paladino?"

"No, what about him? I didn't even know he was still alive."

"With most of his hair intact. Sandy O'Rourke was seeing him. She was his current girlfriend, reportedly. Or one of them. I think that's hitting the news now."

"Really? So maybe Paladino did it."

Ted Alvarez laughs. "Surrounded by that traveling circus all the time?"

19

Vic Paladino was a Detroit name, big famous name from the second, or even maybe third wave of Motown prominence. White guy. The fresh hits were all a long time ago, but everyone knew Vic Paladino. Was he still giving concerts for his aging fans, still belting out his pop songs, still wearing those tight tuxedo pants?

Ted goes, "He's still got a voice, actually."

"I went to see him once, gosh, forever ago." The famous tunes come to mind: "Snowfall Dream," "Another Letter," "Six-Dollar Shoes," and his signature platinum-seller, "Rose Petal Tango."

He was a smooth-voiced son of a gun, with an appealing smile. In concert he joked and laughed between numbers, poking fun at his band, but more at himself. He said he had stage fright, and I guess he did, because lots of times his concerts would start late. I remembered people talking about that. Solid build, bulldog face, but his charisma and talent made the face cute instead of fearsome. I remembered how his thick black hair stuck out boyishly after a few numbers.

"Styles have changed, but Paladino hasn't," Ted says.

"He's losing market share, for sure." I thought that sounded savvy. "But that's the way it goes, right? My mom was crazy for him. She's dead now." The younger public goes for the young stars. All that history flowed through my mind in a couple of seconds.

"He's supposed to do a concert at Masonic in a few weeks," Ted says. "Hasn't performed live in a long time. I've noticed the ads around town."

I want Vic Paladino to have murdered Sandy O'Rourke. I speculate, "But if they actually arrested Gordy—I mean, they must have found—"

"For one thing, he admitted to handling the knife, the murder weapon. Probable cause to arrest him, for sure. It wasn't just that he didn't have a good alibi."

"What else do you know?"

"Nothing, at the moment."

"Our daughter's going to be devastated."

"Mmph."

Cops don't have huge reservoirs of empathy for people they don't know. I don't blame them.

CHAPTER 4

A WARM MUFFIN

It's about a five-hour drive from Balsam Ridge to Detroit, straight down I-75, plus stops for fuel, bathroom, and lunch. I get up early, still in pitch-dark at six o'clock. Before hitting the highway I drop off my philodendron with my friend Connie Blue Smoke, who lives in a shockingly cute cabin on a few acres near town.

Standing in her little entryway, I hand her the plant, which I grew from a cutting Connie herself gave me. I named it Alan. One day I found a shiny black flowerpot in an alley in St. Ignace, so he's in that.

"Can you stay for a cuppa coffee?" She checks her watch. "I got up early and made orange muffins. I don't have to leave for work until eight-thirty." Her place always smelled of good things to eat.

Connie's a nurse at the urgent-care clinic in town. Since forever, she was my studious friend, the one who only drank and smoked weed a little in high school, the one who actually graduated from Michigan State, fairly big deal. A quarter-blood Chippewa from the Sault tribe, she'd inherited the incredibly smooth, incredibly lustrous black hair from her father as well as a hooked nose, which looked pretty good in the long oval face from her mother's side, French-Canadians from generations back. Her black eyes turned down at the corners, and when

I first met her in grade school, I thought she was sad all the time, but she was just serious.

I go, "I'm on a mission," and tell her about Gordy.

"Oh, my God." I was to keep hearing that from people for a while. "That's terrible."

"Yes. Laura's awfully upset."

My friend shifts her voice low and grips my arm. "Bambi. I always worried something bad would happen with him."

"Well, I don't know. Would you please try calling me BB?"

"I worried about you constantly when you were in Detroit. I'm so glad you didn't stay in that marriage." She releases my arm, a thought occurring to her. "Do you realize that could have been *you*, killed there? If things were a little different? Did you realize?"

I had not.

Connie goes on, "His family's going to be so distraught. His mom's got cancer and his dad fell at work or something. None of the kids in that family amounted to anything, except him. Which I realize isn't saying much."

"Ha."

"He held down a job or two, didn't he?"

"He's making six figures now, supposedly."

"Seriously?"

I stand in her entryway, shifting from foot to foot. She cradles Alan the philodendron. I'm the only one who knows his name. It'd be silly to tell anybody I named my philodendron.

"That's too bad about his folks," I say. "If Gordy and I hadn't both been idiot addicts, we might have made a better go of it." I'm anxious to get on the road.

"I think you're kidding yourself." Connie Blue Smoke always spoke the truth. "You're going to Detroit?"

"I just want to be there for Laura. For once."

"Detroit's not a good place for you."

23

"I know. I'll be OK."

"When will you be back?"

"Couple days. I'd rather not abandon my job with Jimmy at the warehouse."

I'd already phoned him and asked for the time off. Jimmy knew Gordy. "No," he said. "I need you to work."

"OK, well, I'm going anyway."

I knew he'd take me back whenever.

Connie says, "You know, philodendrons are hardy. You could stick it in a closet for a month and it'd be fine."

"Oh, I could never do that." My gut actually clenched at the thought. "But ... good to know."

"I'll take care of it."

She wraps a warm muffin in a napkin and hands it to me. Given that today, Friday, was the 13th of the month, I decide to consider the muffin a good-luck charm. Although I'd wanted to leave for Detroit yesterday, I had a major fare lined up of a family of four that needed to get from the Soo airport to Marquette. Six-hour roundtrip, paid in advance.

"Thanks, Connie." I break off a piece and take a nibble of the sweet goodness, practically smacking my lips, which pleases her. With all her domestic skills, plus her good job in town, guys swamped her with proposals. She dated around, but it seemed marriage wasn't in the cards for her yet.

"I don't want to pick up his dirty socks," she told me once.

"Well, you could train him, you know," I said.

"Ugh."

I'm almost out the door when she says, "If there's anything I can do, call me, OK?"

"Hey." I turn back. "You know Gordy's family better than I do. Plus you've kept in touch with the rest of the high school gang. Think you could ask around, and find out if he ever brought this Sandy person up here, eh? I'm just wondering if anybody ever met her, or saw them together, or had any interaction. You know?"

"I can do that."

"I'll owe you."

"Bambi?"

"Yeah?"

"I'm ..." She stands there, lips suddenly tight.

"What?" But I know what she's thinking.

My friend shakes her head and tries to smile.

I'm scared for me too.

Chapter 5

Down to the D

O nce you get on I-75 you can set the cruise control, get comfortable, and just eat up the gas. When you're driving and the day is starting, that's nice.

The bridge is always awesome to me: the mighty Mackinac Bridge between Michigan's peninsulas. Five miles long and tall enough for the biggest ships in the world to pass under, it's painted gray, which makes it seem to materialize and dematerialize at dawn and dusk. In fog and snow, it's like this huge ghost. What a view you get when you're driving over it on a clear day: the blue water stretching away to the west, Mackinac and Bois Blanc islands off to the east. I always tune my radio to the special AM station that tells you conditions on the bridge and the approaches, plus some history about it. When the wind picks up, it's dangerous and you have to go slow. That lady that got blown off.

Mackinac looks like you should say it Mackinack, but it's properly pronounced Mackinaw, which I guess is the French way. Then there's Mackinaw City, which is spelled same as you pronounce it, which makes for confusion for new people. Someone should open a Jewish deli on the island and name it Mackinosh. People would take selfies in front of it.

After the remarkable, gorgeous experience of that bridge, the big water is behind you, and you keep going. You're on your way down the lower peninsula, all the way to the D if you want. It's cool to call Detroit "the D" these days. Probably next week it'll be uncool.

I never get tired of the Michigan landscape: woods, scrub, farms, a line of trees in the distance when you come upon a valley. The terrain is rolling and interesting. Some people think because the land isn't dramatic—it's not the Grand Tetons or something—that it's boring.

It's not boring. It's beautiful. You have to focus to see the beauty sometimes. I mean, if you're the type of person who thinks bare winter trees are ugly, then you won't appreciate Michigan. I think winter trees are as lovely as summer ones. You can see their bones. A big bare tree all by itself, like a huge oak standing in the middle of a snowy field, is just this serious presence, nothing but strength. Bare trees together look soft, though, like brown lace bunched on a silvery dress.

As I drive, I think about the young Gordy, the seventeen-year-old, a year ahead of me in school. He was a decent athlete, the best hitter on the school baseball team. His dream was to play professional ball, but he didn't have the initiative to try and get a college scholarship and make it onto a team where he might be scouted. Apart from that, he was a smartass, he was a stoner, he had this long ponytail. For a white kid the ponytail was somewhat of a rebellion, but not all that big, given that lots of the Chippewa boys wore their hair long too.

We fell in love, just a couple of oversexed teenagers. I was already putting out for guys who bought me things, and I could see a future in that. Yes. That was me, just getting going. Because my aunt Mad told me something when I was about fourteen and complaining about cramps and the whole thing, or maybe I was whining about not having enough money to buy some outfit or whatever. She said, "Honey, you're sitting on a goldmine." That stuck in my mind. Aunt Mad was the most practical person I knew at that time.

I dropped out of senior year when I got pregnant. Nobody made me drop out. I was fed up with school, and it was exciting to go off with Gordy. We got married, then Laura was born. We lived with his parents for a few months, then he got a job driving a county snowplow, the pay stubs from which helped us qualify for a runty apartment. We figured in the summer he'd work in St. Ignace, do restaurant work, or get a job on one of the Mackinac Island ferries.

As you might rightly judge, this wasn't outstanding career planning. I will say the snowplow job paid decent for back then, nine dollars an hour. But the work was only in the winter, and Gordy got hired solely because they needed a warm body behind that wheel. I shudder to remember how many times he went out in one of those massive things while blottoed on pot and beer.

I liked the woods, and thought it'd be cool to become a hunting guide, because I did know those woods. But I didn't have enough hustle in me, then.

Eventually we made our way to Detroit. It's not a bad city if you have your act together, which we didn't.

I make no excuses for myself. While Gordy filled out job applications, I tried to be a good mom by doting on Laura, fixing her hair and painting her little toddler nails in whatever wacky colors pleased her. Buying her pretty things and giving her treats. That's what I thought a good mom did. Except I also drank twenty ounces of vodka a day and did the benzos and coke as well. I was against smoking in the apartment because of her little lungs, so I toasted marijuana in a pan on the stove, then mixed it with honey or pancake syrup so Gordy and I could swallow it, smoke-free, and get high. You can't get high swallowing raw marijuana. Something about the toasting unlocks the inebriation molecules or something. That was another element of good parenting, I thought. Now you can buy legal edibles all over the place, nice tasty gummies and so on. That blows my mind.

Gordy and I managed to stay away from meth and heroin, thankfully. We took pain pills sometimes, but they scared me, seeing all the ODs all over the place. That stuff makes you feel just too good.

I always feel uneasy when nearing Detroit. For one thing, the traffic gets thicker and you have to pay more attention. More dolts going too fast and swerving around for no apparent reason. Bloody swervers. For another, you have to watch the signs because of the high number of roads. It seems the place is nothing but roads, with some buildings sprinkled in.

For another: memories. Everywhere.

I wrangled around the interchanges and got onto the ordinary streets, which are still so shockingly busy compared to any place in the UP. You drive around and you go, there's the stretch of McNichols where I used to pick up johns from the suburbs. Here's the drugstore I hauled out to in my winter coat over my nightgown when Laura had a fever at two in the morning and we had no thermometer or baby aspirin. That store's still there. Here's the bar where Gordy got into a fight and broke out some guy's teeth and then had to have injections because his knuckles got infected. The place I got stopped for speeding when I had eight grams of cocaine in a mint tin in the bottom of my purse but the cop didn't search me. The view down Woodward toward the restaurants and stores, the view that makes you happy if you have a few dollars in your pocket and depressed if you don't. There's that curve from the 94 to the 696 where at night it feels like you're in a space movie (can't explain any better). The streetcorners, too many to remember, where I scored drugs until I connected with a regular dealer. Who then became my pimp. Not a bad guy, actually. I know how that sounds. There's the free clinic on Eight Mile where I got my birth control and once, shots for VD. I pretty much insisted on guys (including Gordy, after I gave birth to Laura) using condoms, therefore somehow I never got herpes, which I dreaded more than HIV, syphilis, or the clap. I did get crotch lice once, which was not fun. They helped me with that there, too.

People say you should be thankful every day. When I think of the diseases and violent lowlifes I dodged, I do feel thankful. It's a cold feeling of dumb luck, to tell you the truth.

I keep driving. I notice a bright billboard for Vic Paladino's upcoming concert at the Masonic Temple theater like Ted Alvarez told me about. I feel reliably anonymous, driving along, having removed the magnetic Jaunty Taxi panels before I left home.

Almost all the cars in Detroit have the appearance of emerging from a disaster movie, covered with that ugly mix of road dirt and white salt powder from the trucks that lay it down when it snows. Every so often I'd spot a shiny clean car, fresh from the wash. I recently learned you can buy monthly memberships at car washes where you can go every day if you want. Imagine that.

One of the gross things around town are the plastic grocery bags that people throw away, or they get sucked out of garbage trucks, and they join the ugly trash mash that lines the streets and expressway service drives. The worst is when trees catch them high up, and there's no help for it. Come spring, at least the trees will leaf out and hide the nastiness to some extent. Nobody's going to rent a cherry-picker and take down ugly plastic bags in trees. Those bags hurt the dignity of the tree.

Due to my early start, I make it to Gordy's house, deep in the city, just as dark is falling. I don't consider staying anywhere else, in spite of the many other humans I know in town. Asking favors right off the bat is something I don't want to do. Plus most of my contacts in Detroit aren't super law-abiding, and I've been working on my life. Of course I don't have a key.

No police tape across the front door or anything. Good there.

I swing the Lincoln into the driveway like I own the place. Gordy had invited me over a few times before I moved back to the UP, to see Laura and I guess for old times' sake, so I more or less remember the layout.

The driveway hadn't been shoveled of any snow for the season so far, I judged, and if you've lived in a cold place you know exactly what that's like: snow and ice, old and new, frozen in ruts, the ice as hard as cast iron, the packed snow in between shaved smooth by whichever car's undercarriage had last been up this way.

I ease the nose of the Lincoln close to the garage, knowing better than to imagine there'd be room in there to park it. Just in case, I haul up the garage door—unlocked—to find the thing empty. I'd figured there'd be the usual junk: a bike or two, a broken refrigerator, lawn mower. Gordy could never keep track of things, never keep anything organized. His car, which he would have parked in the driveway or on the street, was gone, either stolen, or maybe impounded by the police as part of their investigation. The garage might have been cleared out by a helpful neighbor, once the police were gone. (Air quotes around that helpful neighbor.) Would the house be just as empty?

I pull my car in, lift out my backpack and tool kit, and roll the heavy garage door shut. *Boom!* I'd put my little notebook in my purse, along with a pen I got when I opened a bank account in Balsam Ridge. I dig them out and write: *buy padlock.*

The city air is cold and fresh enough. But when you look up at night in a place like this, you get almost no stars. That has always seemed incredible to me. Up north you get practically assaulted by the stars on a clear night. The Milky Way! You feel like a bug on a stump looking up at all that.

I smell burned cooking oil wafting from somewhere, but only a whiff. People's windows are closed against the cold, though some jerk down the block has loud music pouring out somehow. A heavy rock song. The singer sounds like a coyote with his leg caught in a trap.

Most everybody who lives in Detroit is a perfectly nice person. However, to be honest, a fair percentage of the population lives the same way I used to. Not necessarily murderers or rapists, but with an eye out for opportunity, always. And if you're an addict, all bets are off. You could be the church organist, but if you get hooked on something, you'll do anything. You'll steal the pipes off the organ and sell them for scrap. And then when somebody goes, hey, where's the pipes on the organ?, you're like, wow, no idea.

It is now three days since Gordy allegedly came home to find this Sandy's body. Were the police finished with all their forensic work? Could be. Probably. The longer they take, the more chance evidence will degrade or disappear. I learned that on one of the TV shows. Sometimes I read detective books too, which I pick up at the Goodwill whenever I'm in Petoskey. I suppose I'll always have a morbid taste for crime. You understand.

I take a deep breath. Suddenly I'm rethinking this whole trip. I want to help Laura, which is the main given. But what can I realistically do? The feeling of the city is already weighing on me. The bigness, the hardness. The thought of what I might find in this house. Fragments of a murder? Fragments of the killer?

I can't get all anxious. Just get on with it. One thing at a time.

The house is dark, entirely dark, including the back door area, which, fine. On the way down I wondered if the police would just leave the house as is, or if they'd have to turn it over to the landlord or some responsible person, who could be in it. I pound on the door and wait. Nothing. Pound again. Nothing.

The original glass window in the wooden door had gotten replaced with hard plexi somewhere along the line. I try the knob, locked. Sometimes old shrunken doorjambs will be loose enough to let you just force that bolt past the plate if you shake and shimmy it just right. So I rattle the knob hard, ramming my shoulder against the door, but no luck. I could break through the plexi with a rock and the screwdriver from my taxi toolkit, but I don't want to. My feeling is, don't create any more sound and damage than necessary. I've broken into places before. What haven't I done, you may ask? Well, murder and arson. Even in my blackout phases, I'm pretty sure I never did either of those. Armed robbery. Never did that. I was always more of a sneak. Plus I was lazy, so stuff like cybercrime and identity theft were too much work to learn and achieve.

The mansion is crumbling, as I've said. What does that mean, exactly? In this case, not like big pieces falling away, like a gingerbread house mice have gotten at, but everything super crummed up, like the paint coming off anything that's painted, therefore the window frames, for instance, are rotting. Gutters sagging in the middle. That's always so sad, isn't it? Moldy black stuff growing on the stonework, moss creeping up the brick. The place was made of good materials, long ago, whenever that was. The 1920s. The stones, beige stones, were put in around the doors and windows, in like wedges. It's called some style but I can't remember.

And of course poor yard care. With about four inches of snow over everything, it doesn't look so bad, but you could see the shrubs all raggedy and straws of dead weeds poking through the white.

It takes work to keep up a house, for sure. I was barely keeping up my apartment, but at least I'd had the foresight to drop off my philodendron with Connie. The thought struck me that Alan would probably be happier with Connie full-time, so he wouldn't have to always worry if I'd forget to water him. Maybe I should have kept the philodendron with me. How heartless to leave it behind. But what's done is done. Do they make car seats for philodendrons?

CHAPTER 6

LIKE SOMEONE FIELD-DRESSED AN ELK

As I say, it takes effort to maintain a house, and if you're Gordy, the last thing you'd ever think about would be cleaning the filthy windowpanes or cutting back the bushes from around the front door. Only if the pizza delivery guy couldn't make it through the thicket would you try to stomp it back. Because of course you wouldn't have clippers or a saw. And b), never in a million years would you actually repair anything broken, because it's a rental.

Crunching through the dry snow, I evaluate the back windows. Should I have been worried about bumping into some rival prowler? I'd learned a few self-defense techniques on the street, though nothing's better than avoidance. Or a well-oiled and loaded firearm. Actually, avoidance of trouble is way better than having to use a gun and then try to explain yourself from the back of a police car.

The frame of one of the windows is so rotted my fingers sink into the wood. Kitchen window, it seems. I get my bigger slot screwdriver out and pry hard with it, but the window won't budge: the inside latch is engaged. So, gloves back on, I scrape away enough of the frame to lift the lower pane away entirely. That wood was so nice, once.

After setting the pane aside, I hoist my backpack through, hear it thump on the floor, and then climb in after it. I'm fairly agile.

Fortunately the electricity is still on, and fortunately Gordy hadn't sunk so low as to not buy replacement lightbulbs when he needed them. I'd landed in the breakfast nook. The police had left the heat on. Though it's getting dark, I can see well enough to find switchplates and snap on some lights.

The place isn't as wrecked inside as out, though I knew Gordy needed buckets in the upstairs bedrooms when it rained—Laura told me that. She lived with him here for three or four years, until moving out when she started classes at Wayne. She could have saved money staying living with him, but the school gave her a housing allowance, apart from free tuition, so she took off to the student dorms on campus. That way, she could easily walk to class and not even need a car, though she told me "every single one" of her classmates had a car. I was so proud of her getting that scholarship. She'd graduated high school a year early, in the top ten at Renaissance, one of the best schools in the city, along with Cass Tech. She's a determined one.

I don't scare easy, but it's a jolt to walk into that living room and turn on a table lamp.

The couch looks like someone field-dressed an elk on it. Lots of dark blood, soaked and dried into the gold cushions, mostly on one end. One large patch of bloody fabric is missing, cut away in a square. Maybe the forensic people took it. The couch is the same one Gordy and I bought at a junk store when we got to Detroit. Gold fabric printed to look like brocade. Although the blood is dry, a smell comes from that couch, a strong smell like fresh dirt. I force myself to reach out and touch the arm of the couch that doesn't have any blood on it. Almost so as to defy any bad juju that might be around.

It's troublingly easy for me to picture that poor Sandy person dying there, bleeding out, her life over. Death occurred right here. I feel a surge of hatred for Gordy. I feel vengeful, I feel convinced.

The police and wagon guys only left a few bits of litter behind: plastic wrappers, tape, fragments of medical-type stuff. No more blood do I see, or wait, there's some on the rug in front of the couch, yeah, a few splotches, sure looks like blood. "Oh, Lordy," I breathe into the stillness. The black maw of the cold fireplace, surrounded by sandstone blocks, looks like it's gonna disagree with anything good I might try to do.

The wooden parts of the furniture, plus the frame around the front door, seem frosty, but it can't be frost, and looking closer I see it's white dust. Fingerprinting dust, must be. Well, they were thorough. I pick up the litter and take it to the kitchen trash bin. It has a clean liner.

Is Sandy's ghost around? They say people who die violently like to dawdle nearby because of unfinished business. I would bet she's got some, and I wonder what it is. Never having met Sandy in real life, I wouldn't know how to distinguish her from any other ghost.

Though Gordy was no kind of housekeeper, to my relief I don't spot any signs of roaches or rats. I suppose he made an effort against the worst filth when Laura came to live here. Besides, she was old enough to help with cleaning and chores, and I know her to be fastidious about her personal hygiene.

The window I'd removed is letting a river of cold air in, so I remount it and seal it in place with duct tape from the roll in my toolkit.

Besides that, the night cold is sneaking in around all the rotting window frames. Straight through the window glass itself, for that matter. Heat exchange. I remember that from tenth-grade science. In the UP you'll often go in somebody's house and notice blankets and towels tacked up over the windows. They keep a lot of cold out.

This is one of those old houses with a lightbulb in the center of the ceiling of every room. I'm sure in olden days the fixtures were lovely, but the place had been stripped of such niceties long ago. Cheap glass saucers shield the bulbs now. The mahogany moldings and trim are still intact, though, and the place hadn't been looted for pipes and wiring, so hey, a veritable palace.

I take a quick look through every room—nothing shocking other than that couch. Most of the upper bedrooms are closed off and ice-cold, their radiators screwed tight shut. I leave those radiators alone but open the valves wide on all the others. In response, a chorus of metallic groans and the *clunk-clunk-clunk* of awakening steam heat echo through the silent house, rising from the depths. Max out your free heat whenever you can, that's my motto. There is no thermostat. I know nothing of how steam heat works, other than there's always a boiler in the basement and sometimes things go catastrophically wrong.

I almost didn't believe Laura about the buckets to catch rainwater, but now I see the evidence: a stack of galvanized pails in a corner of the upper hallway, ready for the spring thaw. Ugly brown stains on the ceilings.

One of the non-closed-off bedrooms has a twin bed in it and a short dresser: Laura's old room. Plus a little desk. The bed is made up with sheets and blankets. I swat dust off the coverlet. Laura had taped up art posters. One is a slightly traumatizing old-master type painting of two women in candlelight, looking anxiously towards a sound, maybe. The crouching one is holding a man's head partly wrapped in a cloth. I think they killed him, but why take the trophy? A crime of passion, perhaps. The women are plump and young. Maybe they were in love with each other, and the man was the local sheriff who wanted to break them up.

The other picture is of a party from long ago, tons of peasant people mashing faces and drunk dancing. The guys have on tight pants with a special extra pouch in front for their little guy. I've always admired Scottish men and their groin-purses in front of their kilts. They're like, hey, I don't have to show it off, you know? Here's my purse, bet you wonder what's under it.

In the kitchen I find Gordy's junk drawer, crammed with all the usual crap: screwdrivers, a nice-looking multi-tool, buttons, a random fork, some string, rubber bands, a tiny remote control from something like a fan or space heater, an almost empty roll of packing tape, random keys. I scoop up the few keys and try them in the front door lock. The second one fitted. It also worked in the back door, a nice convenience. I work the key onto my own ring in my purse. If I hadn't found that key I would have had to leave the house unlocked and keep most of my stuff in my car trunk. Laura would of course have a key, but I don't want to ask her if I could copy it.

There isn't much to eat in the kitchen, so I get out the second peanut-but-ter-and-banana sandwich I'd packed and sit at the kitchen table near the radiator. I pour the last of my tea into the handy cup from my bottle. It's still pretty warm. I'd eaten the first sandwich at the rest stop south of Roscommon.

I'd brought along a package of salami and more bread, as well as a handful of teabags. My brand is Red Rose, and I hope if you're a Lipton person you won't take offense, but there's no comparison in smoothness. I was sad when Red Rose stopped including the little ceramic figurines in the boxes. You have to buy it online now, to get the free figurines. My aunt Mad once showed me why the figurines had rough flat bottoms: so you could strike your wooden kitchen matches on it when you had to light a gas stove burner. So they were actually like little tools. Olden times.

I eat my sandwich, using the waxed paper for a placemat, and drink the tea. I'd forgotten to bring a book. I just sit in that kitchen absorbing the mood of the house, trying to hunch in on the vibes of whatever happened here.

Wanting to connect with Sandy a little more, I get out my phone and bring up a news article on the murder, which I'd already read. I want to see the picture again. They ran a picture of her, probably a driver's license photo with the blue background and full-face closeup. Most people in their license pictures have either a tense expression or a ridiculous grin. Sandy, however, looked calm, with a natural smile. Clear blue eyes, hair pulled back from her face. A person who looked upbeat and nice.

I sure am sorry you're no longer on this planet, kid.

A sudden heavy pounding makes me freeze in my chair. The pounding stops. I put my phone down, finish chewing my last bite of sandwich, then silently swallow the last of the tea. I listen, and after a moment the pounding starts again.

"Police!" says a hard voice. "Open up."

CHAPTER 7

YOU GRABBED THE KNIFE

I go to the living room and peep out the bay window to see, through a break in the shrubbery, Det. Ted Alvarez standing at the front door, ongoingly hammering his fist on the heavy wood. His profile is just recognizable in the glow from the window. Sharp chin, like a cartoon cop's, and I wonder if he went into police work because of that.

"Ted! My gosh!" I hurry to the door, flip the bolt, and let him in. "Why'd you have to bang so hard?"

"In case it wasn't you in here. I thought it would be, though. Huh. I was driving by and saw the lights." He stamps snow from his shoes and wipes them on the mat.

"You were driving by?"

"Had a feeling. If you came to town, where would you stay? You're always broke." He gives me one of his level looks. I catch his scent: a hint of clove, a hint of end-of-day musk. Still so recognizable.

"I have plenty of friends."

"Not so many anymore." He didn't have to tell me what he meant. You live a rough life, you have rough pals, and the unlucky ones and the dumber ones go to

39

prison or the graveyard at a higher rate than people who have retirement accounts and know which fork to eat the soup with. You know what I mean.

He stands there, holding a small briefcase. When Alvarez joined the force, the height requirement was five feet seven minimum. He must have worn heavily padded socks to the physical, is all I'm saying. Thus he always wore a hat, which added a good inch or two to his stature. Tonight his hat is dark gray with a short brim. The hat, plus his wool coat, makes him resemble a football coach from the 1960s. Those old pictures.

I go, "And I might note that it's not that I'm broke. I'm no longer broke, eh? I'm cheap." I straighten my posture.

"How 'bout that."

"There's a big difference." The only money I owe is $926 to a debt-consolidation place in Sault Ste. Marie. It wasn't that bad of a deal, and I was paying it down to the tune of $125 a month. It's a miracle I avoided bankruptcy. Perhaps there's a mortgage in my future? Someday-slash-maybe. My taxi should hold on for a few years more, given my brother's skill as a mechanic. Bing was good to me.

Ted glances at the gruesome couch. "It's disgusting that you're here."

"Take me out for coffee?"

Twenty minutes later we're settled in a back booth at the Kestrel, an out-of-the-way bar on Conant near Outer Drive. Ted orders Scotch on the rocks, and I go for tomato juice with lemon. The coffee at bars like this is only for if you're having a shot of brandy too, or something, because it's terrible.

"Would you like something to eat?" he offers.

"No, thank you."

"The burgers are good here."

I appreciate his encouragement. "I ate just before you came over. But thank you, Ted." It was about eight o'clock now. The place is dark and not busy, maybe a few guys nursing their third after-work beer before going home. No jukebox, just a couple of TV screens over the bar playing a Red Wings game. Our guys are down a point to the Penguins midway through the second. The Wings were having a pretty good season so far, so I think chances are good they'll score a couple more times. Jimmy at the warehouse keeps track of all the hockey teams, so I know a bit by osmosis.

Ted says, "You're looking well, actually." That *actually* spoke tons. No doubt he's thinking about me from my low days.

"You too." It was true; he hasn't fattened up like so many cops do. A naturally wiry build, I'd call Ted's. He was always plenty strong. A family line from Spain, his people were the crazy ones who bred bulls for the bullfights. One of his uncles had been a semi successful matador, and every time Ted went to the old country on vacation, the family all pressured him to be a bullfighter too, because of his build. He sure has the handsomeness for publicity pictures. Deep-olive skin, face structure suitable for a movie star. Huge eyes, naturally soulful, but as a cop he tried to harden them with a habitual annoyed squint.

"You know I could make your life miserable," he says quietly, his eyes flicking to my face.

"Much worse than I could make yours," I agree in an upbeat way. "What do you have for me?"

He cracks a smile then. "You know I still have feelings for you. Not a lot of feelings. But some."

"You flatter me." I sip my juice and act patient. Men in general, I've sworn them off.

"I'm not going to act on them. Bambi, I regret our affair. It was unethical on every level." He gives me a cool look that tells me he's processed whatever emotions he'd had about it. Good.

"Ted, it was a long time ago. We were both at fault."

"Yeah. But I should have exercised better judgment."

"And it was over pretty quick, actually, once you got a grip."

"Yeah. I will say again, I'm surprised you haven't lost your looks."

Which I understand. While I don't look 25 anymore, I didn't even look 25 when I was 25. I mean I looked definitely wrecked then. But now that I'd achieved some stability in life, clean from the junk, eating better, my face has a little flesh on it, in spite of my advanced age of 37. No gray streaks in my hair yet. My figure's OK, though it was still hard for me to keep weight on, a problem most people would wish to have, I guess. During my super-skinny addict phases, I'd wear padded bras and use concealer on the dark crescents under my eyes. I admit, I deserved to look heaps worse than I did.

"Ted, come on. I'm here on business."

He heaves a sigh. "What you heard was right. Gordy seems to have no real alibi."

"Yeah?"

"Initially, he told the homicide guys he went to a buddy's house to shoot pool. But when they naturally asked which buddy, he said oh, he forgot, that was the prior night. Said he went out to buy beer and chips. So he changed his story within thirty seconds of the first question."

"I saw beers in the ice box. No chips, though." I could have gone for some Fritos.

"Plus his blood alcohol was two-two."

"Point two-two, that's fairly drunk, eh? Could he have driven around town in that condition?"

"Yeah, I don't think he'd have much of a problem doing that, especially if he's been back to drinking regularly for however long."

"Who discovered the body, then—him?"

"That's what he claims. He called 911 at 6:10 p.m."

"Heard the tape?"

"No. The point is, given the time of death being approximately 5:30 p.m.—"

"They can get it that close?"

"If the body's discovered soon, yeah. This was less than two hours, it seems. Change in body temperature, that's how they do it, they jam the thermometer right into the body cavity. Plus other measures, like the amount of rigor mortis."

"Ah. Right. That's interesting."

"Why?" Sharply.

"Oh—not as in, it means something. Just interesting how they figure out that stuff. I like those shows." The police shows. When I think about all I got away with, I marvel.

He eyes me as if he knows just what I was thinking. He rattles the ice in his glass and the barman looks over and nods.

I go, "What's in the briefcase?" He'd brought it into the bar. When he shrugged out of his coat, it fell over the briefcase, but I remembered it was there. I feel hopeful.

"Come sit next to me." He pushes his coat aside and unzips the briefcase. As I slide in next to him, he pulls out a thin computer thing, a tablet, and turns it on.

"I shouldn't be showing you this, but ..."

I guess, "You've seen it already?" He doesn't have to explain to me his every thought process.

"Yes. There's a lot more in it. The lead detective's name is Boris Podyak." He holds the tablet so we can both see it. The barman brings him another drink and takes the empty away.

Together we watch the video of Gordy's interrogation at the DPD.

My ex-husband looked terrible, his eyes veiled by shock and distress. Shock at having committed a murder, or shock at having been brought in so quick? The time stamp was a few minutes before midnight, just hours after he called 911 to report having found Sandy O'Rourke's body in his house.

"God help me, God help me," he muttered to himself throughout the preliminaries. The lead detective looked annoyed, but he didn't tell Gordy to shut up. That's the last thing you want to tell a suspect.

I'm actually surprised Gordy agreed to talk to the police at all, but then I remember all those detective shows where suspects, even smart people with good jobs, just sit right down and start talking to the police without a lawyer there to advise them. The first thing out of a lawyer's mouth to a client in any kind of law enforcement setting is always, "Stop talking."

If Gordy's innocent, it's plausible he'd be like, well, I have nothing to hide, I'm destroyed at what happened. After all, I'm the guy who called 911.

If guilty, he was taking a calculated risk.

The detective, a hefty white guy with Slavic features—high cheeks, narrow eyes—asked Gordy what he'd done that afternoon, and Gordy stumblingly told a tale of relaxing after work by himself in his house.

Cop: After work? What time did you get off work?

Gordy: I only worked a half day today. I got off at noon.

Cop: How come you only worked a half day?

Gordy: It's my regular schedule. I get two half days off, plus one whole day. My days off are—

Cop: What did you do all afternoon?

Gordy: Relaxed at home, mostly.

Cop: What did you do to relax?

Gordy: Well, I—I turned on the TV.

Cop: What did you watch?

Gordy: Uhh ...

Cop: You don't remember what TV show you watched less than twelve hours ago?

Gordy: Well, uh, I ... this has been extremely upsetting, you know... I can't stop thinking about all that blood.

Cop: I bet. Now, what were you watching?

No doubt he was streaming porn, I mean come on.

I imagine how this detective Podyak's night must have gone. He was probably lounging in front of the TV when the call from the uniformed division came in, probably around ten, once they'd sorted out the basics. From the ring tone he'd have known it was dispatch. He'd take the call, memorize the address, put on the blue blazer, white shirt, and dark tie he was wearing on camera, and drive over to Gordy's house, maybe hitting a drive-through first for a coffee to fortify himself against the cold and a bloody murder scene.

He would look over the crime scene with the rest of the team, and he'd talk to Gordy, briefly, on the spot. He'd ask Gordy if he wouldn't mind coming into the station to talk a little more.

His tone was direct but not harsh. As for Gordy, he seemed to believe he was there because the police wanted to hear what happened to him—he went out; he returned to find a dead woman in his house. But once the detective listened to him, they started to have more of a conversation. And I started to think, *Ah, Gordy, how dumb can you be?*

Cop: What time did Ms. O'Rourke come over?

Gordy: She didn't come over, she wasn't there, eh?

Cop: What do you mean, she wasn't there? She died on your couch.

Gordy: I mean, when I left. She wasn't there when I left.

Cop: What else did you do in the house before you left?

Gordy: I heated up some pizza, and—

Cop: And you and your girlfriend ate pizza together?

Gordy: No—

Cop: Did you have an argument?

Gordy: No! We didn't have an argument!

Cop: You had a friendly conversation, then?

Gordy: No! I told you, she wasn't there. I was alone. When I went out—

Cop: What time was that?

Gordy: Well, I don't know exactly. I told them at the house—

Cop: What time?

Gordy: Maybe, like, five o'clock?

Cop: Where did you go?

Gordy: I just—drove around. Just to drive around.

Cop: You told the officers at the scene you went to a friend's house to play pool.

Gordy: I was mixed up, right then. I didn't go over to anybody's house. I drove around.

Cop: In the snow? It was snowing.

Gordy: Yeah.

Cop: Where did you drive?

Suddenly Gordy looked smacked, as if remembering something, or as if catching himself.

Gordy: I don't know—I mean, I guess I went up Woodward.

Cop: And then where?

Gordy: I think I got on 696.

Cop: Going east or west?

Gordy: Uh, west, I guess—

Cop: So if we checked the traffic cam footage, we'd see you driving along there?

Gordy: Oh, God.

Cop: Why don't you just tell me what you did?

Gordy: OK, I better be honest—I drove over to a liquor store on Davison.

I was accustomed to sensing when Gordy was lying. Something was wrong here. He seemed to be trying to come clean, but he was pretending. I wondered if he'd had an appointment or something. An appointment to meet Sandy, or someone else?

Cop: So a minute ago when you said you just went for a drive—'just to ride around'—that was a lie?

Gordy: Yeah. I guess.

I find myself attempting to send ESP waves back through time saying *Shut up and ask for your lawyer.*

Cop: And now you say the truth is you went out to buy some liquor.

Gordy: Beer. I bought beer.

Cop: What kind of beer did you buy?

Gordy: Twelve-pack of Coors.

Now *that* he'd remember: what brand of alcohol he bought. Coors was cheap, but he always liked the taste.

Gordy: And, uh, some chips.

Cop: How much did it cost? Do you have the receipt?

Gordy: I don't know. I don't usually keep receipts.

Cop: What store was it?

Gordy: What store?

Cop: What was the name of the store?

Gordy: King Liquors.

Cop: Did you talk to the clerk there?

Gordy: Well, yeah. I bought a lottery ticket too.

Cop: Where's the lottery ticket?

Gordy: In my wallet. Wherever that is.

Cop: What did you say to the clerk?

Gordy: I don't know, I guess I said I want a lottery ticket as well, for the Powerball for Saturday. And he said OK, and he told me how much to pay and I gave him the money.

Cop: When was the last time you saw Ms. O'Rourke?

Gordy: I don't know, exactly, uh, I guess maybe four or five months ago. I don't know.

Cop: When was the last time you talked to her? On the phone.

Gordy: I guess, uh, around that same time.

Cop: If we subpoenaed your phone records, you think that'd match up?

Gordy: Well—I—subpoena my—?

Cop: Are you strong enough to hurt a woman?

Gordy: I didn't hurt anybody.

Cop: You never hurt a woman in your life?

Gordy: N—no.

Cop: You think your ex-wife would tell us that you never hurt a woman?

Gordy: Bambi doesn't have anything to do with this.

Cop: No?

I catch my breath at the weirdness of being mentioned in this conversation. And how on earth would they know about Gordy hitting me? I'd never called the police on him. At the hospital with my jaw, I said I fell and hit my face on the coffee table. Looking back, I supposed any idiot could see through that.

Gordy: Oh, God, listen! Look, I'm just trying to tell you what happened, I'm trying to cooperate. I came in, I saw her lying there, and I ran to her. I—Oh, my God.

Cop: Go on.

Gordy: I saw the knife sticking out of her chest, and I just automatically grabbed it.

Cop: You grabbed the knife.

Gordy: And I pulled it out! I thought she might be alive, and the sight of that knife in her! I didn't know she was dead. I yelled Sandy! Sandy!, but she didn't move. She wasn't breathing, I saw then. There was blood all over but no blood was coming out. I mean, I think a little came out when I pulled the knife. I put my head down on her to try to hear a heartbeat. But I—

Cop: That's how you got blood on you? On your hands and your face and your shirt?

Gordy: Yes! I told them that before. I don't know who killed Sandy. Oh, God. How did they get in? Why did somebody bring her to my house?

Cop: How did who get in?

The interrogation room door burst open and a guy in a blue puffy parka charged in. "Tarik Ayoub, Mr. Walsh's attorney. Don't say anything more, Gordy." He threw his briefcase on the table, and the detective turned away in resignation.

Ted shuts off the tablet.

At this point I have to decide whether to get up and resume my seat across the table, or stay where I am. Our thighs touched when I first joined him, but I moved my leg away.

If I get up, it might seem like I'm excessively rejecting him. If I don't, maybe it will give the wrong impression. Everybody has these micro decisions to make all the time, don't they? I stay where I am, thinking just don't make a big thing out of anything, you know?

Ted goes, "I was saying before. The reports aren't all in yet, of course, but if she died at around 5:30, he could have done the murder, then cleaned himself up, gone out and cooked up that lame alibi, being seen in a party store. Then he comes home and calls 911, playing the shocked, distraught boyfriend."

"He might have been drunk when he killed her, if he did it, or maybe he started drinking later?"

"Yeah, no way to know, really. They were running forensics on the knife during that interview. His prints were on it, all right, bloody prints, and no other person's were detectable on it. The blood on the knife and on him was Sandy O'Rourke's."

Ted consumes his second drink more slowly than the first. We duck our heads to look each other in the eye, more or less, as we talk.

"Did they find blood in the bathroom?" I ask.

"They did detect some, but not sure it was hers yet. It wasn't in the bathroom, though, it was in the kitchen."

I didn't see any blood in the kitchen; maybe it was just a trace or something. I know they have chemicals to find tiny bits of blood, even when it seems washed away. Luminol, isn't that a good name? The TV shows love to show the ghostly glow it makes. "Doesn't stabbing usually indicate a crime of passion?"

"Oh, for sure. I mean, the person's dead after the first couple good ones to the heart or lungs—or throat, for that matter—but then you keep on stabbing. For what? To try to satisfy whatever anger's driving you."

I pick up a sugar packet someone left on the table and toy with it in my fingers. "And even if you did it, you're still going to be genuinely traumatized, right?" I tap the sugar down to one end, then turn the packet so the sugar settles to the other end. The Wings game is still on, and customers occasionally are calling out hearty stuff like, *Check 'im! Now ram it in! Yess!*

Ted says, "Yeah, murderers often go into a state, like they're confused and stupid. Especially first-timers. Blood simple, they call it."

"I've heard of that. How long does it last?"

"Good question." Ted almost smiles. "I don't know, and I don't think I've ever wondered that."

I say, "What about Sandy's movements that night? Anybody know anything yet?"

"Not yet," says Ted. "Your daughter, did she know Sandy?"

"Seems she did, a little."

"She could be helpful."

"Might could, yeah. She absolutely wants to help get her dad off of this charge."

"Hmm. It seems obvious that Gordy could have gotten jealous of Sandy seeing Vic Paladino, and lured her over for some reason, then killed her."

"Or he could have abducted her," I suggest.

"I doubt that. Seems more probable that he gets her to come over for some reason, he's drunk, they have an argument, it escalates, he loses control. Simple jealousy seems like a reasonable motive." Ted drums his fingers. "Did he ever threaten you with a knife?"

"No, I can't say he ever did."

"Ever put his hands around your throat?"

"Well, once, in a way, but it was more of a cuff than a grip, you know?"

Ted shakes his head. "You should never have put up with that stuff."

"Right you are." I keep fiddling with the sugar packet.

"Do you find the situation disturbing?"

I look up at him. "Well, yeah! The whole thing disturbs me."

"Which side of this are you on?"

"That's what disturbs me. By the way, I saw there was no doorbell cam at Gordy's house, but have the guys checked out houses across the street?"

"Of course. The house directly across has a camera, but they'd leaned a piece of plywood over it and it caught nothing. The other houses nearby didn't have cams."

Before taking me back to the house, Ted talked about the difference between direct evidence and circumstantial evidence, which I sort of knew from TV but not perfectly.

If there's video of you holding a gun to a bank teller's head, and then leaving with a bag of money, that's direct evidence you robbed the bank. If somebody gets murdered in your house and as far as anybody can tell, you were the only person there, that's circumstantial evidence you *maybe* committed that murder.

Lots of people have been put away on circumstantial evidence only. Even for murder. Even without a body. I guess Gordy's prints on the knife were direct evidence. Yet it was true, he could have simply found her dead. What a mess.

I remember how Gordy would get after his fourth or fifth beer, or vodka on the rocks if we had it. I always could tell when one of his rages was coming on: there'd be almost an aura. He'd tip his head back, and get this injured expression on his face, and he'd start to go over his grievances in life. He'd sit and complain, and I'd be there trying to cook dinner, coping with the newborn, trying to take care of him too. Eventually, he'd realize I was the root of all his troubles, and he'd get to yelling, knowing I'd yell back.

What was underlying Gordy's angst in those days? Something he couldn't live with, from childhood or something? Who knows.

I couldn't change him, ever. God forgive me for not getting out sooner, for not taking Laura with me, for not getting clean then.

CHAPTER 8

HOUSEHOLD NAME AROUND THE WORLD

A dark-blue sedan threads its way through the warehouse district of Detroit, on the near east side. It pulls into a deserted gravel parking lot on Atwater near DuBois.

The city is sullen under the January morning. No more Christmas season, no more twinkle lights. Business at bowling alleys picks up a little around now. As soon as the New Year's resolutions wear off, liquor sales go back to normal. Parents haul their kids to hockey practice. Buses splash filthy slush on people waiting, if they're not savvy enough to stand back. Cafés and sandwich places, their windows fogged with warmth, become charming oases: for the price of a cup of coffee, you can hang out for a while and cheer up. There's nothing for it but endure, as you've done for however many years. Fresh snow brings beauty, though. As inconvenient as a snowstorm is, you could hope for that beauty. Fluffy new snow covers up the ugly and turns everything into almost a fairyland.

People manage to find things to get excited about: the football playoffs, pizza and beer pong for the extroverts. Painting by number for a certain category of nerds. You could go to a concert or the casino. If you were a phone zombie or video gamer, the weather hardly mattered anyway.

Chuck Stratton, a lanky guy who used to jump smoke during fire season out West, gets out of the sedan, locks it, and looks around. It's only eight o'clock; this back street is quiet. Breathing deeply, enjoying the dry frigid air, Stratton buttons his maple-colored shearling coat. It is a worn but serviceable coat, and he can't much care if people think he's a cowboy in it. Cold, it is this morning, harsh cold at six degrees above. Clear, though, which sometimes happens when it's this cold. The brightness of the sunshine seems an affront. He wishes he'd brought along his dark clip-ons that go over his regular eyeglasses.

Stratton grew up nearby and although he likes winter, feeling cold is a distraction, so he dressed for it. The thigh-length coat is toasty, as are his wool pants and long underwear. He wears lace-up work boots, the nubby soles of which give decent traction on snow and ice. A navy watch cap keeps his shaved head warm enough. He owns a good backcountry hat with earflaps, but can't bring himself to wear it in the city. He turns up his coat collar and puts on a pair of insulated gloves. He breathes out through his nose in a frosty stream.

Remaining alert to his surroundings, he hikes a little way north on Atwater. His gait is relaxed. The sidewalk had been salted to clear it, overly so, and the leftover rock salt crystals crunch under his boots. The pavement is white with the residue.

He notices the red pillars, emergency call boxes, each topped with a blue light, every 500 feet or so down Atwater. He imagines being a woman and trying to decide whether the call boxes should make you feel better or worse about walking here.

He arrives at a waterfront park with trees and an amphitheater. It used to be called Chene Park, after one of the early French settlers, but after the death of the Queen of Soul, the amphitheater part was renamed the Aretha Franklin. It overlooks the Detroit River and Canada on the other side.

The place will look a lot different come spring, but this assessment has to be done now, and whether it was cold or warm doesn't matter anyway. Stratton has already consulted site plans, satellite pictures, and his own memory. He's worked out distances and noted features he wants to inspect in person. A sudden rattling startles him: a gust clattering through the dead leaves still clinging to young oaks along the walkway. He wonders whether young trees hold on to their leaves more tightly than old ones. Just oaks, maybe. Hadn't thought about that before.

The Aretha arranges itself on the riverfront like the graceful, vibrant singer herself: a white canopy made of a hard composite material that resembled a billowing sail or maybe a scallop shell protects the stage and 5,000 seats. The canopy was rigged taut and well, holding up year after year against howling storms, winter and summer. The lawn is only a sloping strip of ground where a thousand more people could cram in. Stratton came to concerts here when he was younger: everybody played Chene in the summer. Lawn tickets cost less, naturally, as you risked rain and dew, but you could put down your blanket and relax. Stratton preferred the lawn even after he could afford pavilion seats.

He looks at the moat-like pond between the Aretha and the street, which protects the venue from gate crashers in the summer. It is now frozen, and anybody can walk across it, climb the steep berm, and be inside the empty amphitheater.

Stratton stops at the main gate and texts *I'm here.* A big man in a hooded black parka barrels up to the gate. "Stratton?"

"Yeah! Jacoby?"

"Welcome."

"Thanks. Miserable day to be doing this. Sorry to get you out."

"It's like three degrees or some. Saturday, too." But Jacoby's tone is friendly enough.

After that, both men ignore the gusting wind coming off the river, which rarely freezes all the way over because of its depth and steady current. All the lake freighters come through here, passing so near in the shipping channels you can hear the guys on deck shouting if the breeze is right. Any ships to come through today, though, would be on their last run, as the Soo Locks would close within a few days, to reopen in spring.

Jacoby says, "You just need to walk around and eyeball the place?"

"Yeah. Take some measurements as well."

"I have to stay with you." Jacoby stands solid and well balanced on his feet, in police duty shoes.

"'Course."

The men move about the silent open space, their breath puffing white before being snatched away by the wind. Stratton methodically paces off distances and writes in a small notebook now and then. The click of his pen seems loud.

"I hope you're not taking any offense at this," Stratton says, as they move down from the back of the theater toward the stage.

"Naw, I understand." Jacoby is a middle-aged guy with a cropped gray natural that is almost covered by his hood. His face is thoughtful, watchful, with those two deep vertical furrows some people have in their cheeks, almost like knife scars. Carries himself tall. Ex-military, Stratton thinks. Infantry.

Jacoby says, "You're working for Gloria Jensen?"

"No, Vic Paladino. He's letting her borrow me for this." The men climb to the stage and Stratton carefully, patiently, stands observing the place, roof to floor, gazing in every direction, snapping pictures on his phone. He holds up his pen to measure angles. He looks at the black girders and heavily tensioned ties that support the canopy. Nothing has changed since the last time he'd done this.

Jacoby swings his arms. "You're the best, everybody says so. I will note we've not had any violent incidents here. No newsworthy ones, anyway."

Stratton smiles at that. "I'm sure your guys are good at heading off trouble in the first place."

"'Course, the police give us a profile too, especially for traffic out. Let me ask you then. What's Gloria so worried about? Been getting threats?"

"I'm not supposed to say, which tells you."

"Right. Anybody in particular?"

Stratton likes how this guy thinks. "She's being cagey about that. So I wonder. All I'm doing for her is making a security plan for her concert in April. Her team's supposed to take it from here."

"She scared of a sniper?"

"I think so, maybe."

Gloria Jensen, well, household name around the world. Little lady, big lush voice, good songwriter. Tough businesswoman, too, now at the peak of her maturity and influence. Multiple Grammys, gold records still stacking up like pancakes. People call her the white Aretha, which she claims she doesn't like. "There was and ever will be, but one Aretha," she tells interviewers.

Stratton thinks Gloria Jensen must be close to forty, a year or two older than him. He likes her music, which ranges from low-register soul and jazz covers to up-tempo hot pop.

However. While Aretha Franklin was known for her professionalism—commonsense poise gained from hard experience—Gloria Jensen is a fractious diva. Stories abound: shrieking at subordinates, making absurd demands from friends and associates, snubbing fans, the works. One time she even got in trouble with the police for shoving her agent out of the door of a moving taxi in New York City. At low speed, granted, but the guy's arm snapped in two places. And crazy though it seemed, he didn't quit being her agent. Some fans adored Gloria Jensen for such behavior all the more. Stratton could not understand this.

What's more, she churned through husbands and boyfriends like beach foam. Stratton had met and chatted with her a few times, backstage at Paladino's concerts. The most recent time, after a couple of glasses of wine, she'd asked him to take her home. He'd made the excuse of being on duty with Paladino. Apart from the fact that her own escort was standing right there.

Though Stratton hasn't said a word in the last few seconds, Jacoby catches a vibe. "I don't like her, either."

Stratton bursts out a laugh. "Why is that?"

"Friend of mind did some work for her and she didn't pay. Some cabinetry. Said he should be honored to do the work for her for free."

"That makes no sense."

"Agree."

The men go down to the seawall at the amphitheater's rear. Here the bison-thick concrete keeps the river on course. Delicate sheets of ice slink along the wall, slipping under and over each other, sounding like the clicking of insects or maybe dice in a cup. The sun still shines brilliantly, though a line of gray clouds is moving in from the southwest. Stratton squints through the brightness. A couple of gray gulls soar close to shore, hunting for something to feast on, a sodden bag of cookies or perhaps a dead rat. The breeze is stiff.

"Isn't Paladino doing a show soon?" asks Jacoby. "At Masonic, right?"

"Yeah. He's played there before."

"Long time back, though, right?"

"Yeah. Are you aware of any changes?"

"No. I was just commenting on his—inactivity lately. Been three, four years, right? No offense."

Stratton shrugs. "Yeah. He loved playing here. Then he outgrew it, audience-wise. But now ..." he trails off. He kicks a chunk of ice, which skitters to the breakwall and bursts apart. "It's been too long for him to be out of action."

"He's been recording, though, right?"

"Yeah. Writing new songs and getting them out, but sales haven't been great. You gotta tour to make it these days."

The way the Aretha is set up, there's no backdrop behind the stage, no shell, meaning the performers essentially play in the round. The amphitheater crowd in front of you, the river at your back. People run their cabin cruisers in close to hear concerts for free, party, and feel cool being watched by the paying guests. The performers' backs are to you, and the acoustics can't be any good, but that's never the point. The bigger the star, the more boats jockeying around for a spot to drop anchor. Sometimes boats tie up together to make a party barge.

Stratton opens his coat and lifts a small pair of binoculars on a strap around his neck. He pushes his black-framed glasses up on his forehead and trains the binoculars on the opposing Canadian shoreline, about a mile away. Manufacturing plants, storage silos, a commercial distillery. Old smokestacks.

"You'd need field artillery to hit here from over there," says Jacoby, and Stratton smiles to himself: he was right about the infantry.

"Do the Coast Guard or police boats ever come around here during concerts?"

"Once in a while. We don't pay much mind. They like to make busts, but when people are just chilling and not bothering anybody, they don't generally break it up."

"Sure." Stratton puts away the binoculars, adjusts his eyeglasses, and buttons his coat again.

"I like that coat," says Jacoby impulsively.

"It's stupid warm." Stratton glances down at his sleeve.

"Where'd that coat come from?"

"Picked it up out West."

"Made out of sheep hide?"

"Yeah. Want it?" Stratton unbuttons the top button.

Jacoby stares at him. "Oh, my gosh, no. I couldn't take it from you, and anyway, it wouldn't fit me."

"You're right at that." Jacoby has at least thirty pounds on Stratton.

Jacoby peers closely into Stratton's face. Carefully, he says, "You would *give* me your coat, just like that?"

Stratton shrugs. "Well." He pauses, meeting Jacoby's gaze. "You know how it is."

Jacoby doesn't, exactly, but says nothing more.

Stratton says, "So you guys won't mind if Gloria wants to add her own people?"

"Absolutely not. We'd be glad to have a pre-event meeting so we can coordinate. Set up radios. Anything I can do."

Both men know it's impossible to provide perfect security for a celebrity in public. You can have the best people, on the highest alert, and some insane piece of human garbage with a gun or suicide vest can still ruin everything. It doesn't make anybody feel better if the perp gets smoked in the mayhem. You're standing there with your arm blown off, hey great, somebody got him.

CHAPTER 9

QUICK TO STRIKE FIRST

I get up right around six o'clock and take a shower, washing my underwear from yesterday at the same time. I'd slept well enough in Laura's bed. I hang my panties and bra to dry on the shower curtain rod after running a damp rag across it. The rag came away dirty, and there's a tip for you: never trust a strange shower curtain rod.

Before getting in, I'd scrubbed the toilet and sink with some cleanser from under the washstand. I scoured the tub after I got into the shower, swiping the rag around pretty well. Just doing those few things made me feel better about being in the murder house.

After combing my hair, I put on my jeans and sweater over a t-shirt. I let my hair air dry as I make tea and a salami sandwich in the kitchen. First light is still a ways off.

Then I take a real good look around that house. This is Saturday, now.

The police already pawed over the place with their little blue gloves, opening cupboards and drawers, rummaging. Anything interesting they put in plastic evidence bags and took away. However, and I learned this from Ted Alvarez long ago, they don't write down every single tiny thing that's there. They don't remove all the property, they don't look everywhere, especially if they figure they've already got somebody dead to rights. Common sense. They don't necessarily rip up the carpets, unscrew light fixtures, move the stove, crawl into the attic. To do that you'd need about fifty people with hazmat suits for two days, I bet, and who has that level of payroll? This is something they don't make a big deal of on the police shows.

I'm sure they'd be interested in any drugs or bundles of cash. The murder weapon, of course. When I looked for a knife to cut my breakfast sandwich, there weren't any, except for a couple of blunt-tip table knives in the silverware drawer.

In the police shows, things move super fast, and coincidences pop up all the time. Like somebody goes, oh hey, didn't I see that guy in a lineup last week, when Trent had that rape case? or whatever.

Apart from the living-room couch and environs, the crime-scene people had paid special attention to Gordy's bedroom. People generally keep their most important stuff in their bedroom, which makes sense until you realize every criminal knows that because they do it too. Myself, I keep my jewelry, what there is of it, in an empty quart paint can in my front coat closet. I keep any spare cash between the pages of my tenth-grade science book, in the part about mitochondria. The textbook isn't mine, technically—you're supposed to turn them in, but, you know. There's something in me that still wants to understand about mitochondria.

Gordy's things are lying around in some disarray from the police going through it. Some clothes on a chair, closet stuff and shoes on the floor.

A few pictures on the walls would make the place nicer, I thought, as the walls are scarred with nail holes, like pockmarks from tiny grenades. An old paint job is sad, given how easy it is to spruce up a place with paint. Listen to me talk. I've lived in more rat-infested, crummed-up places than you can imagine. I hope that's the case, anyway.

I carefully feel the clothes in the closet. Gordy and I used to hide drugs in the pockets of clothes hung on hangers, whenever we had more than we could consume right away, which was seldom, come to think of it. I don't find anything.

Just curious as to whether he was using. For a time, we hid drugs in the tubular legs of the ironing board, which is a pretty good place, but it gets tedious taking off and putting back the little caps on the ends.

Gordy's fashion sense is the stereotypical "I'm a straight guy and if I spend much time thinking about clothes, it's gay." So his wardrobe is just about as boring as mine. I don't have his excuse. In the past, I dressed cheap and flashy—and way too teenlike—but since getting clean and swearing off sex, I've toned it down a lot. One day, in fact, I decided to go cold turkey, filling a Hefty bag with all my slut gear. I hauled it to a thrift shop and didn't look back. Now I find myself picking up basic comfortable clothes here and there, and it feels good.

The bed is unmade, the impression of Gordy's body clear. He's a sturdy guy, managing to look in shape even when he was using coke pretty heavily. Big brown eyes, furry brows, good hair that he slicked straight back like the finance guys in those various movies. He grew up tough—his dad was a violent bastard—which gave him the perpetual hard-eyed look you see in some people, as if their expression is always saying, "Whatever it is, it's not my fault, and in fact it's probably *yours*."

Gordy, if he sensed trouble from anybody, was quick to strike first. This was a defensive strategy, of course, and it saved him a fair amount of grief in bars and alleys. He knew enough to punch quick, one-two square in the face and get out. If you stand there drunkenly looking down at your opponent with a victorious smirk—that's always a mistake.

For the sake of thoroughness, I go through the dresser and nightstand, though I doubt I'll find anything interesting left by the police. It's a weirdly intimate thing to do, handling Gordy's shirts and socks and briefs after all these years. I shake out his shoes. Take the flashlight from my taxi toolkit and scan under the bed, gulping before I look. You never know. But I only see dust clumps, a couple of old magazines and a forgotten used condom. My flashlight makes me feel competent, somehow. Because even though it's small, it's well made. Heavy black metal, gives a bright beam.

No womanly things, no lipstick in a bathroom drawer, no bras, no thongs. No guns, but of course the police would have taken any they found. I'd never known Gordy to keep guns, though he did have a few badass hunting knives. I do notice that he kept a fairly extensive stash of condoms in a bathroom drawer, plus a half-used tube of spermicidal jelly.

Gordy's home office and gaming station is in a corner of the dining room on the main floor. Evidently the police made off with his computer tower, or whatever those things are called—where your hard drive is, because there's nothing that looks like that. Just a keyboard, two big monitors, and some dangling cables. Dustballs, of course. I hope to come across a vacuum cleaner sooner or later.

I go through a file box on the floor under Gordy's desk and find his tax records. The most recent printout of an IRS filing is two years old, which suggests he's behind. Not that I figured there'd be anything bearing on Sandy O'Rourke, but I'm certainly curious as to what he's been up to. The printout shows a gross income of $132,000. So 'six figures' was true. He paid a bunch of taxes on that, needless to say. But boy howdy, that is a nice income. I'd expected the sun to burn out before either he or I pulled in money like that legally.

I remember Gordy saying he was a "sysadmin" when we last talked, a few months ago. Sysadmin is another one of those words like latte—I don't know what it means, but I don't like it. However, boy, I guess sysadmins must be the aristocrats of the business world.

Why keep living in this sad place, then? Why not spend a couple thou a month on a nice apartment downtown or someplace like Royal Oak where you can walk to a coffee shop or a movie after dark without looking behind you every four seconds?

I wander into the living room and consider what to do about the murder couch. Cover it with a bedsheet? Why not? Just to eliminate the sight of it. Or of the worst of it, anyway. The thing is too big for me to drag out to the curb or garage. It's not exactly mine to dispose of, though it's certainly uncleanable and only fit for the dump. I go and find a white bedsheet from an upstairs closet and snap it open over the couch, letting it billow down. That's better. The gray dawn is creeping through the windows. I welcome the light.

The main thing I'm looking for is one of Gordy's prized possessions: a wooden cigar box where he keeps his grandpa's war medals and other important items.

When Gordy and I still lived together in Balsam Ridge, somebody's apartment in our building caught fire and we had to grab eight-week-old Laura and the diaper bag and run. The fire got put out fast and our apartment was OK. But the experience taught us to put anything we valued near the front door. We hardly owned anything, but from then on we kept a metal cookie box with our birth certificates and whatnot in the corner of the front coat closet. Easy to grab on your way out. That's one of the few things we managed to do right.

Plus, criminals don't expect you to keep your valuables right next to the front door, right? Because, wow, someone could just reach in and go.

Knowing that, how come didn't I start at the front closet? Because if you find something interesting, you can get thrown off from keeping looking. It really is amazing how much I've learned from police shows.

Anyway, I got into that closet now. I take out Gordy's heavy coat and winter boots, which he only wore in the most arctic of conditions, and never did I know the man to own a pair of gloves for longer than two weeks. On Christmas you could give him the nicest pair, leather, warm, and he'd be down to one glove within days.

I yank other crap from the closet, jackets and baseball caps. Gordy had to endure tons of people, the older ones, asking if he was going to play hockey, like Gordie Howe, the great Detroit Red Wings star. Gordy did actually play hockey as a little kid, but quit when a puck caught him in the side of the neck and nearly killed him. I watched him play baseball on the school team, and he was definitely a spark plug. He could always scrape out a hit when circumstances were dire. That was worthy of respect.

Beneath a mildewed sweatshirt in the back corner I find the cigar box.

CHAPTER 10

READY TO BITE SOMETHING

It's a nice wooden job he must have stolen or cajoled from one of the tobacco shops in St. Ignace. I take it to the kitchen table near the window. Though it's a cloudy day and the window is aggressively dirty, plenty of daylight spills in.

I lift the lid and lay out everything, my notebook and pen to the side.

The inventory starts with a velvet box containing a Purple Heart medal. I remember Gordy's grandpa fought in Korea, a war my history teachers in high school barely brought up, not that I was great at paying attention anyway. Reading, I was OK at. Math, though, I found seriously interesting, which set me apart from the other burnouts. I don't know why, but in arithmetic and algebra, something unusual was always going on.

The deep-purple ribbon on the medal is beautiful. It looks like something the king of France would wear front and center. I turn it over.

BERNARD WALSH it says on the back. Gordy's grandpa, who caught a piece of shrapnel in the elbow from a grenade that killed some of his unit. The elbow never worked right again, but he considered himself lucky. That I can dig.

Stashed with the medal are a few campaign ribbons. That's what you call those bars of colors on solders' chests. A war or a big piece of a war is called a campaign, I've learned. Which is both funny and makes sense, because you're trying to campaign for something—what? Land and people, right, just like a political campaign does, except you add bombs and death. Lots of prosthetics, lots of flags presented to the widows at the graveyard.

I fetch my pocket-sized transistor radio from my backpack and set it on the kitchen table and tune it to WCSX, the classic rock station. Janis Joplin's "Me and Bobby McGee" comes on, and I feel less lonely. It's only eight o'clock and full light out now.

Going on, I find a man's gold wedding ring, not Gordy's, not engraved on the inside. Probably his grandpa's. I wondered how come his dad didn't have this stuff. Gordy only showed me these things once, long ago. I'm a little surprised he'd never pawned the ring, at least, for drugs. In retrospect, you might expect I'd have stolen it for drugs myself, but at least I never sank that low.

Speaking of pawning. Folded up with a paper clip are three tickets from Excalibur Pawn, a shop up Woodward I remember from the old days. It's always so funny, the grandiose names these places have. Like as if only the topmost people pawn their stuff there.

They're called tickets, but they're actually whole-page documents, sometimes more than one page, that are like short contracts about the loan. The dates on these are all different, but all within the past five weeks.

Ticket one is for a woman's gold chain necklace, with 14K gold cross pendant, set with a green stone.

The next is for a woman's graduated pearl necklace, sixteen inches long, white gold clasp.

The last ticket is for a woman's gold-tone wristwatch, Seiko brand, quartz movement.

Hm.

None of the tickets are expired yet. I add up the amounts in my head: $125. It's always such a pathetic number. Whose jewelry is this?

In case you are from Pluto or Buckingham Palace and don't know how pawn shops work, basically you bring in an item and they give you some money (usually a check), which is a loan. There's interest on the loan, and this is all made clear to begin with, on paper. Your item is collateral for the loan. If you don't pay the money back plus the interest by a certain date, they keep the item and sell it or give it to their aunt for her birthday. Sometimes they'll buy your item outright if you don't want it anymore.

Also in the cigar box is a piece of jewelry as yet unpawned. A silver-colored bracelet, a cuff-type one with an opening to put your wrist through. It's small; it would fit me. This piece looks and feels cheap, like it was stamped out and not very nicely finished. A picture is engraved on it. I hold it up to the light. The picture is a dog head, mouth open, ready to bite something. Then I see that it wasn't engraved, but pressed in, because I can make out, on the inside, the faint reverse of the head. Also on the inside are stamped-in letters: CADO. That's a funny word. A name? Initials that stand for something?

I turn the bracelet in my hands. It should seem familiar, but I can't think why.

That's it for the cigar box. I put the pawn tickets in my purse, then go up to Laura's room where I'd slept. I didn't go through her stuff. Well, I did, a little. I wanted clues about her, this person I should know so well. I felt awfully sad last night.

This room is a little jewel case of her life, a set of stuff that wants to tell me about Laura. I touch the things, breathe the air around them, breathe in what lingers of my child, her essence.

There's a shoebox of pictures in her closet, pictures printed out from the disposable instamatic cameras Gordy and I documented her babyhood with. A picture of Gordy giving her a bottle, one of me cradling her in my arms with a helpless expression on my face as she cried from colic.

Then me with a triumphant expression, holding her over my shoulder, having gotten her to sleep by walking around the apartment and singing songs from the Joni Mitchell albums my mom used to play so much. "Ladies of the Canyon" worked pretty well as a lullaby. I liked thinking of those ladies, out there in

California somewhere, all of them with their act together, wearing their shawls and beads.

I touch the pictures and sob with guilt and self-hate. I touch my daughter's clothes, the scarves and sandals. As I think I mentioned before, her taste runs to simple things. Not too many of them, so you could pack up your stuff in a garbage bag and head to the next foster house. I believe that was an ingrained habit with her, even though she's been out of the foster system for years now. Going on five years. A few summer clothes hang in the closet, plus some folded in the dresser.

Do you stop being a mom when your kid grows up?

I think Laura believed that. I think she believed we couldn't be mother and daughter anymore, now that she could almost vote. But that's not how it works. You don't stop being a mom just because you messed up so horribly your kid was taken from you. You sure as fire don't.

A schoolkid's bookcase is stuffed with paperbacks and a few hardcovers. Some of them I've at least heard of: the Tolkien books, some of the vampire ones, *Animal Farm* by that anti-commie guy. *To Kill a Mockingbird*. A couple of books on chess. That's impressive. Bing taught me to play when we were kids, and I've always liked the game, though I never could get Gordy to play with me. Laura must have picked it up from one of her foster parents or siblings? I try not to think of Laura's fosters with hate. Senseless to hate people for helping someone you love. But I sort of do.

Also on the shelves is a little section of serious books that aren't novels or about chess. *Siddhartha*. That book looks serious. One by someone named Seneca, which, being a one-word name like Plato, you're supposed to just know who that is. A book on learning Spanish. A book by another one-word name, Epictetus, which ditto. I wonder how you're supposed to say that one: Ee-PICK-teh-tus? Epic-TEE-tus?

Apart from the two art posters I looked at last night, there's a picture of the Greek alphabet, plus one of those history-timeline scrolls, starting with the

Stone Age and going up to 9/11. The posters are neatly stuck to the wall with double-sided tape.

I take the book by Seneca down to the kitchen and make tea. I picked that one because of the shade of optimistic blue on the cover. Being honest here. But also b), because it was the most dog-eared of all the books, meaning perhaps it was one Laura read over and over.

I'm a slow reader. Seneca, I learn, was a Stoic, one of the guys in ancient times who were like, bring on the hardship, we can deal with it. For example, this sentence:

It is not the man who has too little who is poor, but the one who hankers after more.

Seneca, I suspect, never dumpster-dived behind a Pizza Hut at midnight, but I catch his meaning. One thing I've learned in this world, it takes very little to keep body and soul together.

I like to think of Laura reading this book. However, it's also a downer to think of her reading this book, because she should have been happily reading happy books for happy little girls, not grim grown-up stuff like this Stoic guy. *Trusting everyone is as much a fault as trusting no one.* That's another thing Seneca says, early on in the book.

Gordy keeps crossing my mind, and whenever he does, I feel a stab of guilt. I'd promised to stay by him and help him in sickness and health. But I didn't; I got out of prison first and did nothing for him when he got out. Again, yeah, I was deeply messed up, but what if I'd gotten straight sooner and helped him, somehow? I could have helped him and Laura too. Now look what he's facing.

I finish my tea, and for the sake of leaving no stone unturned, take my flashlight down the basement. A predictably gloomy place, bare concrete floor, block walls, lit by a couple of bare bulbs. Plenty of spiderwebs and suspicious shadows. Pieces of ductwork and broken tools strewn in the corners. I force myself to inspect everything, but only find a dead mouse in the dryer. The washing machine seems OK. The boiler is down here, plus a newer gas water heater. I nudge up the temperature of the water heater so my next shower will be steaming hot. The boiler and oil tank look frighteningly corroded, but it was all still working, so whatever. It occurs to me to wonder how long the landlord would be OK with nobody paying rent on this place, but also, whatever. I go back up to the kitchen.

After all that, it's only nine o'clock. I phone Laura.

Chapter 11

I'm Going by BB

She picks up. "Bam? I was just about to call you."

"Hi, honey. I—"

"Something's going on at Dad's house. I'm worried."

"Ah, what?"

"One of my friends from the neighborhood called me a few minutes ago to tell me she thought she saw someone breaking into the house last night."

"Oh! Uh—"

"I asked her if she called the police and she said she did, but she didn't know if they ever showed up. And now I'm scared to—"

"Laura, dear. That would be me."

"What?"

"I broke into your dad's house last night. I drove down yesterday."

"Seriously? You're in town? Why did you—"

"I needed a place to stay, and I'd ... lost the key Gordy gave me."

"He gave you a key?"

"Y—" I clear my throat. "I found a replacement in the kitchen drawer, so everything's good now."

"Oh!" She stops for a second. "But you broke in."

"Yeah, but I fixed where I did it. So. All good."

"OK." She pauses again. "But well, but ... like ... isn't ... I mean, didn't ...?"

"Yeah, it's not the most cheery of accommodations."

"Oh, my God. Is there ...?"

"I'm avoiding the area where ... it happened. Can we meet up and talk?"

"Um, yes. Um ..."

"Not here," I quickly add.

"OK, yes. Did ... did any of my stuff get ... uh ..."

"All your stuff is fine, nobody touched it, far as I can tell."

We agree to meet at a diner called Verna's in an hour. That gives me time to go to Excalibur Pawn with the three tickets I lifted from Gordy's cigar box.

The place is still one of the best pawn shops in the upper-Woodward area: big, well-lit, the stuff nicely displayed on shelves. Racks for the motorcycle leathers and fur coats, glass cases for the jewelry and guns. Guitars and saxophones on the walls behind the counters.

Before leaving the house I put a little lipstick on, brush out my hair, and tie it back with an elastic. My ends need trimming, but that's only noticeable when I wear my hair loose. My outfit is jeans, hiking boots, and a black pullover sweater I think makes me look sophisticated. I also want to look mom-like, but what do you do? If I put on weight—gained a soft mommy-tummy—that could help. But a person's appetite is what it is.

I browse the jewelry, spotting items that matched the descriptions on the tickets, grouped with similar things.

A stroke of luck occurs when a guy behind the counter says, "Help you with anything?" and it's a guy I remember from olden times.

"Isn't your name Robby?" I ask.

"Yeah!" He brightens.

"I used to be Bambi Walsh."

"Oh, cool. What's your name now?"

"I'm still Bambi, but it's Pentecost instead of Walsh. I'm going by BB."

"OK! I remember you being a pretty good source of—various things." Robby rubs his heavy black beard with his fingers and eyes me. He wears a pistol in a brown leather holster on his belt. Smart practice, given all the idiots around who think pawn shops must be easy targets for holdups or grab-and-runs.

"Well, ha, yeah, and maybe you remember my ex, Gordy? Gordy Walsh?"

Robby pushes up his glasses, which are the wire aviator-type. That style seems to be coming back. I push up mine too. Whenever somebody pushes up their glasses, I have to push mine up. It's automatic, and every time I do it I'm like, stop doing that because maybe it makes people feel like I'm copying them. But I never think about it until after I do it. Even when somebody pushes up their glasses in a movie, I do it too.

I'm nearsighted, plus I have astigmatism, and when you're of modest means you wear budget-level glasses instead of having to keep buying contact solutions and all that. Plus the idea of putting pieces of plastic or whatever it is on my eyeballs freaks me out. My frames are plastic tortoiseshell, shaped like old-style TV screens. They're OK.

"Yeah, I remember Gordy," says Robby.

"You know that murder that happened the other day in Boston-Edison? Pretty white woman named Sandy O'Rourke? They arrested Gordy for it."

"Oh. Wow."

"He might be innocent. So I'm trying to help him for the sake of our daughter. He told me where to find these pawn tickets." I get them from my purse and flatten them on the counter.

Robby picks them up. "Yeah." He goes around and collects the pieces and lays them on a cloth-covered board. "You want to redeem them for him?"

I smile as beautifully as possible. "Not at the moment, but would it be cool if I just looked and took a picture of them?"

"Well—yeah, OK, Bambi. Don't see any reason against it."

"Did Gordy ever come in," I ask as I snap with my phone, "with a woman friend sometimes?"

"Not that I ever saw. I'm not here every day, though."

"Right, I was just wondering. Thank you, Robby."

I get to the diner at ten, just on time, take a booth next to a window, and order some tea. The place, on Cass near the Wayne State campus so Laura could walk over, is clean and pleasant. Saturday-morning busy, clanking plates and people talking and laughing in collective Saturday-morning cheerfulness. I don't remember ever being there before.

For years, I've measured my life by Laura's. Before I got pregnant with her, Gordy and I were already partying way too much. Once I knew I was pregnant, I stopped all pills, cocaine, and pot, and only drank a beer now and then. The midwife from St. Ignace was ecstatic with that.

After I gave birth to Laura, my milk didn't come down as well as it should, and the midwife said I just needed to relax about it. "Sit down and think calm thoughts. Drink a beer. Sip it slow." It worked. I suppose Laura absorbed some of the alcohol. These days breastfeeding mothers won't even drink a diet Pepsi. I think that's sad, but not my show.

The server places a large white cup and saucer before me, plus a generous-sized pot of hot water and a tea bag. I put together my drink.

Between Laura being zero and one, we three lived in the bitsy apartment in Balsam Ridge, the one that had the fire. Gordy and I got back into using drugs and alcohol regularly.

Between one and four, we lived in a series of crap-hole apartments in Detroit.

Laura age three was when Gordy busted my jaw.

Then when Laura was four and a half, Gordy and I were so out of control we both got arrested on the same night, me for solicitation and possession and him just for possession, but for larger amounts. These were not our first offenses.

We went off to jail and Laura disappeared shrieking into the foster system.

After twenty months in the Women's Huron Valley Correctional Facility, where I got clean from the drugs and alcohol, I went back to using almost as soon as I got out. Go ahead and judge: I deserve any label you'd care to paste on me. I thought I could handle the booze and pills. Every addict believes that. I thought I'd be able to find a good job—somehow—and rent a decent apartment and get Laura back. Of course I resumed hooking as well. I didn't have my act together enough to go online and make money via video clients who just wanted to see women's bodies and have them talk sweet, or dirty, to them.

The next seven or eight years went by in a blur of alcohol, drugs, and degrading occupations. I understand the urge to be respectful of all humans. That part's OK. Wanting to decriminalize sex work is OK, I guess. I don't know. But anybody who says sex work is the same as any other work is a nitwit whose only knowledge is from the movies. All the hookers in the movies are movie stars. Think about it.

Sex work is demeaning, dangerous, and depressing. It's what you do when your other options are zero. The people you meet, the people you have to deal with, are generally scum: criminals, perverts, losers, addicts. I don't count mentally ill people as scum, but they're pretty hard to cope with in an intimate situation. Take my word for it. The suburban johns with nice cars tend to be cleaner and more careful. Some of them see you as a human being. Psychologically, though, they tend to be just as miserable as any jerk in a back alley.

One more thing. There's this cliché that hookers live a rough life but have hearts of gold. That is generally a crock. The rough life part, yeah. I did meet some genuinely nice hookers, women—and a few guys—who actually had brains, handled themselves professionally, and even tried to be good to other people. They tended to be able to charge more, get off the streets and have a regular rotation of johns, whether through an escort service or whatnot. Mostly, though, when I was a hooker, my heart and the hearts of the other hookers I knew were anything but gold. I sold out anybody for anything, and I got enraged if somebody did it to me. And they did. Our hearts were garbage.

If I could go back in time, I'd punch myself in the face so hard.

Gordy got out of prison a year after I did. He drifted around, then somehow pulled himself together enough to study and receive the certification for being a sysadmin. That took him a couple years to do. He managed to rent the house in Boston-Edison, and that was enough competency for a judge to pull Laura out of the foster system when she was fourteen.

I heard about it and was instantly, insanely jealous, as if I'd been horribly betrayed. Imagine that.

My dopey ex had shown me up, pure and simple.

Shortly after Laura went to live with him, I started the work of seriously getting clean. I won't bore you with the death's-head details. It took three months, and then over the next two or three years I relapsed. Rinse, repeat. I'd be allowed to see Laura sometimes.

When she was sixteen, I left Detroit and went home to Balsam Ridge. With the help of my brother and Connie Blue Smoke, I held onto sobriety. Got the job in Jimmy's religious-supply warehouse. Got my taxi.

I've stayed off all of it.

My brain always adds, *so far.*

CHAPTER 12

YOU CAN KEEP SNARKING AT ME

Laura walks through the door at 10:30. I wouldn't have minded if she'd kept me waiting three hours. I feel my face break open in a crazy smile. I wave. "Laura."

She hangs her jacket over mine on the hook attached to our booth, then manages a side-mouth smile as she slides in opposite me.

I go, "It's great to see you, honey. Been, what, six months."

"More than." She doesn't trust my sobriety at all, which I certainly understand.

"I thought we could compare notes," I suggest. I feast my eyes on her: even lovelier than the last time I saw her. No longer slender as a girl, now she's filled out and strong, with the direct gaze of a woman. She could be an athletic model, in her golden-brown sweater over jeans. Sneakers, in spite of the cold, I noticed before she sat down.

"Do you have boots?" I ask, surprised at how instinctive that felt.

"Yes, I have boots." Irritated.

Her face shouldn't have as much character as it does. Already, a permanent V between her brows makes her look slightly suspicious, or apprehensive. Faint lines around her mouth, and the way she always seems to have a half smile going, from one side, what's the word? Cynical.

All that is my fault.

"Will you have something to eat?" I offer. "My treat."

She picks up the menu card. She scans it, her eyes flicking up to meet mine once over the top edge. She puts the menu down after a minute.

"Look, honey," I say, "I'm here to do what I can. I know it's been way too long since we really talked, really spent time together. And that's on me."

"No, actually, Bam, if you'll remember, the last time you tried to reach out to me I rejected you."

What must it be like to experience basically PTSD when you meet up with your mother? What she just said is true.

A server comes over and Laura looks up. "Steak and eggs. Medium on the steak. Rye toast."

"Coming up. Coffee?" A long white apron is tied around the server's generous waist, like the waiters in a French movie I saw once. She's got on a black t-shirt with the name of the diner on it. Young, open-faced. Everyone here is so young. I notice, though, people who might be professors, crowding in from the cold along with the younger people. What are professors supposed to look like? To me, they're supposed to look intelligent, like they know more than I do, about more than just one subject. But come to think of it, I'm sure I could educate them about a thing or two.

Laura nods yes to coffee, and the server takes off.

I sit up straight. "I wouldn't blame you if you wanted to go no contact with me for the rest of our lives. I was hoping we could talk, though. About our lives, yours and mine."

"I thought we were here to talk about Dad. I have nothing to say to you about ... our lives."

"Well, I have some things I'd like to say to you."

"I don't want to hear them." She clears her throat and glances out the window uncomfortably.

"That's OK. There's plenty of time for us to see if we can have any kind of—"

"We can't."

"—relationship, and maybe work to build something good. But right now—"

"Did you hear what I said?" She bites her lip lightly.

"Yes."

"Fine, then."

"You can speak for yourself but not for me."

That surprises her, my sharp tone.

Her coffee comes, and she stirs brown sugar into it. I like brown sugar too. She sets her spoon on her saucer.

It's nice to have a cup and saucer instead of just a mug, as there's a place to put your spoon after you've stirred. Otherwise you're looking around for a spare napkin, or you just set your wet spoon on the tabletop, which, ick.

I consider how much my approach to life has changed. Before, at the first hint of danger—the snap of a twig—I'd be off and running. I'd disappear through the woods. But here are a pair of headlights bearing down on me, *roaring* down on me, and I'm standing here motionless, fixed. If I get flattened, I get flattened.

I tell her, "I'm going to leave off the I'm-sorrys for a while. You can keep snarking at me. But eventually I might have to ask you why I'm here. You wanted my help. I came. If at any point you want me to leave, I'll leave."

She eyes me, subdued. Says nothing, but she's thinking.

"You look beautiful, by the way. I love how you're doing your hair."

Laura was endowed with a gentle series of waves in her auburn hair, a throwback to my European heritage, I think. Some peasant Pole who mated with an Irish washerwoman, maybe. Me, I came out with a frizzy thatch of copper red, now showing gray hairs if you look close. People comment on red hair. Some people seem to consider you special if you have red hair, while others seem to be annoyed by it. Why is that? There's a stereotype that we all have terrible tempers. Fiery redheads. I like to think I'm a pretty calm person. I've certainly been able to keep my cool in some hella situations.

Laura's hair is shorter than I've seen it, not a pixie, but a swept-back chin-length cut. Her ears show. She looks cute and good, with her pale skin and leftover freckles from childhood.

"You have nice ears," I add.

Patience is my trusted companion. Has to be.

Her steak and eggs come, hot and smelling good. I drink my tea while she digs in. It's nice to see people enjoy their food. She'd ordered her eggs sunny side up, same as I like mine. I feel a wave inside me, like a surge of longing, to cook something for her and watch her eat and enjoy it.

I wonder if she's sexually active and if so, what sort of birth control she's using. I wonder if she smokes cigarettes or pot or drinks alcohol or uses anything else. I open my mouth, thinking to ask something, then immediately shut it.

Outside, a young couple walks by, arm in arm, talking and laughing. Relaxed. I want that for Laura. A nice companion.

"What happened to your hand?" I only now notice the knuckles of her right hand, which are scabbed over and edged by old-looking bruises. "Did you punch a wall?"

She stuns me by answering, "Well, yeah. But only after I punched—" she catches herself. "Let me just say, you should see the other guy."

"Laura. Seriously. Were you in a fight?"

"Bam, you can't take anything too serious in this world."

I sure want to know the story of that busted-up fist, but she's not about to tell me. I do remember that she had temper issues as a toddler, apart from everything else. She hides her hand in her lap, then decides screw it and puts it back on the table next to her coffee mug. The look in her eyes is a mix of defiant and sheepish.

I ask, "Have you been able to do anything, find out anything about your dad's arrest?"

Glad to get onto the subject, she says, "I went down to police headquarters and tried to talk to somebody who knows what's going on, but I didn't get very far. Then I called his lawyer, Mr. Ayoub."

"Good thinking. What did he—"

"That he's in contact with the court, and he's gonna defend Dad to the fullest extent. That was it."

"Well, he's not a public defender, and it seems he's already worked for Gordy, so hopefully he'll be able to devote significant time to this job."

"Yeah."

I talk about her father's police interview, basically summarizing it.

"You saw it? The video?"

"Yes."

"How?"

"I have a friend or two in the DPD." I sip my tea, which was some diner-supply brand, which, whatever. Someday I hope to be one of those tea gourmet type people. Ten dollars for a little tin of tea.

"Well, what else can your friend do for us?"

"I don't know. I'm working on it."

"But Dad didn't confess, though, right?"

"No, not at all. But he did admit to handling the knife. The murder weapon. After the fact."

"Well, that doesn't mean anything after the fact, right?"

"Not literally, but it doesn't look good. It was enough to get him arrested. He had his first court appearance yesterday morning, and they're holding him on $300,000 bail."

She puts her fork down. "That's crazy!"

"Given that he was already a convicted felon, no, it's not."

After a minute, during which we both silently acknowledge that nobody with assets cared enough about Gordy to put up their house or whatever to get him out, she goes back to eating. I tell her about my hunt through Gordy's house, leaving out spying through her things. I pull up the jewelry photos from Excalibur Pawn on my phone. "Do you recognize these?"

"Oh, gosh," she says. "They're Sandy's. I bet any money they're Sandy's. I remember she always used to wear that cross with the emerald in the center. I don't know if it's a real emerald. And the watch, that looks like the one she wore."

"You saw her wearing these?"

"Yeah." She drinks her coffee and stirs more brown sugar in with her spoon, *tink-tink-tink.* A server going by carrying three plates of food trips on someone's scarf hanging from a chair near us and almost drops the food but manages not to. Two people clap for him.

"The pearls?" I ask.

"I don't know. Probably. I mean, I think I've seen her wear a pearl necklace, but I wouldn't literally know if those were hers. Why would Dad have those things, and why would he hock them?" She chews vigorously on a bite of steak, having dredged it in egg yolk first. It's diner-level steak, of course, pretty tough. Still, my mouth waters. I don't want to spend on a restaurant meal for myself, especially as Laura ordered the most expensive thing. Which was fine; I just had to watch my budget. Because I had a growing feeling I might be in Detroit for more than a couple of days. I decide to pour some brown sugar into my tea, just for the calories.

"Well," I comment, setting my spoon on my saucer, "the only reason you hock something is you need money."

"Dad always does seem to be broke."

"Mm. Did he ever talk to you about his job? How much money he made?"

"No, just that it wasn't enough for everything he did. And the bosses were idiots."

Gordy would always be smarter than any boss in history.

"As for you, now," I say, "you're all set up with your own checking account and all that stuff? Where you can deposit your pay from the school and whatnot?" She'd told me she worked part-time as a receptionist at the residence hall where she lived.

"Yeah, Dad set up an account for us. My school pay is direct deposit into that."

"Us? As in—"

"Dad and I are both on it."

"It's a joint account, then."

"I don't know what it's called. The bank fixed it so he can put money in, and I can put money in and take it out. It's my account—it's my money, but he's on it." She looks at me. "So he can keep track of it same as I can. To be on the safe side."

"The safe side."

Something dawns on her right then.

Not wanting to push it further, I go, "What else do you know about Sandy?"

"I was going to ask you that."

"I know next to nothing about her, other than she was twenty-nine years old, and seeing Vic Paladino lately. Was she some bimbo? How did she meet Paladino?"

Laura eyes me over her coffee cup rim. She swallows. "Naturally you'd call her a bimbo."

"I did not call her a bimbo. I'm just wondering if she was some throwaway person *to Paladino*. I might add, bimbo is a step up from what *I* ever was in this town."

"Well, I knew her, some. She was a good person. They told in the news this morning she was a student here at Wayne, did you know that?"

"She was? I haven't seen the papers today." I still say 'the papers' even though it's all online now, practically. Twenty-nine years old isn't typical college age. But I guess anybody can go, if you get accepted. "What else came out today? Did you know that, about her college?"

"Yes. She was studying psychology."

"Huh."

Laura goes on to tell me that Sandy lived in a tiny but OK apartment in Jefferson-Chalmers. "She and Dad met at Dally in the Alley like three years ago."

Dally is an annual food and music fest in the Cass Corridor zone, right near this café.

"What was she like? Did you get along with her?

"Yes. We got along. I mean, she didn't try to pull any stepmom-type stuff with me. We had an argument one time, I was being a brat. She sat me down and said look, I can't tell you what to do, and I'm not gonna try. I just want you to be decent to me, like I'm decent to you. I respected that."

"What did she see in your dad, you think?"

"Well, I don't know. What did *you* see in him?"

"In my case, it was pretty much just a hormonal attraction. And I guess we shared—" I think of our drinking and drugging— "common interests." I swallow some more tea and look out the window. Cars were picking their way through the pothole-scape of Cass. "They broke up, uh, how long ago?"

"Getting on to a year, I guess."

"Do you know why?"

Laura bites her lip. She looks at me and sighs. "From what I could tell, she got tired of him asking for money."

"She gave him money?"

"I think quite a bit. Which he was supposed to pay back but never did."

"How did you learn that?"

She pauses. "He had a few beers one night and got maudlin about her, and he more or less told me."

That's a good word, maudlin. I know what it means, but it's not the type of word you hear every day.

Ignoring the part about the beers, which contradicts what she said the other day about Gordy being straight and sober, I say, "Do you think you could find out more about Sandy? Like any other friends of hers, maybe talk to her teachers at the college?"

Laura rubs under her chin with a knuckle. "I think I could do that. I have a few other ideas too."

"Yeah? Like what?"

"I'll tell you if I learn anything, OK?"

"OK, honey."

"Don't call me honey."

I have to smile at that. "There's a lot I'm willing to do for you. And there's a lot I'm willing to put up with from you, *no complaints.* You calling me 'Bam' is one of them. But so I draw the line at 'honey.' I'll call you honey whenever I bloody well want to."

Raised eyebrows.

I go, "I know you're just in first year here, but do you have an idea of what you'd like to specialize in?"

"It's called a major."

"Right, a major."

"I'm already in the languages program, studying Spanish and Portuguese."

"Oh! That's interesting. Do you—"

"I'm also taking some political science courses. I'm going to double major, if I can."

"Wow."

"I want to be a diplomat."

"My gosh, wow, Laura. That sounds wonderful! Very—"

"Responsible."

"Yes!"

Her plate is clean.

"Before we go," I say, "I want to ask you one more thing. Do you know what prompted your dad to get you back? Out of foster?"

"Well—" She breaks off and considers, knuckle to jaw. "He loved me. He told me that." Her tone turns cold. "Maybe he—you know—*missed me.*"

I don't know whether Laura knew I'd been sending Gordy money to help pay her expenses. At first, when I started the getting-clean process, I sent $100 a month. I worked different jobs. Then I increased it to $125, then $150. It wasn't nearly enough, but it's what I could send more or less regularly. There was no court order for this. I figured when she turned 18, I'd just send money directly to her, to help until she was out of college and into hopefully some good job.

But I've been wondering about Gordy's motives. He was so selfish, always. How come he wanted to all of a sudden be in Laura's life? Have her be in his? Do things for her, look after her? I've wondered a lot about that.

"I'm taking for granted he never hit you, Laura. Is that right?"

"Dad never hit me!"

"Never was abusive?"

"*No*. Well, obviously he'd get mad sometimes. We'd get mad at each other. I mean, you know. But he'd always get ahold of himself, pretty quick. He was never a real jackass to me."

"Never came down on you hard?"

"No. He never needed to ground me, frankly, Bam. I was always so terrified of getting sent back into foster. Worried he'd decide I was too much bother. I stayed away from drugs, boys, just about anything that could get me in trouble."

I go to pay the bill. When I get back from the cash stand I tuck some tip money next to my saucer. I notice Laura's cup and spoon on the table. No saucer. I thought we'd both gotten saucers for our cups. We had. I remember her setting her spoon on hers after stirring in her sugar.

I glance at her, about to say something, but she's looking away. She pretends to stretch her neck.

I hand her coat to her and put mine on.

CHAPTER 13

RICH ENOUGH TO HIRE A HIT

Not having eaten at the restaurant, I'm feeling plenty hungry, so I pick up some groceries at a store up Woodward: more bread, peanut butter, bananas, plus a box of Red Rose, a dozen eggs, some apples, carrots, a block of American cheese, a package of hot dogs. It feels good to pay cash.

Back at the house, I fix myself an egg pancake, this little thing I like to make. You just mix up a couple of eggs, then cook them in one piece in a small pan. Low heat. When they're almost done you throw on stuff, like today I cut up some salami into little pieces, and chopped some cheese off the block I'd just bought. I shake the pan a little to get some of the egg to slop over onto the salami and cheese. Then, when the bottom is crispy and brown, I flip it over so the stuff on top can cook. I like to keep it just a little gooshy in the center. Salt and pepper.

After eating and washing everything up, I dig around the house some more. I search carefully around Gordy's computer desk, and find a bunch of junk, but also an index card that must have fallen behind a stack of magazines next to the wall. It's an important trove, with a list of passwords written on it in Gordy's small printing. The passwords are the same except with the company name in them:

GordyAmex333

GordyCiti333

GordyComerica333

GordyVisa333

GordyVisa-2-3332

GordyVisa-3-3333

GordyWi-fi333

And so on. Gordy considered three to be his lucky number. Now that I have his wi-fi password, I log in to save data use on my phone. I'd brought my laptop, so I fire that up and get on the websites and log in as him, one after the other. Easy as pie.

What I find makes my eyes bug out: a $30,000 balance, roughly, on the Citicard Visa, $50,000 on an American Express. Five more Visa cards, all of them maxed out. More than $170,000 total. The last few statements include sternly worded past-due notices. I'm sure I looked like a cartoon person, mouth hanging open, blinking and shaking my head too fast.

Although I've never owned a credit card legally, I know how they work and what a statement is. The vast majority of the charges in the statements are cash advances. As of roughly three months ago, Gordy couldn't charge any more on those cards. The interest amounts were unbelievable. How did he get all those cards? I go back and look more closely to see if any are in Laura's name instead of his, which none are, fortunately.

Gordy, I knew, liked toys as much as the next manchild, but this was pretty extreme, especially considering his income. And if he wanted toys, why not just buy them with the cards, instead of getting cash advances? And if he *had* bought himself a bunch of expensive toys, where were they?

I phone Laura.

"Did your dad like to go to the casinos? Do you know if he was a gambler?"

"Huh. No, I never heard him say he was going gambling, not that that's proof he didn't. Why?"

"He's got massive credit card debt, for cash advances." I tell her the amounts. "Were you ever aware of that?"

"Nuh-unh. Jeez, Bam."

Gordy knew the casino odds—everybody does—and he also hated to lose, so the gambling possibility didn't make much sense, but it was all I could think of at the moment.

The last account I get into is Gordy's checking at Comerica bank. It takes some time, but I'm able to download his consolidated statements from when he opened the account four years back. I see his stunningly huge pay deposits, every two weeks, and I see the deposits of the little sums I'd sent to help with Laura.

Lots of cash withdrawals of round numbers in the thousands, between five and ten thousand, lots of them.

Back to the main page, I check the balance on the joint account Gordy holds with Laura. It stands at a little over six hundred dollars. I view the auto-deposits from the university, for Laura's receptionist work, and small ATM withdrawals for pocket cash. She was doing some saving already, it looked like.

Next I phone Connie Blue Smoke and tell her I'll be staying in Detroit a few more days.

"OK. How are you doing?"

"Fine. I'm OK. Have you been able to learn anything about Gordy and Sandy O'Rourke?"

"I did ask around. Nobody seems to know anything about Sandy O'Rourke, nobody ever saw him bring a girlfriend up here. In fact, nobody's really noticed Gordy around here for years, it seems."

"I thought he went up now and then, to see his folks."

"Well, I don't know," Connie says. "But listen, when I stopped in at the bar, I saw Prue Walerski there, and we talked. Remember her?"

"Oh, yeah. She was one of the smart ones, like you."

"You were always smart enough."

"Yeah, I know."

"Well, anyway, she said she's not at all surprised that Gordy's accused of killing a woman."

"You weren't all that surprised yourself."

"Right, but listen. Prue said remember Roberta Summerline? And I was like, whoa, what do you mean? And she said she always thought Gordy *knew* something about what happened to her."

Roberta Summerline. A year ahead of me, in Gordy's class. I vaguely remember her, and even more vaguely seem to remember she went missing or ran away. "Wasn't she a cheerleader?"

"Yeah. They were all such sluts. They never learned any good routines, they just stood there and shook their—"

"Ha. And Roberta—"

"Roberta was the sluttiest one."

We snicker in solidarity. "But what *did* happen to her?" I ask. "Didn't she run away?"

"All I know is, she stopped coming to school. Prue said Roberta was having trouble at home. She kept talking—Roberta did—about going out to California where it's warm and the people are friendly and avocados grow on trees."

"They do grow on trees, don't they?"

"I don't know, I guess so."

I say, "I thought she would have taken off for Detroit or Chicago like the rest of us."

"She was dating Wade Kullen at the time, if I remember right. I ought to find out about him. Maybe they took off together."

As we talk, I roam slowly around the house, looking out the windows and holding my free hand over the radiators to enjoy their warmth. The corners in most of the rooms are blurry with cobwebs. I'm going to have to do some cleaning. That was one thing I learned in the various rehabs I went to: keeping yourself and your stuff clean goes a long way. Furthermore, I've noticed that cleaning something gives you a piece of control over it. Like it becomes more *yours*, somehow.

I go, "I don't know if Gordy even knew Roberta. He never mentioned her to me. Did her family, you know, report her missing?"

"Prue says they did, and the police looked into it halfheartedly. Her family was crummy. I don't think they gave a rip."

"Well, Gordy never mentioned her," I say again.

"I always hated those cheerleaders."

It isn't like Connie to be that snarky. I ask, "Did you try out and they wouldn't let you in or something?"

"Ha! No. It was just—remember how they were always trying to make themselves special? Like they'd all buy the same sweater and wear them on the same day? They were the clique of cliques in that school. Remember how they gave each other stupid nicknames?"

"I guess I do, yeah."

"I asked Prue why she thought Gordy would know anything about Roberta's disappearance, or even have something to do with it, and she said something ambiguous about 'timing.'"

"And that's it?"

"She wouldn't really say anything more," Connie concludes. "I don't know if she was playing around or what."

"Like trying to manufacture drama?"

"Yeah. It's interesting, though."

"And you haven't bumped into Wade Kullen for a long time?"

"No, that's the thing. Isn't it interesting that Roberta and Wade essentially dropped off everybody's radar at the same time?"

I thank her, and she promises to keep her ears open.

As I'm thinking about all that, Ted Alvarez stops by. I welcome him enthusiastically, because I have no idea what to do next.

"Learned anything more?" he asks, tossing his coat on a chair. He glances at the sheet-draped couch and gives me a grim look.

I pull cushions from the two armchairs and say, "Let's hang out over here." We sit on the rug in the dining room, in a patch of sunlight. The cushions make things comfy enough, and we don't have to look at the murder couch. I tell Alvarez about the pawned jewelry and my conversation with Laura. "Plus I hacked into Gordy's credit card accounts."

"You did? I'm impressed."

"Yeah, *aaannd* the jackass was borrowing big-time. Cash advances, maxing out cards."

Ted extends his legs in front of him and leans forward to touch his toes, grunting softly as his lower back gives in to the stretch. "The department's getting a search warrant for his financial records, so they'd learn that soon."

"Who knows what he did with all that money, though?"

Still in his stretch, Ted says into his legs, "Well, extortion's a possibility."

"Right. Apart from that, I think Vic Paladino needs to be looked at seriously."

Ted straightens up. "Why?"

"Well, just because Sandy was seeing him, you know?"

"He's got a tight alibi for that day. And there doesn't seem to be any reason for him to have wanted Sandy O'Rourke dead."

"Well, stuff goes on between people."

"I know, Bambi."

"Have the homicide guys checked her apartment?"

"Yeah, of course. I don't believe they found anything of interest. No struggle, nothing to indicate she was abducted by force."

"Was Vic considering asking to marry her?"

"Who knows? He's got a string of ex-wives, so I imagine he's on the hook for a lot of alimony. Or maybe they all just took cash lump settlements and be done with it."

I think about wives for a minute. Wondering about Alvarez's wife, Darlene, the one I threatened him about when we first talked. I wonder how good their relationship is at the moment. Hope it's good.

"What's Paladino's alibi?" I say it tough-like, TV cop style.

Alvarez snorts in amusement. "He was with Jason Givens that day from midafternoon until midnight."

"Who's Jason Givens?"

"I wondered if you knew the name. He's a detective sergeant in the DPD."

"Oh. Never came in contact with him."

"Givens took Paladino target shooting in a gravel pit somewhere until it got dark, then they went to Givens's house for some food and drinks. They watched the Pistons game on TV."

"So they're like buddies?"

"Yeah, Paladino's a police buff, you know the type. Givens worked one of his concerts a few years ago, and I guess they struck up a friendship."

"Paladino wants to be a tough guy?"

"Yeah, and he loves Givens because he takes him out to do insane stuff, like go shooting outdoors in the dead of winter."

I go, "But Paladino's rich enough to hire a hit, of course."

"Yeah, but like I said, for why? This woman wasn't threatening him, she wasn't out of control in the relationship. By all appearances, they were enjoying each other. There was no obvious benefit to Paladino for her to be dead."

"That you know of."

"That's right."

"Could she have been pregnant?"

"They tested for that, negative."

"Insurance policy?"

"There was one, with her father as beneficiary."

"Ted, really? I almost didn't ask about that, because she was so young. For how much?"

"Five hundred."

"As in thousand? Five hundred thousand? Are you guys looking at the dad, whoever he is?"

"The investigators talked to him. Nothing jumped out at them. He seemed genuinely upset, grieving, for whatever that's worth."

"Did he know Vic Paladino?"

"I don't know, Bambi. Look, why don't we get that couch out of here?"

"Seriously?"

"Yeah, why not?"

I jump up, grateful energy surging through me. I remove the sheet so we can get a grip on the frame. Ted takes the bloody end.

"Ever the gentleman," I comment.

"Let's go."

We half shove, half wrestle the thing to the front door. I prop the door open with the brick Gordy used as a stop, and once past the tight squeeze of the doorframe, the process gets easier. We bump the couch down the few stone steps to the walkway. At that point we're able to actually lift the hideous ruin and carry it to the curb. By the time we get it there and drop it in the remaining ratty snow, a couple of cars are already slowing down, the better to evaluate the find.

Thinking aloud, I go, "Maybe we should cover up that stain with a rag or something."

"Bambi, this is Detroit."

"Right you are."

Chapter 14

Unfazed as a Cat

A butler greets Chuck Stratton at the front door of a large house overlooking Lake St. Clair, in Grosse Pointe. It's eleven o'clock Sunday morning.

"OK to leave my car there?" Stratton's Ford sits under a generous portico at the apex of the curving drive.

"Certainly, sir." The butler, a flawlessly groomed guy of about 35, takes Stratton's heavy shearling coat. He indicates a spacious living room, or sitting room, or whatever it is, off the marble-floored foyer.

"Ms. Jensen will be in shortly. My name is Helmut. May I offer you something, Mr. Stratton? Coffee, tea, something stronger?"

"Glass of water would be great." Stratton carries a letter-sized portfolio under his arm.

"Certainly. Ice?"

"Sure."

The house is one of the classic old ones, just a couple of miles upstream from the Detroit city limit. Fancy wood and pretty colors in this living room, a feminine energy to it. Windows that make the place bright and pleasant, even though the day is dreary. Stratton remains standing, relaxed on his feet, near a fireplace with one of those gas apparatuses that shoots a modern-looking curtain of flame up from some invisible origin. A slot in the fire bricks?, Stratton wonders. The fire looks nice.

He'd spent an hour on Saturday afternoon writing up his security plan for the Gloria Jensen concert in the spring. The singer hadn't wanted Stratton to email her the plans, fearing, she said, hackers. So here he is.

Helmut delivers the glass of ice water with a small cloth napkin on a silver tray, and Stratton thanks him.

Gloria Jensen sweeps into the room, one hand extended to Stratton, the other trailing behind. "Here's my boy!"

Statton was neither a boy nor hers, but he only says, "Hello, Ms. Jensen." He takes her hand, shakes it once, then drops it.

"Oh, call me Gloria! Well, how've you been? You're looking *quite* well, I must say."

"Fine, thank you. I have for you—"

"So good of you to come over on a Sunday. You were at the Aretha just yesterday?"

Helmut goes away.

"Yes." Stratton draws an envelope from the portfolio, which is of thin leather, soft with wear. "I printed everything out. There's a flash stick in here as well with the plan, including all the pictures I took." He holds out the envelope, but Gloria arranges herself on a flower-print couch and pats the place next to her. Properly, he should have delivered the security plan to Gloria's security guy, but Stratton learned she had dismissed him a month ago and not yet hired a replacement.

Gloria Jensen certainly is a looker, still. Smooth face, the skin not weirdly tightened with plastic surgery or injections, a ready smile, nice figure, not too thin. Good legs for sure, shown off by the leotard pants she wore, topped by a body-hugging tunic of shiny cloth.

She twinkles at him and again pats the cushion next to her. "Here, let's go over it together." Her speaking voice is as rich as her singing voice, big and luxurious.

Stratton obliges, because that's what he's getting paid for. He opens the envelope and shakes out the papers on the coffee table in front of them. The cushions under his thighs are pleasantly firm. Couches that swallow you whole are no good.

He smells her perfume, and of course she lays a hand on his back as he leans forward to spread out the materials. Of course she does. He sorts through the papers and explains everything, pointing out one thing and another with two fingers. He's aware of his big hands and tries to use them with a modicum of grace.

"It shouldn't be a difficult job," he concludes. "Jacoby's crew will work with yours."

"Jacoby? I don't know him."

"He's a sterling guy. They've never had a serious problem."

Gloria caresses Stratton's back, feeling his muscles through his shirt. Her other hand, red-fingernailed, moves along her own thigh, up and down. Her fingernails are perfectly done, though too long, Stratton thinks. He likes practical women. But he does like them good-looking, and Gloria Jensen certainly filled that bill.

He clears his throat and stands up, gently shrugging off her hand on the way.

"Chuck." Sultry tone, low in the throat.

He turns to her. "I thought you were going to try to hire me away from Paladino."

Her eyes widen. "Well, yes! That's the idea. I'll double your pay, whatever it is."

"But not the only idea."

"Ha! Caught!" She fingers the necklace at her throat, a string of colorful gems, and smiles widely, twinkling all the way. Then she turns pensive. "I just can't get you off my mind."

He catches himself before he sighs too heavily. "You're a very nice lady, and a terrific performer." He used the word performer deliberately. "I'll be glad to answer any questions that come up."

"But Chuck. Please." Her face gets sad. "I'm frightened. You know that. I need you more than Vic does." Seeing him look around for his coat, forgetting that Helmut had taken it, she cuts to the chase. "You *handsome* bull."

"You haven't actually been threatened at all, have you?" That was a ridiculous thing to say, he thinks too late. They all get threats on social media.

"Oh, but I have, I have!"

"You've gotten law enforcement involved, then?"

Slight pause. Checkmate. "Yes! Of course!"

"Then I couldn't really do any better for you. I need to go."

"You're not afraid of me, are you?"

Enough. "For crying out loud, ma'am. I think you're a lovely lady, but I'm not available."

She was as unfazed as a cat. "Oh? You're seeing someone?"

"Don't make it hard on me, ma'am."

Gloria Jensen flings herself back on the cushioned couch. "Oh, all right. You're a tough man, Chuck."

Helmut is already in the foyer holding Stratton's coat. As he offers the coat, Helmut's eyebrows barely flick, just a hint of sardonic understanding. "Thanks," says Stratton.

CHAPTER 15

IF YOU LIED TO THE POLICE

Vic Paladino looks up from his lunch as Stratton enters his study. A police magazine lies open on his desk in front of him. The way he takes off his reading glasses and folds them into the breast pocket of his jacket gives a clue as to his meticulous demeanor. Stratton has observed this before. He closes the heavy oak door and turns to his boss.

"Sit down, Chuck. How did it go with Gloria?" Paladino flips the magazine closed.

Stratton eases himself into a leather club chair. The room is a wood-paneled masculine affair with green drapes and so on. "She wants to hire me away from you, and she wants me to make love to her. The security plan for the Aretha was just a fake-out. Did you know that? Were you in on it with her?"

Paladino doesn't laugh. "That's classic Gloria, all right." His speaking voice is resonant, his enunciation clear.

"I don't appreciate being put in that position."

"Man, I didn't know. I wouldn't do that to you. Anyway, what's your problem with Gloria? She's pretty hot."

"There's something about her that's—desperate."

"Well, yeah, the clock's ticking for all of us."

Normally, Stratton thinks, Paladino would be all hyper-jovial about Gloria Jensen making a play for him. But Sandy's death has shaken him up, badly.

"I miss the Aretha," says Paladino. "I felt like I hit the big time there." He pauses thoughtfully. "No, it was more of an acceleration for me, that venue, that beautiful place, the energy of the fresh air and the audiences. The ramp up, and I knew it, and I enjoyed it. I miss that place."

"You wanted to see me," Stratton says. "How are you doing?"

"Not good, Chuck, not good."

"I know you cared for Sandy quite a lot."

"I did. I loved her, man. And she was a doll, Chuck, she was a doll in so many ways. She loved me too. It's horrible."

"Yes. I thought she was a nice person, a genuine person."

"I wanted to marry her. But I didn't propose yet, it would have been too quick. I was stupid about women in the past, when I was young. Selfish. Arrogant. Sandy was so different, I wanted to take it easy with her. She was trying to look out for me."

"In what way?"

No answer.

After a moment Stratton says, "It takes time to ... contend with something like this."

"Well, that—that's the thing." Paladino pushes his luncheon salad away. He takes a drink from the glass of mineral water he likes to have with his food, then sits back in his swivel chair.

Stratton looks at him, gathering his mental energy. "What is it?"

The famous singer's face has always been a full one. His head is large, and his chest is big too. The face stops short of being jowly, saved by a wide mouth and expressive eyes. His bushy eyebrows, decidedly arched, help as well, pulling his face upward, as it were. He could fit in as the cheerful plowman or baker all the village girls go for.

"Well, I might not be ..." Paladino pauses, going into the middle distance with his gaze, "... entirely in the clear on this."

Stratton has listened to many a startling confidence in his day, but this is exceptional. He sits back in his chair. "You'd better tell me everything."

"Well, I can't. But—I wasn't with Jason the whole time, like I said I was. To the detective that came by."

"Vic. You lied to the police? If you weren't with Jason, where were you?"

"*Not* at Sandy's old boyfriend's house! I didn't kill her!"

Stratton waits.

"I need help, Chuck."

"Why can't you tell me where you were? If you lied to the police, I doubt I can help you."

Paladino buries his face in his hands. Stratton thinks he might be crying. But he looks up, eyes dry. "I keep remembering playing the Aretha when it was Chene Park, when it was just a slab and some pillars. People came. They clapped. I love that place, you know?"

Stratton says, "What's all this nostalgia? What do you want me to do for you?"

"Well, first off, I just need—somebody to talk to."

"And somehow at this moment, Sunpod isn't able to fill the bill."

Paladino looks up, exasperated. "Oh, Chuck, gimme a break."

Sunpod is Paladino's spiritual counselor, that's what he calls her. As far as Stratton can tell, Sunpod is a useless hanger-on who spews wisdom from fortune cookies and self-published poetry books. Though in fairness, she did handle a bunch of stuff at the house, managing the cleaning squad and the landscape guys. Sunpod likes to wear long dresses made of white gauze fabric, with a strip of leather tied as a belt. It is unclear to Stratton, actually, whether Sunpod is a she for sure; Sunpod wears her ice-blond hair cropped short, and her jaw is markedly square. Yet she seems to have breasts, and speaks in a whispery high register. Stratton sticks with 'she' in his mind for the sake of clarity, and to be agreeable.

"All right," Stratton says. "Did Jason Givens have anything to do with the murder?"

"No, no, of course not. Well—" Paladino stops. "I don't know, literally, OK? I wasn't ... I didn't have eyes on him all that afternoon and night."

"So, what did you guys do?" Stratton picks up a smooth stone from a side table and hefts it in his hand. The cobble is butterscotch in color, and feels nice. He needs to keep his cool and think. His job is to help his boss, but not to dive under a bus for him. Abetting a crime after the fact is out.

On the other hand, Stratton has successfully bent laws now and then, with great care and forethought. A former boss was about to get framed for money laundering by a scumbag who wanted to save his own skin, and Stratton was able to reverse the tables. A bit of cash, a bit of reasoning with an honest but ill-informed witness.

He hefts the smooth cobble from hand to hand.

When Paladino stays silent, Stratton says, "Look, if neither you nor Givens had anything to do with Sandy's death, and some other guy's in custody for it, what's there for you to worry about?"

"Do you think there's any way you can, like, find out for sure if that other guy did it? Because if it turns out he didn't, maybe they'll take a harder look at me."

Stratton sets the cobble down. "Is there something else going on with you that's ... illegal? Is that what you're worried about? Police scrutiny in general?"

"You have a very sharp mind, Chuck."

CHAPTER 16

DR. PELTZ-SPRAGUE

At 10 a.m. Monday morning, Laura Walsh makes her way to an auditorium in the General Lectures building. She checks her watch. Dr. Emily Peltz-Sprague is teaching there and will be finished in a few minutes. Laura slips into the back and stands with her shoulders against the concrete-block wall that forms a pleasant arc around and down to the podium. The room is brightly lit. Fifty or sixty students sit in upholstered seats with those writing-panel attachments, typing notes into their electronic tablets. A few, Laura observes, write by hand with styluses onto their tablets. She scans the room with a small feeling of anxiousness until she spots one student—a single renegade—writing in a wire-bound notebook with a ballpoint pen. He sports a green school sweatshirt and jeans. Laura prefers to take notes by hand as well, and likes anyone else who does, just on principle.

Dr. Peltz-Sprague's course is called, "Transgressions: The Universality of Post-Traumatic Stress Disorder in Emerging Populations." Laura knows what PTSD is but she doesn't exactly know what an emerging population is. The professor is telling the students something about a research trip.

"—and we'd no sooner made contact with the nucleus group when Peterburg's gaggle showed up."

A soft groan goes up from the class, which evidently has been following this tale for some time.

Dr. Peltz-Sprague noticed Laura come in. She paused for just an instant, then went on with her lecture.

"Yeah," says the professor, "here they came in their canoes, carrying on like an Alabama frat party, shouting and taking pictures. *Taking pictures* before their first dugout even touched the mud bank!"

Chuckles and scoffing from the students, the collective tone a mix of contempt and pleasure.

Laura kneads her shoulders on the hard concrete wall. She'd swum that morning, did a mile, and her traps are a little sore. She takes off her anorak jacket and rolls it up under her arm. The hard wall feels good through her thick oatmeal-colored wool sweater.

Dr. Peltz-Sprague adjusts her hairstyle, a poufy gray cloud. Generous of figure, the professor wears a black long-sleeved t-shirt, wide pants, and a roughly styled copper necklace that looked like it used to be a valve assembly for an engine.

"I mean, Peterburg's cameras were these weapons-grade *Leicas* with all these telephoto lenses, virtually a bunch of *howitzers* pointed at every child and adult on that riverbank." She smiles wryly. "Need I tell you this grand entrance succeeded in undoing everything my team had so far accomplished! I'll be writing about this," she adds, glaring defensively, it seemed, up at Laura, as if maybe she were a Peterburg spy.

A soft chime draws Dr. Peltz-Sprague's attention to a black phone on a table next to the podium. The students begin to stir as she concludes, a little more loudly over the stirring, "I'll tell you on Thursday how we regained control of the situation, as well as preliminary findings. Read chapters eleven to fifteen in Beekman and St. John. And if I were you, I'd be nearly finished with my two-thousand-worder by now."

Laura waits as the students file out through the doors, checking their phones.

Two students stay behind to talk to the professor, then they leave, and Dr. Peltz-Sprague, who clearly had remained aware of Laura, glances up at her again. Laura starts down the aisle as the professor gathers her computer tablet and phone into a canvas briefcase.

"Dr. Peltz-Sprague, hello," says Laura with a smile.

The professor eyes her suspiciously, which puzzles Laura. She's just another student, just a kid here at Wayne. Laura takes a step back, hands loose at her sides, and Dr. Peltz-Sprague seems to relax.

"My name is Laura Pentecost. I'm a student here, in the languages program. I'm looking into what happened to Sandy O'Rourke. I knew her. I wonder if you'd be willing to talk with me a little bit. As her graduate advisor, you were like a mentor to her, I bet. Right?"

Laura has learned that not every graduate student-advisor relationship is close, but some are quite cordial. Worth poking into.

The professor's face changes, as Laura expected, into an expression of pain and bafflement. She looks as if she might well up, but she simply closes her eyes for about a three-count, then opens them.

Laura says, "I'm sorry for intruding into your workday. I was just hoping you could—"

"Why didn't you email me first?"

"—spare me a few minutes." Laura had not wanted to explain a whole lot about this in advance, which might give the professor a chance to think of an excuse to say no. Laura chose here to use her mother's last name, though her legal name was Walsh, same as her dad's. No need to reveal that relationship here.

Dr. Peltz-Sprague looks her over: the girl's open face, long neck, firm figure in her jeans and sweater. She hesitates.

"To tell you the truth, I'm—" Laura suddenly thinks of a possibly really good angle. "I've just been so upset. I—she and I were friends. We were swim buddies, down at the Y. And you know how in the locker room, you just talk about anything, while you're changing and everything?"

The professor nods, picking up on Laura's emotion.

"—and she didn't really know this, but—I—I just really admired her. I admired her very much. In that I basically ... ohhh."

"Yes? In that you ...?"

Laura blinks. "I looked up to her. I really did." She shakes her head. "And now she's *gone!* And I'll never see her again. Never get to ask her anything about hair or makeup or studying or a career!"

"And you—"

"I just want somebody to *talk* to about her!" Laura chokes back what might be a sob. "Somebody else who knew her, you know? More than just, like, classmates, you know? I was so interested in her work here at Wayne. There's so much more I would have liked to know about her."

"Yes." Compassionately.

"I have no one."

"I'm sorry."

"And I want justice for her. I want her death not to be in vain."

The professor perches herself on the table next to the lectern. Excellent. The setting is private for the moment. "I want justice for her too. What would you like to know about Sandy?"

Laura isn't comfortable talking in such a big space, but she says, "I'd like to learn about her course of study, for one thing. I thought it was so interesting!"

Laura had read in the school paper online a couple of quotes by this professor in a story about Sandy, saying the expected things: Sandy had been a good student, sweet person and all that. The singer Vic Paladino was not mentioned in the school article, but Laura thought this professor might be a link to explore.

Dr. Peltz-Sprague says, "I can't tell you any confidential information, of course."

"Of course." Laura pulls herself together. The swim-buddy story is true. She and Sandy shared a lane at the YMCA downtown, early mornings. Sandy had gotten Laura interested in swimming last year. Laura thought swimming laps was badass, and Sandy had given her some tips to smooth out her freestyle stroke. Although they were both entitled to swim at the university's pool, the swim teams used it in the mornings. Sandy's swim-gear bag sported a mermaid tag, and she gave one to Laura too. They decided they were a two-member mermaid club.

"I'd happily see that piece of garbage rot in hell," the professor says with sudden vehemence.

"That may well happen. You're talking about the suspect, Gordon Walsh, right?"

"Yes. I never liked him."

"You knew him?"

"Just from what Sandy told me."

"What did she tell you?"

"Oh, just that he—wasn't all that interested in her as a *person*. He was older, you know. She was twenty-nine, and I think he was over forty. That's quite a gap."

"Mm. And I'm like, why did he do it? Why?"

"Why, indeed." The professor hesitates slightly, gauging her audience. "Men can be *such* pigs."

"Oh, I agree. Definitely."

More surely, the professor says, "They're responsible for so much chaos in this world." Still sitting on the lecture table, she swings her legs. Black chunky shoes, somewhat salt-stained from the winter sidewalks.

Laura inclines her head agreeably.

"Well," says the prof, in a lower tone, "I really need to know more about who you are and what you're doing."

Laura runs a patient hand through her hair. Another idea occurs. "The thing is, I don't think the police or the prosecutors have a clue as to the underlying *psychology* of the situation—" she observes Dr. Peltz-Sprague's eyes brighten and sharpen— "and Sandy was studying with you, and I would estimate you to be a woman of great insight." She puts this out in a warm, even tone that could be interpreted almost any way at all.

"Ohh," scoffs Dr. Peltz-Sprague, but she continues to listen intently.

"The police," Laura goes on, "have their suspect, but I want to make sure they're not overlooking anything. Doctor Pelz-Sprague, given the horror of Sandy's death, it seems a person has to go beyond the facts, once you're sure of them, and into the realm of thoughts and emotions." She is pleased to have used the word *realm*. It just popped into her mind.

The professor's whole face opens up and her upper body relaxes; neither Laura nor she, it seems, realized she'd been rather tense.

"The law can only go so far," says Laura. "I'm like a soldier, in a way." But the professor's expression darkens ever so slightly. Laura says, "Actually, more of an elf." The professor's expression lightens. "I'm essentially an elf here, scampering around gathering details that the justice system considers trivial and unimportant." The professor likes that. Elves are better than soldiers. Remember that.

In the quiet, the air handler chugs to life. It settles to a low hum. Laura feels a warm updraft from the ducts.

"Sandy occupied a strange rung on the ladder of Detroit celebrity," says Professor Peltz-Sprague. "The news reports, most of them, when they noted that she'd been involved with Vic Paladino, considered her to be one of those ..."

"Throwaway bimbos?" Laura suggests.

The professor smiles in acknowledgment of that bluntness. "Yes. But she was a serious person. A serious scholar, and I admired her, too, frankly. She had more initiative than most students. Well, she'd worked for a few years before starting her graduate degree, so she was more mature, for one thing."

The professor feels something similar in the spirit of this young person. Something welcoming? No. This Laura is one of those older young people, mature beyond her years. Quite a few other students at Wayne are similar: not from families that could help them go to U of M or some higher-tier school. Those kids, especially ones who'd come through hard times, broken families, are not consumed by the usual frivolities. A rare few embodied a strange calmness, as if disaster had grabbed them by the shoulders and stared deep into them, and *not gotten them.*

Dissatisfied, those kids might be, perhaps even resentful. But without the anxiety that was all over the place these days. This one, this Laura, was one of the tough calm ones, Dr. Peltz-Sprague perceives.

As the professor is thinking about these things, all at once, as people do—Laura is thinking too, and realizing that Sandy O'Rourke hadn't only been a role model for her, she'd been a role model during Laura's most formative years, the recent ones. Sandy, yeah, whose hair was in fact sandy in color, who had a good figure, had worn nice clothes and shown Laura how to shop for things that fit and looked right together—even on a tight budget.

"Now look," Sandy said one time when they were combing the sale racks at the Gap. "You know the only kind of women who look good in fine-gauge sweaters?"

Laura didn't. She fingered a soft green crewneck.

"Small-busted women. You'll see women with big chests wearing fine-gauge sweaters, and the sweater clings real sharply, and then it looks like they're trying too hard."

"Wow, yeah," said the 16-year-old Laura, totally getting it.

"So! As long as you stay under a C cup, you'll be fine with these. You develop to a C, you start looking for a different style. But I bet you'll be fine."

Laura asks Professor Peltz-Sprague, "Where did she work before starting her studies here, do you know?"

"Well, I think the same place her father works, Lomastar."

"The pharma company?" Laura knows this.

"Right. As I was saying, she had a lowly place in the show business pecking order, being intimately involved with a star such as Paladino, but not being a celebrity herself."

"I see."

"After she got her master's in social work, she wanted to go for a DPhil. Research, which is where I came in, was starting to fascinate her in a serious way.

She saw the possibilities for developing the knowledge base of the field, and she saw how that can lead to new therapeutic approaches. This is boring to a lot of people."

"Not to me! I like to learn how things work." Laura makes a mental note regarding *DPhil.* The slangier way to say doctorate. "How did she get involved with Vic Paladino, do you know? Was he paying for her schooling?"

"Oh! You don't know. She was studying him. That was the whole point."

Pause.

"Uh, can you tell me about it, please?"

Laura listens as the professor sketches out Sandy O'Rourke's recent activities. She'd gotten into the graduate psych program with the initial goal of pursuing a clinical degree so she could work as a children's therapist, then she became interested in performance anxiety.

"So, Paladino," Laura says, understanding. "Really bad performance anxiety."

"Debilitating. She read everything she could about the subject, then when it came time to decide on a narrower course of study for her thesis, well, she decided to boldly go—so to speak!—into performance anxiety. Used to be called stage fright, and that, of course, is the real reason Paladino's career has been ..."

"On the skids?"

"Ha! Yes, all the excuses about back spasms and sore vocal cords were just stories. I guess he always had trouble with fear of audiences, from when he sang in neighborhood talent shows when he was a little boy. He overcame it by brute force, he told Sandy, and he tried to pretend it was under control, but the famous incidents are almost beyond counting now, like when he cancelled concert after concert in Europe, always an hour after he was supposed to go on, and the time when he actually ran out of the dressing room and into the streets of London in a panic. Word was he was so afraid of the crowds, he hallucinated that he was Henry the Eighth and he had to go save Anne Boleyn from being beheaded."

"*Save* her from being beheaded?" Laura had read a history book or two in her time.

"He was hallucinating. Then of course the most famous and embarrassing incident of all, right here on his home turf."

"I don't know about that one," Laura says, as if she *has* heard about the others.

"Well, simply that he kept a sold-out crowd at Pine Knob waiting for an hour and a half while he hyperventilated and obsessed that he'd forget the lyrics. To songs he himself wrote."

"Did he ever go on that night?"

"He did, but it was a disaster. He stopped and started songs, he fumbled the microphone, he apologized. People thought he was on drugs."

"Might should have been."

"Ha."

"It was too bad. What a voice! What a man." Laura observes a parade of emotions cross the teacher's face.

A student walks into the auditorium. The two stop talking. The student lifts a hand in greeting, throws down his backpack, tumbles to the carpet along the back, and curls up for a nap. Two more students come in.

Dr. Peltz-Sprague says, "Are we finished here?"

"No."

"Well, OK." The professor hesitates, then goes ahead. "Would you like to get a cup of coffee?"

Laura would.

Over hot javas at Verna's, the professor tells Laura that Sandy O'Rourke came to her last summer and asked if she thought it would be a good idea for her to make a study of Vic Paladino. She needed subjects, and he was the biggest, most famous sufferer of performance anxiety in the world, practically.

"Sandy figured simply studying him, with his cooperation, could yield a trove of insights into the condition—though not broad-scale data, of course. She wrote a letter to Paladino through his agent, and surprisingly, he answered. He agreed to let Sandy interview him, but with strict rules as to what she could do with the material. If she wrote about him, she couldn't use his real name—although anybody could figure it out in two minutes."

"I see."

"According to Sandy's reports, he was working hard to try to get past his anxiety. He had a vocal regimen, he had a physical conditioning program—you know. And he had—advisors."

"Yeah? An entourage. And Sandy observed all this? And then things took a romantic turn?"

"Exactly. I should have seen it coming. Sandy was attractive and young, and although I think she fell for him early on, I tend to believe she was nobody's fool."

"Was it a happy relationship?"

"Well, it shouldn't have been a relationship at all, of course. A researcher isn't supposed to let her subject ..."

"Bang her?"

The professor laughs aloud.

Talk of love makes Laura think of a girl in her Spanish class, a stunning beauty with a self-assured manner and a quick wit.

Students and faculty people hurry or saunter past the restaurant's wide window, depending on where the clock and their schedules stood. None carry books in their hands; everybody has a backpack or messenger bag. Laura uses an army-green canvas bag from the surplus store up on Gratiot. At least half the people walking by are looking at their phones.

"Was Sandy a good student? I mean, was she conscientious and—honest?"

"What an odd question. Well, yes, I never had any reason to suspect that she was falsifying any of her research, if that's what you're asking."

Laura doesn't know for sure why she was asking the questions that come to her. "And conscientious? A hard worker?"

"Of course Sandy was conscientious. My gosh, even when she had a broken ankle, she hobbled all over campus to her classes. Never missed turning in any work."

"When did that happen?"

"Not long ago, actually. Maybe four months?"

"How did she break it, do you know?" Laura had known of Sandy's injury, and helped her in the locker room when she was able to swim, but not walk on it, yet.

"Slipped and fell in the shower. One of those things. She was badly bruised up, as well, but she didn't let that stop her."

"Bruised up?"

Seeing Laura's gears working, the professor folds her arms. "If you're thinking what I think you're thinking, you're wrong! You're wrong!"

"I'm not thinking anything."

"Vic wouldn't hurt anybody. He's brokenhearted."

"Is he? I heard he gave Sandy a black eye once." This is just a shot in the dark, based on the broken ankle. Laura learned long ago that a lie can jog forth the truth with some people.

"What! Where did you hear that?" The professor bangs her cup on her saucer.

"I've been talking to a couple of other folks who were acquainted with her."

"Who? I don't believe it. I never saw her with any black eye." A red flush crawls up the professor's neck, up from her grayscale scarf. "Who?" she demands. "And when would that have been?" Are the professor's hands trembling?

"It's just hearsay, I admit," mutters Laura, recoiling from a fleck of spittle launched from the professor's lips.

"I should say so! I don't believe he was jealous enough to experience a psychotic break and stab her to death!"

Laura swallows and smiles gently. "I don't mean to upset you."

"I'm not upset!"

Laura sits back in the booth. Beyond the window, bits of blue sky shimmer beyond the hazy high clouds. What if Sandy found out something compromising about Paladino?

Dr. Peltz-Sprague is looking at Laura calmly, and with a new light in her eyes. She's collected herself.

"I'm sorry," says the professor.

Laura smiles again, reassuringly. You're in love with Vic Paladino yourself, she thinks. You're a fangirl yourself. That's what this is about.

Or wait a minute! Maybe you were in love with Sandy.

Hm.

Maybe you were in love with both!

Laura asks, "What can you tell me about Gordon Walsh?"

"I don't know why she kept up with him for as long as she did. They were off and on for gosh, huh, I think something like four or five years?"

"Did he pay for her school?"

"I don't think so. She was here on a graduate professional scholarship, I believe. No, she didn't sponge from him—it was more the other way around."

"Yeah?" Laura knows this too.

"Mm-hmm. He borrowed money from her and never paid it back. She was angry one time, told me that he took some of her jewelry, saying he was going to get it cleaned or something, but she never saw it again."

"Did Sandy ever seem afraid of Mr. Walsh?"

"Well ... maybe, sometimes. He was so irresponsible. She liked his daughter, she said. Fun, smart kid, she said. God knows how things are going for her now."

"Yeah," says Laura. She can't think of any more questions. But a sudden idea comes together. "Professor, did you ever go with Sandy to any of her meetings, or interview sessions, with Mr. Paladino?"

"Well, once, yes. I admit I was starstruck."

"Where does he live, then?"

Dr. Peltz-Sprague signals their server for their check. "You'll allow me. I don't know where his house is. The interview I attended was in a lounge at a recording studio, uptown somewhere."

"I see. Thank you."

"Laura? Ah, you know, you can call me any time if I can do anything else to help." She smiles in a pretty, almost happy, way.

Laura sees the professor appraise her, looking her up and down, from the top of her head to her hands around her coffee cup on the table. Suddenly self-conscious, she places her hands in her lap. Dr. Peltz-Sprague is a not unattractive middle-aged woman; her mouth and chin are firm, her eyes bright, if a bit pouchy. She gives Laura a slight, sideways nod and a quirk of her eyebrows. Laura isn't precisely sure what that means, but she can tell it's supposed to mean something, apart from what they've been talking about.

What else do you know? Laura wonders.

CHAPTER 17

THERE'S ALMOST A SMELL TO THEM

Laura returns to her dorm room, throws her coat on the bed, and logs into her laptop. Searches 'Vic Paladino real estate.' Everybody likes to see how their favorite celebrities live. Nothing comes up, though. She plugs Paladino's name into the property records in Wayne and Oakland counties, but finds she'd need an address before being able to fit it to a name. Moreover, she realizes a public figure like Paladino wouldn't necessarily buy big things under their own name. Don't they have lawyers and so on?

Then she gets lucky with a hit on 'Vic Paladino lifestyle': an article in the *Free Press* from two years ago, just a fluff piece about a summer charity party he hosted. The address wasn't in the article, but pictures were. Laura studies the photo of the huge back patio, or terrace as the article called it. Paved in flat stones that sprawled out to grassy acreage, it featured white tents for the party, and a large bean-shaped pool in the ground. A tennis court a little ways away. According to the article, Paladino's multi-million-dollar house was in north Oakland County. Perfect for parties for big donors to the latest charities.

All Laura has to do is open maps, then mouse along in earth view, starting at the northern Oakland county line. The house probably isn't as far away as Holly, but maybe Clarkston or Auburn Hills. She proceeds methodically, noting roads and intersections to keep track of where she looked. The orientation of the pool, terrace, and tennis court: that's the key.

Laura does not find this work tedious, though after an hour her eyes get tired. She grabs a bottle of Faygo Rock & Rye out of the mini-fridge and scoots her chair so she can put her feet up on the window ledge. She sips the cold drink, gazing out the second-story window. Rock & Rye is a good flavor, sweet but with a solidity to it. She watches students surging along and traces the buildings and upper outlines of the winter trees with her eyes, feeling the relief of long focus. The cold of the windowpane seeps through her socks, and she moves her feet to the heat vent just below the sill.

Like many children who survive bad parenting and the instability of the foster system, Laura's growing up was compressed. Some foster kids trusted no one. She'd been like that for a while. When a family was nice to her, she didn't believe it. Children don't have a lot of time to wait for trust to build.

But being distrustful was its own kind of hell, Laura found. You had a choice: either protect yourself as much as possible by trusting no one—and accepting the ice-rock loneliness you get with that—or give in to the impulse to try to figure out who might be OK, and open yourself to the possibility of injury or friendship.

As she progressed through childhood, Laura got better at judging people, at reading the cues. Everybody gives off cues. Even truly bad people give off cues, though they don't think they do. The psychopaths, the sociopaths—there's almost a smell to them. Not everything can be reduced to eye contact and body language.

Laura found herself able to handle pain better as she got older.

One family was especially nice to her. Gave her new, good clothes and a phone and a computer. A room to herself! This family tried hard. A mom and a dad and two bio kids. *They* trusted *her,* just on some strange principle, without testing her in any way.

When she got caught shoplifting bottles of nail polish and was not punished for it, she went into her room and destroyed all of those nice things. The mother apologized for failing her and they gave her back to the state. She thought occasionally about those people and how they could never understand her. And now she was beginning to understand that it didn't matter whether anybody understood her, because nobody understands anybody. That was life. You could still have friends. She's been getting better at the friend thing, but progress on that would have to go on hold while she's helping her dad get free.

She goes back to looking for Vic Paladino's terrace and pool. The more she looks, the more she wants to find it. Her fingers fly over the keyboard. The minutes stretch on. Every empty patch of ground, every wrong house seems like a door closing, another chance for her father gone. *Patience. Patience. If you rush, you could miss it.*

After another whole hour of careful scanning, a particularly large house on a road pretentiously called Monteleone Manor Drive creeps into view. The spatial relationships between the terrace, pool, and tennis court are perfect. The satellite image, from the summer, even shows a blurry someone sunbathing on a lounge chair next to the pool. Laura shifts to street view and notes the façade of the house, a three-story brick job that was trying hard to look old and classical. In spite of an iron fence guarding everything, she makes out the address, written in letters above the front portico: Sixty-Two.

CHAPTER 18

V IS FOR VIC

The next day after classes, Laura asks a favor from one of her roommates, Becka, who owns a car, a little Toyota. The Beckster is short and square-built, with the super straight bearing short people seem to automatically develop. A computer science major, she likes punk music from the 70s and is a cheapskate. If you gave her gas money and bought McDonald's or gyros, she'd drive you anywhere. Moreover, she is not intimidated by Detroit traffic and can find a free parking spot almost on demand, which is saying a lot.

Laura tells Becka to pull over a couple hundred yards from Vic Paladino's house.

Becka settles down to eat her second lamb gyro and finish an extra-large order of curly fries as Laura gets out. Other excellent reasons to ask Becka for the ride today: she's calm and non-judgmental, and not likely to ask too many questions.

The country lane is quiet, the day gray and cold. Laura feels solitary, still thinking with some uncertainty about her plan, like a hunter looking for a clear game trail.

She presses the call button at the front gate. Although there appears to be a speaker through which someone might talk to her, the gate simply gives out a hornet-like buzz and rolls open sideways.

Laura follows a brick walkway that had been spread with white de-icer pellets. A layer of snow a couple of inches thicker than the one in the city covers the lawn and shrubs. She has on her ankle boots, good jeans, and her black parka.

The front door, wooden, carved with rosettes and leaves, is a double-wide one, like you could move a piano in without taking it apart. Half of the door swings open and a tall bald man in a navy turtleneck sweater stands there.

"Are you here—" he begins—

Laura speaks quickly so as not to lose her nerve and run away. "I'm here to see Mr. Paladino."

The man smiles slightly. His face is rumpled like an outdoorsman's, with deep crinkles at the outside of his eyes. She can see this even though he's got on black plastic glasses like the old rockers. "Well, he's not handling these interviews directly. You're here for the chef position, correct?"

Chef position. Laura's mind churns. "Uh, no. Uh … I have this …"

The man's expression hardens. "Then you have to leave immediately."

Before he closes the door all the way, Laura says, "Wait, sir! Please. My mom's an incredible fan of Mr. Paladino's, I mean I am too, but she's an *incredible* fan, and I want to surprise her for her birthday with an autograph! Would Mr. Paladino consider signing this record cover?"

As she opens her messenger bag, the tall man takes a step back and moves his hand to his waist. Laura pulls out the only Vic Paladino album the second-hand-record shop near campus had, a ratty-looking copy of "V is for Vic." All the tunes are ones the singer wrote himself.

The man's gray eyes behind the glasses are hooded and intense but not to the point of crazy. His brows are wiry clusters of dark gold, mixed with a little gray. "You shouldn't just show up to people's houses uninvited," he says, as if wanting to help her out with a bit of advice on adulting.

"I know. I'm sorry. But—"

"Mr. Paladino will make an appearance at the Masonic theater next month. You could try to meet up with him there and get your autograph." He turns away. Beyond his figure, Laura can make out a bright foyer with an enormous chandelier hanging high above. The chandelier is a modern starburst type, made of tubes of metal with lightbulbs on the ends.

"But the party's tonight! My mom's birthday party!" Laura's tone veers too much into panic. *Get a grip.* "I need this now," she asserts, more calmly. "Please, sir. If I could just meet Mr. Paladino for a minute—"

"No. Tell you what. I'll take this and see if he has a minute to sign it." He reaches for the record.

But the whole point here is getting an audience with Paladino. Laura believes in her ability to read people. She's gotten so good at it, so good over time. A few minutes with Vic Paladino could tell her if the guy is sweating out this girlfriend-murder-situation for good reason or not.

Because Laura doesn't believe psychos roam among us invisibly. She believes most people are oblivious to psychos: they don't want to admit there are monsters in our midst, so they don't permit themselves to see them. Pure denial.

Paladino might not be a psycho, and if he isn't—if he's just a guy who wanted his girlfriend killed—he'd show more emotional weirdness than a psycho would. Especially if she got the chance to simply say, "I know what you did." That single, basic accusation can put just about anyone out of touch, if only for a microsecond, with their public-facing self. And such a thing will show. For a microsecond. Maybe Paladino is innocent. That would show, too.

But Laura isn't getting into that house, and she won't be able to lob a truth-seeking missile at Vic Paladino. So she hands over the LP, why not.

"Wait here." The man, darned handsome, she suddenly perceives, shuts the door. Broad shoulders in his black sweater, narrow hips. Bald guys can look scary or dumb, but this one looked kind of sexy. Prominent Adam's apple. Could he be Paladino's enforcer: the guy who smoothly takes care of the boss's problems?

If she can cross Paladino off her list, fine. But Professor Peltz-Sprague's excessive protesting when it came to a question of Paladino perhaps being violent to Sandy, that was something that simply demanded exploring.

What is this about a chef's job? They're interviewing? Could she pivot on this, somehow?

The tall bald man opens the door again and hands Laura the album. Paladino's signature is there, across one corner in thick marker, V-squiggle, P-squiggle.

"Please tell Mr. Paladino thank you," this enthusiastically and warmly. "And thank you, sir, for not just slamming the door in my face."

The man glances about. "Where's your car?"

"Oh, just down the road. Thank you!"

The door chunks shut behind Laura as she hurries off. A car pulls up as she reaches the road and a woman gets out, carrying a small canvas roll tied with a string.

Laura says, "Are you here about the chef job?"

"Yes!" Pert-looking thing, round face, round glasses. "I'm a little early for my appointment at—"

"I'm so sorry! They just hired someone, I'm afraid."

The woman's face falls, but she peers past Laura to the house. "Well, I should at least—"

"No," says Laura firmly. "I wouldn't. Seriously." Laura turns her death stare on the woman. "Don't chase after heartbreak."

The woman slinks back to her car as Laura knew she would, and Laura takes off down the lane to find the Beckster relaxed and happy and ready to drive back to campus.

CHAPTER 19

I AM NOT A CHEF

I figure the police would reasonably have done all sorts of door-knocking the night Gordy was taken into custody. They learned whatever they learned, if anything. But what if not everybody was home? What if somebody saw something that didn't match the police narrative so far, which was Gordy luring Sandy to his house before slaughtering her?

Today is Tuesday. While thinking about the neighborhood, I start the morning by cleaning the house more thoroughly, beginning with the laundry machines.

I didn't used to be a morning person, what with working the streets at all hours—plus of course hangovers from booze and drugs—but I've turned that around pretty well. Now I like rising early. Seeing the dawn makes me feel like I'm getting on top of the day.

I run some towels through the washer using hot water and vinegar, then feel all right putting my clothes in. Gordy has a box of powdered Tide on hand, which I appreciate. They could make a cologne out of it and I'd buy it.

Gordy, my man, you really messed up your life, somehow. If you murdered Sandy, that says it all. If you didn't, there's still a reason it happened in your living room. You can rip out carpet that has blood in it, you can throw out a couch, but what's the dirt beneath all that? What and where?

I remove the dead mouse from the dryer and clean the drum with a rag and more vinegar, then I wipe it down with rubbing alcohol I found in the bathroom. For sure I let it air out before putting the towel load in.

The vacuum needs a cleaning before I can use it. Gordy had gotten hold of a cheap upright, but at least he did that. The dust cup is packed full, the filters are clogged, and the brush on its spindle is strangled by hair and rug fibers. That takes some time to sort out. I run the machine around the upstairs, then quit for something to eat.

While drinking my tea and eating my sandwich, I think about what I was just doing. Almost smiled at myself. Gordy, I can clean up your house, but can I clean up your life?

After eating, I go out and knock on doors in the neighborhood. I practiced emitting bright, friendly vibes in the bathroom mirror before I set out: eyebrows raised a little, wide clear eyes, corners of mouth turned up.

I hit four houses on either side of Gordy's, the corresponding row across the street, as well as the house directly behind, plus the ones on either side of them. Only two open their doors. The first is a young fat guy who invites me in, and when I say no, I just wanted to ask if he knew Gordy or if he saw anything on that night last week, he calls me an ugly bitch and slams the door. Is he just a jerk, or is this neighborhood on edge?

The other person who answered the door is an old woman in a fabulous cable-knit sweater and slacks who says she was home that night but wasn't aware of anything wrong until she saw the police lights on the street. However, she was slightly acquainted with Gordy, who occasionally borrowed a bucket of heating oil from her.

"He borrowed a bucket of heating oil?" I repeat stupidly.

"People do," she says, "when they're hard up. You need a funnel to get it into the tank."

"Well, gosh," was all I could say. He was literally that broke, sometimes?

On my way back to Gordy's house, Laura phones.

"Bam, we've *got* to get closer to Vic Paladino."

"Well, maybe." I let myself in through the back door. "But I don't imagine he could tell us—"

"OK, you agree. Here's the thing. He's looking for a personal chef. I found the listing on Konnect-A-Chef."

"How did you—"

"Long story. Listen. You have to get that job. I'll send you the link. I can help you fake a résumé."

"Honey, there's no way."

"He wants a French chef, it says."

I consider. "Well, there were a few occasions—in the past—when I was asked to be a French *maid,* uh, you know—"

"Ugh."

"—and I kind of was able to bring off a convincing—"

"You can cook, can't you?"

"I'm not all that—"

"You can cook all kinds of stuff! I remember!"

"I am not a *chef.* Even I know you have to have all kinds of specialized knowledge—and experience!—to be a chef. My goodness. Especially a French chef!"

"You've got to get that job!"

"Why are you so fired up about Paladino?"

"Look, I think he might have beaten up Sandy in the past." Laura tells me about her talk with Sandy's professor. "And she did that 'protesteth too much' thing when I asked if he ever got rough with Sandy. So I think there's something there."

"Well, even if I did get the job—which, honey, there's no way—what would it gain us? What would I learn as this singer's cook?"

"Never call yourself a cook! From now on, you're a chef. You could snoop around the house and try to find something that ties him to the murder. Are you dense, Bam? Like if he hired somebody to do it, there could be evidence of that. A notebook with names and numbers. I don't know! You know?"

I think of my standard diet of sandwiches, fruit, and egg pancakes. The occasional pork chop or pot of spaghetti. When Gordy and I were married, I threw together whatever. None of us were picky eaters.

"No. Let's keep trying to learn more about Sandy and other guys she knew. What about her computer?"

"I'm disappointed in you, Bam."

"Wait until this is all over before you say that, all right?"

It was worth a call to Ted Alvarez. I leave a message, and he calls me back half an hour later to say the police didn't find a computer in Sandy's apartment. There was an adapter and charging cable plugged into the wall, but no laptop. Nothing in her car, either, which had been towed from her apartment lot and searched.

"In general," says Ted, "we're only interested in text messages and email, and they have Sandy's phone, which will yield that stuff. One of the investigators hinted that they found something of interest in a text message, but I haven't been able to find out what it is."

I call Laura back. As we talk I heat water for tea, clumping back and forth on the kitchen linoleum in my hiking boots. It's hygienic to go sock-footed indoors, but that place was pretty drafty. My wool socks and boots are keeping my feet comfortable. Before coming inside, I always cleaned any snow or dirt off my boots with a whisk broom I found in the front closet. I'll scrub that kitchen floor when I get a chance.

"If it wasn't in her apartment or car," Laura says—

"The killer could have it," I go.

"For some important reason."

"Could her dad have it?"

"Sure. Maybe she left it with him or some other trusted person. Maybe she thought she was in danger!"

At least I've gotten Laura off the French chef thing.

I ask, "Would Sandy have had an office or a little cubby or something on campus? Given that she was being a PhD-er and teaching a little bit already?"

"Hm."

"Maybe the police asked around already."

"I don't know, but—" Laura stops.

"What, hon?"

"Nothing."

CHAPTER 20

NEW FOSSILS GET EXPOSED

Chuck Stratton eases through a gap in a chain-link fence, pushes through some brush, and stands, hands on hips, looking down into a limestone quarry. On this Tuesday afternoon an expressionless white sky is hanging over this vast pit, half a mile across, with a series of ramps cut into one side for trucks to come and go.

The quarry is reaching the end of its life, Stratton learned, which meant the workable layers of stone are pretty much gone. Limestone is used to manufacture cement. But there is still some left, and a reduced crew is employed to take it out.

What might he uncover in this place? Such a big scar on the earth, its neatly terraced sides going down like steps to nowhere. Maybe a hundred fifty feet to the bottom, Stratton judges. Hard to figure the depth realistically, given today's overcast. No shadows. Is that truck way down there one of those giant ones, or a normal sized one?

Warm in his shearling coat and watch cap, he ambles around the pit's perimeter to the guard shack at the main gate. He taps at the shack's side window, startling the guard, who, upon seeing Stratton, smiles and shakes his head.

Stratton goes around to the door and lets himself in. "There's a gap in the fence," he says, "about a hundred yards down, that way." His glasses fog up from the warmth of the guard shack's heater. He takes them off briefly.

"Yeah," says the guard. "Have a seat if you like. They'll be here shortly. How've you been?"

"Fine. Working for Vic Paladino these days." The men worked together on security jobs here and there when they were younger. The guard's name is Silva. He wears a navy watch cap like Stratton, and a high-viz hoodie. Though drafty, the shack is comfortable enough, with a space heater running in the corner, its coils glowing orange.

"You like working for him?" Silva asks.

"It's OK for now. So, you weren't here that afternoon or evening?" Still in his coat, Stratton leans against the wall near the door.

"I was here until we closed up after day shift, three-thirty. This teacher's got permission to bring students in here after the equipment's been shut down. Nobody but workers came through this gate that day, though."

"How does the teacher get in, if the main gate's locked?"

"They usually come in just before we close, so I let 'em in. See that side gate over there? They go out that way and it just locks shut behind them. If they come after we close, they get in the same way you did."

"So, anybody could walk in through that gap after hours?"

"You'd have to know about it, but yeah, that's right."

"And off-duty police come in here sometimes and practice their shooting, right?"

"Well, really just Jason Givens, like I said on the phone. There's a place, a big gravel pile, in the northeast quadrant. He shoots targets in front of that. Sometimes he brings buddies. Obviously when nobody else is in the pit. We're OK with it. It's a favor he appreciates."

As Stratton watches, a red minivan rolls to a stop outside the fence and a spare-looking man in a ski jacket gets out. Silva hits a button and the gate rolls open on heavy wheels. Stratton goes out to meet the man, who turns and nods at the van. Four teenagers pile out, dressed in thick jackets, jeans, and boots. They carry rock hammers and canvas tote bags. They stand in a semi-circle, waiting, three boys and a girl, breathing white vapor into the cold. They look ready for the cold.

Stratton introduces himself and explains, "I'm doing some private security work. Silva was nice enough to tell me you were coming today."

There isn't room in the guard shack for all of them.

The teacher wraps his checkered scarf better around his neck. "Yeah, he said someone wanted to talk to me. I'm Andy Bonetti, I teach at the high school, and these are my honors science students. What can I do for you?"

"I understand you and your students come and go from here quite a bit."

"Yeah, is there a problem?" Andy Bonetti hooks his thumbs, in leather work gloves, in his jacket pockets. He carries a canvas tote under his arm same as the kids.

"Not at all. You guys study the rocks, the geology?"

"Partly that, but mostly we look for fossils. Limestone quarries are great for certain kinds of fossils." After a slight pause, he adds, unable to stop himself, "Primarily from the Ordovician and Silurian periods."

Stratton likes the guy for that. "You come here all through the winter?"

"Yes, fairly often. The exfoliation in the winter is more aggressive, so new fossils get exposed on the vertical faces and in the waste piles." The students stamp their feet to keep warm.

"Do you have a record of the days you come here?"

"Yes. What's the issue?"

"I'm looking for possible witnesses of something that might have happened here last week, on Tuesday. Were you here that day?"

"Yeah, I think so. We tend to come on Tuesdays and Wednesdays, given the school schedule." The teacher pulls out his phone and consults it. "Yeah, we were here that day. We got here after Mr. Silva was gone, so we came in through the busted fence." Bonetti, slightly apprehensive, looks at Stratton. "We've done it lots of times."

"Cool, that's fine," says Stratton. "My main question is this. Did you guys see anybody else here that afternoon?"

The students and teacher look at each other and shake their heads.

"No."

"Nope."

Stratton detects no off-key vibe. "You didn't see anybody over by the gravel pile? Probably around four o'clock or so? Five o'clock? Two men?"

They hadn't.

Andy Bonetti says, "We got here at about 3:45 and left when it got dark, shortly after five."

"Hear anything unusual? Gunshots?"

Their eyes widen, but no. "We certainly would have heard shots, if somebody discharged a gun in this quarry," says Andy Bonetti. "Excellent acoustics!"

CHAPTER 21

A MERMAID STICKER

The next morning, Wednesday, Laura Walsh locates Professor Peltz-Sprague's office on the 7th floor of a cool old university building, stone floors, mahogany doors and all that. She gets off the elevator and looks around, to see the professor herself walking down the hall away from her, toward the lavatories. This is worth a shot.

Laura moves quickly and finds the professor's office door ajar.

Fortunately Dr. Peltz-Sprague wasn't one of those pack-ratty profs where as soon as you go in their office you get claustrophobia, what with the walls being covered with every diploma, certificate, every group photo from every conference, and stacks of papers and keepsakes. Professors seem to love small toys, Laura noted. Little figurines, things you can fiddle with. Also, things that show erudition, like a human skull (hopefully fake), a bust of Darwin, a geodesic model. That picture of Einstein with his tongue sticking out.

Heart accelerating, Laura rams open all the drawers in the professor's filing cabinet, one after the other, slamming them closed, no laptop. The professor's own device is on her desk, open to an article or something.

With intense, quick focus, Laura continues to scan around. Wooden shelving, another little table, and then—hm, a gap between filing cabinet and bookcase. She reaches into it. Her fingers brush something cold and metallic. She fumbles for just an instant, then pulls out the tucked-away laptop. And there it is: a mermaid sticker, exactly the same as the tag on Sandy's swim bag. Exactly like the one she gave Laura to put on hers. This is it.

Footsteps in the hallway, pat-pat-pat.

Laura slips the device into her messenger bag.

She turns to go. The professor is in her face.

"Hello! What are you—"

"Professor! I just stopped in to ask if—if—you'll be teaching that class about PTSD next term."

"You mean summer term? The schedule is already—"

"No, fall term."

"Yes, I think so. Why? Are you—"

"Thank you! Gotta run!"

CHAPTER 22

THIS IS ABOUT DRUGS

Laura and I settle at the kitchen table in Gordy's house. It's mid-afternoon on Wednesday, and a pot of water for tea is heating on the stove.

I knew what she was about to produce from her book sack, but when she excitedly pulled it out and set it on the table, I nearly said out loud, *Here is a thief after my own heart.*

Stealing stuff is a rush, I get that very well. Wrong, but feels so right!

The laptop powers on. Check.

An icon of an eye appears, looking for Sandy's face. Unexpectedly creepy moment here. Laura clicks to the password option, checks something on her phone, then keys in a number on the laptop. The screen welcomes Sandy to her online world.

"How did you know *that?*"

"She let me use this laptop one time when mine was in the shop. It didn't recognize my face, of course, so she told me her passcode. I made a note of it."

"Because ...?"

"Because you never know when a piece of information might come in handy. She could have changed it, but I thought it was worth a try."

"And if—"

"If it didn't work, I have a buddy in IT support at the school, and I think he could get into anybody's computer. They're all issued by the university in the first place. You'd be surprised how much those guys know about everybody's business."

"Just informally."

"Yeah."

I brew tea and set out some vanilla cookies I'd picked up.

Funny, I thought. All my life I'd been anything but vanilla. Now I want nothing more than to be as basic, plain vanilla as possible.

Sandy's schoolwork—her lesson plans for her assistantship classes, plus her uploaded reports and papers—all that, we find, is behind another password-protected portal, something specific to the department. Laura tries the same trick, but it doesn't work.

"No matter," Laura says cheerfully. She munches a cookie. "We've got access to her Word files, all that stuff, plus her email. This'll keep us busy. If we decide we want access to her department account, I'm sure I can get it."

"Well, let's dig in."

Side by side, with Laura operating the keyboard, we skim the names of file folders, then file names in said folders. Lists and lists of notes, reports, on and on.

"This is a lot of sheer volume," I say. "Don't you agree we should focus on her work related to Paladino, plus whatever might have her dad's name attached to it?"

"Her dad?"

I tell Laura about the insurance policy Ted mentioned. "Half a million to her old man. Tax-free. I wouldn't count him out, as horrible as that is to think of."

"Wow. Yeah."

After an hour and a half, I make more tea and fix peanut-butter-and-banana sandwiches for us.

"You used to make these when I was little," Laura says, chewing.

Maybe she is chewing around a faint smile?

I feel comfortable being so near her. I want to hug her, hold her. I gauge her vibe towards me, which amounts to caution. Which is a thousand times better than fear. Or contempt.

The daylight fades through the curtains.

We keep working, taking turns writing notes while the other searches the laptop. I'm surprised to see how much Laura's handwriting looks like mine: smallish, jagged letters that crowd into one another. Legible enough.

Laura gets out a charging cable from her bag. "It's the same one for my computer."

"That teacher's gonna know you took the laptop. She probably noticed it missing as soon as you left her office."

"Irrelevant. She can accuse, I'll deny. There's no evidence."

"I see you've learned the power of denial."

She fixes me with her clear young gaze. "Absolutely, Bam."

The first rule of misbehavior is don't get caught. The second rule is deny. Even if somebody tattles or there's an eyewitness, you deny. And never offer alternative explanations.

No. It wasn't me.

But you were seen.

It wasn't me.

But we found the water-balloon launcher in your room, pointed out the window.

I did not launch any water balloons.

You knocked that kid off his bike.

I did not.

Yes, you did.

No, I didn't.

Well, who did, then?

No idea how that kid fell off his bike.

Obviously denial can only go so far in something like a criminal case. Still, it's a good baseline strategy.

We look for names, any names. A name can be searched on. A name that comes up repeatedly could be significant.

We open Sandy's master folder for her doctoral thesis and skim around the files. I'm impressed with the language, the technical terms and all. *Pedagogical. Repertoire. Aryepiglottic.* Very strange word.

Laura shakes her hair back. "This is pretty scant, given that she's been working on this degree for supposedly two years already."

"Yeah?"

"It's a bunch of notes about Vic Paladino's vocal technique and some stuff about his pre-concert routine, if you can call it that."

"Seems interesting to me."

Laura says, "For a doctoral thesis, you're supposed to put a whole lot of stuff together, like gather other people's prior work and theories and stuff. Then you do your own thing, and you're supposed to like build on what's been done before, or go in a different direction."

"How do you know all that?"

She shrugs. Her shoulders look smooth and right in her close-fitting sweater, her arms nicely shaped. Fingernails short but not ragged, which tell me at least she doesn't have the nervous habit of chewing them. "I've been talking to people. It's not hard to make friends with the PhD people, especially if you're taking their courses. I mean semi friends. You know."

"Do you think you want to get a PhD someday?"

"I might."

We go back to skimming files.

"What's this one?" says Laura. "The Efficacy of Schedule I, II, and IV Controlled Substances on Performance Anxiety and as Performance Enhancers, as Used by Prominent Contemporary Entertainers."

"Well," I go.

The document was written, or being written, by Sandy O'Rourke. Laura and I read it. The document refers to Vic Paladino and other top entertainers, using pseudonyms. It seems to be a highly technical study, oriented towards brain chemistry and medicine.

I say, "This is about drugs, pure and simple." I push up my glasses, which I notice have gotten smudged.

Laura goes, "I think this is the real thesis."

We take the time to read pretty much the whole thing.

"Most of this technical stuff is beyond me," I say, "but it seems her real goal with Vic Paladino was to study his drug use."

"I agree."

My legs are tired from sitting. I get up and pace the kitchen, up and down. I wash my glasses at the sink and dry them on a towel.

"I don't want to sound too street here," I remark, "but I thought practically *all* the big entertainers use drugs, you know, to get up for shows and down afterwards. Especially somebody like Paladino, who carries his whole show himself. I mean, he's got a band and a couple of backup singers, but it's him in front."

Laura is fiddling with her phone, holding it up and squinting at it.

"What's the matter?"

"Oh, this phone's just being a pain. I'm trying to adjust the glare from the light. I can do it best at eye level." The overhead light is quite bright.

"Do you want to use mine?"

She fusses a few seconds more, then puts it down. "No. Thanks, though."

I go, "It seems Paladino's a major pillhead, like, you know, Elvis and Michael Jackson and whoever. And I'm gonna bet that he doesn't consider himself a junkie."

We discuss the second half of the report, which focused on Sandy's theories about drug formulations. There's data in there about current anti-anxiety drugs.

"Sandy's dad's a chemist or something," I say. "He works for Lomastar, it's a drug maker."

"This thing is going in—"

"Several directions now."

"Yes."

Laura sits, chin in hand. Slowly, she thinks aloud. "If Sandy had uncovered this much about Vic's drug use ..."

"What else might she have uncovered? And who might ..."

"... be willing to ... "

"... kill to keep it quiet?"

CHAPTER 23

KONNECT-A-CHEF

The next morning I got Ted Alvarez to agree to interview William O'Rourke, Sandy's dad, for us. Ted was impressed by Laura's and my skullduggery, and decided he could afford to step in a bit. Rationalization: Alvarez worked narcotics, and the pills Lomastar made found their way onto the black market with increasing regularity.

"What we need to know, Ted, is what this William O'Rourke is doing, exactly, in his job at Lomastar. I know he's been interviewed already about Sandy. But can you, like, do another one? And somehow find out what his projects are? Or assignments, or whatever?"

"I can do that."

"Oh, super. But without, like—"

"He'll never know my angle."

"Thank God for you, Ted."

An hour later, around eleven o'clock, Laura shows up. "Bam, you *have* to get into Paladino's." She shrugs her coat off and plants herself, feet apart, school bag in hand, in the living room. "You just have to. The chef job."

"They've hired somebody by now, I'm sure." The blackened fireplace, strewn with old ashes and a broken grate, looks on disapprovingly. I don't know why it sort of developed a personality to me.

"It's only been a day and a half since I learned about it. Two days. The listing's still up on Konnect-A-Chef."

"What is that, anyway?"

"A website for professional chefs. People put want ads up, and chefs put their profiles up."

"No."

"Well in that case, look here." She beckons me to the dining-room table where she gets out her laptop. She keys in some stuff. "You already *have* a profile on Konnect-A-Chef, and nine hits on it since it went up this morning, by the way, and you have an interview at Paladino's house at three o'clock."

I can only splutter. There's my picture! A shot of me from the waist up in my black sweater, sleeves pushed up, hair askew, held in a loose mess with a pencil I'd stuck in crookedly. I'm looking directly into the camera, an eyebrow quirked up.

"You look busy and intense," says Laura admiringly.

"You took this—"

"Yesterday, while you were pacing around. I even managed to get the pantry shelves in the background! You're a busy chef in a private kitchen!"

"When you were pretending to have a problem with your phone."

She is quite pleased with herself.

"I can't be a professional cook! I can boil water but I can't even—"

"You are a chef!" She makes a curlicue in the air, then kisses her fingertips. She scrolls down so I can read my résumé.

"My name is Celeste LaPorte?"

"Yeah, get used to it."

"The Escoffier School of Culinary Arts? Did I even say that right?"

"It's pronounced Ess-coffee-ay. Say it fast."

"Ess-coffee-ay. In Paris. Of course. This is insane, honey. And I worked at, what, is this a Michelin star restaurant in California?" I did know how to pronounce Michelin, because of the tires.

"Yeah, Bam."

"I was born in Toulouse?"

"You pronounce it Too-loose."

"Well that fits, I guess."

"Actually, it's more like Too-looz."

"I don't even—is that a village in France? And who's this Baron Elmshot I was supposed to work for until last month?"

"Well, I made him up. English guy. He lives in a stone mansion in Surrey. Two kitchens. Former ambassador to Belgium."

I go, "There is absolutely no way I could pull this off."

"There are risks, granted," says Laura thoughtfully. "But I bet they won't check your references."

"Why not?"

"Just a feeling I have. Just in case, though, I did go to the trouble of creating a phone number with an exchange for England. It forwards to my phone, so I can handle a call to Baron Elmshot's house manager, if that comes up."

"This is insane, honey."

"Stop saying that." My daughter fixes me with the calm, direct gaze I was getting used to. "Isn't your motto fake it 'til you make it? I put your profile together last night, using, you know, stuff from other chefs' résumés. And I got in touch with Paladino's contact person this morning, pretending to be someone from some French agency. They want to see you!"

I lean on the dining table with both hands. Its surface was pretty banged up, but the wood was nice. Some type of dark wood.

"What happened to the previous chef, do you know?"

"Took a job on a cruise ship."

"You figured that out online?"

"Same website, yeah. Is that your phone?"

I glance at it. "It's Ted." I pick up.

"Two pieces of news," he says.

"You talked to O'Rourke already?"

"Yeah, I had some time and went over there. First piece of news, William O'Rourke is working on a drug. A new synthetic anti-anxiety drug. As he explained it, this drug's supposed to give the patient a major boost of energy like an amphetamine, yet also the mellowness—the euphoria, like—you get with a medium-strength narcotic or benzo. Only, safer than either one. Non-addictive."

"A safe speedball. Every junkie's wet dream." A speedball, you may know, is a combo of an upper and a downer. Heroin together with cocaine is a time-honored classic. Lots of celebrities have died from speedballs. Heroin plus meth is even worse. Some older junkies call them goofballs. Not that there are many older junkies around, just as a category.

"Every *dealer's* wet dream. Every *manufacturer's* wet dream." Ted pauses. "If a company could perfect and produce something like that—"

"You could make a killing."

We think about that. A safe speedball, incredible. A drug that could change everything. But was it connected to Sandy O'Rourke's murder? And if so, what role did her father play in it?

"The other thing," Ted says, "is regarding Gordy."

"Yeah?"

Laura leans in to listen.

"The prosecutor's going for first-degree murder all the way. Life without parole. No deals."

Laura's head drops helplessly. A second later she lifts it and stares at me with blood in her eyes.

"OK," I go. "OK."

Chapter 24

Celeste LaPorte

V ic Paladino's kitchen is just like the ones in magazines, unbelievably spacious. There's an outdoor kitchen on the patio as well, closed now because of winter.

Between the main living area and the kitchen is a huge dining room, plus a smaller area called a breakfast room with a countertop and a kitchenette of its own and a fridge and everything, so people can get their own breakfast or just a cup of coffee any time, without feeling like they shouldn't still be in their PJs. High ceilings everywhere. The rich like high ceilings. Is it to show they can afford the heating bills?

Man, the kitchen. Stainless steel everything, crystal clear lighting, egg-cream walls and cupboards, gray stone floor. An incredible gas range with a huge griddle to one side, definitely restaurant quality. Wall ovens, plural, a duo of enormous refrigerators, and a freezer any serial killer would envy. Plus of course a pantry the size of a 7-Eleven, with extra storage and a wine cellar in the basement, I was told.

More ingredients than I could ever imagine are there, but I notice the cans and bags on the shelves aren't organized nicely, and when I peer in the first of the three fridges it's the same. A bunch of good fresh food, meats wrapped up in butcher paper, vegetables and whatnot, but rather messy. The glass fridge shelves are gummy. I don't know how to turn on the grill, but I can see it needs a cleaning. The whole kitchen wants a good re-ordering.

Vic Paladino—yep, him in the flesh—says, "Hey. I thought you could fix me something to eat, as a tryout. Like a croissant, with maybe some escargot. Or a soufflé." He looks older than in his publicity pictures—naturally—and more worn. Big guy, but not fat. Thick arms and legs, deep chest, confident posture. He's smiling slightly, showing his entertainer-level white teeth.

A soufflé. Oh dear.

I hold up my hand firmly. "*Stop.* This is unacceptable."

Paladino raises his furry eyebrows. His forehead makes three perfect ridges.

"I will cook something for you," I tell him severely, "but *not* until this kitchen is clean!" I toss my head. "It's filthy. Filthy!" I stalk to the griddle, run my finger along the edge, and hold it up. "Grease!"

Paladino looks at a strange womanlike individual dressed all in white, who shrugs. She'd met me at the door, not bothering to introduce herself, and showed me into the kitchen. She carries a clear plastic cup filled with a gray semi-liquid substance that looks like chopped tadpoles in root beer. She sips from it occasionally.

"Sunpod," Paladino says, "can we get this place cleaned up, you know, properly?"

I nearly shout, "No! I will clean."

"But" says Paladino—

"I will clean, I will bring this—this *pigsty!* to standard, and *then* I will cook for you. And *then* I will show you and *you*—" I point at this Sunpod person— "how I cook. Filth," I mutter, turning away, then back to them. "Where is soap, where is bleach, brushes, cloths! I begin now!" I smack my hands together, and both of them literally flinch. Then Paladino laughs.

"Oooh! Well, haha! A fierce one here! Ha! I like her, Sunpod." He turns to me. "What's your name, again?"

"I am Celeste LaPorte."

"Celeste LaPorte." He belts out an impromptu rap: "Celeste LaPorte! Celeste! The best! She'll put! The kitchen! To! The test!"

Before driving myself there, I had a lot to think about. At first I didn't know how I was going to make my personality work. Maybe my normal self with just a hint of an accent of some kind? A fake French accent was out, though. I'd sound ridiculous, and no way could I keep that up in any long-term sense.

But a combative persona came to me, and so did an accent. One of our neighbors back in Balsam Ridge was a factory-tough Hungarian lady who'd worked in the dog-food processing plant in Escanaba her whole life. Imagine retiring to Balsam Ridge on purpose. But after forty years of grinding up horse intestines or whatever, I guess a quiet life in Balsam Ridge wouldn't be half bad. Property values were always on the buyer's side in Balsam Ridge.

Anyway, this lady, Mrs. Graznak, babysat for Bing and me quite a bit when we were little. Both of us picked up on her hard-edged eastern European accent and imitated it behind her back, thinking we were hilarious. Basically you just speak all your consonants extra clear and stern. I figured if I just talked that way—super clipped, is another way to describe it—and if I emphasized the wrong parts of words once in a while, I could keep that up, in the unlikely event I got this job.

I tried out this way of talking on Laura, and she thought it effective.

Also, given my totally unstable base as a chef, I needed a strong persona that would bridge as many gaps in my skills as possible. Any sign of nervousness or insecurity would be fatal. I reminded myself that this chef thing was just a quick ruse. Even if I had just a couple of days inside Vic Paladino's house, that could be more than enough.

The idea of rage-cleaning came to me while preparing to drive up to Paladino's. As I think I've noted, when you clean something, you stake somewhat of a claim on it. Cleaning Paladino's kitchen with fierceness would be a way to assert dominance. And I was sure no other chef applicant would be so ballsy as to criticize the guy's kitchen and talk mean to him.

146

Also, I'm afraid to say I drew on my experience working the streets. The richer johns from the suburbs, they tended to be used to people who worked for them being nice and smarmy to them. The height of thrilling, for them, was to get confronted by a hard woman who could make them quake in their Vuitton loafers in a hotel room.

I'm not exactly talking about masochism, which is a kink with rules and a distinct flavor profile, to borrow a term I learned from Connie Blue Smoke. We were drinking cream soda on her porch one hot day, and she commented that its flavor profile was distinctly vanilla, with a hint of caramel. After thinking about it, I had to agree.

I was going to either flame out or succeed spectacularly.

I phoned Connie on the way.

"You gotta help me, pal." I told her the whole thing in a minute. "So," I finished, "I have like twenty minutes to learn from you how to make something French, or at least convince people I know how to make French food. I know it's demented. Especially because I don't even like all that silly dainty food they supposedly eat in those restaurants. But if I get the job I'll be able to buy time in order to learn more. I'm planning on a shock and awe approach."

"Wow," said Connie. She was quiet for a moment. "Well, you know, just make your egg pancake for him. That's an omelette."

"No, it isn't."

"Yes, it is. It's an omelette *rustica,* which means rustic, like peasant food."

I eased around a beer truck rumbling along in the middle lane of Woodward. "Really? Even though I don't fold it over like in restaurants?"

"I swear, Bambi. *Rustica.* Throw, you know, ugly mushrooms into it, throw in plenty of cheese. Trust me." Connie was warming up to this.

"Rustica." I said it like she did, roostica. It occurred to me that someone fancy like Paladino might appreciate a rougher style of food, so long as I could sell it as French. Maybe.

Connie said, "You got this. Use lots of butter no matter what it is. And pork fat, if it's a savory dish. That means not sweet."

"I know what savory means."

"OK, well, I never know with you. Pork fat, is all I'm saying."

"What if they ask me complicated questions about food and oven temperatures and whatnot?"

"Fake it, pal!" Connie knew me, that's for sure. "Faking it is what you're best at, Bambi."

"Let's not get carried away with the praise here, Con." If I had a dollar for every orgasm I faked as a hooker, I'd be hiring my own French chef.

"Look, I'll help you. We can talk more tonight. I can give you ideas and help troubleshoot."

"Yeah, OK."

"And there's YouTube."

"Right."

"YouTube's a trove. You can carry this off a hundred percent. Call me tonight and tell me how it went, OK?"

Now, seeing Paladino's pleased expression, I feel a warm sense of victory. I'm the Stone Bitch Chef.

CHAPTER 25

A MUTUAL ALIBI

Chuck Stratton walks into the Daybreak Café in Royal Oak. He looks around, unbuttoning his coat. The café is a train-car type, long counter with stools, and booths along the windows. Clean place, welcoming. It's early, 6:00 a.m., and breakfast rush hasn't hit yet. Maybe five customers. A man dressed in a maroon sport coat with a sweater underneath sits in a booth at the far end. From there he can take in the whole place at a glance.

Stratton understands why Detective Sgt. Jason Givens would choose that seat. Awareness is a top value if you're a cop.

The place smells good. The heavy-faced cook is busy frying meat and potatoes, and the server has just hit the brew button on twin coffeepots.

"Sit anywhere you like," she tells Stratton, brushing back a wisp of strawberry-blond hair.

He observes Givens for a second before approaching. The detective happened to be looking down at his phone when Stratton came in. Givens was a guy who liked to work out, and even though he carries a bit of a gut, he's strong and competent looking. Squared-off mustache.

Givens looks up as Stratton's boots sound on the floor.

"Morning, Jason," says Stratton.

Pause.

"Chuck." Givens puts his phone down.

"Like some company?"

The detective pauses again. "Sure, have a seat."

The server comes over with a mug and a coffee pot, and Stratton nods. "What can I get you to eat?" She's maybe fifty, quick and efficient. Black apron over an old-style pink service dress.

"Just the coffee, thanks."

"Your order's almost up," she tells Givens.

He nods in thanks. His overcoat is folded on the seat next to him. Stratton keeps his unbuttoned coat on, the better to indicate that this shouldn't take long.

The men were acquainted through Paladino, who noticed Givens five years ago when he was a patrol officer, working off-duty at one of his concerts. Givens, assigned backstage, bantered with Paladino man-to-man after his first set. The singer invited Givens to his after party, and from then on Givens was a side pal.

Genuine machismo fascinated Paladino; Stratton observed this over and over. It was probably the main reason Paladino had chosen the rangy security man as his personal bodyguard. Apart from being a smoke jumper, Stratton had worked as a paramedic, a bar bouncer, and a firearms instructor.

"I need to talk with you, and I didn't want to call," he tells Givens.

This simple sentence informs Givens that Stratton doesn't want there to be any evidence of their conversation, for both of their sakes.

"How did you know to find me here?"

Stratton notes that Givens could have hit a button on his phone to record whatever conversation was to come, but he didn't. Recordings can backfire. Cops know this better than anybody.

Furthermore, Givens is certainly aware that Stratton is being extremely courteous, meeting up with him as if by chance. No appointment on a calendar, no text message, no awkward moment on the Givens house doorstep, with Mrs. Givens wondering who this stranger is and what he might want.

Stratton says, "I remembered Vic telling me, all impressed, that you go out for the same breakfast every work day: a pound of sausages, plus eggs and a plate of tomatoes, because you never knew if you'd have a chance to eat again for the rest of the day. So I stopped in at diners between your house and headquarters at breakfast time until I found you."

Givens nods. "What's up, then?" The man has an edge to him, but also that valuable quality of steadiness in the face of just about anything. You don't survive past your rookie year as a Detroit police detective without those attributes.

The server sets three plates of food before Givens, one piled with steaming sausage links and fried eggs, one stacked with four oval pieces of buttered toast, and the last heaped with sliced raw tomatoes. Givens looks at Stratton, and both smile a little. The detective picks up his knife and fork and spears a sausage.

"Looks good," says Stratton.

"Want some?"

"No, thanks, man. What's up is a good question." He glances around; no one is near; the server is busy behind the counter. Stratton lowers his voice. "Has to do with Sandy O'Rourke's death."

"No, it doesn't."

That's a quick response.

Stratton considers what Givens literally might mean. "OK," he says, "to be exact, it has to do with Vic Paladino's whereabouts that night."

"Does it?"

"Look, Jason, I don't want to make any trouble for you. I think you realize that."

Givens nods, biting into a piece of toast.

Stratton continues, "Vic told the investigators he was with you. That you guys went shooting at the quarry, then over to your house to watch the Pistons game. And you, when asked to confirm, must have said yes, that was true."

If Givens is unsettled by this conversation, he's not showing it. He chews and swallows his food steadily, meeting Stratton's eyes but not over-meeting them like a person who's striving to appear natural.

Stratton drinks some of his coffee. Decent coffee. "Well, here's the thing. Vic's worried, and I don't understand it. I'm wanting some reassurance, if you can give it. Or some insight? He's worried about police scrutiny. I don't know why, and he won't level with me, saying it's best I don't know too much. Yet he wants me to help him."

"He say how?" Givens shovels an overly big forkful of tomatoes into his mouth. His table manners are a bit rough, but Stratton doesn't care. The meals he ate like an animal in the thick of fire season out West were too numerous to count. Hunkered on his heels with the other men, wolfing meat and bread spiced with smoke, chugging coffee. He missed those days, the adrenaline of it, the rawness every day brought. The marrow-depth fatigue that set in the moment they pulled you off your double shift.

"He wants me to make sure the suspect, Gordon Walsh, is guilty. He's concerned that if Walsh gets off, or if there's enough doubt, law enforcement could look harder at him, because he was seeing Sandy O'Rourke. And that makes him nervous."

Givens nods and keeps eating.

Stratton considers. "So I'm looking into things on my own." He gazes out the window at the parking lot. An elderly couple, hand in hand, are on their way in. The man holds the door for the woman, and she smiles at him over her shoulder as if they're on a date. Their faces are creased and worn, but their grooming is good: nicely combed hair, tidy overcoats. The woman sports a leaf-green scarf around her neck.

The sight of the couple gives Stratton a lift. He says, "I know that neither you nor Paladino were in the quarry that day."

Givens raises his eyebrows and stops chewing.

Stratton goes on, "Maybe you and Vic went to your house to watch the basketball game, but I doubt it. I'm guessing that wherever you were, you guys weren't together, either. I think you're both using the same story, for different reasons."

The detective's fork hovers over his food just a second longer than necessary before he resumes eating. Stratton notices, but doesn't make comment.

"If neither of you had anything to do with Sandy O'Rourke's murder, but if you were up to something illegal, you know it'd be better to come clean about it now."

Givens gives Stratton a cold glare. By now he's put away a substantial portion of his breakfast.

"I'm not threatening you," says Stratton, "because I have no idea, and the last thing I want to do is stir up anything. I'm just trying to help out my boss." He drinks some more coffee. "I'm guessing you guys cooked up a mutual alibi," he continues, feeling more comfortable. "Who knew Sandy would get killed that same day? Who knew that you guys' activities that afternoon and evening would come under any scrutiny at all? Just a bad coincidence." A thought strikes him. Occam's Razor. What do married guys do that needs hiding? "If you were shacking up, and all you needed was something to tell your wife—"

Givens surprises him by bursting out laughing.

Stratton finishes, "You probably told her you were at Paladino's after the quarry, right?"

Collecting himself, Givens says, "We oughta have you on the force."

Stratton smiles.

Givens collects himself. "OK. My wife was on me to take down the Christmas lights. That's how this whole mess started. Here we are, after New Year's, right, and I hadn't done it yet. I'd put in for the day off, middle of the week, because I had a long dentist appointment, root canal, and I get nervous about that stuff. But that morning the dentist office calls and they have to reschedule. I wasn't about to waste the day off, so I tell Nancy I'll take down the lights."

Givens wipes up some egg with a piece of bread. The café is getting busier, more retirees and blue-collar guys coming in for the bacon-and-egg special.

"But something else came up," says Stratton.

"Right, my girlfriend texted me." He shrugs. Stratton keeps his face neutral.

"She lives in Chicago," Givens says, "and she'd just flown into Detroit for a morning meeting. She's a building materials rep, makes good money. Anyway, she's got the afternoon and evening off."

"I see."

"Usually I just tell Nancy I have to work late, but that wouldn't do this time. I need a good excuse, fast, so I get in touch with Vic and say hey, can you cover for me? I'm going to tell my wife you called and you want me to go shooting and then get something to eat, OK? And he says, sure, you can tell her that."

"Your wife likes Paladino?"

"She's crazy about him, she brags that him and I are friends. He's been over to the house."

"OK ..."

"So, everything goes fine. I meet up with my woman, my wife knows nothing. But then the news breaks about Sandy's murder, and the investigators in charge question Vic. He tells them he was with me, like we agreed. And now instead of him backing me up, now it's me backing *him* up, and we're both lying."

"Uncomfortable situation."

Givens looks down at his food, about a third of which remains.

"Do you know what Vic was doing instead of being with you?"

"He wasn't murdering Sandy O'Rourke, but I suspect he was up to something he shouldn't have been."

Stratton is a patient guy, but this was pushing it. "For God's sake, what was it?"

"He won't talk to me about this particular time. But OK. He likes to play cop, you know that."

"Yeah."

"Well, I think he went out to play cop that evening, and things got out of control."

"Something that hit the news?" Stratton asks.

"Yeah."

Stratton considers. "The fight at the shopping center?"

"Yeah."

Fifteen or twenty young people got into a brawl out back of Somerset, the upscale mall north of the city. Presumably the fight was about drugs and money. Weapons were pulled, and a kid or two got shot.

"I thought that was a gang thing," Stratton says.

"Well, I'm betting he mixed himself up in it."

"As in, trying to stop it? Like stop the drug dealing in the first place?"

"I think so."

"A kid died, correct?"

"No, he made it."

"Did Paladino shoot him?"

"I don't think so. He hasn't been identified as being there, to my knowledge."

Stratton says, "When he's with you, does he talk a lot about, you know, wanting to keep the streets safe? That kind of stuff?"

"Yeah, I think he was developing an obsession about it, frankly." Givens wipes his mouth and drains his coffee cup.

CHAPTER 26

ONE OF THE BRIGHT LIGHTS

I phone Connie Blue Smoke on Friday after her shift at the urgent care center.

"Did you get the job?" she asks excitedly.

"It seems so." I fill her in on how it went at Paladino's. "So, after I spent two hours cleaning, with the almost useless help of his personal assistant, I told him this was just a start and I'd need a lot more time to do a thorough job. Then I made an egg pancake, with three eggs, butter, some Camembert cheese, which I'd never tried before, but some was in the fridge and wow, it's good, plus mushrooms. I fried the mushrooms separately, then put them in like usual. Salt and pepper."

"You sauteed them. Never say fried."

"Understood."

"And he loved it, right?"

"Yeah. I got the distinct feeling he liked being slapped around by this little nobody. I acted the stone bitch."

"Wish I could've seen it. Did he ask you anything difficult?"

"I think he tried to. He goes, 'What's the first ingredient in an aspic?' Of course I have no idea what an aspic is."

"Well, what did you say?"

"I go, 'I do not make aspics! They are poor for the digestion! You will never see an aspic come out of this kitchen!'"

"Excellent, Bambi."

"I was ready to say something about enzymes, but he dropped it. I think he wants a French chef only because it sounds classy. I start Monday."

"Oh, thank goodness."

"Which, yeah, because I can practice and learn stuff all weekend."

"We can do a video call tomorrow, and I can show you a few things, once we both pick up some ingredients. I'll make a list."

"Great!"

"By the way, I still haven't found anybody who knows anything about Gordy and Sandy O'Rourke, but I did learn something offhand."

"Yeah?"

"Which might be of interest to you, just separately."

"Yeah?"

"OK, so I bumped into Leif Olson, remember him?"

"Isn't he a cousin of Gordy's, right? Few years older?"

"Right, so I stopped in at Marco's yesterday after work, I'm picking up my pizza, and this gigantic, brand-new pickup truck pulls in behind me on the street. And Leif jumps out, and we say hi, and he goes how do you like my new truck? And I'm like, man, that is some truck. Didja hit the jackpot at the casino or something?"

"Ha, yeah, none of those guys ever accomplished anything on their own. I can't imagine he could ever get enough credit to even get under payments on one of those."

"Yeah. I'm embarrassed to say I dated Leif for a while, back when I didn't know any better."

"Ugh."

"Yeah."

"Everybody makes mistakes."

"Anyhow," Connie kept on, "he says this is thanks to his uncle Eric. He left some money. And I say that's nice, and then it occurs to me to ask if he left any for Gordy. Because Eric Olson is Gordy's uncle, too, right?"

"Yeah!" Uncle Eric was one of the bright lights in Gordy's family, on his mother's side. After a career in the Merchant Marine as a captain of one of the lake freighters, he retired out and started a charter fishing business out of St. Ignace, just for fun. Did very well with that. Never drank, saved his money, wife died young of cancer, no kids.

"And Leif said, well, he didn't exactly leave it to me, he left it to my kid."

"Well, that's different."

"And that's where it gets interesting, Bambi."

"OK."

"Leif says, Uncle Eric died five years ago, and he put up all these trust funds for the kids, for college. But, he says, my kid's not going to college, at least not just yet."

"Oh, my gosh. How did Leif get his hands on it, then?"

Connie says, "Yeah! I asked that, and he said once his kid turned 18, the money dumped from the trust into the kid's bank account. But the lawyer that handled it didn't notice the account was joint with Leif."

"And Leif just waltzes into the bank and takes out the money."

"Yep."

"What a piece of scum."

"Yep."

"Well, how much was it? Do you know?"

Connie says, "Leif said he got sixty thousand dollars, but the truck cost sixty-two, and he had no credit, so he had to scrape up the last two grand somehow. I think he thought I'd be impressed. I go, what about your kid? And he says Ricky's working the gas fields over by Alpena, making good money, six figures, won't even miss it."

Everybody, it seemed, was making six figures these days, even kids just out of high school. "Well, that is some story. Did you ask—"

"I sure did. He thinks there must be an account for Laura. I don't know if it'd be the same amount as for Leif's kid, but you'd figure. Uncle Eric didn't leave anything to his nieces and nephews, said they seemed to be doing all right. Just their kids, he left money to. The great-nieces and -nephews. Eight of them. That's what Leif told me, anyway."

"Ohhh, Connie."

"Yeah."

"I can't thank you enough for telling me that."

"When does Laura turn 18?"

"April first." An easy birthday to remember, all right. Thank goodness the midwife didn't prank me somehow, handing me a gorilla doll wrapped in a blanket instead of Laura. These things occur to me.

CHAPTER 27

PABLO SAW A MAN

Laura Walsh waits quietly, watching the street-hockey game until the ball flies over the curb near her. She hustles to get it.

A few kids, tweens and teens, played this game after school and on Saturdays, even in the winter if the streets were clear enough. Laura has joined in now and then.

She jogs back with the hard black rubber ball and, still holding it, asks, "Did you guys hear about the woman that got killed over there?"

The five kids heard of it. One, the tallest of the bunch, says, "What about it?"

"Your name's Tremaine, right?"

The boy nods.

Although some recent sunshine cleared away most of the snow from the streets, it's still cold: everybody's breath comes out in white streams. The boys are panting and have shed their jackets.

"I'm—"

"Laura," Tremaine says.

"Yeah." She smiles at being remembered. "I knew her, her name was Sandy. They think my dad did it, but I know he didn't. I'm asking around if anybody saw anything. Like if anybody saw the woman, Sandy, come to the house, and who was with her."

They all gaze at the house.

Although the boys are getting cold, no one moves, as for one thing, Laura still has hold of their ball. For another, yeah, the dead lady. One of the boys shuffles impatiently, eyeing the ball but not saying anything.

The belief that no one talks in the 'hood is a myth, unless it's a gang thing, a drug thing. People keep their mouths shut about that stuff. But plenty of witnesses talk about plenty of crimes.

"Pablo saw a man," says Tremaine at last. "He said he saw a guy come out."

This was the thing: who listens to kids? Nobody talks to the neighborhood tykes.

Laura breathes evenly. "Where's Pablo now?"

A fireplug of a kid with close-set eyes says, "When the snow's good, you could try the Aretha."

"The Aretha," repeats Laura.

"The berm there, you know."

Back at her dorm, Laura digs the crummier of two skateboards out of her closet and lays it deck-down on her desk. The board is fairly chewed up. She gets out a skate tool and removes the wheel assemblies. She adds some grip tape to the deck. This isn't going to work at all, in the practical sense, but that doesn't matter. She checks the weather reports.

CHAPTER 28

BOOK DUST AND CURIOSITY

I couldn't believe how complicated fine cookery is. Take potatoes au gratin, which I learned how to make over the weekend from Connie Blue Smoke and YouTube. Properly, you pronounce it oh-grahtin, not ow-grahtin. That was thing one. Then you need eleven ingredients and two hours because you don't just throw cut-up potatoes into a crockpot with some cheddar and milk. You need two kinds of cheeses you've barely heard of—Gruyère? That was one of them.

You're supposed to simmer onions, garlic, and shallots (which were also new to me, and is that not overkill anyway, since they're basically mini onions?) in heavy cream, slice potatoes paper-thin with a terrifying device called a mandoline, arrange the slices in a DaVinci-like spiral, pour over the liquid stuff, then bake it for a long time. After that, then and only then, do you add a whole bunch of the Gruyère on top and so forth and *then* broil it. Broil it? That's what it says. The whole process was like rocket surgery, for gosh sakes.

"You can make it a day before you need it," Connie told me. "Except the cheese-broil step, you do that just before you serve it."

Which was a godsend, now that I thought of it. I could make any number of dishes ahead, work all night if I had to. No one need know. A small servant's suite was assigned to me in case I wanted to sleep over at Paladino's house any time, depending on what he needed. That was fine with me; I planned to start sleeping over immediately.

As far as I could tell, I'd only be cooking for Paladino and his house gang in the immediate future. No huge parties, so that was a blessing.

I kept reminding myself that cooking wasn't my real mission here, but I did have to keep my job until I could learn whatever there was to learn about Paladino's possible involvement with Sandy O'Rourke's murder.

As the weekend progressed, I grew more comfortable with my persona of Celeste LaPorte. Let's just ride this beast until we can't.

It helped a lot to remind myself why I was doing this: for Laura. Not for Gordy, not for some ideal of justice—but for Laura.

I wanted a book, though, too, a real cookbook I could flip around in. Not being able to prove a Detroit address, I wasn't going to be able to check anything out of the library, and I didn't want to risk stealing from there. So on Saturday afternoon I ran over to King books, the used-book shop I went into once or twice when I was genuinely trying in life.

As you've gathered, my information bank is spotty. I like to read well enough, but I read slowly. So I haven't read as many books as most people. And of course, there were years when I could sit and read, but not be able to remember anything two minutes later. Being straight now, though, my memory's improved quite a bit.

I've always liked figuring. I can keep score in pinochle in my head.

King Books is huge and old. Every floor smells like book dust and curiosity.

In the cooking section I nab a copy of *Mastering the Art of French Cooking*, the book by Julia Child that everybody's supposed to have. I take the book to the checkout counter.

Then something amazing occurs. A guy comes in with an armload of books to sell, and he starts laying them on the counter. One of the books is a smallish hardcover with a picture of a deer's face on it, and the title says, *The Original Bambi*. The next line says, *The Story of a Life in the Forest*.

"Hey, man," I go. "That book."

He, definitely one of those professor-looking people, salt-and-pepper beard, turns to me.

"That says 'original,'" I say. "Does that mean the book was before the movie?"

"Yes." He stops what he's doing and looks at me. At first he seems irritated, then his face smooths into something like patience. He says, "It's a social allegory written in the nineteen-twenties by a persecuted Jew named—"

"You mean Disney didn't invent Bambi in a cartoon?"

He laughs in an actually friendly way, not condescending as I've experienced. "Nope, a guy named Felix Salten wrote it. This is a newer translation. It's pretty good."

"Oh." I had to take a second. "Well, how about that."

The man seems to be checking to see if I want to hear more.

I look into his face enthusiastically. "I'm not sure what an allegory is."

"Oh!" says the man, whose bald spot—I suspect—is covered by a skimpy-looking black beanie. "Well, an allegory is a story that makes a point, or develops a moral theme."

"Like a sermon in church?"

"Not exactly. No. Well, some poorly written ones are! But no, a quick example would be, oh, the fable of the ant and the grasshopper. The ant's industrious, while the grasshopper fiddles away the summer, and—"

"And doesn't save up," pipes the clerk behind the counter. She's old with wrinkled hands.

"And then he's sorry come winter," I put in. "And the moral is you should save up and not expect handouts from society."

"You're quite right," agrees the professor, and I can picture him saying that exact thing to kids at the college. Everybody sitting around a table talking about literature with cups of coffee. You're quite right.

He goes on for a minute more, telling how the real, original story of Bambi was about innocence and bravery and people not fitting in and people being ignorant and mean, and the pogroms of Europe around the time of World War One. "Salten used the forest and the animals as substitutes for governments and populations."

Pogroms is another word I learn from this guy, who looks at his watch and takes off after I keep asking questions.

I buy the book for five dollars.

CHAPTER 29

DEFINITELY A TOUGH GUY

I get to Paladino's huge house at six in the morning for my first day of work. A security guy in a thick shearling coat meets me at the rear service gate. He introduces himself as Chuck Stratton, and tells me to park my red Lincoln under a carport behind the garages. He shows me the two rear entrances to the house.

"This is the personnel entrance. Let's go in here. The other one is for deliveries." Even though he's got on thick glasses, his gray eyes are unnervingly piercing. He shows me how the electric pallet lifter works, and how to secure both doors. Next, he gives me a code to use on the rear gate and the personnel door. "It gets changed every week."

"Right."

"You'll be informed."

Having adopted my Celeste LaPorte persona on the way there, I was properly in character. I give this Chuck Stratton a cool look, which he returns. We hang our coats in a closet off the receiving room.

"Have you been shown your room?"

"I was shown it Friday. It is all right. I will require cleaning supplies."

That amuses him. Slight eye-crinkle.

I flip on all the lights in the kitchen, and in spite of the pitch-dark beyond the windows, the room comes to life bright and huge.

Using the center kitchen counter as a desk, Stratton lays out a W-9 form for me to fill out, as well as an American Express card with my name on it. *Celeste LaPorte.* Beneath that, it said *OneTrack Inc.* Paladino's company name.

"You can use this to buy food, beverages, and whatever else you need in the kitchen. The bill will be paid."

"How did you get this so fast, with my name on it?" I ask, dumbfounded, but covering it with a quick layer of suspicion.

He just smiles.

I fill in the W-9 with a fake address and made-up Social Security number.

I ask, "What is my budget per month?"

"For food, no limit. For wine and liquor, just try to keep it real. Vic goes over the books himself, so he'll know. If you want to buy something high cost, just talk to him or me first."

Besides giving off massive competence vibes, this guy is nice to look at. Straight build, slim but not skinny. Deep-set eyes, prominent nose, full lips. The nose was too big, for real, but it saved his face from being pretty.

"I will shop after breakfast."

"Fine. Keep track of your mileage for taxes."

I nod as if I know what he's talking about.

Stratton tells me the names of two stores that deliver.

"OK. I must go to market myself."

"Fine, whatever you want to do."

"How many for breakfast?"

"Three today, maybe four. Everybody comes down at different times, though."

"OK." I asked on Friday whether anybody had any allergies or food limitations, expecting to learn that Sunpod was a vegan. As it happened, Sunpod was worse than a vegan. I was told she mainly consumes liquid food—the chopped tadpole

167

mixture, some special formula she buys online and keeps in a refrigerator in her suite.

As Stratton and I interacted, we sized each other up. It was kind of funny: I could tell he was doing it, and he could tell I was doing it, and we both could tell we could tell. His main job was being Paladino's bodyguard, but it seemed he was a bit of a house manager as well.

Definitely a tough guy. Bald head—shaved? Takes care of himself, works out, no doubt. Flat stomach, good shoulders, strong neck, not too long of a neck. Large hands and feet. Calm vibe. Could be a great nightclub bouncer—maybe was, at some point. The guy who quietly and effectively explains why it's best for you to leave now, you personally. You right now. Forty years old, I guess, and I wonder what his ambitions in life were when he was twenty.

This guy could be a powerful ally to me. That, or a dangerous enemy. If Paladino was involved in Sandy O'Rourke's death, Stratton could have been heavily involved as well, in any number of possible ways: the assassin, bagman for the assassin, driver, lookout, anything.

Or, of course, he and everybody in this house could be innocent.

"What do you like to eat, Chuck Stratton?" I push up the sleeves of my white chef coat. I went to a restaurant supply store on Sunday and picked up this coat, which I revealed in all its blinding-white authority when I flung off my parka in the entry room.

"For breakfast?" he smiles a little. "I like French toast and bacon. Coffee. There's a coffee machine over there in the breakfast zone."

"Breakfast zone." I like that.

"Everybody can make their own," he says. "The coffee. I've had a cup already."

"You are hungry?"

"Sure am."

"Get out now and I will work."

I root in the fridges and pantry for fresh ingredients, locating two loaves of decent sliced bread in the freezer and some fairly new eggs and milk. I make 16 slices of French toast, using maple syrup to flavor the milk, and the huge griddle to cook them. I make sure to use a high ratio of eggs to milk, adding a few extra yolks, as Connie Blue Smoke advised.

"Let the liquid soak in real well," she added, "and cook the slices low and slow so everything gets browned and done all through. Be patient. Never let your French toast be raw or cool inside. The secret's low and long."

I discover a warming oven in the side kitchenette, so I store the completed French toast there, piled high, with a pair of wooden tongs so people will be able to serve themselves. We're not going to call it French toast, however. I set up plates, silver, and napkins on the counter, then get going frying a couple of pounds of bacon. I'm betting Stratton's a big eater. I fry the bacon slowly, making coffee meanwhile. There's a canister of reasonably fresh-smelling coffee beans next to a grinder on a counter. I grind a bunch of beans, heat water, and use a French-press pot to make coffee three times. I rinse out a large insulated carafe and pour the coffee in there, sipping a little myself along the way. I prefer tea as you know, but coffee seems more favored in France. I make a second carafe-full.

It's now almost seven. Nobody down yet. I set to work on a pineapple, cut that up, strow some plain sugar over the pieces, as they're fairly tart. I mix the sugar in well, so it disappears. I set that out with a serving spoon on the breakfast counter.

As I work, I consider my mission. Getting to be on buddy terms with every-body in the household is job one. Too much of a stone bitch persona could work against me, so I'd decided to be a caring stone bitch. It seemed to work well enough on Stratton.

One by one, Paladino's household made their way to breakfast.

Sunpod shows up, carrying her clear plastic cup of gray liquid.

"Good morning, good Sunpod," I say briskly. "Coffee for you?" I reach for a mug.

"I don't usually drink coffee." Her voice is annoyingly wispy.

"But you will have some now because it smells so good," I order. "What do you take in it?"

"Nothing." She reaches for the mug. She looks like she was born to a pair of greyhounds with eating disorders.

"What is that ... liquid you drink?" I ask as I tidy things, as she watches.

"It's a special mix, made just for my biome." She mentions a company name and something about the lost coast of California, whatever that is. "They test your hair follicles, then they know the whole story of a person, and which kinds of food materials are best. Then they formulate it."

"Food materials."

She gazes at me with enormous neutrality.

"Well," I go, "I have cooked some food materials you will enjoy. Toast Alsace. Help yourself from the warmer."

Sunpod says, "I don't usually eat breakfast."

"But you will taste my Toast Alsace." Connie taught me how to pronounce it, like *all-sauce*. "You must eat, my dear. I hate to tell you this, but that is not food, there, in your cup. It is not food. How does it make you feel when you drink it?"

"Well ... OK. I feel OK."

"You do not."

She stares at me. Chuck Stratton appears in the kitchen entryway, behind her. He holds a plate piled with bacon and Toast Alsace, and he's already taken a bite.

"Ask Mr. Chuck Stratton how he feels eating my Toast Alsace."

She turns to him, her diaphanous white outfit flowing around her.

"I feel good," he says, smiling and forking up another bite.

I'm making an impression.

I tell her, "I am responsible for the well-being of every stomach in this house. You will listen to me. You will eat."

"In the French style?" suggests Stratton, still smiling.

I glance at him sharply. "I will cook French food and American food. The best world cuisine is French. Next best is American." I take Sunpod's arm. She doesn't flinch away. "You will eat properly," I order, staring deeply into her eyes, which engage with mine willingly. Her arm is like a Q-tip. Little soft hand at the end.

Stratton sets his plate on the work counter and continues to eat, standing up, watching me putter around. Sunpod goes to the breakfast zone and comes back with a piece of Toast Alsace on a plate. She gives it a suspicious look, but lifts a corner to her mouth and nibbles it. Her eyes widen.

After another few minutes, Paladino shows up in the kitchen, carrying a plate of Toast Alsace, bacon, and pineapple.

"I heard you all talking. Good vibes in here."

"Yes," I affirm. "Even better with you now." That was easy flattery, but people appreciate flattery, what the heck.

I fuss around and listen as everybody eats. They all talk about Paladino's upcoming concert. Advance ticket sales haven't been as strong as we might like. That's concerning. At one point Paladino mentions someone named Joe.

"I called him," Sunpod says.

"He's coming, then?"

There is no talk of Sandy O'Rourke.

I observe Paladino as closely as I dare. *Are you a guilty man? A grieving man? An innocent man?* The only thing that strikes me is that he seems a bit thinner than I remembered from when I met him just a few days ago. Maybe not thinner, but a little less *full*, somehow, less energetic. Maybe he just needs the morning coffee to kick in. I check out his skin tone, the skin on his face. Is it slacker than one might expect from the publicity photos?

As soon as he came into the kitchen, Sunpod handed him a heavy wine glass, like what I would call a goblet, filled with at least 15 pills of different colors. Where had that come from? Perhaps she'd prepared it in the breakfast zone. I can't get a close look at the pills. Paladino's hands tremble a little as he handles the pills and the glass of water I serve him.

"Vitamins," Sunpod says to me, noticing my interest.

"Yes," I agree.

"And for my blood pressure," Paladino says. He tips about five pills into his mouth at a time, and washes them down with gulps of water. He seems more centered now. He drinks his coffee and eats his food without hurrying.

"After eating my food for one week, you will not need so many vitamins," I tell Paladino sternly.

He smiles sadly. "To tell you the truth," he says, "I like taking pills."

A stroke of fortune broke when Sunpod tells me about the private refrigerators in everybody's suite of rooms. "You're supposed to keep them stocked with whatever we want. Right, Vic?"

I go, "Certainly." I grab a pen and pad. Paladino wants bottles of gourmet spring water, yogurt, and berries; Sunpod requests a brand of water I'd never heard of that is reportedly "ionized," plus organic grapefruit juice, and Stratton says he'd like tomato juice, veggie sticks, and hard-boiled eggs. Clearly, these are the snacks they knew they should have, as opposed to what they really wanted. I tended to believe Stratton, though. He looked to be in pretty good health.

After loading one of the two amazing dishwashers and starting it, I go to the nearest Kroger and buy a ton of fresh groceries. Aside from all the basic stuff I wanted for making smothered pork chops ("Viande de la Marseilles"), meatloaf ("Boeuf du Corsica"), my omelettes rustica, and so on, I buy two huge bricks of Velveeta, a few jars of brown gravy, cake mixes, refrigerator dinner rolls to bake-n-serve, toffee-chocolate cookie dough (ditto), and loads of fresh fruit and cheeses, including Gruyère. I also pick up some fresh gourmet bread, which I figure I'll need to do every day. I can warm it in a low oven to generate proper aroma (another Connie tip), then bring it out to the table with some flour dusted on my forearms. Of course I make sure to pick up everything for the personal fridges.

Upon returning from shopping, I see a man leave the staff entrance at Paladino's. Vigorous guy, he seems: spring to his step, bareheaded, dirty-blond hair flopping around. Silver-colored puff coat, hands jammed into his pockets. He glances around, sees me, ignores me.

Before I can park and talk to him, he jumps into a tricked-out white Mustang that wasn't in the carport when I left. The Mustang zooms to the gate, the guy punches in the code (because you had to use it both coming and going), and the gate opens for him.

In the kitchen, I find a plate with a couple of crusts of Toast Alsace on the counter, plus a used coffee mug. I'd left a few slices in the warmer. I hurry to stash the groceries, taking care to hide the cake mixes and my other cheater ingredients in the remotest crannies I can find.

Every minute I can keep up this charade could be another minute closer to discovering ... something ...?

Truth?

Something.

CHAPTER 30

TALKING TO SOME KIDS

Everybody in Detroit has a love-hate relationship with snow, reflects Laura Walsh as she rides the Q-Line streetcar down Woodward to the waterfront. Snow is falling now: nice thick-flaked fresh snow, falling straight down. It is Monday, two in the afternoon, and her classes are over for the day.

The snow is beautiful and cleansing. That is the love part. The hate part is having to drive in it, or afterwards trudge through the increasingly dirty ruts and ice. The main drags get plowed or treated with salt, but in the neighborhoods you just have to mush through it. The worst experience as a pedestrian is getting splashed with filthy slush while waiting at a corner. Every place she's lived, Laura has made a point of memorizing where the worst of the slush pools form. Because some drivers know too, and take pleasure in aiming for them in order to drench pedestrians. This to Laura is one more proof that God is not just. God is God. On any given day you can get a fair shake or a filthy ice shower.

The seats on the streetcar are hard, but so what. God had nothing to do with that design choice.

Laura gets off the car downtown and walks the rest of the way to the Aretha Franklin amphitheater on the waterfront, carrying her modified, wheel-less skateboard. The snow is accumulating quickly, maybe three inches by now, and it's still falling plentifully. Perfect. The temperature is in the high 20s, frigid enough for the snow to stick, but not tooth-shatteringly cold.

She stops at the edge of the Aretha property. The white canopy over the pavilion is invisible in the falling snow. About four guys are snowboarding down the berm between the lawn and the street. The berm slopes sharply down to the frozen-over canal which in summer acts as a barrier to the property. In winter, who cares? The pavilion is empty, except for the flat bare stage platform.

The berm is surely a pathetic place to board, but it's right there in the level city, meaning you need no transit to a ski area, no money for a lift ticket. You can at least carve a couple of turns, try to do tricks. The guys have stripped off their coats and are running their boards down the good part of the berm, then hauling back up on the sides, so as to save the best snow. A couple of guys wear fabric neck gaiters pulled up over their lower faces against the cold.

Laura trudges up to the top, angling from the street.

"Hey," she says.

"Sup."

"Hey."

When she gets the chance, she drops in on her ridiculous board. She stays upright, trying to simply edge down the slope, but one boot slips off the deck and she spills halfway down.

She gets up, shaking her head.

"Are you an idiot?" says one guy as he zips past.

"Yes, I am!" she answers brightly. The others snicker.

"You need bindings on that," says another guy, "at least."

"You're right," agrees Laura. She stays where she is, in the center of the run. Smiling widely, she calls, "Pablo here today?"

She is pretty enough and seemingly hapless enough that the guys pay a moment's worth of attention to her. A guy wearing a yellow knit hat and a basketball jersey over a thick sweatshirt drops down to her and stops. He pulls down his neck gaiter and wipes snow from his glasses with a gloved finger. Blinking through the wetness, he looks about fifteen.

"I'm Laura."

"I know your name," he says. "We played pickup together couple times. What do you want?"

"Talk for a minute. About the woman that got killed on Boston." Laura gets on her board and manages, with the help of the grip strips, to edge her way to the bottom. She kicks along the frozen canal a little ways, Pablo following. The snow keeps falling, settling in fluffy whiteness over their shoulders and heads.

She turns to him. "Man. Hey. I knew that woman. Been asking around. The guys said you maybe saw a guy leaving that house? Is that right?"

"Yeah. I didn't know him, you know?" Pablo speaks in fast clips. "I was walking up to Woodward, OK? And he kind of caught my eye, even though it was getting dark. He, yeah. He was in a hurry." A blackwork tattoo creeps up Pablo's neck to his jawline. Something in script; Laura can't make it out without staring.

She says, "What did he look like?"

"White guy, gray jacket with the hood up. But I caught a look at his face. Big face, kind of moon face."

"Light gray jacket or dark gray?"

"Light gray."

"He came out the front door, then?"

"Yeah. He slipped and fell on the ice. I hear him go *uff!* and I look over and see him down. I think maybe he's knocked out, but he gets up. His hood falls off when he gets up. He drops a bag. He was carrying a bunch of stuff, yeah, and it was windy."

"You guys made eye contact? Would you recognize him if you saw him again?"

"He gave me a *look.* I might know him again. Can't say for sure."

"Do you happen to remember the exact time you saw him?" Laura blinks as snowflakes settle on her eyelashes.

"Naw, naw. I kept walking."

"You say he dropped a bag? What kind of bag?"

Pablo glances up the berm, anxious to go again. "Garbage bag, black garbage bag. It broke open, some stuff fell out, then the bag blew into the tree, and he was mad! Oh, he was mad over that, yeah, you know? He cussed and stomped."

"Hmp." Laura thinks about that. "Have you noticed if the bag's still in that tree?"

Pablo hasn't.

Laura asks, "Was he carrying other stuff?"

"Another bag same, but it didn't break open. He picked it up."

"And then which way did he go? Did he get into a car?"

"Laura." The young man looks at her directly. "If I'd've known it was important, I'd have looked at him longer. But it was cold, you know? I kept walking."

Laura nods. She slips him a McDonald's gift card. "Twenty on here. Thank you, man."

"No need. But I appreciate it." Pablo flashes her a wide smile, zips the card into his pants pocket, and heads up the berm.

The snow is chasing pedestrians indoors, and the city as a whole is decelerating, withdrawing to wait out the snowfall. Only gotta-do vehicles like buses and delivery trucks are plodding onward, carving trenches in the streets.

As Laura nears the streetcar stop, a man materializes out of the whiteness right next to her.

"Hello, Laura."

Instinctively she recoils, skipping a step sideways, almost stumbling. Her breath catches, pulse spikes. This stranger knows her name.

"It's all right," he says in a courteous tone. "I'm sorry I startled you. I'm a friend of your mother's. My name's Ted Alvarez." It seems he's been out in the weather a fair amount of time; an inch of fluffy snow has collected on his fedora hat, and snow has clumped on his shoes.

She collects herself and walks on. Ted Alvarez falls into step with her.

He says, "I'm a detective with the DPD. I'd like to talk with you for a minute."

Laura doesn't know whether to feel reassured. "You must have been following me."

"Yes. What were you doing at the Aretha?"

"Talking to some kids."

"You're working on your father's case, aren't you?"

"I can do what I want." Her guts clench with apprehension, though there is a funny shard of euphoria in there as well. Being told by a cop that she is working on a case is one of the most grown-up things that has ever happened to her.

"Yes," says this Alvarez, "and you're doing fine. I'm not supposed to help you or your father. I have my suspicions about the case. That's why I'm talking to you ... quietly. Is there anything you've learned that you'd like to tell me? Anything that could help?"

They arrive at the streetcar stop. No one else is there. Laura peers up Woodward. The streetcar isn't in sight, but she can almost hear it. She stares into the snowfall.

Alvarez says, "You don't know if you can trust me, right? I just want to tell you, I can speed things up, if you come across any evidence or witnesses that could help. Ask your mom about me." He hands her a card.

"Dude. Sir. Why are you doing this?"

But Detective Alvarez is walking away quickly through the falling snow, and in a moment he's invisible.

CHAPTER 31

I PRETEND NOT TO WATCH

I play it cool at Paladino's house, keeping to myself the rest of my first day, fixing lunch and dinner, cleaning up. Having all the time in the world to cook definitely took the pressure off. I make a big Niçoise salad for lunch, with warm bread and gourmet butter. I do the slight dusting of flour on my forearms and nobody questions the bread. Paladino loves the lunch. Everybody loves it. All Niçoise is, is tuna, hard-boiled eggs, and some specific vegetables, dressed in vinegar and oil. I used red vinegar and olive oil for that. I caught my reflection in a glass cupboard door and thought, *yeah, baby*. Chef.

In the afternoon I plan meals for the next few days, then set to making dinner, which is going to be Boeuf Bourguignon, or beef burgundy for us yokels. I go down to the wine cellar, which is eye-popping: there must be a thousand bottles in there. Needless to say, none bear labels I'm familiar with, like Thunderbird, Night Train, Riunite. I pick one that says Burgundy on it, open it, and slosh some into the pan. To make the sauce richer, I drizzle in a fair amount of beef gravy from the jar, plus a big handful of Bac-Os, which plump up in the sauce appealingly and add lots of flavor.

More warm bread and a huge pot of smashed potatoes rounded out that meal. I cooked the potatoes with the skins on, threw large amounts of butter and sour cream in, plus salt and pepper, and smashed everything carefully, using the bottom of the wine bottle and leaving lots of chunks and lumps. Rustica.

Another hit meal. Even Sunpod, in her customary outfit that looks like it was made out of bleached seaweed, comes in to say thank you as I'm cleaning up.

How am I going to nose around this house, get into places I'm not supposed to be in? So far, I haven't seen any interior cameras. Outside, there are several, mounted near the doors and at the corners. Sooner or later, Paladino has to go out, with Stratton at his side, plus, I hope, Sunpod. The three are the only full-time residents, unless there's some disfigured stepchild hiding in the attic.

The next morning, Tuesday, Sunpod tags after Paladino into the kitchen as I'm prepping to make omelettes.

"Oh, my mouth is watering," he says, inhaling the warm bread aroma. His large head swivels to take in the bowls of ingredients I was lining up on the counter. I'd already fixed an omelette for myself, topped with wads of Velveeta and some canned mushrooms I fried up in some butter. It was good. If you press all the water from the mushrooms, you can fry them—er, sauté them—in butter and some salt and pepper, and they'll be tasty. And you say it soh-tay, not saw-tay.

Sunpod, however, says, "No bread for you, Vic. No omelette."

I look at her questioningly.

"He gets only coffee and something small right now."

Twisting his fingers longingly, Paladino says, "Aw, Sunpod, but don't those omelettes smell good?"

Sunpod looks to me for help.

"Fruit?" I point to a bowl of apples. "They are washed."

"Yeah," says Paladino, taking one.

"Your vitamins," says Sunpod, handing him the goblet of pills.

He stands at the counter and snaps a bite of apple. "I'll be working in the studio this morning," he explains after chewing and swallowing. "Can't have a full stomach. Need a little something in it, though." He looks optimistic, if not bright-eyed. Obediently, he swallows the pills as Sunpod portions them out to him like candies.

I pretend not to watch closely. One of the candies is Dexedrine, the unmistakable orange-and-brown spansule. Definitely. It's a good upper. The rest of the lot seem to be supplements. Fish oil and the like.

"Very fine," I say. "You will be singing?"

"Yeah. Working on some new music for the show."

"I will cook a special omelette for you after your singing session. You will sing well. You should strive to have a Montmartre stomach!" I pronounce it more or less correctly, *Moh-mart*.

"Ooh, what's that?" He sounds like such a little girl with that *ooh*. I feel slightly embarrassed for him.

"Twenty-five percent full," I say. "Like the boulevard men, the singers along the boulevards." I saw *boulevardiers* in the French phrasebook I picked up along with the cookbook, but I'm not confident enough to pronounce it. "Also," I add, "the gondola men in Venice!"

The both of them buy all that, made up by me on the spur of the moment.

Paladino says, "Are your accommodations all right?"

"I cleaned. I stay." I put my hands on my hips. "You will want some light refreshments in the studio. Show me where it is, Mr. Vic, thank you very much."

He likes my caring-bitch persona. Smiling a little, he leads me deep into the house to an incredibly large professional music studio on the basement level. I say basement, but we're not talking concrete-block walls. The place was as swanky and professional-looking as you could imagine, with climate control and all sorts of equipment, instruments, everything. Control booth for recording.

"How many will be with you?" I demand.

"Uh, two or three others."

I go away, thinking about dexies, which in the spansule form that Paladino has are great. Spansule just means time-release capsule. Dexies come in tablets as well, which give you a jolt of energy and brainpower, but the spansules are better if you want the effects to last. Doctors give those to ADD kids, among other stuff like Adderall and Ritalin, which are good too. Street meth is an upper along the same lines, except much more raw and dangerous. You can get brain damage, which if you're desperate you don't care about. Neither do you care that the meat will shrivel off your bones, your teeth will fall out, etc. Pharmaceutical drugs are always better.

I return to the studio in half an hour, pushing a cart loaded with plates of fruit, cheese, and crackers, plus two hot-bottles full of a warm drink I concocted from Sprite, ginger juice, some lemon, and honey.

Paladino is in the room with Sunpod and two men. One is the guy I saw yesterday, the one who left in the Mustang. The other is a mustachioed gent who looks like what I imagine an opera singer to be: portly and elegant, with an intelligent expression and big rings on his fingers.

Given that I'm a servant, I figure I shouldn't expect to be introduced to these people, but of course I want to know who they are. I'm about to say something when Paladino announces, "This is Celeste, my new chef!" Enthusiastic tone. Which is great, but neither guy speaks to me. Mustang Guy, burly and confident, goes over to an electric guitar and picks around on it, head bowed, watching his fingers. The guitar just makes a thunking sound, as it isn't plugged into an amp.

I talk to the other guy. "You will let Mr. Vic know anything else you might need, Mister ...?"

"My name is Walter Razkowski," he says in a voice that reminds me of a smooth brass horn, one of those ones where the tubes make a circle? Super clear but not obnoxious.

Paladino adds, "My vocal coach."

"Ah," I go. "I like music very much."

"What is this drink?" Paladino asks, licking his lips after pouring himself some.

"Boisson de Paree." I'd looked up the French word for beverage. "Full of goodness, but a little naughty around the edges."

Everyone in the room smiles and wants some.

Mustang Guy and I look at each other. His face seems faintly familiar, but I can't place him. He sure doesn't seem to recognize me. Well-built guy, blocky body, just a little fattish around the middle. Fair skin, blondish hair in a clean cut, ruddy cheeks.

"That's Joe Myers," says Paladino. "He's a friend."

"Ah. Mister Walter, Mister Joe, a pleasure to meet you." Mister Joe grunts in reply. I hold my head high as I leave the room.

In the privacy of my little suite, I phone Ted Alvarez. "I think I know the answer to this question," I begin, "but how come you're dogging Laura?"

"To protect her."

"She called me. You slightly freaked her out."

"I know. That's part of the deal."

"You're saying she should be scared of nosing into Gordy's case? This isn't some big conspiratorial thing."

"Isn't it?"

"What do you mean?"

"Frankly, Bambi, I don't know. What are *you* up to? You haven't been at the house."

"I'm ... I'm ..."

"Don't tell me you're with Paladino."

"I won't."

He chuffs, "I knew you'd weasel your way in there somehow."

"Just leave me be for right now, OK?"

No response.

"By the way, how's Darlene?"

Silence. "I'll leave you be."

CHAPTER 32

DEVIL TAKE THE HINDMOST

Laura Walsh stands, hands on hips, before the enormous oak tree fronting her father's rental house on Boston Boulevard. The tree is positioned on the center greenbelt, quite a lush stretch in summer. It's lucky there's so much snow on the ground, maybe six inches accumulated in the past couple of weeks, the better in case of a fall.

The young woman gazes up at the twisting intricacies of bare branches, black against the overcast white sky. The black plastic bag is there, still, this long after the murder—two weeks, has it been? Well, this is *a* bag, at least; hopefully the same one Pablo saw blow away from the man in the gray coat. Luckily the tree is an oak, with gnarled, clutching fingers, instead of something smoother, like willow or chestnut.

Weather is trying to occur: wind, tiny granular snowflakes blowing around.

Laura wears running shoes laced tightly, and leather gloves she borrowed from Becka, whose hands are small. Tight gloves are a must for climbing a frozen tree. When you want to hide, a tree's a great place to go. There was almost always a good tree for Laura to escape to, even near the various foster homes in the city she found herself in. Tree climbing isn't all that hard. You find holds, you trust your feet, your hands help you along. If you fall, you fall, and you try to go Zen on the way down and hope for the best. She'd gotten the wind knocked out of her a few times. No big deal.

Laura glances around. Sparse traffic; nobody out on foot at the moment.

The tree is roughly 30 feet tall, and the bag is lodged two-thirds of the way up. Two stories, about.

Laura eyeballs the tree. A good route becomes clear quickly: shinny up the trunk, stand on the biggest low branch, and reach around the back for the next hold. There are plenty of good branches along the way; the crux move would be the first, to get up the trunk to that first horizontal. She decides monkey style—that is, butt outward—will be better than huggy-bear style, given the thickness of the trunk.

Might there be invisible ice, somehow, somewhere on the bark? Doesn't seem so, but you never know.

"Well, devil take the hindmost," she mutters, and starts up. Once you commit to a route, anxiety goes away and you just keep reacting to the environment. The tree bark is cold and hard and furrowed, and the furrows are deep enough for her gloved fingers to grip. She takes it slow, but not too slow. You don't want to overthink it.

She inches cautiously out on the limb that captured the plastic bag. Takes a moment to study the black clump. Anything in it? Maybe only traces of something useful. Maybe nothing. But based on what Pablo said, the seemingly empty bag had been important to that man. She fishes in the chest pocket of her anorak, pulls out a clean food storage sack, inverts it, thrusts her arm in, and grabs the black plastic bag with it. After a moment of tugging, the bag comes free. It's tattered and clumped with ice. Laura shakes off bits of ice and snow, then draws her clean bag up over it, ties it off, and drops it to the ground.

After downclimbing easily, she hangs by her arms from the lowest branch for a few seconds, feeling that great full-body stretch. Then she drops down, knees flexed. She stands next to her bag of evidence and phones Detective Ted Alvarez.

CHAPTER 33

I FORCED THEIR TROUBLES OUT OF THEM

Over the course of the next couple of days, I cook, serve, and learn. Stratton is of particular interest, being Paladino's bodyguard and somewhat of a sounding-board, it seems. Sunpod, though, seems always to be at hand, like a flimsy shadow.

I stock everybody's fridges, thereby getting a good look at their personal spaces. Still, I can't just paw through their stuff while they're home.

It was easier to get to know the crew than I expected. In spite of the beverages and snacks in their own quarters, everybody came to the kitchen multiple times a day, just like in ordinary houses! I don't know why I thought it'd be different in some rich person's house.

"Unless the chef's a nasty cat," said Chuck Stratton when he came in to get a snack on the second afternoon. I'd designated one refrigerator for snacks—open season—and the other for chef-only stuff, like raw meats, eggs, and so on. I stashed the Velveeta in there, having disposed of the outer boxes.

Furthermore, I stocked a deep drawer with wrapped candies and bags of potato chips and cheesy curls. They were instantly popular.

I had just remarked something to the effect that everybody loves the kitchen, and Stratton came out with that.

"The last chef?" I inquired.

"More or less," said Stratton.

Paladino found reasons to come into the kitchen when I was working, which was awkward, because I had to quickly hide whatever cheater ingredient I might be handling. However, I was delighted that he felt a sort of attraction towards me. Sunpod was always hovering around with her fake Buddhist-calm persona, beneath which I quickly spotted anxiety and neediness. She made me watch a video on her phone of some health guru who was selling herbal gargles. Telegraph that one around the world, boy.

Only once in those first days did I almost blow it. I was trying to make chicken cordon bleu, per a recipe from the cookbook I'd picked up, when it all came apart horribly. I just couldn't get the stuffing inside the chicken breasts without them looking like they barely survived an airplane crash. In frustration, I chopped everything up and pressed it into a baking pan, then strewed loads of cheese and breadcrumbs on top. I threw it into the oven and hoped for the best. It actually came out pretty good. With the help of the internet, I called it Délice de Poulet. Chicken delight.

But as they were all sitting down to eat, Paladino asked, "So! What wine will we be having tonight? What do you think would be best?"

I'd forgotten about wine.

"Maybe an Albarino?" suggested Paladino. "Or a Malbec? What do you think?"

Holding up a finger, I said, "One moment. I have selected the best. The wine needed extra time. Patience!"

I raced to the wine cellar and looked up 'expensive wine for a chicken dinner' on my phone. Even though my signal was faint down there, I was able to match a recommendation with a white wine from the cooler, a Pinot Grigio from Italy. I had no idea how to pronounce it, so I presented it silently with an extra-dramatic flourish. I was proud that I had the presence of mind to look up the correct type of wineglass as well.

They loved everything.

Whew.

Fairly quickly, I realized that Paladino was much weaker than he appeared on stage and in interviews. He could sing beautifully and work an audience but in reality he was a manchild who needed a strong presence to boss him around, to organize him. That's the best way I can describe what this guy came across like. Sunpod was just a groupie who dispensed clichéd wisdom. Given that Sandy O'Rourke had been Paladino's lover, I wondered if Sunpod filled that need for him now. I doubted it, but you never know. It seemed Paladino wanted her to be his anchor of strength, but I thought she was just about as weak as he was. Therefore, my presence as the forcefully capable Celeste LaPorte was attractive to them both. Initially I'd expected Sunpod to see me as a threat, but her own neediness overcame that. I got the impression that I could spew any sort of wacky philosophy, and they'd buy it.

More helpfully, the people in that house started to tell me their troubles. Actually I forced their troubles out of them. I used the same technique with this band of oddballs I used with johns when I did sex work.

With the higher-end johns, once we were in the hotel room, if he seemed nervous or hesitant, I'd talk a little about this and that, as in some movie I'd seen, or I'd ask him about his favorite fast food or liquor or cigars, anything to get him to say a couple of sentences.

Then I'd say, "Hey, handsome. You seem a little troubled. What's going on? Tell me."

And he'd relate a little bit, and I'd cuddle him, and it would be roughly four minutes of him spilling out that his boss was an idiot and he was afraid he wouldn't be able to make payments on the pair of jet-skis he acquired after the divorce, and his kid doesn't want to spend time with him unless he buys her a horse. Once he stops to take a full breath, I'd say, "Hey. Don't overthink it." Aaannd he realizes he's ready.

Some guys will absolutely talk you to death, and you have to remind them of the time. Some seriously just want to talk. Not that they hired you for that. But when he starts talking, and you listen, sometimes he decides he just wants to talk and that's it. For some lonely guys, talking to a woman who *listens* is literally better than sex. I mean, if you're a stone loser, you can always jack off to porn, but how many women will listen to you attentively and say supportive things? You can go to a strip club and the women will smile at you, but you can't have a conversation of any depth.

Once in a while the john will do more than complain: he'll confess something, like he sabotaged his brother's career because he was envious, or he ran over the neighbor's dog on purpose. And he feels guilty, but better for having talked about it, and then we get on to business.

Don't overthink it was always my standard advice. Which is so vague but yet so basic, I guess, that everybody seemed to find various levels of profoundness in it. They could interpret it to mean anything from *I deserve that new BMW* to *No one will care if I miss my kid's school play* to simply *Live for today.*

So that is the exact model I followed in that kitchen. To summarize, these are some bits of conversations I had in the first two and a half days.

Me: You are out of sorts today, Mr. Vic.

Paladino: Oh, I'm all right.

Me: No. You are worried.

Paladino: I have many issues on my mind, Celeste, many issues.

Me: You are sad for your lost love.

Paladino: I cry for her. I cry in the shower.

Me: Your fears should be spoken and be done with. Do not overthink your fears, Mr. Vic.

Paladino: I've done some things in my life.

Me: People do things. What have you done?

Paladino: Irreversible, Celeste, irreversible.

Me: Good Sunpod, where did you meet Mr. Vic?

Sunpod: Oh, at a retreat in California. We did forest bathing.

Me: Forest bathing.

Sunpod: Right, and we especially bonded during Silent Day.

Me: Ah. It seems you have powers to calm and restore Mr. Vic.

Sunpod: I do, I do.

Me: And yet. *And yet*, Miss Sunpod, you are not confident. Why is that?

Sunpod [stunned]: I'm still trying to figure my life out.

Me: What is the problem?

Sunpod: Well, I just don't know if Vic will keep me around.

Me: He pays you well. [Total guess, but good odds.]

Sunpod: That's the trouble. [Bingo.]

Me: You've been good for Mr. Vic, but that doesn't mean you can stay forever, does it?

Sunpod: It seems things are slightly ... tight, financially.

Me: Right. I say to you, Miss Sunpod, don't overthink it. Do not overthink your life. Do you worship?

Sunpod: Uh ...

Me: Whatever spirit you may pray to, will guide you in this.

Sunpod [thrown sideways by the course of this conversation]: I might need to ... move on. But that scares me.

Me: Don't overthink it. I will prepare for you now some cinnamon toast and good tea. You will wait. You will eat. You will feel better.

--

OK, I thought, so Paladino has some variety of dirt and perhaps even blood on his hands, and although Sunpod might be a lamebrain, she has an instinct for self-preservation.

Something, but not enough.

CHAPTER 34

THIS SENECA GUY

Stratton comes into the kitchen on Wednesday night, about ten-thirty, looking for a beer and some chips. "I want junk." I had to smile.

I'd figured out how to dim the kitchen lights and was sitting at the little built-in desk in the corner, reading the Seneca book under the lamp there. It was a pleasanter place than the cramped sitting area in my suite, plus I wanted to be on hand for as many hours in the day as possible.

I set down the book and open a bag of kettle chips while Stratton helps himself to a Budweiser from the snack fridge. I pour a generous pile of chips into a bowl and fetch a couple of napkins.

"I could cook you something," I offer. "Chips are not much sustenance." I'd picked up that word from Seneca, or the guy who translated him, anyway. "Hamburger?"

Stratton notices the book. "You're reading Seneca."

"Yes."

This Seneca guy was helping me quite a bit. He was like the anti-addict of his time. Addicts are always indulging themselves, lying and cheating to get their next hit or drink, and then blaming all their troubles on other people. When you're an addict, the problematic people in your life are the ones who stand between you and your drugs, and b) who want you to take responsibility. For something. For anything. Which is the last thing you feel like doing.

But Seneca, now, this ancient Roman guy was all about being OK with no drugs. He was all about being OK with no anything. If you don't need anything, you're free. You can take on duties and responsibilities. He wrote about a lot more ideas, but mainly his basic thing was do your best, don't chase after your cravings, and never complain. If you're one of the sorry wretches at the bottom of the luck barrel, well, it's better to be matter-of-fact about it than a crybaby. Seneca was an original Stoic. I hadn't known anything about the Stoics. I thought stoic was just a word. Not like a branch of thought.

"I like the Stoics too," says Stratton. "What's that other book you've got there?"

"Oh, nothing." I nudge the book with my elbow towards the back of the little desk.

Stratton leans in closer, hovering over me. "Bambi," he says, and I practically jump, but collect myself instantly.

"Yes," I say in my harshest Celeste LaPorte tone. "It is a book. You may know it. A gift from a young friend."

"Ah."

He consumes his beer and chips quietly. I've seen him go out running in the afternoons, which haven't been much warmer than the icy mornings.

"Do you run to eat," I ask, "or do you run for self-punishment?"

He laughs, but I don't exactly understand why. Then he goes quiet for a minute, and says, "To be honest, it's a little of both, plus I just like to test myself."

I nod approval. "Good."

"What do you like about Seneca?" he asks, leaning against the counter and sipping his beer. His voice is upper-chest resonant, clear and entertaining. That's a funny way to put it, I realize.

"I haven't read the whole book yet. But I like the idea of going after hard things. I like that it's OK for life to be unfair. Take it and go with it."

"Yeah."

He pushes up his heavy-looking glasses. I push up mine.

"Mr. Chuck, why are you working for Mr. Vic?" That question just pops out of my mouth, and the next thing I say surprises both of us. "You are more splendid than this work."

He knows exactly what I mean, but asks anyway with a quirk of his sandy eyebrows.

I go ahead. "Holding the hand of an overgrown boy and probably cleaning up no end of his messes."

I half hope he'll laugh, taking my words lightly, but he doesn't. He looks at the floor.

I say quickly, "I've given offense."

"No. I have a push-pull in my mind about working for Vic."

"Meaning, Mr. Chuck?"

Stratton sets his beer down. "Meaning so much of this world—so much of what people want—is fake and gaudy."

"Yes," I breathe.

"And powerful."

"Yes."

OK, here's a pretty deep look we're exchanging, and we both want to keep talking, but we're both a little spooked by that deepness. He finishes his drink and leaves the kitchen. I sit in the soft light thinking about Chuck Stratton's presence. Squarish face, close-set ears. I like the way he moves: deliberate but relaxed. His glasses, those square black frames, make his face look even more rawboned. I was thinking his brain inside that shaved skull must be pretty big, which I guess is why I blurted that question about working for Paladino. But there's something more, a special simplicity about him. Leading a simple life is good. Seneca says so.

Fifteen minutes later, Sunpod stops in to get "a little something to help Vic with his supplements." She clenches a goblet of pills in her hand.

I say, "Something, as in ...?"

"To help push them down."

"Of course." I toast a slice of bread and slather it with butter and orange marmalade. Sunpod watches my every move, as if learning how to make toast with butter and jam for the first time.

I plate the bread and say firmly, "This will do. There is fresh water in Mr. Vic's refrigerator."

Sunpod agrees, takes the plate and leaves, but not before I noticed two Oxycodone 30s on the top of the candy-like heap in the goblet. Those little blue pills pack a wallop of a downer, especially two at a time. Does Paladino know what he's taking? Or does he simply trust Sunpod to manage his life as easily as she pours those pills down his throat?

It's cool to be learning what I'm learning, but I need to seriously clear the house of people for a while. Kitchen fire? I could certainly create a modest one, and I could raise the alarm and get everybody out, but my private time in the house would be short-lived. The gang wasn't going to stand around in the cold indefinitely, and someone would call the fire department, of course, even if I shouted that I had everything under control.

Some kind of special cleaning involving dangerous fumes? A cleaning gimmick would work with my personality, but how would I convince the gang that although they had to leave, I could stay?

My worries come to an end when Paladino, next morning, tells me I have the evening off. "Gloria Jensen's show at the casino? We're going, and we'll eat there. I forgot to tell you."

"Thank you, Mr. Vic. No problem. Everyone will go? Mr. Chuck, Miss Sunpod?"

"Yes. Uh, by the way, you might want to give some thought to my show at the Masonic."

I quirk an eyebrow.

He says, "I'm throwing an after-party in my dressing room, and I want you to do the food for it."

"Oh. I see!"

"All my old friends will be there."

"Ah. And, uh, roughly how many guests might fit into—ah-haha—your dressing room?"

"Oh, well, it's actually quite a large space! I'll invite I guess twenty or thirty people. We'll need some good food, easy to eat, you know, and drinks, of course. Plenty of champagne!"

"Sir. Thank you for this opportunity. I will require help. A vehicle, of course. I will make a list."

"Whatever you need, arrange it. Just keep Stratton informed, OK?"

"Excellent, Mr. Vic."

Of course, I have no reason to think I'll still be in Paladino's employ ten days from now, but hey, I'll spin this charade out as long as need be.

CHAPTER 35

NARCAN COUCHES

That evening I watch as Paladino, Sunpod, and Stratton pile into a big black SUV, Stratton at the wheel. I run out, acting like I almost forgot, and hand them individual boxed snacks of mixed nuts, cheese cubes, olives, and bottles of water. They are happy. Plus pre-moistened towelettes.

I've wondered about other staff, but all this house had was a cleaning squad that came in every few days. That's what Stratton called it: the cleaning squad. There were three people in it, they wore blue uniforms with their names sewn on, and they attacked the dust and grime in that house like the Marines landing on Iwo Jima. I saw a movie of it.

Although I haven't noticed any cameras or microphone-looking things in my various comings and goings around the house, I know they're probably here, and I expected Stratton, at least, to have a phone app that would alert him to anything unusual going on. Well, devil take the hindmost.

I beeline to Paladino's study and just start carefully tossing it. Desk drawers, small file cabinet. No laptop. Seems he just used his phone for everything, which would be interesting to poke through. The study yields a bunch of gun and police magazines, but no diaries, receipts, notes on how to murder someone and pin it on somebody else. I don't see a safe, but you'd figure there must be one somewhere, hidden. I knock on the paneling, but no one knock produces a different sound than any of the other knocks.

I look for little red LEDs glowing out from crevices, but see none. Whatever. Everything through the house is pretty clean and uncluttered. Modern furniture, the stuff in magazines that looks uncomfortable. Just to see, I sit on some of it. It feels OK. Firm cushions, but with enough give so you can relax.

When I flop down on one of the couches in a nook off the living room, something pokes my thigh, and I reach down to find a small box that was crammed between the cushion and the arm. I draw it out. Narcan nasal spray, the two-pack. I put it back.

As I spool around the house I keep an eye out for more such boxes, and find one stashed in every couch, between a cushion and an arm. A few armchairs as well. Nicely systematic. If somebody goes down, one of those puppies is within a few paces anywhere in the house. All you have to remember is *nearest couch, right-hand cushion.* In case you're not familiar, Narcan is used to bring people back from an opioid overdose. Anybody can give it. You just rip open the package, roll the person face-up if they're not already, and squirt the stuff into their nose. If they wake up, you're golden.

How many times has Paladino OD'd? It seemed his dosages are well monitored by Sunpod, but anything can happen.

Besides the Narcan, I do locate the glory hole of Paladino's drugs: a small metal cabinet in Sunpod's sitting room. It's the only thing I come across that's locked, so I figure that has to be it. I jimmy it open with a screwdriver and a thin metal ruler I found in a kitchen drawer. Quite a stash in there. Besides the Ox and the Dexedrines I saw in his pill goblet, there's a tasty selection of other uppers, downers, and painkillers in varying doses. Good pharmaceutical stuff: Xanax, Librium, Seconal, Adderall. No street meth, cocaine, heroin, or anything that looked psychedelic, like mushrooms, peyote, or acid tabs. No syringes. A small black cloth case, for travel, perhaps.

Everything is in prescription bottles, all under names that are not Paladino's. Most of them say Joseph Myers. That would almost certainly be the Joe Myers I was introduced to, the guy with the white Mustang who sat toying with an unplugged guitar in Paladino's studio the other day. Some of the prescriptions are under the name Karen Short. Might that be Sunpod? Nothing in Stratton's name, nor the vocal coach guy, Razkowski.

Most addicts want their drugs handy, thus they keep them at bedside or toilet-side. But if Paladino doesn't trust himself not to take too much, then somebody else should watch over his supply. He's smart enough to be OK with that. A fairly well functioning addict, then.

I smile to see, as well, a whole host of vitamin bottles: multis, extra Cs, B complex, and a ton of fiber capsules. If you take painkillers, your gut stalls out and you get constipated. Keep up your fiber and water. I re-lock the metal cabinet.

After carefully combing through Stratton's rooms—finding nothing relevant to my mission—I linger. I like his stuff. Stacks of books in a case. A nice android tablet, which I turn on, but of course the screen is locked. I look into his sleeping room, the neatly-made bed a twin that looked extra long. That's a statement. Mister hermit here. There's a couch in his sitting room—equipped with Narcan, of course—and I inspect it to see if it is, perhaps, a pull-out double sleeper. It is. Nice contingency setup.

Stratton's clothes are simple, all in black, gray, or navy blue, no other colors, not even a red ball cap or something. Basic dude bathroom stuff, Gillette, Old Spice.

Nowhere in the house do I find anything at all incriminating towards Paladino or anybody. No papers, no files. No scribbled messages about "the caper" or "the job" or anything. No diagrams of Gordy's house with an X in the living room.

Laura calls as I'm standing in the living room thinking what to do next.

"Bam, I found something interesting. I've been going through Sandy's laptop some more."

"Yeah?" I flop down on one of the Narcan couches.

"It's a copy of a life insurance policy, and it seems to be the exact one the police mentioned, where William O'Rourke gets five hundred thousand if Sandy dies."

"Oh! Well, that's cool. It's good to know that's solid."

"Listen, though! The person who *bought* the policy was Sandy!"

"Whoa." I sit up straight.

"Yeah! She bought it, she paid for it, and she named her father the beneficiary!"

"Whoa. OK. Maybe somehow her dad convinced her to buy it."

"Maybe. But I'm thinking, well, OK, Sandy's put herself into this famous star's life, and she's working on this secret drug project, and she knows there's this guy, Paladino's dealer, around somewhere. And maybe she understands she's putting herself at some risk, and she's worried about her dad if something happens to her. Maybe she really loves her dad."

I pause.

Laura goes, "Some girls just love their dads."

"And are afraid of them too."

"That makes no sense."

"You know it does."

No response.

I go, "I'll let Alvarez know about this."

"You can't! That could make O'Rourke look better! Besides, the police must already know about this."

"Don't give them too much credit. They knew about the policy, but who can say if they actually got a copy of it and read it? Or whether they just questioned some insurance agent on the phone who skimmed over a file while they were on hold?"

"Yeah, I guess."

"Let me think about this."

I return to the kitchen and fix myself a small chopped salad, then a ribeye steak with fried potatoes. I eat slowly, savoring the food in the quiet kitchen. Long time since I had a steak. I drink some soda water with a piece of lime in it. I think about Sandy's insurance policy, but come up with no new angles.

After cleaning up, I fix a mug of tea, lower the kitchen lights, and settle at the desk to read *Bambi: The Story of a Life in the Forest* under the good lamp there.

As I read, it hits me hard: Bambi wasn't just this innocent fawn I remembered from the Disney movie. He was a survivor, hardened by loss and the brutality of the world around him. I understood that. Both Bambi and I, we had to grow up fast. I'd say I made more mistakes than Bambi ever could. But we both had to fight to live.

The gang isn't home by the time I go to bed at ten.

CHAPTER 36

I REALIZE I'M SWEATING

When I come to the kitchen at five-thirty to start breakfast, Stratton is sitting at my little desk there.

Just by the way he's sitting, I know he knows.

I stand looking at him.

Finally, he says, "Bambi Pentecost."

Even though my trouble mantra has long been *deny, deny, deny,* there's no point.

"I'll get my things," I say in my normal voice, and turn to go.

"You will not." He's on his feet.

"Yeah, but—"

"No."

I sigh. "Let me guess, you want to talk."

"Right."

"How did you—"

"Not here."

He grips my arm as if to perp-walk me into the pantry, but I go, "At least let me fix us something to eat. There's time."

I swear he forced back a micro smile. I could breathe.

Quickly, I scramble half a dozen eggs with salt and pepper and toast four thick slices of bread. I butter the toast, divide the eggs, and fix plates for us. The kitchen now smells like morning. I manage to grab forks as Stratton practically levers me into the pantry.

"Well, go get us some coffee, then, OK?" I say hurriedly. "Black for me. I'm not going anywhere."

He stalks out and returns with two steaming cups. There's plenty of time before anybody else will be looking for breakfast.

The pantry, as I've said, is big, lined with commercial shelving uprights. A work table in the center makes it easy to get stuff out and line up ingredients, tools, bowls. Nice bright lighting. I set our plates on the table and we stand.

Suddenly I wonder if I should look for a weapon. There's a stone rolling pin on the equipment shelf, but the thought of little me trying to swing a short club at this big competent human is ludicrous. I guess I could have grabbed a can of tomatoes, if only for show.

Stratton positions himself between me and the door.

He slides my plate and says, "You eat on that side. Don't be afraid." He forks up some eggs and takes a bite of toast. He swallows and eats more eggs while they're hot. "I am hungry," he comments.

We drink our coffee. The pantry is silent except for the clinking of forks and our blowing on our coffees. I force myself to swallow some eggs, pretending to be casual, or at least wry. Is that the word: wry? When people in movies make a wisecrack even when they're hanging by their elbow from a helicopter?

I wait. One's next move, when denial isn't possible, should always be to keep your trap shut.

"I know you're not a French chef," he begins, "though you're a better cook than I might have expected. This is killer toast." He takes another bite, chews, and swallows. "For a while, I thought maybe *you* murdered Sandy, in order to try to ingratiate yourself into Vic's life."

I go, "The fatal-attraction-fangirl thing." It's a relief not to have to talk like Celeste LaPorte.

"Yeah. But no, the timing was off."

I don't know what he means, but I keep quiet.

He eats some more, wipes his mouth on a paper napkin from a stack on a shelf, and says, "You're not a psycho."

"Thank you."

"I checked your plate and VIN the day you came to—um, audition, so it was easy to figure out your real name and address. Far from here."

I nod.

"As well as your arrest records, pleas, convictions, incarcerations ..."

"Right." I go ahead and ask my main question. "You never saw me as a threat?"

A stifled laugh. "Look, Bambi—"

"Call me BB."

"I didn't out you right away because I wanted to see what you wanted here." He speaks almost gently. I realize he thinks he can maybe learn something important from me. "What were you looking for last night?" he asks. "Of course the house is wired."

"Right."

"You had to have thought of that."

"I did."

"But you went ahead poking around anyway."

"Yeah."

"Come on, then. I can't force you to cooperate with me, but if you don't, I can make trouble for you. And I'd rather not."

"How come?"

"Because I have a feeling we might be able to help each other."

I consider myself a fairly sharp person, but this knocks me back. "Really."

"You have to level with me, Bambi Pentecost. Now."

He pushes up his glasses, and I push up mine.

I realize I'm sweating. I blot my upper lip with the white sleeve of my chef coat. "How in the world can I be of help to you?"

"Tell me what you're after."

"What are your assumptions?"

"Don't make me laugh."

I go, "Yeah, OK, fair enough." How to begin. "Can I assume you looked over the court records on my divorce?"

"Yes."

"Then you know who my ex is."

"Yes."

"And where he is now?"

"Yes. And I know you have a daughter. Is she the one who came here that day with the record album?"

"What?"

He laughs. "Maybe she's as cagey as you are."

"OK, whatever. I think Gordy could absolutely go up for this. But our daughter—her name is Laura, by the way—she's convinced her dear daddy couldn't possibly have stabbed that poor woman to death. Granted, he rescued Laura from the foster system, so she worships him. Of course, rescuing your own child from the foster system is a lot like pulling them out of a bonfire you threw them into."

"Yes," agrees Stratton, finishing his eggs. He certainly has a big appetite.

"I did even less for her. Well, anyway, given that Paladino and Sandy were lovers, I was thinking maybe he had something to do with her death, and if I could *some*how find *some* form of evidence, maybe that could get Gordy off the hook."

Stratton again pushes his heavy black glasses up. "That's a pretty big reach."

"Well, yeah." I tell myself not to push my glasses up, but my hand just does it. "Laura and I've been looking into other people connected with Sandy, like her prof at Wayne and so forth. Sandy's dad. This chef opportunity came up and I went for it." I explain how Gordy's alibi is screwy, which is why the prosecutor's office was happy enough to charge him. Stratton listens.

204

I finish up. "Personally, I have nothing against your boss. I'm sorry."

Stratton folds his arms. "What have you found out about him?"

"Like everybody, he's complex. He's achieved a lot in show business, but he's slipping, and he's scared, and bottom line, he's a little boy still trying to grow up. He's a police groupie and a pillhead. That Joe Myers guy is his supplier. Myers doctor-shops for all that stuff, doesn't he? And who's Karen Short? Sunpod?"

Stratton stands there, thinking, I guess. He paces to the end of the work table and back again.

"Why do you want to help your ex?"

I stare at a row of pasta boxes. "I stopped loving him fifteen minutes after we got married. But I want to improve my relationship with my daughter, eh? She flat-out gave me the option."

"She'll love you again if you set her dad free?"

I pause. "Not necessarily love me again, but despise me less. Which, believe me, would be a level of magnitude above now."

"OK."

"So. There are my cards. Why did you let me toss this house, risk me finding the drugs?"

"They're not street drugs. They're all legal prescriptions."

"And you're OK with that?"

He looks at me flatly. "No."

"You don't like your job."

"That's right."

"You waffled about that before."

"Well, I'm not waffling now."

At last we're on the same frequency. I say, "OK. What do you want?"

"First of all, I want you to stay on."

My hands are clinging to my coffee cup as if it can ward off witches' spells. The cups are nice: halfway between a teacup and a mug, cream-colored china with a blue line around the middle. I liked them a lot and wished I could take a few with me when I pack up to go. Whenever that's gonna be.

Stratton goes on, "Vic likes you. I won't tell anybody who you really are. Here's the thing. While your ex's alibi—"

"Gordy."

"While Gordy's alibi for Sandy's murder isn't so hot, neither is Vic's, to tell you the truth. He had nothing to do with the murder, I'm certain of that, but he was up to something illegal that afternoon and evening. Somebody got hurt."

"Oh!"

"Do you know who the Pope is?"

"Uh—as in the Catholic Pope, the king of the church guy?"

"Yeah. He goes out at night dressed as a regular priest in a black outfit, and he helps the street people, and they don't recognize him. He wants to be among them."

"Are you Catholic? Why are we talking about this?"

"I wasn't brought up as one. I'm a seeker, and so are you." He smiles a wide free smile as I drain the last of my coffee. He says, "Vic fancies himself a warrior of the people. His name—Paladino—comes from the Paladins, this set of ancient knights."

"They were idealistic?"

"Yeah, I guess so. Sometimes Vic goes out at night without me and tries to protect young people from drugs and crime. He wears a witless disguise and the kids don't recognize him."

"That's unhinged."

"He doesn't consider himself an addict, and he thinks he can handle himself in rough situations."

"Then why does he need you around?"

Pause. Stratton slowly takes a sip of his coffee. "He knows I'm a layer of genuine protection."

"You know, his drug problem's going to kill him sooner or—"

"Right. I want you to convince Vic to get clean. This upcoming concert is stressing him out. He's not working hard enough to prepare for it. I feel responsible for him, even though he makes his own crappy decisions." Stratton changes the subject suddenly. "Are you still trying to cast doubt about Gordy's involvement in Sandy's murder?"

"It's too late for that. They caught him literally red-handed. His fingerprints are on the knife. The only way is to expose the real killer without the shadow of a doubt."

"Maybe he could still win a jury trial."

I think about that. "Be a high-risk bet."

"True."

"So," I ask, "how can you help me with this?"

"For one thing," he says, "I can go talk with Sandy's father. I think he knows more than he said to the police."

"I've been thinking that as well. But they've interviewed him at least twice."

"Well, I've been looking into him. There's some stuff in his background I think I can use. I'm not a total stranger to him, and I might be able to manipulate a conversation where we can learn something. And for another thing ..." He hesitates. "I can protect you."

"Dude, what?"

"I'll leave it at that."

Having somebody else in my corner couldn't be a bad thing, let alone somebody with Stratton's sheer masculinity and confident ways.

"OK," I go. "What do you want me to do with Vic, exactly?"

"You've been straight from drugs and alcohol for how long?"

"Few years. Couple."

"Yeah. It still shows in your face."

"Thanks."

"You know what I mean."

"Yeah. I do."

Stratton drums his fingers on the steel tabletop. Large hands, hairy on the backs, the nails clean. "I think a frank conversation between you and him, at the right time, could turn him around. He doesn't listen to his doctors or me."

"Sunpod?"

"She knows little about anything that counts in life. He keeps her around out of ..."

"Pity?"

"Ha. I think if Vic doesn't get straight soon, he might never get his career back on track."

I look steadily at my new friend. I feel I can start to think of him that way.

He returns my gaze, puzzled.

I explain. "Chuck Stratton. Look. Vic is tired of the show. He's bored with it. He doesn't much *want* to get his career back on track. But he's confused. He's got everybody telling him he needs to sing and sing some more. Some stars are so greedy for cheers and record sales that they'll do anything to keep the show going, even when it's a sad version of what they used to do. We've all seen this in show business over and over. I think Vic hates his life. He doesn't have the guts to walk away from all this and try something new, so he takes refuge in his drugs."

Stratton stares at me, stupefied. His forehead is a map of interesting creases, plus a scar or two.

I say, "Vic's gotta get clean, but not so he can refresh his career. So he can refresh his *life*."

It's funny how a person's eyes can be looking at a shelving unit full of bottles of olive oil and vinegars, just a few feet from their face, but you can tell they're looking at something far away, maybe as much as a mile into the past or future.

Stratton blinks and comes back to the moment. "I think you're right. But how do you know that? You've barely spent—"

"He's no different than dozens of people I've known. He's no different from me. He's no different from you. It's obvious."

We stand in silence for a minute.

I go, "And now let's get to work. You're gonna help me figure out who killed Sandy O'Rourke, right? We know her murder wasn't random."

"Who else is working on this?"

"Besides me and you, plus Laura, well, there's a police detective who's sort of—quietly on our side."

"That's good. When will you talk to Vic?"

"Well, not before the concert."

"You think he'll crash and burn?"

"He might. And if he does, that'll give me the perfect opening." I check my watch. "I gotta cook."

"Right."

"You know, of course, there are no guarantees about Vic. He'll only get clean if he wants to."

In a suddenly low voice, Stratton says, "Yeah." He clears his throat.

"Why do you care about him?"

"I just don't like to see a person suffer that way."

CHAPTER 37

NO WAY OUT

L ast time I was in the Wayne County jail, I arrived in cuffs and went through booking via the fortress-like garage. The dirt of the jail, the relentless screaming of my sister detainees, and the drain flies were nothing compared to withdrawal from my drugs. If you have to ask what drain flies are, you are fortunate beyond belief.

Mighty different, things are, now. Not only am I free, the jail's new. They built a whole fresh one on Russell Street, all together with a juvenile hall, sheriff's office, plus courts and so forth. Walking through the place felt surreal, like I could be a lawyer in some TV show. No anxiety, no outstanding warrants.

I sit across from Gordy in a private interview room, nicely arranged by Ted Alvarez. My chair is cold metal, but I'm so glad to be there as a visitor, I could be sitting on ten porcupines for all it mattered.

"I know I look like hell," Gordy says, seeing my face.

"Been tough."

He shakes his head, but the truth is plain. "Thanks for coming."

I'd gotten the day off with the help of Chuck Stratton. I ask, "You've seen Laura, right?"

"No. I think she's afraid to come here."

"They have video visits."

He shrugs. Though shaved and clean, he is thinner than I've ever seen him and very frightened. His mood is different from someone who's waiting for a minor plea deal or a trial on a crime that will involve a few months if found guilty. Different too, from someone new to being locked up. Gordy knew the rules of jail: keep to yourself, don't get into anybody's debt, and don't let anyone get in debt to you. Never escalate anything.

However, he's desperate now. Gordy was never one of those deeply philosophical people who can turn the worst sorts of situations into peace and acceptance. He was no Seneca.

I go, "First of all, I'm not against you."

"Alvarez told me. That's something."

"Mainly, whatever I do is for the sake of Laura."

"Fine," he says in a tight voice.

"What can you tell me?"

He clears his throat, and I watch him pull himself together. "You know I'm innocent," he begins.

I nod.

"Do you remember when we used to watch videos together? Movies on video-tape?"

I look at him. Suddenly the atmosphere is different. "Yeah. I do."

"We used to watch so many."

"Yes." I wait, open to whatever he's trying to tell me. You don't just sit there reminiscing randomly in a situation like this.

Gordy says, "We had our favorites we used to watch over and over. My AA sponsor, Ethan, has all those tapes now."

"Yeah?"

"I gave them to him. He has them. He never throws anything away."

Collecting and watching old VHS videotapes was one way Gordy and I amused ourselves without spending much. We shoplifted some from the last existing rental stores and dickered down boxes of them from garage sales. When Laura was born, I found some children's movies and we all watched them together, with popcorn. I haven't thought about those videotapes for years. We must have had a couple hundred.

I prompt, "Uh-huh, yeah?"

"That one called 'No Way Out.' Remember that one?"

"Oh, for sure. How could you forget Kevin Costner running around in his white sailor suit? Did Ethan get the player from you as well?"

"Yes, he did! It'd be extremely good if you would get that tape from him and *watch that movie.*"

"OK. I have his number in my phone."

"Good."

"But can't you just tell me—"

"No. I'm not—comfortable." He glances around meaningfully. These visits are supposed to be private, but neither of us would put it past the authorities to screw us over. We never had good lawyers. However, Alvarez told me that Gordy's current one, the guy I saw in the interrogation video, is OK.

Gordy drills his eyes into mine and says, "There's lots of good stuff in that movie. At the beginning. Important stuff."

Before I leave, I tell him that I put forty dollars on his commissary account so he can get brand-name candy bars, chips, meat sticks, and so forth. "You can get the twenty-nine-dollar food pack," I say. "It's junk, but at least it tastes good and has calories."

"God bless you." Everybody gets a little more religious in jail.

I well remember the one single time I got a food pack in the lockup. My then-pimp arranged it as a farewell gift. Those goodies changed my life, for a couple of days.

Four hours later, I press the play button on a vintage VHS machine I hooked up to my laptop with a special connector.

Ethan still had the tape, to my relief, and he even knew where to find it. He handed it to me as I stood in his foyer in Cornerstone Village. Every tiny bunch of streets in Detroit is now called a neighborhood and has an interesting name. Cornerstone Village, Sugar Hill, Woodbridge. I don't quite know how that happened.

I asked Ethan about the player, but he said it was broken. "My kid used to watch the cartoon videos on it, and he recorded some off the TV, but then it started chewing up the tapes, and I think he more or less destroyed it the rest of the way trying to fix it." Ethan is a wide-set guy, thirtyish, with a spiky black haircut. He was calm and concerned.

"Well, Gordy just told me this movie was special to him, and I realized he was communicating something. When did you get these tapes from him?"

"Two or three years ago, I guess. They're starting to be collectors' items now. I figure someday I'll be able to make money off them. You know, you can get that movie on Netflix or whatever."

I stared at him. "Dude. It's not the movie, it's the tape."

"Ah. Right."

"By the way, Gordy told me to tell you hi and he hopes you're well."

"He did?" Ethan's broad face lifted. "Cool!"

Gordy said no such thing, but I knew my lie would make Ethan feel good for a minute, so what the hey.

I found, at Excalibur Pawn, a VHS player for twenty bucks with the promise they'd take it back in a day if I didn't trash it.

Why, any thinking person might ask, a videotape? Why wouldn't Gordy use the digital tools on any computer or phone these days, and make a video that way? I well knew the answer: It's quite hard to alter an individual videotape after it's recorded. It's not *impossible* to open a cassette and do some cutting and splicing, then carefully wind the tape on new spools and reassemble the case, but those changes you've made to the physical tape are obvious. Gordy and I saw it on a police show once.

I made some tea, set up the player and my laptop on the kitchen table at Gordy's house, and got my notebook and pen ready.

And now I press that button. The machine whirrs, and I hold my breath as I watch the first couple of scenes of "No Way Out" on my laptop. I got a capture connector at the pawn shop, so I'm recording what I'm seeing on a flash stick, for insurance's sake. The movie's a fun thriller, with Kevin Costner playing a Navy officer told to track down a Soviet spy. It's got a super twist at the end. About two minutes in, Gordy's face appears.

I shout, "Yes!" in the quiet kitchen. This is it.

Where he got a VHS camcorder, I have no idea. But a video of him sitting in a dark room looking face-on at the camera now replaces the movie footage, and he starts talking.

"I'm making a videotape because you can destroy it but not alter it. If something happens to me, I want this video to be made public." He'd been drinking, clearly. Scared, bad scared. Apart from seeing him in jail today, I'd never observed that expression of terrified desperation on his face.

"Wade Kullen has to pay for what he did," Gordy goes on. "The whole thing started back in Balsam Ridge when we were teenagers." He stops and wipes his face with his hands. "Oh, God."

The video switches abruptly to a Bugs Bunny cartoon. "Baseball Bugs." My stomach drops. Wait, what? I watch the cartoon, in which Bugs Bunny plays every position on the diamond and outwits the gorillas on the other team. I watch carefully, looking for symbolism. Another Bugs Bunny follows, then another, and I realize they were taped from the Cartoon Network, which ran marathons of classic cartoons.

The cartoons end after three more Bugs Bunnies, and Gordy's face reappears. "I was out of it, but at the same time I was aware, like in a fog. He took her away. When I woke up for real, I was by myself. My nose was broken. She was gone. Wade knows where she is, there's no doubt in my mind. So." Pause, while Gordy scrubs his face in his hands again. He looks up. "That's the whole story as I know it. The key to the rest is Wade Kullen."

I take my glasses off and lay my head down on the kitchen table for a while.

Then I get up and make some more tea. I phone Ethan. "You mentioned your kid. Might he have taped over some of those movies with cartoons?"

"Oh, yeah, that could be," says Ethan. Downbeat. "Yeah, he learned how to block the port that keeps you from recording over—"

"Yeah. Was Bugs Bunny a favorite of his?"

"Oh, yeah! He wanted to *be* Bugs Bunny. On Halloween he—"

"OK, thanks."

"Wait, what did you find out?"

"Not enough, friend, not enough."

I sit there thinking. Kullen was a name from the Upper Peninsula. My brother, Bing, hung out back then with the thuggish Kullen boys, got into a scrape or two with them. Fortunately, Bing didn't have any lasting damage, such as a prison record. He got his head straight, earned his mechanic's certification, and found a good job. Now he runs his own shop. His wife, Glenna, is a nice person. She guides hunting and fishing trips for women, which is highly cool.

Gordy, too, knew the Kullens. There were the Balsam Ridge Kullens (main clan), the St. Ignace Kullens, and I thought I remembered a branch of them in Marquette. I never knew Wade Kullen, though I remembered Mickey and Donnie from high school.

The Kullen family's roots ran deep and trashy in the UP. Whenever two or more Kullens got together to drink, their cumulative IQ went down. They'd jump from one boneheaded scheme to another: drugs, snowmobile stunts, car theft, burglaries. They loved to fight. At least one of them got a job on the St. Ignace police force, which was hard to believe but true. The Kullen girls were exactly what you'd expect: cigarette-smoking tattooed divorced moms of five or seven little Kullens, always scheming to borrow money from anyone dim enough to listen to their sob stories.

On top of all that, the Kullens looked more or less alike, all pale in their coloring, with high, protruding foreheads. Powerfully built, the women as well as the guys. Any one of them could have been a good athlete if they tried a little bit. I don't know if their common look came from their original Nordic ancestors or what. The guys hated to pay for haircuts and razor blades; they peered out at you from the ragged thicket of their bangs and beards like wolves.

After a few more sips of tea I remember Connie mentioning that Roberta Summerline, the supposedly runaway cheerleader, dated Wade Kullen.

Was that just before she took off, or went missing, or whatever it was? Could the "she" Gordy mentioned in the video be Roberta? She was gone when he woke up? I'd never heard Gordy mention her before, that I remembered. He certainly could have known her in high school.

I look around online and see that Roberta Summerline has nearly zero presence anywhere, no social media, no white pages address, no mug shot, no obit. I look her up in the state prison system, nothing. However, there's one hit on her name: a reference in the Balsam Ridge Argus, the town paper, just a photo of the cheer squad at Balsam Ridge High and a squib about them going to a regional cheer competition. There was no follow-up piece, so I guess they didn't make it to the finals. But there they were, the whole eight of them, with Roberta on a knee in the front row. Hands buried in her pompons, cute pleated skirt, school sweater, big smile. Huge eyes, Roberta's were, huge young enthusiastic eyes. *I'm on the freakin' cheer squad, one of only eight girls in the whole school.* Roberta was a happy young thing when that picture was snapped.

I always liked that the owner of the paper called it the Argus. Although it was just a few crummy sheets of newsprint with town council reports and some ads, the name sounded classy, and I knew it was a reference to some mythological person—or thing?—from actual mythology.

There are, I see, other Summerlines on social media. No mug shots for any of them.

Wade Kullen pops up here and there. He's got a few stale social media accounts. Last posts from about four years ago. Nothing all that interesting, just stuff like blurry pictures of guys drinking beer in a hunting cabin, whatnot.

I go ahead and put $9.99 on my credit card to start a subscription to a people-search website that's supposed to give you arrest records and so on.

And yep, six arrest records for him. The first four are split between Balsam Ridge and Sault Ste. Marie for the usual stupid unnecessary criminal stuff. The next one was for a drug bust in Detroit, the last for a sexual assault in Livonia, west of the city. The court records show he pleaded guilty to simple possession of meth, presumably in exchange for information on another dealer or dealers. The sexual assault bust must have been dropped or dismissed. It didn't say there was a weapon involved, which could be the reason.

So. Wade Kullen had made his slimy way to Detroit too. I find no current address, job profile, or anything else that might lead me to him.

CHAPTER 38

A CURRENT OF DOUBT

Back at Paladino's house, I cook dinner for the boss and Sunpod. Stratton had the day off. He told me he was going to do some research. I'm looking forward to seeing what he spades up. I heat French onion soup from cans, with some white wine poured in and boiled down so it's almost getting a little thick. Buttery grilled toast rounds on top, generous handfuls of grated parmesan strewn on from a bag, hot oven, it gets all brown and oily, serve it, everybody goes wow.

I also put out some sausages with a topping I thought up of mustard (Grey Poupon, because even I know enough to use that instead of the yellow store brand) and Worcestershire. Mix those two things together, drizzle some over the hot sausages, call it *saucisse St. Pierre* and yep, it's fabulous. I tell Paladino and Sunpod a little story about making the dish for the prime minister of Austria one time and he gave me a tiny crystal swan. I actually have a tiny crystal swan at home, but I got it for free when I bought some yarn from a shop that was going out of business in Sault Ste. Marie. Haven't made anything from the yarn yet. I feel like a culinary genius.

But I notice Paladino picking at his food.

He stops in the kitchen as I'm clearing. He stands here, shifting from foot to foot, looking like he's wishing for something. Wanting something. He's haggard, his face drawn down by heavy evening stubble. Sunpod has gone upstairs.

I take the initiative. "Sit, Mr. Vic." I nod curtly to the chair at my little desk. He sits, looking relieved to be bossed. "You have been off your food," I tell him. "Is my food not—"

"No! It's good cuisine, Celeste. Excellent. I've dropped a few pounds, it's true, my appetite hasn't been what it ..." He hesitates.

"Talk to me, Mr. Vic."

He wants to talk. He doesn't feel right.

I go, "When you are in show business, Mr. Vic, you must be one with your emotions."

"You're right, Celeste. I'd say an entertainer's emotions need to be available at will. Available and quashable! Ha."

"I understand." I set my hips against the counter comfortably and fold my arms.

"Do you? I feel you do, but I wouldn't know why."

"I too have been in ..." I hesitate. "Show business."

"You have?"

"After a fashion." Yeah, for sure I learned how to put on an act. When you're an addict, you lie constantly and your life can depend on being convincing in your lies. Furthermore, working as a prostitute is about the oldest form of acting, right? The acts I've put on, boy howdy. I'm not even talking about role playing during sex—that's generally easy. The thing is showing the john you enjoy him. Most johns are so desperate to believe you like them—love them—that they convince themselves. However, the better you are at it—the more you touch their insecurities and make those insecurities go away for a while—the more gigs you'll get from them, and the more OK they are with price hikes.

Paladino says, "Do you think I look unwell, Celeste?"

"Are you unwell?"

Silence. Is he fighting back tears? After a long pause, he says, "Sometimes I'm not sure who I am anymore."

I let that sit there.

After a minute I go to the cooktop and pick up the kettle. "You will have tea with me."

He sits there gratefully. I make tea, and we talk about this and that. I make up cozy stories about my schooling in France. "... and from then on, the little dog always came around when he smelled those cheese puffs. I made sure he got some, every time."

"That's sweet, Celeste." Sad smile.

"Mr. Vic, all troubles can be made better, even big ones. You know that, don't you?"

"Be nice to believe that. But it's not true. We both know it."

I don't argue. That was a fairly unintelligent thing to say, I admit. But I was trying to be a helping presence. I learned something right there.

Out of the blue, Paladino arrives at it. He meets my eyes deeply, like a large dog who's exhausted, and says, "My meds help me feel ... normal." Deep down, he knows I get it. Good. But does he truly understand that he's an addict?

They always say something more if you keep quiet.

"I—I think my life is too ..." He doesn't have a word.

"Soft?" I suggest boldly.

A minute ago his eyes were filled with sadness, but a spark has just come in.

"My God." He takes a deep breath, as if testing the idea by making himself a little bigger in the world. "I think you might be right. Sometimes I do crave ... hardship." He looks surprised that he's said it out loud. "Does that sound ridiculous to you, Celeste?"

"Of course not."

Could it be that simple?

I watch a current of doubt sweep over him. He shakes his head, but the idea has come into the open.

"And," he says, "I'm tired of singing the same old songs."

"New songs?"

"My fans want the old ones! That's what they all yell for. When I sing something new, they don't clap as hard, don't cheer as loud. They want 'Rose Petal Tango'. They want 'Another Letter.' 'The Streets of Pontiac'. They want all those old ones."

"Mr. Vic, you know your fans love you. By the way, I think 'Rose Petal Tango' is a fine song."

He smiles so sadly I almost reach for his arm, to pat it as you would a heartsick old man on a park bench.

"They don't know me." Great big sigh. "I remember what it was like when I played the bars, the small rooms, before I got my first recording contract."

"Tell me."

His tone changes. "Are you here to help me, Celeste?" He sounds younger, somehow. That's not it. Eager. Hopeful.

I don't know what he means, but I keep my Celeste matter-of-factness going. I think about Seneca, the Stoic guy. Keep it simple. Maybe Paladino thinks I was sent to him by the spirit world.

"Yes, Mr. Vic, I am."

"I loved that time in my career. I was writing songs, people enjoyed them. I felt free."

"Yes."

He clutches his hands together like a boy. Funny, this masculine guy—solid build, heavy jaw, strong hands—is looking lost. I nod, trying to encourage him.

"Probably the best I ever felt was the first time I played Chene Park—the Aretha, they call it now." He added that last part knowing I'm from France or wherever. "Chene Park, that was a step up for me. And I sold tickets! I got 'em in the seats, they came to see me as if I was *somebody!*"

"You have a great talent, sir."

"I love that venue. But listen, Celeste, that was when I started working with kids!" He brightens up still more. "Yeah! I worked with kids in the music programs in the schools. I helped them, I really did. I got them excited about learning their instruments and writing songs."

"That is super happening, Mr. Vic." I say it deliberately, like I'm trying to sound tuned in. He smiles.

"And I saw what those kids are up against. So many of them. The temptations of street life."

"Drugs." I hear myself say it with the flatness of Bambi Pentecost, recovering addict. "But you don't work with kids anymore?" I adjust my glasses.

"Oh, I do! Just in a different way. The music kids, I'm not cool enough for them anymore. They're into the younger musicians, the rap stars. I'm a dinosaur to them."

"Dinosaurs are cool."

He laughs, mouth wide, teeth looking as good as any T. Rex's. He looks around as if worried someone might be nearby. We're alone, though. He lowers his voice. "I still work with kids, but on the sly."

I raise my eyebrows.

"I know the dangers of drugs," he says. "I grew up poor. I'm not so sophisticated as people think. I probably should have gone to the police academy. I'd be a detective by now! Ha!"

"But—"

"Everybody says 'but,' Celeste. I have talent along other lines besides just music."

"Yes?"

"Well ... maybe not talent, yet, but desires. I desire to work with my hands, for instance."

"As in with ... wood? Metal?"

"Yeah."

Nothing more happens in the conversation, but that was plenty. Things are easy between us, and I'm pretty sure that fact will be important soon.

CHAPTER 39

WHEN A COLLABORATION GOES BAD

"Thank you," says Chuck Stratton to a biochemist from Kalamazoo. "I think you've saved me from making a big mistake."

The biochemist, an attractive middle-aged woman who knows the score in the pharmaceuticals business, nods and pockets Stratton's card. She heads for one of the several bars set up in a ballroom of the Marriott hotel in Grand Rapids. A few hundred scientists, doctors, and marketing people are on hand for a conference named something complicated but basically it's about the future of the drug business. By the time of the cocktail gathering on Saturday evening, nobody is checking badges; Stratton had simply driven to Grand Rapids and walked in.

He looks around and locates a sixtyish fellow with a swept-back, iron-gray hairstyle at a stand-up table near the hors d'oeuvres. The man's attention is half on a folded program, and half on one of the curvaceous servers moving about.

Conveniently, the man is alone. He sips from a glass of red wine.

"Evening, Mr. O'Rourke," says Stratton, setting his own glass of wine on the little table. The room is noisy with conversations and not too-brightly lit. Pleasant enough.

O'Rourke focuses on him. "Who are you? Oh. You're—"

"Chuck Stratton. I work for Vic Paladino. We've met."

"Yes, I was just recognizing you. What are you—" He looks around, just beginning to grasp that something uncomfortable is about to happen.

Stratton speaks quietly but clearly. "I want to talk about Sandy and Vic. What was her real purpose in getting close to him?"

O'Rourke's mouth falls open. He shuts it, and his jowls harden. "I've said all I have to say to the police."

"No. You haven't."

"If you want to talk, you can talk to my lawyer."

"Come on. I know what happened when you were at—" and he named the big pharmaceutical company. "I won't hesitate to make a few phone calls. You might not wind up in jail. But your life could get ugly. And expensive."

"What do you know? You're bluffing me."

Stratton hardens his gaze and drills it right into O'Rourke's eyes. "I know that you falsified data, and probably stole patents, too. You embezzled close to a million dollars. Other people know, but they have their reasons for keeping quiet about it. I don't. You—"

"How did you hear—" he stops himself.

It was easier than it should have been. O'Rourke's online profiles included mention of a high-level position in new product development in that dominant company. Why did he leave that plum job? There was a funny gap, which coincided with a few oblique references in the professional journals to a major company sweeping something under the rug. Stratton had spent a few hours online looking into all that. Couldn't get clear details, but he felt they were out there.

Then, once he got to the hotel ballroom, Stratton approached the nice woman in the beige suit, who'd worked for the same company. He told her he was quietly vetting O'Rourke for a venture capital outfit, and he pretended to know more than he did about the scandal.

With her help—for she was no longer working there, had not signed a non-disclosure agreement, and had nothing to lose—he pieced together that O'Rourke had been busted in an internal investigation for falsifying research data, plus it seemed he'd stolen money outright, with the help of a crooked financial officer. The financial officer went up for it; O'Rourke didn't, but he paid restitution and left the company. It had all been kept very quiet.

"It's precarious, though," said the woman. "Scientists falsify their data often."

"For reputation, for money?"

"Both. And then companies have to cover. If investors learn of it, they'll dump that stock in a heartbeat, which could—"

"Kneecap the company."

"Not just that. The whole sector could take a dive."

"Ah."

Stratton assured the scientist that not only would he keep her confidentiality, he'd be delighted to do her a favor or two in return. Having made her way in the increasingly cutthroat world of emergent pharma, she thought it rather thrilling to have a solid IOU from a security professional as good-looking as Stratton.

Now he's talking to O'Rourke and he's got him on the ropes. The mid-level ruckus of conversations and clinking plates continues. A server clad in catering black stops by with a tray of appetizers. Her apron bears witness to a spill or two so far this evening, but her vibe is upbeat.

"Is there any coffee?" Stratton asks. He'd taken a glass of wine to help blend in when he entered the room, but he didn't want it. "Black's fine."

"Certainly, right back."

"So," says Stratton as O'Rourke stares down at his glass of merlot or whatever, "I know Sandy was working with you at Lomastar. I think things went wrong, and she became a liability to you."

The air goes out of the man as if Stratton had punched him in the chest. He tries to pull himself together, stays silent.

Stratton goes on, "I'm trying to help someone."

"Paladino."

"No."

"What do you want from me?"

William O'Rourke is one of those medium-sized guys who wear big wrist-watches. Stratton is not attuned to the current wristwatch scene. He wears a plain wind-up watch left to him by his father.

"As I understand it," Stratton says, "you and your daughter were working together on a new anti-anxiety drug in the labs at Lomastar."

"That's right."

"And Sandy was studying Vic Paladino, and he was going to be some kind of test subject for the two of you, wittingly or unwittingly."

Stratton looks imposing, in his turtleneck and herringbone sport jacket, his hands laced on the black cloth table cover. A bald guy with a good head. O'Rourke's swept-back look appears to require hairspray to stay in place. The server delivers Stratton's coffee and leaves, engulfed by the room's hubbub.

"I don't think you murdered your own daughter, and I don't necessarily think you arranged it, but I think you know why it happened." Stratton understands that when a collaboration goes bad, it's often because someone has a change of heart. Something emotional.

He goes on, "You were OK with your daughter going into a dangerous situation. You were OK with her literally risking her life to advance what you all were working on."

"But I didn't—"

"Was Sandy starting to have doubts about what you were doing?" Stratton starts to sip his coffee, finds it too hot, and sets it down.

O'Rourke's silence tells him he's on the right track. Eventually O'Rourke says, "She ... it wasn't so much that ... well ..." He looks up into Stratton's intense face, those glasses. He continues in a low, angry tone, "We agreed she'd study the guy. That's not a secret. I didn't tell her to fall in love with him!"

"And that changed the dynamic."

O'Rourke nods. "She went from being all in favor of using him as a test case, to 'Oh, my darling shouldn't be using drugs at all.'"

"Because she started to see the toll his pill routine was taking? And she was starting to turn against you, right?"

"Then you already know. She tried to sabotage me—and our work!"

"How?"

"For one thing, she pretended to accidentally lose a significant amount of our data. It was no accident. And all of a sudden she's telling me I'm evil."

"The new drug."

"The *better* drug. You know, you holier-than-thou types make me laugh. Sitting there ingesting a caffeine infusion, maybe with a pack of aspirin in your pocket, and a bottle of booze at home! Drugs!"

"Yeah, yeah, I get it. But between a cup of coffee with brandy in it, and a pharmaceutical speedball, is a lot of road." Stratton waves off another server with a tray of goodies. "I don't imagine you wanted to shut Sandy up, exactly."

"No! I was just kidding around. I just kinda wanted him to scare her away, that's all. I was just kidding around, I swear."

"Him who? And instructions were misunderstood? Or things got out of hand? Him who?"

"I can't ..."

"Look, man," Stratton says calmly, "you've built a hell of a career, and you're still rolling. You didn't need Paladino as a test subject, although it strikes me that he'd be a great spokesman for you, whenever the product came out. Your own daughter turned against you. She became a threat to you. I understand. What were you supposed to do? All I want from you is the name of the person who went to shake up Sandy."

"I didn't murder my own daughter."

"I know you didn't." Stratton studies O'Rourke like an insect pinned to a board. The man, in spite of his rakish hair, is deeply insecure, unhappy, confused, regretful. And yet, there's a particular, vibrant self-interest rolling around inside him, a useful narcissism. This characteristic, Stratton reflects, is what fuels so many great escapes, whether from a padlocked dungeon or from an uncomfortable cocktail conversation.

Stratton decides to go ahead with it. "How much did Myers want for whatever he was supposed to do?"

O'Rourke flips his eyes to Stratton's, and therein lies the confirmation.

Because, of course, if Sandy had turned against Paladino's drug use, she'd have become no friend to Joe Myers.

CHAPTER 40

I THROW GASOLINE

Two unusual things happen as I'm checking over my grocery order for Paladino's after-party Saturday night. It's now Monday afternoon, and I have the week to prepare. Basically, I'm going simple yet big, if that makes sense. For instance, in the short time I've been a French chef, I've discovered that everybody loves hot, seasoned meatballs on toothpicks. No sauce. If you buy the Italian-seasoned mini meatballs frozen in bags at the market, you're golden. The key is to buy and prepare huge quantities, so no one feels they have to exercise any restraint. If you don't heat them for too long, they're plenty juicy, yet there's no sauce to drip on anybody's outfit. I call the meatballs *morceaux de paradis,* or 'morsels of heaven.' The internet's been a big help.

For the vegetarians, I'm planning on mini sandwiches of good baguette bread, hummus, and roasted red peppers. All of it from the grocery store, needless to say. You slice the bread thin, plaster on some hummus, lay on a slice of the roasted pepper, then maybe throw on a basil leaf, top with more bread and hummus. This item was suggested by Connie Blue Smoke, and I've already served it at the house to great acclaim. You can make these as double-deckers, which look impressive, but then they're harder to eat. I'm planning on assembling at least two hundred of these, which I'm calling *collation royale.* Royal snack. Mountains of them, no matter how tight the guest list is. No matter how many skinny, mineral-water-sipping persons will be on hand. They'll eat them, all right.

But I'm most proud of my mini *pâtés en croûte,* which are simply wads of liverwurst wrapped in the crescent dough that comes in tubes in the cold case at the grocery. Bake and keep hot. I should buy stock in Pillsbury. I'm ordering 30 tubes for the party, plus twelve pounds of liverwurst, which should make 240 pieces. The household seriously went mad for these things when I made a test batch. The hardest part has been keeping all my trickster ingredients hidden in the pantry and fridges. I'll fix a few trays of raw veggies and some version of dip as well.

Oh, plus there'll be lots of champagne bottles sticking up from ice chests, so people will be able to grab refills at will, like a frat party at some upscale college. Grab a whole bottle, eh? We got plenty.

Laura has agreed to help me on Saturday. Between us we'll be able to handle prep, transport, serving, and cleanup. I've reserved a catering box truck to haul all the food, drink, and equipment. She's antsy about what she sees as lack of progress on proving Gordy's innocence, but hey, maybe we'll learn more during that party. I already have a few ideas.

The first unusual thing that happens while I'm working on all this is Paladino comes in and hands me a little box. It's a lusciously blue box with a white ribbon around it. Just by looking at that box, you can tell whatever's in it must be costly.

"I was out and about," he says, "and this made me think of you."

Which is peculiar.

"Mr. Vic," I demand in my best Celeste LaPorte butcher-block tone. "What is this now?"

"Open it." He's standing there like a prom date who's spent all his allowance on a corsage.

I undo the ribbon and open the rectangular box to behold an astonishing bracelet, gold and diamonds (reasonable assumption) in a swirly design, as if the gold links are water and the diamonds little suns captured in the eddies.

"W-wow," I go, almost forgetting to stay in character. My breath catches for real at the sheer beauty of the thing. In a second, I get a grip. I remain sitting.

I give him a cold stare. "Mr. Vic. Explain." Is this a crush gift, or maybe a bribe? Or maybe some bizarre apology for something he's done that I don't know about yet?

His eyes are shining, I swear they're almost glittering. Is he high? I don't get that sense.

"Put it on. I think it will look—"

"Explain."

He smiles even bigger. "Nothing to explain, Celeste. It's just that I think you're a special person. A great chef! But not just that. Whenever we talk, you and I, I feel—good. Better, best!" He smacks his hands, his main expression of enthusiasm. "I just want you to have this. Do you like it?"

I turn the bracelet over in my hands. "It is beautiful." I drape it over my wrist.

"I think it's perfect in every way. It's imaginative, but refined, don't you think? And totally genuine! Just like you."

I cough slightly.

He beams.

"Mr. Vic, I'm afraid I have given you the wrong—"

Another voice breaks in. "Celeste, is there any—oh, excuse me." Chuck Stratton stops short. Looks at me holding this sensational chunk of treasure, then to Paladino, then to me again. We're all pretty calm.

"Yes, Mr. Chuck. What may I do for you?"

"I'm interrupting something."

Obviously. With my eyes, I try to communicate *I have no idea what's going on.*

"I'll stop back." He exits quickly. I hear his work boots clumping away.

"Is he sweet on you?" Paladino asks.

"I doubt it."

"Well, take this gift for what it is: just a gift. No strings."

"Mr. Vic, there are always strings."

"Not this time."

"In that case, thank you."

"I'll let you get back to work."

Is this a tip? How would I know? Paladino actually having a crush on me is beyond improbable. This gift is all to the good. He'll listen to me, when the time comes.

The next unexpected thing that happens, as I'm still sitting there staring at this amazing object, feeling its weight in my palm, the smoothness of the gold, is my phone bleats and I answer because it's a 313 code.

"It's you, isn't it?" says a woman's voice that's familiar. She's talking all hard and angry. "*You're* the one he likes." Very accusatory.

"No. Who is this?" I lay the bracelet in its box.

A laugh that says *I look down upon you.*

Again I ask, "Who is this?"

"This is Gloria Jensen. Why don't you just keep away from him?"

Oh. The voice that pours from a billion ear pods. Strange to hear her speaking, not singing. I go into redline Celeste LaPorte mode. "I'm working in his house," I inform her harshly. "He is my boss."

"It's not his house. Don't you know anything? He is *not* your boss."

"Wait a minute, him who?"

"You know very well. *Chuck.* Come to think of it, they're probably both in love with you."

"Only someone who's never met me could say that."

A snort of ridicule. I thought it was a pretty good line.

"Ms. Jensen, you are completely mistaken." I don't bother asking how she got my number.

Stratton reappears, striding into the kitchen, and thankfully he overhears me say 'Ms. Jensen,' because he stifles a laugh and mouths *Speaker.*

So I hit speaker and hold the phone up, and we hear Gloria Jensen in an ongoingly ugly tone: "Chuck doesn't know his own mind. You're nothing to him."

I can play this game. "Then how come you're calling me?" I hook my arm over the back of my chair.

"He said he was seeing someone. And when Vic went on and on about *you*—" she said it like *yewww*—"and I saw the look on Chuck's face—"

"When was this?"

"After my show at the casino! Don't pretend you don't know what I'm talking about!"

I throw gasoline on her fire. "Ms. Jensen, you have been drinking." Stratton and I are rewarded with a moment of stunned, confirmatory silence, then a stream of unimaginative swearing and name-calling. I mouth *Wow* to Stratton. He nods, biting back more laughter, and I hit the end call button.

"You owe me an explanation, man."

He relaxes against the counter opposite my desk, turning his neck a little bit, loosening it. His glasses flash in the lamplight. "She has the hots for me and can't understand why I'm not panting after her in return."

"She'd be an easy lay."

He grants that with a nod. "I remember what it's like to be a horndog that'll screw anything. But a woman like her brings a lot of expectations. Things get transactional pretty fast. She doesn't even know me."

Transactional. I like that word. Very clear.

"Speaking of which," he goes on, "what just happened with Vic and that thing?"

The bracelet is sitting there in its box on my desk. Lovely glowing robin's-egg blue box.

"Wait a minute, pal, back up. What did you say to Gloria Jensen about me? Or more to the point, about you and me?"

He chews his fleshy upper lip for a second. "Not that I expect you to believe me, but OK, Vic wanted to go to her concert, and of course I had to accompany him. I wasn't looking forward to it. Of course she invites us backstage after, and in the midst of the party she makes a beeline for me. I'd turned her down before, but this time I told her explicitly that I'm seeing someone."

"Yeah?"

"And Vic barges into the conversation and says something like, 'Oh, we're both fighting over my new little French chef!'"

"What!"

"I had no idea why Vic said that, because he and I have never discussed you in that way. I told Gloria I was seeing someone just to get her away from me. But, 'course, why would she be put off by that?" He sweeps his hand ironically. "She's Gloria Jensen!"

"I see."

Stratton sighs, folds his arms comfortably, then smiles a little. "The fact is, I think you're pretty neat."

I blink. "'Pretty neat?' What are we, fourteen?"

Little bit more of a smile. His teeth are crooked, I suddenly notice. Quite crooked, jammed together, askew. I decide it adds to his attractiveness. If his teeth were perfect, he'd be able to get jobs as a movie actor and he'd look fake and become conceited.

But I say, verging on Celeste-like again, "Let's clear this up now. I think you're 'pretty neat' too, but I'm not interested in relationships. Nothing's going to happen between us. I didn't think that needed to be said."

"Of course. Fine." Is he amused now? I find that insulting, but it's not clear enough to call him on it.

I go, "So Vic does have the wrong idea about me."

"Seems so."

"I'm an easy distraction from his grief about Sandy."

"Therefore the bracelet."

"I admit my first thought, given my current bank balance, was *I wonder how much I could get for this at Excalibur Pawn.*"

"Ha."

"There's very little that's beneath me."

"Right."

"You weren't supposed to agree with that."

"Right."

CHAPTER 41

SO JUMBLED AND UNCLEAR

Stratton and I talk some more that night, and I learn about his conversation with William O'Rourke. Neither Stratton nor I have seen Joe Myers lately. Evidently Paladino's well supplied with drugs for the time being.

Stratton wonders aloud, "How do we suppose Myers and O'Rourke got in league with each other?"

"OK, Sandy's the connection. Myers could easily glean from some overheard conversation that Sandy's working with her dad. He hears about this new drug. He gets in touch to see what kind of leverage he might be able to gain over Sandy via William. He can do that without revealing much about himself. If nothing comes of it—"

"He's no worse off."

"Right."

I message Ted Alvarez to call me when he can.

Next morning after breakfast I slip out and head to Gordy's house. Something's trying to knock through my skull, triggered by that bracelet from Paladino.

I let myself into the quiet murder house, hardening my nerves against the creepiness, even though it's a bright enough morning. It's cold in here: I'd screwed down most of the radiators before leaving to be Paladino's chef. I dig Gordy's treasure box out of the closet and open it on the kitchen table. There's the bracelet, the silver-tone band with the dog head embossed on it. I finger it, and it's as cold and cheap as I remembered, yet in a way more real than the glittering ornament Paladino had given me. This one had a different kind of weight—the kind that comes with secrets.

I open my phone and look up Balsam Ridge High School. Our mascot was the timber wolf. The cheerleaders would chant, "Timber Wolves! Timber Wolves! Go! Go! Go!" followed by a drawn-out "Owooooo!" Nothing rhyming or clever, but what word possibly rhymes with 'wolves' anyway?

The line drawing of the mascot on the website is exactly what's on the bracelet. Same exact outline, dog head in profile with teeth bared. Again I read the stamped lettering on the inside. CADO. I phone Connie Blue Smoke.

"Con. Thanks for picking up."

"I'm on break. What's happening?"

"Do you remember what Roberta Summerline's cheerleader nickname was?"

"No. It was something silly, they all were."

"Could it have been Cado? Like avocado? Remember you told me how she wanted to go to California and eat avocados off the vines or something?"

"I don't know. You want me to ask Prue Walerski?"

"She might remember."

"I'll try to call her now. How did you—"

"I found something. Call me back as soon as you talk to Prue, OK?"

Why would Gordy have Roberta Summerline's cheerleader bracelet? Could he be innocent of one murder but guilty of another? I fix a cup of tea and write some things in my notebook, stuff I want to remember. I try to get down facts, but everything seems so jumbled and unclear. Writing things down helps, and I realize I should do it more often. Detectives always write stuff down in their pocket notebooks. Did Gordy and Roberta date at some point before he and I got together, and she gave it to him as a keepsake, like a promise trinket? If so, why would he keep it all these years, in his special box with his most important, meaningful possessions? According to Connie Blue Smoke, our old classmate Prue Walerski thought Gordy 'knew something' about Roberta's disappearance. Could Gordy have murdered Roberta for some reason, then kept the bracelet as a souvenir of the crime? Killers on the police shows do stuff like that. We were all so young back then.

Alvarez calls while I'm writing these thoughts down, and I tell him about Stratton and how he cornered William O'Rourke at a conference.

"The name Joe Myers came up strong. O'Rourke more or less let on that he and Sandy were arguing about their research, and he might have sent Joe Myers to straighten her out."

"And things went wrong?"

"Well, yeah, if that's what legit happened. But why at Gordy's house? I can't get over that."

Ted asks, "What else do you guys know about Joe Myers?"

"Nothing. He's just this guy who comes and delivers drugs to Paladino. He's not on the payroll, so Stratton doesn't know his address or anything. Paladino must pay him on the side in cash. Prescription drugs under different names. One of the names is Karen Short, who I think is Paladino's assistant. She goes by the name Sunpod."

"One of those."

"Yeah. I'm betting she helped Paladino get his drugs before Joe Myers came along. She was probably glad to be relieved of that duty."

"That's plausible."

"Hey, and b), can you get me in to see Gordy again, with as much privacy as possible, and c), has anything come from that plastic bag Laura found in the tree?"

"Bambi, I don't know. Does he want to see you again? And yes, there were DNA traces in the bag, but they're still working on it."

"I have to ask Gordy some more questions."

"Is it stuff his lawyer can answer?"

"No." I tell Ted about the messed-up videotape. "It has to do with a guy we knew from back home, named Wade Kullen. I need Gordy to—"

"Wade Kullen?"

"You know the name?"

"Well." I hear Ted rubbing his face. "The forensic analysis of Gordy's banking showed he was making payments on the regular to a Wade Kullen. I'd guess some kind of extortion."

"Oh, boy. OK."

"Find out anything else you can about Joe Myers and let me know, OK? If he comes to Paladino's house again, call me immediately, all right? I'll see what I can do on my end, and I'll see about getting you in to see Gordy again."

"It would seem a conversation with Kullen would be beneficial."

"Well, yeah," Alvarez snaps. "Question is where to find him."

"You've looked."

"We're looking, with no success."

"Have you gotten any help from the state police up north?"

"We've asked, but nothing's come from them."

Ten minutes later, I've fixed another cup of tea and am staring into space when Connie calls back.

"It was just like you said. Roberta's nickname was Cado, because she liked avocados."

Before I leave the house, Alvarez calls to tell me Gordy's down sick with something like the flu, so no visitors for now.

"'Something like the flu?'"

"He's sick for real, they don't screw around. I can maybe get you in next week."

"Next week is a long time from now."

CHAPTER 42

RISKS EITHER WAY

A few days before the concert, I ask Sunpod, "Have ticket sales picked up?" She's hanging out in the kitchen with me after breakfast. Paladino's gone off to work with his band, driven by Stratton. The Masonic is pretty big, more than 4,000 seats.

She gives me a hard look, which is unusual for her. I'd noticed she wasn't particularly good at making eye contact. She could get there, but it was more of a sideways glide into it, like a shoplifter going into a liquor store near closing.

I keep my expression open, yet still Celeste-like. Sunpod's gaze softens to sadness, then upshifts to anxiety as she considers unemployment if Paladino's career doesn't ramp up. Paladino had an accountant and a lawyer somewhere, and Stratton told me they were ready to drop the anvil on Sunpod. Or is it axe? I think it's drop the axe. It seems the accountant and lawyer were doing a decent enough job for Paladino, but good as they were, they couldn't spin gold out of nickels.

Later I ask Stratton if he thinks Sunpod has morphed into the role of sex doll for Paladino.

"Well, he's a healthy man. He's used to having sex, and Sunpod's always there."

"She seems so unsexy. Like if I tried to paint a picture of lack of libido, she'd be it."

He laughs.

"I mean," I go on, "if I had his fame, I bet I could sure find somebody juicier. Sunpod, she's like an aluminum chopstick."

"Yeah." His chuckles subside. "I think it's a little early for Vic to be looking for a real girlfriend."

"Right, of course." I avoid jumping into the next hopscotch square of asking Stratton what he's doing for romance. There's romance, and there's simple sexual release. As a former streetcorner bangtail, I knew that difference well.

Over and above everything else, I'm familiar with Sunpod's type: an underachiever who learned to make her way in life by pleasing men. There are definite similarities between letting a man support you in exchange for comfort and being a regular hooker. Is one better than the other? You'd think, well, why *wouldn't* you want just one client, not having to get out and hustle night after night?

Looking at it from a business standpoint, there are risks either way. If you're hustling freelance, risks abound: you can get beat up, robbed, infected, messed with in any number of ways. But you're diversified. With just one client, as long as it's good, it's good. But if he gets tired of you or angry with you, or his wife finds out, you can be standing in your boots and nightgown on some corner in a snowstorm at midnight with ten dollars in your pocket.

In any case, it's not like you've been paying into some pension program, or even Social Security.

Sunpod was a one-client gal, and she now was realizing the potential costs of that.

Chapter 43

But Murder's a Big Deal

On Thursday afternoon I get a call from Alvarez, who wonders whether I'm free to meet him for coffee.

"You have news?" I ask.

"Yeah. It's a little complicated, and I'm hoping you can help."

"Absolutely. Do you want Laura too?"

"No. Can you come to the Sparkplug within the next hour?"

"Yeah."

Alvarez is there, cup of coffee before him, when I walk into the café, which wasn't too long of a drive south on Coolidge. His coat is crunched next to him in the booth, his hat on top. The place is an older diner, decent coffee, big windows, quiet with dusty afternoon light. I decide to have coffee for a change. Once I get settled and order a cup, Alvarez pulls a sheaf of folded papers from his coat pocket. Thin sheaf, three or four pages.

"These are phone records."

"You got these from the investigators on the case?"

"More or less."

"I've always liked the cut of your jib, Ted." I learned that phrase from one of the nicer hookers I knew back in the day.

243

We smile a little together. My coffee is delivered by a server whose t-shirt and hair are both bright maroon. Magenta? Is that a color, or is it a spacecraft material like Kevlar? Cheerful server. The place smells of grilled cheese and onions.

Alvarez takes a pen from his pocket and points to things on the papers. "Here. These are calls and texts to and from Sandy O'Rourke's phone. This column is the time. And over here, to and from Gordy's phone."

"There's a third number in here."

"Right. Unknown whose."

"Burner phone, deactivated now, right?"

"Yep."

"OK," I go. "From what Stratton says, we're betting Joe Myers had something to do with Sandy's murder, but then there's this seeming extortion of Gordy by Wade Kullen, right?"

Ted laces his fingers together.

"Ted, what exactly do you want from me here?"

"We need a scenario. I have my own ideas, but I want to hear yours." He clanks his cup and saucer. "You've always been good at street logic."

"I'm flattered."

"The lead investigators just aren't all that interested in digging into this stuff. They feel they have enough on Gordy. They have timing of these calls and texts, the body at his house, the blood literally on his hands, his evasions about what he was doing that day."

"Well. OK, but I'm no cop." I study the pages. "What about GPS?"

"They haven't bothered. But Gordy's lawyer might be on that, if he's gotten a straight story out of him."

After going back and forth from one page to another, I start thinking out loud. "OK. Day of the murder. Are we assuming each person is carrying their own phone?"

"Yes."

"We have a call from this unknown phone to Sandy's at 4:30 p.m. Could be random, but we have to bet it wasn't. I think it was the murderer trying to set something up."

"OK."

"We have a text from Sandy to Gordy at 4:45 p.m. *I need you to come over right away.* He texts back, *Why?* No answer to that, so he calls her at 4:48."

"Minute-long call."

"Right, quick call, but whatever she said, it was enough for him to go over to his ex's apartment, in spite of not having seen her in what, at least six months? How long would it take in the snow for him to get there?"

Alvarez considers. "At least twenty minutes. Half hour, maybe, with grabbing keys, getting the car going, parking."

"That fits well enough. At 5:20, he texts her. *I'm here. Buzz me in.* But she doesn't, because then he calls her at 5:22, and she doesn't answer, or can't answer. What would he do? He sticks around for a few more minutes, then leaves. He thinks, is she pulling a trick on me for some reason?"

"But we think he didn't leave."

"Right, I'm thinking different, OK?"

"OK."

"He leaves."

The server comes by and refills our cups. We pause our talking. In an upbeat tone, verging on cute, the magenta-shirted guy says, holding the pot off to his side, "I'm so bored! Aren't either one of you hungry?"

I shake my head with a smile, but Alvarez answers, "Bring us each a grilled cheese, would you?"

"Fries?"

"Yeah. Smells too good in here."

The server bops away and I thank Ted. He says, "Even if you don't eat, I could probably finish them both."

I reflect on the fact that I've eaten quite well since starting work for Vic Paladino. Gonna be hard to get back to normal. Haven't had a peanut-butter-and-banana sandwich in days. Been missing them, actually.

I continue, "So what's Gordy gonna do but go home? Maybe on the way he in fact stops at the beer store like he said on the video."

"Yeah, beer, chips, and a lottery ticket. We did find the ticket in his wallet, time-stamped 5:44 p.m."

"OK, that fits too. He then gets home, finds Sandy's body, and freaks."

"But maybe," Alvarez objects, "she was in the bathroom or something when he arrived at her apartment, and she did let him in eventually, and then he abducted her to his house."

"Well, yeah, that's what your comrades on the force are saying. No doubt they're saying that. But here's what I think, based on the fact that there was a guy seen leaving Gordy's house, and losing a trash bag in the tree. The witness didn't get a good look at the person, and maybe it was Gordy, leaving the house to dispose of evidence. But we don't need to keep pounding nails into Gordy's coffin, right?"

"Yeah."

"By the way," I say, "do you know if the insurance company has paid out on Sandy's policy yet?" I shift in my seat, appreciating the comfy vinyl upholstery. Padded seat *and* back in these booths.

"Oh, I highly doubt it. She was murdered, there's an active investigation, which usually holds things up. In normal cases, it usually takes a few weeks after the beneficiary files a claim before they get the money. In a case with some ambiguity, it's gonna take longer."

"OK. I'm thinking it could be good to keep an eye on Sandy's dad's banking records. He knew about the policy, obviously. Very handy for Sandy to have arranged it herself. Incredibly idealistic of her, I'd say."

"Or naïve."

"Yeah, probably both. What if O'Rourke promised the money to the killer, as payment? Some or all of it."

Alvarez thinks about that. "We'd need a solid reason to get a warrant for his banking records. Just wanting to know what he does with the money isn't enough. At least at this point."

"Keep it in mind, though?"

"Yeah."

"It's pretty plain Sandy knew her killer, and it was a setup. If I wanted to frame Gordy for a murder—whether Sandy O'Rourke or anybody—I'd think, 'Boy, how perfect to do the murder in his house.'"

Alvarez listens, his large dark eyes darting from mine to the pages on the table then back again. The man had lashes. "Obviously," he says, "but—"

"If I was a lowlife—" I stop myself. "If I was *still* a lowlife and in possession of some shred of IQ, I'd get a gun and *use* it but not shoot it. I'd go over to Sandy's and tell her she and me and Gordy need to have a talk. She knows trouble's coming, she doesn't even want to talk to whoever this is. Let's say it's Joe Myers, eh? Let's just say that for a minute."

"OK," Ted agrees.

"If I'm Joe, a.k.a. Paladino's supplier, and Sandy's gotten all holy all of a sudden, I'd want her out of the way because Paladino's the grandest client I've ever known. But murder's a big deal, even if I'm a scumbag. You don't just kill somebody without trying to come up with a less dangerous alternative, or b) come up with a major gain from doing it. And a major gain is money. Major money."

"Hence you're wondering about the disposition of the half-a-mil insurance money."

"Hence. OK, so if I'm Myers, I go to her apartment, get her to let me in based on some lie or other. Once inside, I tell her, 'OK, we need to have a little chitchat, you and me and Gordy. Call him up and tell him to come over.' She doesn't want to, she senses big trouble. Hence—"

"The gun."

"He holds the gun to her head, she makes the call. Maybe even Gordy hears the stress in her voice and that sets off *his* trouble alert. So he goes over to her place, to maybe protect her from whatever mess is trying to go down. As soon as Myers figures Gordy's on his way, he says to Sandy, 'Change of plans, we're going over to *his* house. I'll tell him.' And he—"

"What reason does he give for—"

"No reason, Ted. He's holding the gun! So he makes a fake call."

"This all sounds quite good, Bambi."

I'd given up trying to get anybody to call me BB. "Myers rushes Sandy over to Gordy's. She's still got her key, he made sure to ask that. Otherwise he'd have to break in, which would screw up things. Or maybe somehow he made a copy of Sandy's key to Gordy's when they were still somewhat friendly, bumping into each other once in a while at Paladino's."

"Even if he had to break in, Gordy could be accused of staging it to suggest an intruder."

"Yeah, so that's actually irrelevant, good point." I stop and without planning to say this, I go, "Isn't this *interesting?*"

Ted smiles.

I keep on. "Myers gets her to calm down and have a seat. On the couch. He's back in a second with the kitchen knife, which is already probably gonna have Gordy's prints on it. He's wearing at least one rubber glove to hold the knife with."

Ted and I sit for a moment, thinking about what happened then, whether by the hand of Myers, Wade Kullen, or whoever. Traffic streams by steadily on Coolidge. A pedestrian dashes across, zigzagging from lane to lane. Young guy, brainlessly fearless, thin denim jacket.

"The killer's thought about this all, he's planned it pretty well. He brought his own knife, but ideally he's going to use a weapon of Gordy's. Knife, lamp, fireplace poker. The knife was great because it looks like a passion killing. Messy, but he felt he could handle it."

Our sandwich plates come, wafting delicious smells that make you want that meal every day for the rest of your life. We dig in. I'm hungry enough, turns out. The server brings more coffee.

You know how when you're sitting near a window and the light hits somebody's eye sideways and shines through the colored part? Ted's eye nearest the window glinted rich brown, almost amber for a moment. I think it's so beautiful when that happens.

Although we feel the cold trying to come in through the window, fingering its way around the weatherstripping, the microclimate created by our hot food and coffee makes things cozy enough. I warm my hands on my coffee cup. One of the little comforts of winter.

We munch a few bites. The cook had pressed the sandwiches with his spatula just the right amount, so they weren't too flat but flatter than just grilling and flipping. Ideal. Plus he didn't skimp on the cheese.

"The killer," I propose, "needs to get out as fast as he can. But he got blood on his shirt or pants or arms. He rummages through the kitchen, finds a couple of garbage bags, puts his bloody clothes in one, runs upstairs, wipes himself on a towel or two, grabs pants and a shirt from Gordy's closet. Now he's hurrying, cuz he knows Gordy's probably on his way back. He puts the bloody towel in another bag. They're small bags."

"And as he's leaving, he slips on the ice, drops the bags, one splits open—"

"They're cheap bags. I've used that brand. The box is still in Gordy's kitchen."

Ted says, "And it gets blown up into the tree, which we know. Except we actually *don't* know for sure if the bag Laura found was the exact same bag the kid saw blow into the tree."

"Common sense says it is. Plus the lab's still testing it, right?"

"That'll tell the tale. Soon, too, I think."

"OK, OK, let's just keep going. He scoops up his stuff and beats it. Gordy comes home, finds the body, he's telling the truth when he said he didn't know if she was alive or dead. In his panic he pulls the knife out, then calls 911. He lies to the police about his actions, because he certainly doesn't want to say he went to Sandy's place an hour ago for any reason."

I eat a few fries. "If Gordy had been better about clearing the ice off his front walk, Kullen wouldn't have fallen, lost the bag, and drawn the attention of the kid. Pablo."

Ted chews and swallows. "That's pretty good," he says again.

I sit back. "Yeah."

CHAPTER 44

THE LITTLE BLACK CLOTH CASE

"Bam, this is amazing." Laura stands in Paladino's kitchen, hands on hips. We're pretty much done packing up the food for the after-party, having worked all day, preparing the hundreds of pieces of finger food, making runs out to pick up the rented food service box truck, the rented chafing dishes and Sterno cans, the linens, plates and glasses. Nothing disposable, all very classy.

"It does all look grand, doesn't it?" We share one of the mini roasted-pepper sandwiches, then load everything into the truck Laura parked outside the service door. The truck's equipped with ovens so we'll be able to bake the liverwurst-in-dough pieces on site and run them in hot, then set them over the Sterno.

At the last, Laura grabs the stone rolling pin from the pantry and stuffs it into one of the equipment bags, along with a huge spoon fit for stirring a cauldron of buffalo stew.

"Why?" I ask.

"It just looks good for our image. The rolling pin. It looks professional. I just like it."

"I've never even used it." The pin was made of marble, I guess, and was as heavy as you'd expect.

Paladino worked hard through the week, rehearsing with his band and consulting with the vocal coach guy, Razkowski. Close at hand was Sunpod, whose role seemed to be pharmacist-in-chief as well as number one flatterer. She was like a human service dog, always measuring Paladino's mood and anticipating his needs before even he knew what they were. Maybe she did have special powers, gained in the mystical magical forests of California.

I introduced "Laura LaPorte" to Paladino and the team as my daughter, knowing the plan would work better that way. "She is," I told them, "a recent graduate of Le Cordon Bleu, preparing for work in private service under my supervision." Laura smiled serenely. They were charmed.

Laura, riding shotgun, and I, driving the truck, get to the loading dock behind the Masonic Temple downtown two hours before showtime, which is 8 o'clock. Paladino's there as well, getting ready to do final sound checks with the band. He's nervous, trying not to show it, pacing and talking out loud about what a great concert he's going to give.

Stratton helps us unload the stuff we'll need first, then goes back to keeping his eye on Paladino. A hair stylist and makeup artist have already done their work, though the star hasn't yet donned his signature outfit of perfectly tailored tuxedo and patent leather slip-ons.

Backstage here is identical to any backstage I ever saw when crashing rock and folk concerts, everything pretty utilitarian. Except the atmosphere! You can feel the energy in the air from all the ghosts, and from your own adrenaline that keeps rising with every minute until showtime. It's cool in the bare corridors, and the air smells pleasantly of floor-sweeping compound: resinous, like faintly of turpentine. If you've worked with it you know the aroma. We used it in Jimmy's religious-supplies warehouse to keep the dust down.

Conveniently, there's an empty dressing room next to the one assigned to Paladino, where Laura and I organize our stuff. I managed to leave the rolling pin and spoon in the truck. Paladino's dressing room is big, with nice lighting and comfy seating, and that's where the people will hang out for the party. To get to it, we'd had to go up from stage level via either stairs or elevator. The elevator will be convenient for running the hot food in from the truck. It's the old kind, where you have to work a lever to tell it to go up and down.

I'd written out checklists like mad, with timetables down the left-hand margins. The ovens in the truck are on low preheat. Laura looks pert and serious in her auburn wavy bob and black outfit. She's even added a black bowtie to her black blouse, the sleeves of which are rolled up to mid-forearm. Ready for action. I've got on my chef coat over a t-shirt and black jeans. We each have on a black cook's cap, low and flat, which keeps your hair out of the way and looks neat. After a moment's debate, we decided to bring our purses in, instead of leaving them somewhere in the truck with our coats. We stashed them in a cubby under one of the makeup tables.

I'd rented a stainless-steel ice chest on wheels, this double-walled box the size of a coffin. Now, Laura and I fill it with bag after bag of ice from the truck (which also features a refrigerated compartment, super convenient). I add a couple of gallons of water. The thing must weigh a hundred and fifty pounds. We look at each other and nod.

Last night Stratton clued Laura and me in on Paladino's concert-night meds routine. Stratton ducks in now, and the three of us check our watches. It's seven o'clock, an hour before show time. Stratton says, "Just before you guys got here, she put it in there. On the little makeup table, front and center. Black cloth case, like for toiletries. Paladino's on the stage right now with the band." The star will want his first dose of pre-show amphetamines in about fifteen minutes.

"I can handle this," says my daughter resolutely, squaring herself and taking a deep breath. While Stratton keeps watch in the corridor, Laura puts her weight behind the ice chest and pushes it into Paladino's dressing room as I hold the door. I follow with a case of champagne, which I set on the floor in a corner. Off from the dressing room is a bathroom and shower. All looks good. The little black cloth case is sitting by itself on the center white countertop, just as Stratton said. I exit, leaving Laura alone.

Stratton and I wait in the corridor. A couple of tech guys trot by in their noiseless stagehand sneakers, and we hear Paladino telling the band some last thing on a hot mic that's piped through the backstage areas.

After a few minutes an impressive crash occurs in the dressing room. It sounds like the last moment of some legendary glacier as the final iceberg rips away. Stratton and I look at each other.

"One more minute," I murmur. We stand calmly until we hear a weak cry. We rush in.

I yell, "Oh, no!"

Laura's lying on the floor, one leg seemingly pinned under the overturned ice chest and the mountain of wet ice cubes it spewed. Paladino's pill satchel is missing from the table.

Sunpod comes running in, her white outfit flowing behind her, followed by Paladino.

"What happened?" Paladino is aghast. Sunpod stands there tensely. Coach Razkowski trails in.

I kneel with Laura as Stratton squats and hoists the ice chest off of her. Everybody's talking at the same time.

Me: "Oh, my God, honey, are you hurt?"

Sunpod: "Where is it?"

Laura, dazed: "What—what happened? I must have—"

Paladino: "Is she OK?"

Laura: "I must have—"

Me: "Is your leg hurt?"

Stratton: "She'll be OK."

Sunpod: "Where is it?"

Laura, slowly: "I think I'm OK. I'm so sorry."

Sunpod: "Where is it?"

Paladino: "How on earth did that happen?"

Laura wiggles out from the mountain of ice. Freezing water and ice cubes have sloshed all over, soaking into the rug and pooling on the tile nearby.

Sunpod's eyes are huge with panic. Her gaze darts around the room, settling on the ice mountain. As soon as Paladino realizes what she's upset about, he closes his eyes and takes a deep breath.

"Find it, Sunpod."

She drops to her knees and starts pawing through the icy mess. Stratton and I avoid looking at each other.

"Where's what?" Stratton asks. No one answers.

I help Laura into one of the lounge chairs. "What happened, honey?"

"I don't know." Laura rubs her leg through her sopping pants. "One minute I was pushing that cold case in. Then I wake up and I'm under it."

"Oh, no! Did you have another seizure? I thought your new medication was working!"

Laura looks up at us all, confused and sad. Gradually coming out of her dazed state. Slowly. Doing a really good job.

Sunpod literally screams, "Oh, my God!" She pulls the little drug satchel from the bottom of the ice pile.

It's been crushed.

And soaked.

A black fabric pancake.

"Open it!" Paladino orders frantically. "Maybe some of it's still—"

Sunpod fashions the case back to some semblance of square and gets at the zipper. Sodden, crushed, dissolving pills pour out, falling into the ice pile in a colorful, useless, pharmaceutical slurry. Pieces of broken plastic bottles as well.

Perfect.

"I thrash around," says Laura. "I know sometimes I thrash."

"Does she have epilepsy?" prompts Stratton.

I nod reluctantly.

Laura goes, "Well, I have a *form* of epilepsy. It's called—"

"Never mind that!" Paladino knows he must, at least, not panic. "We've gotta get Joe here! Immediately! Sunpod!"

She was already getting her phone out.

Nimbly, Laura gets to her feet, amazingly recovered. I clap my hands. "Let's get this mess cleaned up! Bring two pots and some towels from the truck."

Laura hustles off. I kick the ice into a tidier pile.

Sunpod talks rapidly into her phone. "Thank God you answered. Vic's whole kit just got destroyed. The—everything, Joe."

Vic yells, "We need everything!"

"Uh-huh, the whole contents. Catastrophe. Emergency. There's no time for somebody to run home, and anyway, he needs—"

Paladino interrupts, "I don't even *have* everything at home! We packed almost all of it."

I notice the portly, elegant Razkowski off to the side, wringing his hands, literally wringing them. His expression isn't panicked so much as sad. In a vague way I wish I could get to know him better, just personally.

"Yeah, the Masonic," says Sunpod. "Dressing room one. The main one. Every-thing, Joe, bring everything." Pause. "What do you mean you're in Flint?"

Paladino looks like someone just whacked him with a pool cue. Flint's at least an hour away. I stay quiet and watch his expression morph in an astonishing sequence, over the course of a few seconds. It's all on his face, I can read what he's thinking like a comic strip. Despair, first off. Then in an instant he's trying to get over it. He's thinking, OK, I can't get my drugs in time, but I got this! I'm man enough to do my show without drugs. He tries to square his shoulders and convince himself.

One more instant, though, and he deflates. He knows he's screwed. Fear. Pure fear.

"Ohhh," he moans. "What's he in Flint for?"

"Well, get here as fast as you can!" Sunpod shuts her phone off. "It'll take him—I don't know. You'll have to do the first half, at least, cold."

I meet Stratton's eyes. Stroke of luck, right there, Myers being an hour away. Not essential, but helpful.

Laura returns with the pots and towels, and she and I set to work scooping up ice and mopping. The ice thunders into the metal cooler.

"That ice'll be fine for keeping the champagne at temperature," I assert. "We'll fill the other smaller cooler with fresh ice for drinks."

Somehow Laura's pants are smooth and dry, whaddaya know? A clean pair must have made their way into the truck. Socks and shoes as well. I note with happiness that she won't get chilled from staying in wet clothes. She and I might both get murdered tonight, but at least she won't develop hypothermia.

Paladino is making a huge effort to calm down. This is not helped by the vocal coach Walter Razkowski, who says, "I'm very disappointed. Very disappointed in you, Vic. You told me—"

"Get out of my face," snarls his pupil.

I suggest, "Mr. Walter, it might be best if—"

But he's already leaving the room. Slams the door behind him. I'd say this isn't the first time Paladino has sworn to Raczkowski he's off the drugs.

"Here, sit down, Mr. Vic." I take his arm and lead him to a chair like you would a child. "I'll fix you a nice snack."

"I don't need a snack, Celeste." He checks his watch. "Oh, God."

"Let's get you dressed." Sunpod shoos us out.

"I'll watch for Joe," says Stratton. He's wearing a sport jacket over his habitual turtleneck, and I know he's got a gun under there.

CHAPTER 45

WE'RE BOTH SHIVERING NOW

W hen you're an addict in your lowest depths, you know Job One is getting clean. Of course you put it off for as long as possible. You avoid admitting you're killing yourself, and you refuse to even think about accepting help. When you finally decide the pain of getting clean will be less of a problem than dying, you're on your way. Getting clean becomes your whole focus.

Then you wake up one day and realize that you have to stay clean, which is as ghastly as getting clean in the first place. Because you have to keep making decisions not to drink or use, constantly. The recovery program people say you only have to decide once, but that is so easier said than done.

So then you find yourself staying clean, and you realize you still have a lot of work to do. You have to start living a normal life. An honest life. You have to take care of business and stay off the streets. Normal life is terrifying when you've never really done it.

For us lucky ones, there comes a day when you realize you've gone over some sort of hump. You think you've got a chance to make it, make it long term.

I could see a long road ahead of Paladino, should he wish to set off on it.

I duck out to the loading dock for privacy and call Alvarez. He doesn't pick up. Shivering in the cold, I leave a message about the impending whereabouts of Joe Myers.

Laura meets up with me. "It's looking … well, sparse out there. The crowd."

"You peeked into the auditorium? It's almost showtime."

"Yeah. I mean, there's a lot of people in the seats, but the place isn't full. He's panicking back there, Bam. I feel sorry for him."

"So do I."

"But I mean, come on. How hard could it be to do a show without drugs? You just get up there and sing. He's given hundreds of concerts, right?"

I stare at her. She seems startled by my intensity. I change my glance to the distance, down the back parking area. I look at her again, with less hardness. "Come here." I lift my arm so she can come under it and keep a little warmer. She looks at the ground and stays where she is. All right. I drop my arm and she hugs herself. I feel a stab of sadness.

"Although I've never been a pop star," I begin, "you know I've been an active addict. I can tell you exactly what it'd be like to do a show without the drugs you're used to. Paladino's pre-concert cocktail no doubt consists of one part speed—or coke, whatever—and one part benzos. That would take care of it."

My daughter goes ahead with a question. "What would it feel like?"

The simple fact of her asking that question gives me such incredible relief I can't describe it. How come? Because only a non-user would ask that question.

It's cold out on that loading dock, but somehow neither of us is shivering now. Neither of us wants to break off our conversation.

"The speed makes you fearless," I tell her. "You're filled with energy, and you're exceptionally sharp, brainwise. You're like a human razor blade. That mental *zoom* is what I miss most about cocaine or any of the pharmaceutical speed I ever took. Plus you get creative. When that speed kicks in, your brain suddenly goes, right, throw anything at me, make any demand of me, and I will handle it better than Einstein. Or some astronaut commander, or hey, Picasso. And it stays that way for hours. Combine all that with the anti-anxiety med, and it's like you're all that wrapped around the core of a Zen monk."

Laura nodded. "I see."

"It's great. I swear."

"But." She knows enough.

"But if you're used to being able to skip in and out of that state, and you make commitments based on it, and suddenly you're just ordinary *you* ... talented you, OK, accomplished you, OK, but weak, anxious you at the center—forget it." I see Laura listening closely, she's fascinated, blowing into her hands, hugging herself again. I go on. "You're going to struggle to remember your own birthday. Your brain will be racing in circles. Nothing will feel right, nothing will be right. Our friend Vic here will make mistakes and hope nobody notices. He'll go too slow or too fast. His judgment will be shot. He'll make desperate decisions he knows he'll regret before he even makes them."

"Decisions?"

"What's a performance but a series of decisions?"

Laura stands there, getting it. "Wow, Bam."

Even I have to admit that last bit was pretty inspired.

We're both shivering now.

"And that's the cold truth of it." I open the backstage door and we go in. The warmth hits us like a soft wall, but the place was buzzing with nerves and last-minute prep. The contrast feels like we stepped from one world to another: chaos, wrapped in the glow of stage lights.

CHAPTER 46

A TERRIBLE FIRST HALF

When I return to the dressing room at ten after eight, one of the Masonic managers is in there talking to Paladino in a clear, hard voice.

"Your contract says promptly at eight! Nobody's opening for you! You're going to be out a lot of money if you don't go on. *Now.*" He's got a coffee cup in one hand and his clipboard in the other. Good-looking black guy, named Tony. A gym junkie's upper body. "No? I'll tell your band *and* the audience you've canceled, and you'll be on the hook for every dollar." He turns to go.

"OK, OK!" Paladino shouts. "I'll go on." And Sunpod practically leads him from the dressing room. He was perfectly groomed and dressed, but he looked like death, he really did. Sunken eyes and all.

Although I knew he'd have a terrible first half, I found myself hoping he'd do great. You just root for people, you know?

Detroit's Masonic Temple is this enormous old complex that includes a theater as well as tons of rooms for meetings, banquets, athletic stuff, and so forth. There's a church in it where people get married. What do the masons even do? Is it supposed to be Masons, with a capital M? Strange and elaborate place. I remembered going to a concert there years ago and having to wait forever in line for the bathroom, but the gothic décor almost made up for it. The neighborhood's not all that great anymore, but whatever.

In the midst of the splendor, Vic Paladino, formerly great singer, stammers and stumbles through his first half like a sixth-grader who hasn't practiced for the talent show. The band knew what was up before Vic came on, and you'd think maybe one of them would have had *something* in his kit Paladino could make use of. Evidently not. The cliché is that all musicians are on heroin, which used to be semi true for the jazz cats. I'd say today a fair number of stage musicians use weed and uppers, but Paladino's crew was pretty clean, I guess.

I did see the star toss back a gulp of vodka from a pint bottle produced by one of the stagehands as he got ready in the wings. Just a desperate measure.

The applause was big when he came out, naturally, and it sounded like a full house. It wasn't, though, as I've said. After each song, the applause meter went down and down. We backstage even heard a few boos. That had to have hurt.

Paladino is at the moment a washrag of a man. Soaking with sweat, agitated, hopeless, talking to himself, sitting there in the dressing room. "I gotta get up, up, oh God, where is he?" Sunpod tries to soothe him, total futility.

As I'm arranging our still-wrapped trays of food, Laura pops in to whisper to me that half the audience is leaving. She pitches in to help.

"Furthermore," she continues, "Gloria Jensen is sitting out there front and center, with a frozen expression on her face. At least she's not bailing."

"I'm sure she's guessed exactly what's going on. Did you recognize anybody else on the party list?"

"No, but I saw some guys who have that old-musician look to them."

"'Old-musician look?'"

"You must know what I mean."

"Yeah. I guess you've been to a club or two."

"Yes, Bam, I have."

She's too young to recognize these exact guys by sight, but it's true they all have the look: some combination of unconventional hair, graying naturally, extra-big or extra-small eyeglasses, seamed faces that need a shave and that tell you of a lifetime of late nights, drugs, liquor, and as much sex as possible. The ones who went too far are either in the graveyard or drooling into their oatmeal at the nursing home. Those here tonight are the ones who valued themselves enough to get it together and survive into middle or even old age. They've decided the high of performing outstrips love of the other thrills. I go out to take a peek myself. Yep. A few iron-tough women in that mix as well: decidedly still blonde, pudgy-but-I've-earned-it bodies, costume jewels, makeup a touch heavier these days. I found myself loving them, the singers and saxophonists and guitarists who ran their bands from the front with as little extra personnel as possible. Gotta keep an eye on your overhead. I learned that in my own businesses, early on.

So, for Paladino tonight, disaster. Laura and I continue working, setting out dishes and utensils, pouring ice, wrangling champagne bottles. I keep an eye out for Joe Myers. Stratton's watching for him too, but he can't be everywhere. I'm guessing Myers will try to get in through the backstage door, but it's possible the security guys would tell him to go around front. Has Stratton given the security guys Joe's name?

My phone buzzes and it's Alvarez calling back. Gratefully, I duck out to the corridor and just start talking.

"Did you get my voicemail? Joe Myers is almost here, I think, he's on his way, and at the very least you can bust him for drug possession, because I can assure you he's coming into this theater with enough of a stash to knock an NFL team on their—"

"Hey, Bambi, listen," he interrupts. "News on the O'Rourke murder. The lab found Sandy's DNA—from blood—in that bag. Also DNA from Wade Kullen. I don't know if it's hairs or what. They had him in the database from that rape arrest in Livonia that never went anywhere."

"Oh, now." I think on that. "OK, so maybe Myers hired Kullen for some reason. Possible?"

"Possible."

"Or they worked together, or Kullen's DNA got into that bag randomly and he had nothing to do with it, no matter what Gordy was trying to say in that video that got deleted."

"Yeah. That goes against common sense, though."

"I know. Well, look, if you want to talk to Myers, he'll be here any minute. Backstage at Masonic, the big theater."

"OK. Sit tight."

I return to the dressing room and resume party prep. Laura consults our schedule cards. "Almost time to get the hot food going in the truck," she tells me.

"Right."

Tony the stage manager shows up looking resigned, like he knows the night can't be salvaged. "Mr. Paladino, five minutes was announced ten minutes ago. I'm standing here ready to drag you onstage myself, because I'm a fan."

Paladino says something into his hands.

I tell Tony, "You're being remarkably calm."

He looks at me. "I get a paycheck, not a percentage. I have no skin in this game."

"Ah."

"It's beautiful, actually."

"Would you care for one of these little sandwiches?"

"Thank you." He indicates for me to set the sandwich on top of his clipboard. I do so.

Holding the clipboard and sandwich (which I'd professionally served with tongs on a napkin) horizontal, Tony starts to somewhat yell something else to Paladino, when the door from the corridor blasts open and Joe Myers charges in, holding a blue backpack.

Where's Stratton? I thought he'd be right with him. Where's Alvarez? Not time enough for him to get here yet. Paladino practically falls into Joe's arms, sobbing his thanks and reaching for the backpack.

"Hold on, hold on," laughs Myers. "Gimme a minute." He glances at Tony, who takes the cue and goes out, throwing a threatening look over his shoulder. Myers says, "You're pretty happy to have a guy like me on your side, eh?"

I'd seen the guy once from a distance, then met him briefly in Paladino's home studio. I'd not heard him talk until this moment. His voice, his tone, the rhythm, tugged at something deep in my brain. That place I'd left behind in the UP?

Yes! He talked like people talk at home. So many white people in the UP talk different from people in the lower peninsula: the Canadian influence, for sure, although you noticed that in the Detroit area too. The "Eh?" for sure (which rhymes with "hay," in case you're uncertain). And in Balsam Ridge, enough old Finnish immigrant blood remained that there was sort of a vocal micro-zone. People tended to talk in a—how do I describe it? Like a mid-range tone, quite flat, almost Russian in flavor. I guess I talk somewhat that way normally. This guy, Joe Myers talked like that. When he said, "You're pretty happy," it sounded like, *You're prdiddy hoppy.* That's an exaggeration, just so you get the idea.

I grab a couple of table linens and pretend to fuss with the setup. I lay the cloths on the unused makeup counters as he opens his pack. I hand Sunpod a bottle of spring water, who passes it to Paladino.

I stare at Joe Myers.

Canadian? No. Kullen.

The realization hit me like a bucket of sleet in the face, his voice replaying in my mind, overlaid with teenage memories of Mickey and Donnie, wild-haired boys with their too-wide foreheads and too-fast fists.

This guy has the beefy family build, thick chest and shoulders. Never got skinny from drugs; probably didn't use much, if at all. His hair got darker with age, dirty-blond now with gray streaks. Cut nicely, combed back with something like a matte gel, exposing that prominent Kullen forehead. Pale, clear skin. Guarded blue eyes.

A mouth that sets into a line when he sees me staring at him. He turns to Paladino and Sunpod and dumps an assortment of zip baggies on the makeup table.

"Oh, good, good," breathes Paladino, grabbing the packets. I can't watch him gulp his doses down; I turn away.

And when I turn back, Wade Kullen is a foot from my face. Cousin of Mickey and Donnie.

"What are you up to?" he whispers.

"Nothing." I draw away from him.

He turns and moves fast out the door. Doesn't glance my way again. I didn't remember ever meeting up with him in Detroit, outside of Paladino's place. He couldn't have recognized my slight UP accent, as I've been talking as Celeste LaPorte. But he had dirtbag instinct, the kind of sixth sense you're born with, the kind of thing you can't even pay a cellmate to teach you. You bet he had that.

CHAPTER 47

REALLY SUPER POOR CALCULATION

Stage manager Tony is waiting in the corridor, aware of exactly what just went down between Paladino and his dealer. Not his monkey. "You getting your mojo back, now, Mr. Paladino?" He'd eaten his sandwich in a few bites while Kullen came and went.

Ten minutes later, Paladino sweeps out of the dressing room like a proud bride. Perspiration mopped, fresh shirt. Off he goes, followed by Sunpod and Tony.

Chuck Stratton appears panting in the doorway. "Where is he?"

"Just took off. I don't know which way."

"He must have come in the front. I told the security guys about him, but there's been too many people coming and going." He hustles away.

So Wade Kullen became Joe Myers when he got to Detroit. Does he think I know who he is? Does he think I'm the only one who knows?

Within a minute, three uniformed Detroit police officers arrive, followed by a detective I didn't know. The officers are a microcosm of diversity: one black, one Latino, one white. The white one's a woman, tough-looking and heavy, like she'd be able to hold her own in a chaotic arrest situation. Maybe not, though. I've seen meth-crazed criminals haul three arresting officers around like a lumberjack playing with his kids. The detective was black, and sported a nice stingy-brim hat with a red feather cluster on the band.

"I'm Detective Sergeant Phillips. We got word from Lt. Alvarez to show up here. He's on his way. Where's this Joe Myers?"

"I don't know, he just left this room, uh, a couple minutes ago."

"What was he wearing and what does he look like?"

One of the officers pipes, "And what kind of car does he drive?"

"I think his real name is Wade Kullen." I describe him. About six feet tall, burly, the bulging forehead, the hair color, the silver puff jacket, same as when I saw him the first time at Paladino's. "And the other week I saw him driving a white Mustang with those black stripes on the hood. Fancy wheels. I don't know the plate number."

I tell the guys who Stratton is, and they take off, Sgt. Phillips giving orders.

Laura stood silently through this. "I bet he's long gone."

"I bet you're right."

"I'm confused. Who and what—"

"I'll tell you all about it later. We gotta get the hot food ready."

Cautiously, we head to the food truck. All quiet. The rear of the building is lit well enough for us to see that no one's around. There's fencing around the parking area, which is for working trucks only, but I can't tell if the gate is fastened or what. Laura unlocks the back door of our truck and we climb in. We unwrap and shove the first batches of mini meatballs and *pâté* rolls into the two ovens, which I'm unreasonably happy to note are at proper temperature.

"I'll wait here," I tell her, not wanting her to be all alone back here, despite the nearness of the police and Stratton.

Reading my mind, she jams her fists on her hips. "I can take care of myself."

"Oh, honey, if there's one little old college student in the city of Detroit who can take care of herself, it's you. Give me the keys anyway."

She almost—almost!—smiles. Hands over the keys, or rather, key, plus a fob with buttons on it. Such bright eyes. The fob was for the ignition, the key for the back door. The slight weight of them reminded me, somehow, of all the times I hadn't been there for her. But now? Now we were in this together.

"You hold down the fort," I tell her. "Light the Sternos and make sure everything looks good."

She takes off, and all goes well from then on. I run the first hot trays in. The show concludes, and Paladino takes a bunch of curtain calls before coming to the dressing room.

Pumped up and smoothed down by his drugs, Paladino played the second half almost like his old self—he'd even forgotten to have stage fright. The audience that stuck with him were rewarded. Laura, who'd peeked out a couple of times, said, "He hit the high notes, and his—what do you call it between numbers—"

"His patter?"

"Yeah! Good word. He was like effortless. Even Gloria Jensen looked relaxed and happy for him in the front row." Laura pauses. "Maybe she was too relaxed and happy? I saw her slugging from a flask."

"Ha, that might have helped."

"It was good that he saved 'Rose Petal Tango' for the second half. Plus the people seemed to love the new one, 'Scars and Shadows'."

"Cool."

Alvarez is there. "We missed him," he says glumly. "But we'll find him, if you're sure he's Kullen."

"Yeah, I pretty much am."

Stratton comes in, followed by Sgt. Phillips.

Stratton says, "I can't believe how fast he got out of here." He paces around. "Funny thing is, his car's parked just around the corner on Second. The white Mustang."

"Hey," I go, "I bet he saw the police pull up and went the other way. I bet he's on foot out there, or he ducked into a bar or something."

Phillips goes, "My guys are looking around. They'll run a check on that car if they haven't already."

Paladino's face is pink with happiness. He ducks into the bathroom to freshen up as guests start streaming in. Corks pop, plates get loaded, the party gets going. The Old Musician guys and gals clap when Paladino's band members come in, and they clap when Paladino comes out of the bathroom in track pants and a t-shirt, towel around neck. It's like he's in a fog of amnesia about the first half. I can forgive him that. It seems his friends do too. Everybody's jovial and friendly. Someone lights up a doobie and passes it around. Even coach Raczkowski materializes, smiling, having been listening from the wings.

The mood changes a little bit when Gloria Jensen glides in. "Hey, kids, what's up? Who do I have to screw to get a drink around here?"

She sees me, tosses her head dismissively. I happen to be standing close to Stratton at the moment. His Adam's apple jumps and I catch him muttering something like, *Oh, Lordy.*

Gloria gives Paladino a big hug and a smack on the cheek. She brays out, "Not a bad show for an old loser! Huh!" The other guests mostly turn away with tired expressions, embarrassed for her, knowing her. She came in with no escort; I thought she must have a driver outside, at least.

Laura offers Gloria a glass of champagne, which she accepts. The diva then makes a beeline for Stratton. I move away.

A minute later I hear one of the guests say, "This French food's pretty good." That makes me feel wonderful.

As Laura and I circulate with trays, I see Gloria standing practically against Stratton, like she's a pleasure yacht trying to dock up next to a Coast Guard cutter. Actually, it occurs to me, they would make an attractive couple if you just went on looks alone.

Except he keeps trying to make eye contact with me. As I avoid trying to notice this, I see Gloria seeing it. I see Alvarez seeing it. I mind my business, checking on the food, rearranging things, keeping Laura moving.

At one point I hear Gloria loudly announce to Stratton and anybody else within a mile, "It's true what that guy said on his podcast! I got more money than God!" Class act, there.

After chowing down some food, Alvarez and Sgt. Phillips leave, telling me they'll do a last sweep of the concert hall. Lots of nooks to hide in here, it's so big and old. The Masonic would appeal to that writer, the guy who wrote all those scary stories. Edgar what's-his-name Poe. Ed Poe.

I wonder if Wade Kullen's Mustang is still out there. I'd be fifty miles away in a stolen car, never to see that pretty pony again.

Stratton takes me aside. "I don't want either you or Laura going out to that truck by yourselves."

"We'll be fine."

"You'll let me take you."

"You know he's miles away."

"What about his car?"

I shrug impatiently. "Probably still there. He's stolen or jacked another one."

"Oh. Right."

"You know, for a tough guy, you can be pretty innocent."

He smiles. I like people who know when you're fooling around. Who don't get all butthurt about every little thing.

"Anyway," I assure him, "we're set for now." I'd brought in almost everything, only holding back a tray each of the sandwiches and meatballs, plus a small veggie tray. I have to admit, it made my heart feel good that Stratton wanted to protect Laura and me.

"I thought you would have fired her by now." That was Gloria Jensen's hyper voice cutting through the general, genial hubbub. I turn from filling fresh champagne glasses. She's standing now with Paladino, gesturing at me.

"Why would I do that?" says our host.

In answer, she lets out a sharp cry and spits out a mouthful of food. Right on the rug. Everyone stops talking. She stares hard at me.

"Ugh! This food is spoiled! She's serving rotten food. Everybody, don't eat those little puff things. They're terrible!"

All eyes turn towards the food table, then to me, then to Laura, who was circulating with a tray of mini sandwiches. She is now standing still. A flush creeps up her neck.

I keep my poise. The guests have stopped chewing and are looking doubtful. I don't know what to do, but I have to do something. I square up my shoulders and unleash my sternest Celeste LaPorte voice. "The pâté puffs are not to your liking, Ms. Jensen?"

"She's trying to poison us!"

Still holding it together, I respond, "That is not true, of course."

An Old Musician murmurs, "I've eaten five of those so far."

Gloria stalks two paces to Laura. She points to the sandwich tray. "Look! I just saw a maggot!"

Laura shouts, "You did not! My mom's food is good and you know it!" Her face is bright red and I notice her hands holding the tray trembling. She sets it down on a nearby side table and pushes herself tight in to Gloria. "What are you trying to do?"

Gloria's not backing down. I sure would, in the face of that fury from Laura.

This is not a professional situation. I have to change the dynamic.

"Laura, we will take this food away."

"Wait, no," says Paladino, who is as startled as anybody. I notice Stratton moving quietly around the side.

To my shock, Gloria shoves Laura in the chest with both hands. "Get out of my face!"

Super wrong move.

Really super poor calculation.

Everything speeds up.

Laura flexes her knees as I shout, "No!"

She rares back and, with her open hand, whacks international singing celebrity Gloria Jensen upside the head. Hard.

A couple of the Old Musicians say, "Whoa," or something, but they're a pretty chill bunch. Guys in general, I've noticed that they'll usually just stand there and watch a fight, not automatically try to separate the fighters. After all, who knows for sure who might deserve a whupping here? Everybody in the room is still. There's a clink as someone sets a glass down.

Gloria staggers into the side table and manages to sweep the tray of sandwiches to the floor, where they break apart all over the place. She lunges at Laura, but Stratton is now in action. He reaches Gloria from behind and wraps her in a bear hug, pinning her arms. How's he going to finesse this one, I wonder?

Laura stands there glaring.

"Great Spirit!" shouts Sunpod, waving her hands in some artful pattern. "Bring peace to this place!"

Incredibly, Gloria struggles and kicks. One high heel goes flying. Laura ducks it. Gloria grunts like an animal.

"Come on," says Stratton in a hard voice, holding on to her. "Relax."

I know if this goes on for a second longer, I'll do something bad. I try to take Laura's arm. "Come away."

She shakes me off and holds her ground. Worse, she shouts at Gloria, "You bitch! What's the matter with you? Why do you want to make trouble for my mom?"

There's a crazily satisfied look on Gloria's face, and I'm like, Oh, right. She's just managed to get Stratton to hug her. The harder she fights, the tighter he'll have to hold her.

I leave the room as Stratton calls, "Wait!" He's still holding onto Gloria Jensen.

The corridor's deserted except for a couple of stagehands hoping for leftovers and wondering what's going on in there. If I'm not in that dressing room, I can't say or do anything stupid or criminal.

What I can do is check on the food in the truck and maybe run another tray of something in, unless the party's over, which it probably is after a buzzkill like that. I know Laura's OK. Stratton won't let anything else happen. I get the truck key and fob thing out.

Thoughts swirl:

My girl stuck up for me.

Gloria Jensen is out of control.

My girl stuck up for me.

Could Gloria be as insecure as she seems? Stars, they can worry about every-thing: losing their talent, losing their voice, getting sick or hurt, losing their wealth from some trusted person stealing from them or their own stupidity, losing their fans to newer performers. I can get all that.

The back door of the truck is unlocked. It's closed but unlocked. Did I forget to lock it? This is not right.

I climb in and look around carefully. Nobody's here. Nothing missing, far as I can tell. OK. I set the keyring on the little counter over the cold cases. Just breathe, calm down, check on the stuff in the warming ovens.

As I move to that side of the truck, I trip on something soft, like a pile of linens, that wasn't there before.

The pile grunts.

CHAPTER 48

DON'T PANIC

I catch myself from falling, but my heart staggers in my chest.

Before I can leap away, the rag pile erupts like a shrub zombie in a horror movie I saw. The title was in fact *Shrub Zombies.* Sequel to the better-known *Tree Zombies.*

I dodge, but Wade Kullen's arm is around my neck. He flings me down, grabs the keyring from the countertop, and jumps out. The side of my head hits the floor, but I don't go unconscious. I see Kullen with a focused, intent look in his eyes, as he slams the door shut before I get to my feet. I hear him quickly insert the key and turn it.

I throw myself at the interior latch, but I'm locked in. You'd think there'd be a fail-safe latch somehow, like in car trunks these days, where a person can get out.

"Hey! Hey! Let me out!" I pound on the door, not because I think he has any intention of opening it, but in case anybody else can hear.

The cab door opens and closes, the engine starts up, and off we go.

It's all pretty clear. Kullen, upon leaving the theater and seeing the police cars, and maybe even spotting cops walking around, fled to the rear, saw this box truck as a great hiding place, tried the back door, found it unlocked. No doubt he was checking his watch and deciding when it would be safe to jump out and get away. Maybe he fell asleep back here.

Whatever the case, due to my negligence, I'd given him everything he needed: a hideout, and now a getaway vehicle with me as a prisoner. Slick of him to grab the keys.

The truck rumbles forward. I hang on as it sways and picks up speed, cornering into the street. I shout some more. Maybe somebody will hear and call 911. Not sure how soundproof this box is.

"I'm being kidnapped! Help! Fire! Call the police! Stop this truck! I'm a prisoner!"

I picture people on the sidewalks on their way here or there.

"Huh, did you hear that?"

"Yeah. Unusual."

"Yeah."

"Huh."

I bang on the side. The truck is distinctive, painted bright red, with the name of the rental company on the side in white. Not the greatest getaway vehicle, but of course when you're on the run, you switch vehicles as often as you safely can. He'll want to ditch this truck soon.

Don't panic.

It's gonna make no sense for Kullen to kill me.

One thing about murder, though, it really is an effective problem-solving tool. You have to admit it. You might cause yourself a whole raft of future problems, but you've solved the present one, at least. You come home unexpectedly and find your wife in bed with your bestie? Now that's a problem. Bang-bang shoot-shoot, problem solved. Suddenly a slew of new problems. Maybe you can deal with those. Maybe you won't get caught. You're smart, you're not an idiot. You can figure out what to do. Right. Some do. There are thousands—millions, maybe—of killers enjoying life out there.

A hooker pal of mine told me how she beat her pimp to death in Kansas City with a chair, skipped over his body there on the motel rug, blotted her lip where he'd split it, left town that night, and was free ever since. Never apprehended, never questioned for it. I'm sure she didn't brag about it much, though. She overdosed a few months later. Narcan wasn't really a thing then. Rhonda was her name.

So I'm tumbling around in here with these odd thoughts going through my head, but in another minute I get my mental act together. From the suddenly smoother movement, I figure Kullen has gotten us onto an expressway. Hopefully he'll get stopped for speeding or something, but he's probably being too careful for that. He's gonna have to get himself out of this truck, though, before it hits the police radio.

I find my coat and put it on. I grab a serving tray and jam it into the door latch, then I arrange some other stuff. When Kullen opens that door, he won't find me helpless.

CHAPTER 49

THIS WASN'T SUPPOSED TO HAPPEN

It took a little bit of time for Stratton to sort out the catfight. Gloria Jensen screeched about assault, but Stratton, backed up by Paladino and several Old Musicians, got her to understand there were twenty witnesses who saw her start it.

Now an Old Musician—thin face, soul patch, gold earring—convinces Gloria to let him escort her to her car. Doing everybody a favor.

"I do feel tired," she says, patting her hair as if reluctant to go. However, the full force of her embarrassment has broken upon her. She exits.

A few other guests trail out, but some stay to visit and gossip. This little incident will go down as a characteristic part of her legend.

As Laura comes fully out of her fight stance, her eyes meet Stratton's. "Keep the party going," he tells her with a smile. "I'll check on your mom."

Truck's not there. No Bambi. He calls 911 and explains the situation while hunting a little bit for Bambi, but he knows she's gone. He phones Alvarez and Sgt. Phillips. He talks rapidly and clearly. If there's one thing he can do, it's keep cool in a crisis. You face enough thousand-acre wildfires, you learn to stay calm, quit, or die.

In the dressing room, he has no choice but to inform the party.

"I can't believe it," says Paladino. He's sitting, shoulders down, exhausted, in one of the lounge chairs.

"Vic, listen to me." Stratton stands with his feet apart, fists on hips. "Joe Myers is an alias for a guy named Wade Kullen. He's wanted for questioning in Sandy's murder. I believe he's abducted Ba—uh, Celeste in the catering truck."

Laura gives out a tight sound and rushes to see for herself. Stratton likes her: an unpredictable spirit. He likes her mom too. Defiant, determined women, both of them. Not sophisticated. Which is fine.

Following after Laura, he asks about Bambi's phone.

"Ah!" They return to the dressing room and Laura scrambles for it, hoping maybe Bambi took it with her, but no, there it is in the cubby with her wallet.

"We have to go after them!" Laura almost shouts in her panic. "Where's your car?"

Stratton wishes he could pick her up and soothe her like he would a puppy. He takes her cold hands into his. "We have no idea which way they went. The police are our best option right now. They'll find that truck quicker than we ever could."

The party guests clear out; the theater needs to close. The stage manager, Tony, who's been clued in about the truck and Celeste, produces a large tote bin for the leftovers. "The staff will appreciate it."

Laura paces the dressing room desperately.

She's gone.

Bam is gone again.

Left me again.

Taken?

Alive?

Dead?

This wasn't supposed to happen.

I thought we were safe.

At last.

Sunpod comes forward from the corner she'd retreated into after calling upon the Great Spirit. "Here, now," she says kindly in her weightless voice, "let's tidy all this up together."

Laura stares at her.

Sunpod tells her, "It's better to be busy."

Laura looks to Stratton. He nods gravely.

They're right.

She catches a glimpse of herself in one of the mirrors.

You look stupid. You're not a child. You've been through this before.

You know you can take care of yourself.

"Yes." Laura joins Sunpod, who knows just what to do first, second, and third.

The two women shift the leftover food into the tote, and Tony ducks out, saying, "When you guys get things straightened out, call me and we'll arrange for you to pick up all this food equipment." Sunpod and Laura stack trays and warming dishes, extinguish Sterno cans, and collect plates and napkins.

Stratton helps, watching Laura out of the corner of his eye. What is she thinking, what is she feeling? After a few minutes, she cracks. He saw it coming: the quivering face, the clenching hands. Laura retreats to a wall, crouches sideways against it, and forms herself into the smallest ball possible, burying her head in her arms.

Sunpod goes to her. "Hey, hon, hey."

"Leave me alone."

Paladino, who's been continuing to sit in a funk, says halfheartedly, "Everything's going to be all right."

Sunpod squats next to Laura. She places her hand on the back of her neck. Laura lets it be. Sunpod sweeps her hand firmly down her spine to her butt. Then she repeats it. To Stratton's eye, the gesture seems odd, heavy. But perhaps somehow better than gentle patting. One more time, slowly. Three times total.

Incredibly, Laura snaps out of it. Lifts her head.

"You're all right," Sunpod tells her. "We need you to be up." Sunpod's coming through here.

Laura looks around. Everyone is quiet.

"Take your time," says Stratton.

Laura sits, then rises up tall.

"You're all right," Sunpod repeats.

"Yeah," she agrees. "What did you just do?"

"I hit all your chakras."

"My what?"

CHAPTER 50

OF COURSE HE'D HAVE A GUN

After twenty or thirty minutes, with multiple turns, stops, and starts, the truck slows. The ride turns jolty, and I'm guessing we're on dirt or gravel. I hear the tires crunching.

The woods.

Somewhere.

I listen as Kullen kills the engine, climbs out, fiddles with the key. The serving tray I'd wedged in there gives him little trouble. He flings open the box door.

Cold night air rushes in. It's pitch-dark in the truck, but there's a wash of faint light behind Kullen in that doorway. I'm crouching behind the barricade I built of champagne cases, trays, pans, rags, and the like. Peeking over the top. Normally, the overhead light in the box goes on automatically when the door is opened. I'd reached up with the weighty stone rolling pin Laura had insisted we bring, and broken it out.

Kullen's silhouette is bearish in his winter puff coat. I duck down as he lifts his arm in a gesture we've all seen a million times in the movies.

Pop! Pop-pp-pop! Pop!

Sharp and sudden. I thought he might do that. And I hoped my barricade would keep me safe from the bullets. Depends on how powerful his gun is.

Whenever anybody starts shooting, your heart jumps into hyperdrive, though mine already was going pretty fast.

How did I know he'd have a gun? All lowlifes like him carry a gun, if they can possibly afford or trade drugs for one. Of course he'd have a gun.

As soon as the first *pop* happens, I scream. I hear the bullets bouncing around the truck box. I cover my head with my arms. A champagne bottle explodes. When the shooting stops—just a few seconds—I moan loudly in pain, then trail off. My ears are ringing, and I expect his are too, but I think he can hear me.

My would-be killer stays silent, waiting. He can't tell exactly where I am, but he fires once more, for the heck of it, I guess.

I didn't have a ton of choices here. I could have tried to push past him as soon as he opened the door, but he could have grabbed me. If he didn't catch me and I took off running, then great if he didn't drill me with a bullet in the back. Plus, I had no idea whether I had any place to run to. Where were we?

He's got choices. He could walk away now. He could check on me. But he can't see in here very well, so he'll have to kick around to find me.

Every bullet you fire risks attracting attention. The gun's a semiautomatic, no doubt, with at least a few rounds left in it. Seems we're in a fairly isolated place, but you never know who might be around.

I'm ready either way. I can't afford a struggle, I can't win a fight.

Kullen climbs into the truck box, I feel the movement. He takes a step forward, then another. I hear him breathing now, panting with excitement and fear.

This guy is not a battle-hardened supervillain. Somebody like him would naturally be in a state of tight panic, making it up as he goes, trying to force his brain a step ahead of his situation.

From my squatting position, I throw a serving spoon past him. It hits the side wall, and he turns toward the clang. I bounce up and whack his head with the good old stone rolling pin.

Oh, baby, I connected! Got him smack in the side of the skull. My timing was perfect. He staggers and reaches for me, but I'm quicker than he is now. I wallop his head again, same side. He crumples.

Excellent.

Having noted that his gun was in his right hand, I scrabble around and find it, loosely clutched in his fingers. I yank it away and now everything is much better.

He's unconscious, but he'll surely come around pretty soon, unless I killed him, which is possible. That would complicate my life for a little bit, but oh well. I chuck the rolling pin into the woods.

I hunt through his coat pockets, find his phone, yay, find the key and ignition fob for the truck. He's slumped over quite a bit, so I can't reach the rest of his pockets to see if he has any other weapon or even perhaps a second phone.

He moves a little, groans. It's only been 20 seconds or so that he's been out. Definitely less than a minute. I jump out of the truck.

His phone is locked: the fingerprint symbol appears when I fiddle with it. No bars, besides. I'd love to get in touch with somebody, anybody.

Do I have the guts?

No time to think.

I've seen it on the TV shows.

I climb into the truck. My heart is hammering so hard I can feel it in my head. I fish for Kullen's right thumb, grab it, and mash it onto the screen.

It works. Open. I try 911, but no dice. Dead quiet, zero signal, which I usually only see in certain parts of the UP. A bit of bad luck here. I keep the phone open by swiping around on the home screen every few seconds.

I've never owned a gun, but Connie Blue Smoke has three. She took me out shooting a few times, having first given me safety lessons. So I know enough.

We're in a wooded place. The night is clear and there's a moon, nearly full, so I can see. My eyes adjusted to the dark of the truck during the ride. The moonlight filters through the bare trees overhead.

It's freezing, and my shoes crunch over a thin cereal of snow and forest litter as I look around. Just woods. I can't see any lights or houses in the distance. There are plenty of patches of scrub and woods like this on the outskirts of metro Detroit. Places that haven't been developed yet, little scrubby preserves. These night woods smell of cold earth. The kind of smell that makes you want to be indoors next to a wood-fire stove.

The gun is indeed a semiautomatic, black and tough-looking. I press the magazine latch, and the bar of ammo drops into my hand. I can tell that it's about half full. I ram it back in. Carefully, I keep my finger off the trigger.

I doubt Kullen would have a second gun on him, but he might have a knife, which he could throw, I guess.

"Hey, Wade!" I call. "Wake up."

To be honest, I'm glad we're in the woods. I feel safer here than in the city. It's easy to run in the woods, it's easy to hide if you don't mind getting dirty. The most dangerous thing you can encounter in the woods is a drunken hunter. Wear blaze-orange during deer season, that's what I do. Even in town.

These woods are winter nighttime silent. I know the bare trees will whoosh a bit if a breeze comes up. Animals moving around make their noises in the dry frostiness. Not much activity right now, though. A hungry owl perched up high might be watching all this, wondering if I'll stir up a mouse or two. Nobody's moving around for fun.

"Get alert, I'm talking to you." I've been thinking fast. "Wade, Wade, we gotta talk. You OK? I know you can hear me."

Sounds of movement in the truck box. He's sitting up, feeling his head. Wonder if it's bloody. Probably is. Another groan.

"I'm pretty sure the police will be around here soon. So let's get some stuff clear. I can help you out of this mess."

"How?" Ah, there he is. Husky voice, lowered to sound tough. Practically everybody in Balsam Ridge grew up talking like that.

"I already know you killed Sandy O'Rourke, and about half a million reasons why."

A snort, a scoff. A scrabbling sound.

"Nice juicy insurance policy, shared by Sandy's dad with you. I have your gun, by the way." After a pause, the scrabbling continues.

I fire off a round into the ground.

The scrabbling stops. A despairing grunt.

"I'll let you go. Drive the truck out, take off on foot, whatever. I'll wait here. We'll talk first, though."

I'm sure glad I have my warm coat on. "You and William O'Rourke will split up the insurance money when it comes in, right? Nice of Sandy to take out that policy. Maybe you'll manage to get it all. That'll be nice. Hopefully that'll happen. O'Rourke could go back on his word to split the money with you, saying, hey, I'll turn you in for killing Sandy. But all you'd have to tell him is how you'd implicate him as well. And then that money, if the insurance company can't get out of paying, would get spent on lawyers. For O'Rourke, not you."

"I won't go down alone for this."

Righto. "You think I'm a threat to you, but I'm not, I'm actually on your side. Do you know me?"

"No."

"I was married to Gordy Walsh. I'm Bambi."

It was like talking into the mouth of a cave.

"Why don't you come out of the truck? Sit down in the doorway, OK? Yeah, that's it."

Kullen makes his way unsteadily, shuffling. And now, as he weakly sits himself down on the doorsill, I see him well enough in the moonlight.

He looks pretty lousy. Blood shines down half of his head and neck. But he's staring at me and pulling himself together.

"Wade. You've got something over Gordy. I want in on it."

"Why?" OK, no denial.

"Money."

"There's no more money. Why did you hit me?"

"Dude. Seriously. You were shooting at me."

A scoffing grunt.

"Listen. Gordy and I got divorced. We had a daughter. He abused her, it was terrible. I hate his guts and will keep hating his guts until I die. I'm glad you framed him for Sandy, but there's a problem with that."

"What problem?"

So right! OK! No denial of framing Gordy. It's astonishing what people will give up without realizing.

"Listen. I'm getting my act together. I know he's been paying you for something. Here's the thing. Are you listening?"

"Yeah."

"There's more money. A lot more."

"From Gordy? How would—"

"No. From our daughter. She's coming into some money soon. A relative died. Big amount of money. But Gordy's going to have control of it. Even in prison, he'll have control. I know it's insane, but that's what the judge says."

"How much money, and why would—"

"A lot. Close to a million dollars. First, I need to know how come you were shaking him down. It has to do with Roberta Summerline, doesn't it?"

Long silence. Bingo.

Eventually, "Gordy killed her."

"He did? Ha, I knew it."

But of course I didn't know. Huge reveal here. So now we know Roberta's not missing. She didn't run away from home, she didn't run off with Wade. She's dead. And Wade knows she's dead. That's a puzzle piece right there. Who else knows she's dead, besides me, now?

I strongly doubt Gordy murdered Roberta. The 'she' Gordy talked about in that video, that had to be Roberta. Had to be. *When I woke up for real, she was gone.* According to Connie, Roberta was dating Wade just before she disappeared. I demand through the cold darkness, "Tell me how it happened."

"Why?"

"First of all, I have your gun and could easily end your life right here if you act stupid to me, but just listen. Like I said, something's come up that ties you to the murder of Sandy O'Rourke. It could completely muddy the water around Gordy's guilt. Do you know who Ted Alvarez is? Detective Alvarez of the DPD?"

Kullen shifts uneasily. "No." His voice has pain-strain in it. Yeah, he's hurting.

"Well, I know him well, and to be honest, I'm running my own little scam on him. There's evidence against you, and I could—"

"What evidence?"

Pause.

"I think you know. Did you lose something afterward?"

"Afterward."

"Yeah. Well, right, the thing you lost? It got found. And there's a tiny bit of evidence in it."

Silence.

"And someone saw you lose it, as in there was a witness. You fell, and it blew away. I could arrange for it to get lost again. It won't be easy, but I'm pretty sure I can do it. Did you think the police around Masonic were looking for you because you're Paladino's supplier? No, man. It's because they're suddenly thinking you killed Sandy. You, not Gordy."

"Get to the point."

"Right, well, besides that I can help you get off the hook for Sandy. *And, and,* now this is a big *and,* we need to use the Roberta Summerline thing against Gordy *now*. Because I need him to stay in jail. Our daughter needs him to stay in jail." Pause. "So I have stakes here." I learned about stakes from a TV show on how TV mystery shows get made.

My real stakes, of course, are the opposite of what I just said. And I'd already won some. I'd exposed Kullen, hadn't died doing it, and now have the upper hand. If I can help the police with anything incriminating against Kullen, anything more than what they have already—well, Gordy will have an excellent chance of walking. And Laura's angst will be relieved. And maybe she'll let me, once again, be her—well, let's not get ahead of ourselves.

I go, "You can help me, and I can help *you* in two ways. One, I make that bit of solid, DNA-soaked evidence against you go away, and I share my daughter's money with you. And in return, you give me the info I need to feed the police about Gordy and Roberta Summerline."

Silence.

"Dude. Every detective wants to solve cold cases. Come on. You used your leverage on this to squeeze money out of Gordy. Let's just get to it." I touch the record button on his phone screen.

Something rustles in a tree overhead. Some night bird, leaving, right. Got bored listening to this.

At last Kullen launches into the story I've been wanting to hear.

CHAPTER 51

I MEAN, SHE WAS DEAD

Big huge sigh from Kullen. "Me and Bobbie were together, eh? You know. And Gordy was buying drugs offa me. You and him were together then."

Pause.

"Right, Wade." Encouraging.

"So he calls me up and wants some weed. Except I'm not home. Bobbie's there."

"Roberta takes the call."

"Gordy, his car's not workin'. He needs a delivery."

I must have still been living with my parents then.

I go, "So Roberta—Bobbie—makes the delivery. She has access to your stash."

"Yeah. She leaves me a note. I get home. I wait. She don't come home." To whatever cruddy apartment.

"Sooo." Kullen sighs again. "I go over there, I know where he lives. Nobody answers the door, so obviously I kick it in."

Obviously.

Pause.

"Yeah?" I say.

"Well." Kullen makes a gesture like, *Well, that was it. Obviously.*

I give him another few seconds, then go, "Man, what? What happened?"

"You don't know?"

"No!"

"They were together."

"As in they were having sex?"

"Yeah, I mean they heard me come in and they tried to pretend like they weren't, but it was obvious."

"OK, so you caught them. Then what?"

"Well, obviously I go after him."

"You guys fought?"

"Yeah. And for just a second I'm on the floor, eh? And Gordy, he gets his bat and he bashes Bobbie's head in."

"He bashes her?" Which makes no sense.

"Yeah, and she don't move no more."

Pause.

"She died? Right there?"

Pause. Long pause. Is he convincing himself of a lie? A lie in the past he's told to himself over and over again?

Kullen goes on. "So Gordy, he killed her. I mean, she was dead. I saw red, man, I just saw red. I get the bat—yeah, I get the bat away from him, hey, and I smack him. I smack him so hard, man. Didn't kill him, though, as it turns out."

When I woke up, she was gone.

"What did you do with Bobbie?" I figured it was worth the guess.

"I got her out of there. But she was dead."

"Yeah? You *carried* her out?"

"Obviously. And I took her someplace only I know where."

He dumped her body! But this wasn't adding up. Why dump her if Gordy killed her?

Because Gordy didn't kill her.

No time to mull that over. In a cheerful tone, I ask, "Where's that?"

291

"Not telling *you* yet."

Right.

"I took the bat too, with Gordy's prints on it."

"Ah, I see."

"It's all been pretty convenient."

OK. He busted into Gordy's apartment, already mad, caught Gordy and Roberta in the act, or maybe just suspected they were in the act, didn't matter. His anger spikes. Gordy grabs his bat, but Kullen gets it away from him, knocks out Gordy, and takes Roberta and the bat with him. Given that it seemed she was cheating on him with Gordy, he kills her with the bat. Naturally. He then dumps her in some remote place. Gordy's prints are on the bat, which is woodburned with his initials, by the way. I remembered that. Kullen knows where the bat and the body are. And oh, yeah, if Gordy and Roberta had had unprotected sex, his semen would be in her vagina. But if her body's in some ravine, it's just a skeleton by now, at best. That's a puzzle I don't pursue at the moment.

"Why," I ask, "did you dump her instead of just call the police?"

"Baaambi," he says. "Baaambi."

I cut the recording on his phone.

"Oh," I go. "Drugs. OK, so you have what it takes for the police to nail Gordy for Roberta Summerline. This is excellent." I don't ask him how he'd explain any number of details.

"And you were blackmailing Gordy about this."

"I wouldn't call it that, exactly. He paid me voluntarily."

"I'm sure he sees it different."

We hang there for a minute.

"You gotta see a doctor," I tell him. "Let's get out of here. I think we could take the truck, ditch it in the nearest parking lot, and grab us something else to drive. OK?"

"OK." Hard breathing. "I'm not feeling so good. I think I'm gonna vom."

He's slumped against the doorframe, legs hanging down.

I flip the gun's safety on and stick it in my coat pocket. A few quick steps and I'm on him. He looks up, surprised. I grab his legs and sort of hike him into the truck box. While I'm shutting the door I get the key out, stab it into the lock, and he's safe in there for now. I hear him retch.

I take a minute to smooth myself down.

Then I climb into the cab and start her up.

CHAPTER 52

THEN THE STORY DIVERGES

Upon depositing Kullen into the cordial arms of the team at police head-quarters, where he was immediately booked on vehicle theft and kidnap-ping (of me), with other charges pending, I briefed Alvarez about the Roberta Summerline story. I played the recording from Kullen's phone.

I said, "This is part of it. He'll probably repeat all this to you guys, blaming Roberta's murder on Gordy. But until now, nobody but him knew she was dead."

"Right," said Alvarez.

"I'm pretty sure this wouldn't be admissible in court, right?"

"Actually, I'm not sure. You're a witness to what he said."

"Yeah, but I had a gun pointed at him."

He gave me a flat look. "Did you?"

"Shutting up."

Huge smile from Alvarez.

Stratton came and gave me a lift to Paladino's, where Laura waited. She prac-tically knocked me over with a shrieking hug, and I stroked her hair and just let her emotions be. Carefully.

"I love you, honey," I murmured into her hair.

She mumbled something I couldn't catch. That was OK.

My charade of being Celeste LaPorte was over, thankfully.

"I knew it all along," said Paladino, looking glum in the kitchen, where we'd all gravitated to.

"You did not," I said. "Aren't you happy about your concert? Has the glow disappeared so fast?"

"It has."

Stratton gave me a little look, knowing look.

Now I'm in an interview room at the jail on Monday, with Alvarez and Gordy. Detective Podyak, the lead investigator on the Sandy O'Rourke case, is there as well.

Also crammed in with us is Tarik Ayoub, Gordy's lawyer. I recognized him from the interrogation video of seemingly so long ago.

Gordy needs a haircut. Is there a barber in the jail, to clean up guys when they have to appear in court? My ex's face is pale, haggard, his expression almost slack. Yes, I would say his past mistakes—and the contemplation of them from a locked cell—have taken a serious toll on him. Oh, yes.

We're all hunched on hard chairs around a small steel table. A bottle of yellow Gatorade sits in front of Gordy and he sips from it as we talk.

Podyak, a white guy in a sharp suit and polished black shoes, goes, "We're pretty sure you're innocent of Ms. O'Rourke's murder. We're looking at somebody else."

Gordy lets out a long breath. He looks at Podyak, incredulous.

Podyak says, "Do you know who it is?"

"I sure hope it's Kullen."

Now everybody breathes out.

Ayoub says, looking reproachfully at Podyak, "The lack of blood spatter on Mr. Walsh should have been given more weight at the outset." Podyak shrugs.

Alvarez, sharp of chin but relaxed of manner, says, "Kullen's talking to us about another murder."

Gordy looks at his lawyer.

Ayoub, a stocky guy in a white shirt and tie but no coat, says, "I've already told you not to say anything. But if you want to go ahead, I can try to advise."

"I want to talk about this." Gordy's energy seems to be building up. He gulps the sweet drink and rubs his arms. "I'm a victim and a witness, not a killer."

I go, "I think it's your best chance, right here. The videotape got ruined. What did you say on it?"

Deep breath. Gordy tells a story that matches up with Kullen's to a point. Roughly twenty years ago Roberta Summerline arrived at Gordy's apartment with some marijuana. They lit up together, one thing led to another, and they had sex. Kullen busts in. Then the story diverges.

"He was out of control, eh?" Gordy shakes his head. "I heard him breaking in. I jumped out of bed and put on my pants. I grabbed my bat but I never had a chance to swing it at him. Roberta tried to get it away from me, and that slowed me down. You've seen Kullen, he's an ox. Least he was then, anyway. Twenty-two-year-old ox. He got ahold of the bat, and that's the last thing I knew for sure. Lucky he didn't kill me. I was on the floor in like a fog."

He takes a breath or two, remembering. "I was aware of them leaving, he hustled her out of there. She was scared, she was crying and struggling. Next day I went to the doctor's, my head hurt so bad. He said I had a concussion and a broken nose. My head and my face hurt for weeks."

Gordy takes another gulp of the drink, wipes his mouth on the back of his hand. "I went looking for them after I left the doctor's the next day. Didn't find either one of 'em. Asked around. A week went by. A month. Nothing. The other Kullen boys didn't seem to know anything about Wade. Probably lying. Roberta's family? Scuzzbags, all of them. That stepmother, ugh. You knew them."

I did, well enough. I ask, "Why is Roberta's cheerleader bracelet in your box at home?"

Pause. "You found that, eh?"

"Yeah."

"How did you know what it was?"

"Connie Blue Smoke and I figured it out. You remember her."

He leans back, scrubs his face in his hands, then looks up to me. "I found it on the floor. It must have come off when he grabbed her to go. I don't know. I kept it to remind myself of my failure."

"Failure?" asks Alvarez.

"To protect myself."

"And her?" I prompt.

"Yeah."

I go, "Deep down, you knew—"

"Something terrible'd happened to her. I didn't act forceful enough. I guess that was partly why I got into the booze and drugs so bad. Trying to keep that down."

Alvarez says, "So you and Roberta had sex that day. Did you wear a condom?"

"No."

I wince. Was hoping for a yes there, given the possibility of semen evidence. But what about the body?

Gordy goes on, "Kullen told me about the evidence only he knows about. He's been squeezing me for money since he got to Detroit a couple years ago."

Detective Podyak says, "Why did you pay him?"

Gordy scoffs. "You know, it's funny. He didn't come for me. I went after him. I heard he was in Detroit, and I tracked him down. It wasn't all that hard, you know, a couple people here knew him. He came to town to try his hand at something, anything different from the dimwit stuff he'd been doing up north."

Everybody in the little room is listening closely.

"I confronted him about Roberta in a bar. I remember that clearly. You wouldn't believe how that went. He was glad to see me!" Gordy's voice spikes up. "He admitted to killing her! After he took her out of my apartment! I go, *I'm gonna get you.* And he goes, *No, you idiot, I'm gonna get YOU.*"

Pause. Gordy takes a deep breath, collects himself. "Wade remembered how he used my bat—the old wood one, with my initials burned in! Fingerprints, well,

297

them too, I guess, but who cares, it's my bat. He took the bat along with Roberta. He kills her with it, dumps her, way back then. And now, OK, he's in Detroit, things aren't going well for him, he's back to dealing drugs but he's made a few mistakes."

I go, "Do you know if Roberta's body was ever found?"

"I don't know. He says it was, and she was a Jane Doe. No ID on her. Maybe my DNA's somewhere in some database, eh? I don't know if he was lying. But I was scared. I was pulling my life together and I didn't want it ruined. He said he'd gladly keep quiet if I gave him ten thousand dollars."

"Wow."

"I paid him. I knew that wouldn't be the end of it, though, and it wasn't. I considered killing him, I honestly did. I sure hope he goes up for Sandy. But this other thing ..."

The rest of us in the room all go like, "Yeah ... yeah ..."

"Eventually I was broke. I told him I don't care, go ahead and tell the police I killed Roberta. Bring forth your evidence. He didn't, though. I think he might not be so sure of himself on that one. Makes me sick, all the money I gave him."

We sit and think about that. Podyak and Alvarez leave the room to confer.

As the lawyer Ayoub makes some notes, I decide to get at something else.

"I need you to admit something, Gordy." I drill him as hard as I can with my eyes. "Why did you get Laura out of foster?"

He looks at his hands on the tabletop for a long time. "Well, she's my kid and I love her."

"That's not an answer. She was always your kid and you were always supposed to love her."

Uncomfortable silence.

"So, how come?"

"You're playing a game with me."

"Yeah, and you're losing. Look, I know about the money from uncle what's-his-name. Uncle Eric. You know Laura doesn't."

Silence. Direct hit. Ayoub looks up from his writing.

"You got her back with you when you found out about that trust money," I go. "You set up a joint bank account with her. When she turns 18 on April first, you're gonna help whoever's holding that money—Uncle Eric's lawyer or whoever—dump that money into that account, and then you're gonna drain it. And you engineered all that before Kullen came at you for the blackmail money, so you can't use him as an excuse."

Silence. It's so satisfying when you can stop a scumbag.

"Here's one thing you're gonna do. In exchange for me not telling Laura your plan, you're—as soon as you're out of here—you're gonna tell her to set up a bank account in her name only. Make up a reason, eh? You'll tell me that account number, and when I get back to Balsam Ridge, I'm going to give that information to the lawyer."

"So." Quietly. Head down. "Laura won't know."

"She won't know. You'll still be her hero for getting her out of foster. Cuz you love her."

"OK."

CHAPTER 53

A JUNCTION OF INTERESTS

Wednesday morning, now, Gordy's house.

The neighborhood is calm this day, the house silent except for the creak of my footsteps and an occasional shudder from the radiators. I stand in the living room. "Well, Sandy, it looks like your killer will get his due," I tell her loud and clear. "That should help you rest easier, right? No need to ever think of haunting Gordy, right?" I sit down on a cushion on the dining room floor just to think for a while.

One other thing we all learned from Gordy was how Wade Kullen, as Joe Myers, found his way into Vic Paladino's inner circle. Simple. While extorting money from Gordy, he happened to meet Sandy, then Gordy's girlfriend. When they broke up, Kullen knew about it. He thought Sandy was hot, but by the time he got around to tracking her down, she'd hooked up with Paladino. Seeing a possible new drug client with loads of money and connections, he wormed his way, via his acquaintance with Sandy, into Paladino's life. For a lowlife criminal, he acted smart about it all, clean-cutting himself up, and making himself likable to Paladino. He did all the doctor-shopping necessary to acquire the right pills, bribed the right corrupt pharmacists to fill fake prescriptions. He did all the exact correct maneuvers somebody like Paladino couldn't do on his own.

One conclusion here is, it's a lot easier to weasel your way into a famous person's life than you might think. There just has to be a junction of interests. And then a bit of just the right leverage.

Not every last shred of business is finished here, but I can only take so much of Detroit at one time. Understatement of the year.

I get my clothes and toiletries stowed in my backpack, then I check over my toolkit. Everything's there except my flashlight.

I know I used it to scope around the basement, also in the front closet where I found Gordy's treasure box. I look around. I go upstairs to Laura's room where I slept the last few nights, having moved out from my suite at Paladino's. The handy, heavy little thing is nowhere to be found. I like that flashlight. One of the more quality things I own.

You know how sometimes when you lose something you just have to be super methodical? You start looking in places you know it's not, but sometimes, well, it is, because your brain jumped the tracks for a minute.

I run my hands over the bed, under the pillow. I'd laundered the sheets and towels early that morning and remade the bed, so I know the flashlight isn't there. I take every book off the shelves of the little bookcase. There's dust, so I run a cloth over the shelves before putting the books back. No flashlight. It's only 10:30, so there's time to keep looking. I can just about get to Balsam Ridge before full dark if I leave in the next hour.

I open Laura's small bureau drawers, having already snooped through them. No flashlight. I sit down at her desk, imagining her studying here. I open the drawers, three of them on the right side of the kneehole. School papers, a red plastic pencil box with a broken hinge. A few lipsticks, some little figurines of cartoon people.

The bottom drawer sticks when I tug.

I yank harder, and it scrapes open. My throat goes tight. A stack of envelopes, no, two stacks, addressed to Laura in my handwriting, so many that they made the drawer bind. The notecards I'd sent her over the years, some forwarded through the foster office before she got back with Gordy. They fill the little drawer with—what? Cheer? Sadness?

I decide she kept them out of hope. I thumb through one of the stacks. It would seem she held onto them all, hauling around a growing pile of birthday cards, Christmas cards. Notes and letters just to say hello when I was thinking about her and missing her so much, in my disjointed way, in spite of my ridiculous, selfish, addict, prostitute behavior.

Like I think I said before, I had some nice Gwen Frostic notepapers, then when those ran out I bought cheap, goofy cards, sentimental cards with rhymes about a dear daughter and how much she's cherished, yadda. I'd stick a little money inside when I could.

Did it hurt her to receive these cards? I imagine it did. *Oh, here's a card from my mom who can't even keep herself sober for my sake.*

If she threw the cards away, she'd be throwing little splinters of me away. Of herself?

Why am I crying? Joy? Same old regret?

I go down to the kitchen and fix myself one last mug of tea, to try to calm down before hitting the road. I sit sipping in the soft light of the kitchen. Goodbye, old crummy mansion. Goodbye, strangely heartless fireplace. I suppose I could have gathered a few sticks from somewhere and tried to make a cheery blaze, but I never wanted to hang out in that living room much from the get-go.

A pounding on the front door.

Alvarez?

I open it, mug in hand.

Stratton. Lanky in his sheepskin coat and work boots.

"I need you," he says, looking intense.

"I didn't think we'd have this conversation so soon."

"It's Vic."

"Oh."

"He's in trouble. Will you come with me, please?"

"Why me?"

"He likes you, you know that. Your way of talking to him is ... good."

I look at him. His face is hopeful. Soft smile. "I'm tired, Chuck. I want to go home."

"Please."

I set down my mug and get my purse.

As we zip along Woodward towards downtown in his car he tells me, "I found him there once before when he got like this."

"Got like what?"

"You'll see. I hope he's there."

The city is winter-tired, with none of the few pedestrians smiling as they trudge along the sidewalks. Today's sky has gone from the dead-white of thin overcast to a scudding show of bluish-gray clouds ramming in from the northwest. People's coats are blowing about.

"After Sandy was killed, Vic was scared," Stratton tells me. "He lied to the police investigators about what he was doing that day."

"What was he doing?"

"Playing cop. You know he's got this thing where he sees himself as a friend to kids? Wants to protect them from drugs?"

"Don't make me laugh."

"It's real. He got himself in the middle of a scrap between a bunch of rich-kid dealers back of that mall they hang out at, Somerset. A kid got shot. Didn't die. Fortunately Vic didn't have his gun on him, and he got out of there right away. He was in his street disguise—hat and sunglasses, basically—and nobody recognized him, which is good on one hand. But on the other, he couldn't prove where he was the afternoon and evening of Sandy's death."

"How totally ridiculous."

"Yeah."

As we're nearing the riverfront, Alvarez calls me.

"The police got a warrant to search Wade Kullen's apartment," he says, "which yielded a pair of boots with four or five small drops of blood on them, plus a shirt and pants belonging to Gordy."

"Blood on his boots?"

Stratton nods, gathering what this is about.

Alvarez says, "Yeah, that's a biggie. The lab's working on it now. I have little doubt that blood is Sandy O'Rourke's."

"Makes sense." I gaze out the window as the downtown storefronts and building lobbies slide by.

"Yeah. Kullen figured out quite a few details in advance, but he didn't think about his boots. They were brown, and I guess the blood wasn't really noticeable on them. He had to have taken them off to change his pants, then put them on again. The blood wasn't smudged as if with a rag, so he must have thought he was clean. That, on top of the plastic bag with DNA, was enough for the police to ask the Wayne County Prosecutor to charge Kullen with Sandy O'Rourke's murder."

"And drop it against Gordy."

"Yeah."

"When will they let him out?"

"Whenever the prosecutor's satisfied and gets the paperwork done. Day or two, I guess?"

According to Alvarez, the investigators put pressure on William O'Rourke to admit that Kullen showed up after the murder to demand all the money O'Rourke had.

"'I solved your problem, now you solve mine,' he supposedly said."

"So," I go, "it's one guy's word against the other, though?"

"Yeah, but—"

"It would be a cherry on top if you guys arrest O'Rourke for conspiracy. That would be fine with me."

Alvarez laughs and we hang up. I fill in Stratton. "What a stupid mess, eh?"

"Yeah," he says, driving. He goes east on Jefferson, then jogs down to Atwater and left on that.

"With Kullen locked up," I comment, "now where's Vic gonna get his drugs?"

"He's got a stash at home, but it won't last long. He wanted me to help him develop some other source, and I told him to kick rocks."

"So he's freaking. He needs to get to inpatient treatment right now."

Stratton pulls over at the Aretha, cold and desolate on the waterfront.

"Oh," I go.

"What?"

"He talked to me about how much this place means to him."

We get out of the warm car into the raw wind of the riverfront.

At the moment no kids are snowboarding the berm. Laura had told me about that. They'd worn the snow down to the dead grass and would have to wait for another storm.

"Let's keep quiet," says Stratton. We make our way across the frozen moat, our boots squeaking softly. We hike up the berm, going diagonally for easier walking. At the top of the slope we step into the deserted amphitheater. The ice-white canopy with its serious rigging hovers overhead. Makes me think of angel wings, only the angel is feeling very stern at the moment.

Something catches our attention on the stage platform.

Have you ever seen a sad buck deer? The ones who lose a fight are depressed for a while. They stand without real strength, head down. Same with elk, I would guess.

Vic Paladino is standing just that way, in the middle of the platform.

He's got on a black wool jacket, no hat. Black pants and shoes. He's staring down, hands in his pockets. I can't tell what his expression is.

Stratton motions to me, and we slowly set out down the steps towards the stage. Halfway there, Stratton's boot scuffs a step and Paladino looks up.

"Hi, Vic." Stratton's tone is calm and easy.

"Oh, it's you." Paladino focuses on us, then his eyes drift away. We keep going down towards him. It looks like he's been pulling at his hair, it's all askew in tufts.

I've seen people in catatonic-type states from insanity plus drug withdrawal, but Vic here isn't giving off that same vibe. He's more in touch.

"Mind if we join you?" says Stratton. Without waiting, he climbs onto the platform, turns, and gives me a hand up.

We're all standing now on that cold, bare stage, looking out at the frosty, empty tiers which are lined with chairs during concert season. I feel like we should build an igloo. Although the wind can't knife its way through my parka, I know my face is gonna turn to marble in about five minutes.

The light in here is as flat and bare as everything else.

Stratton clears his throat, then seems at a loss. He looks at me.

"Mr. Vic, sir!" I exclaim. "It's good to see you."

Even though he knows I'm someone named Bambi Pentecost and not Celeste LaPorte, he doesn't know who Bambi Pentecost is.

I ask in a brisk tone, "What are you doing here?"

He focuses on me with a soft smile. "I used to love it here. I used to love it here so much."

I nod encouragingly. It strikes me that nobody has to fix everything right now. Just one little thing at a time.

I go, "It's the dead of winter. We must leave and find hot drinks right now. Mr. Vic. Am I correct? I am correct. We go."

With a grateful glance at me, Stratton says, "She's right. A hot drink's the thing."

Paladino shakes his head. "I don't want to leave here."

We all stand still, our breath coming out in white streams that zip away in the wind from the river. Gotta be patient.

Vic says, "I'm done. I know it now."

"With music?" I ask.

"I'm spent. I still love music, but as a performer, I'm spent. That concert proved it. To me," he adds, as if ready for us to argue.

"It's very cold here," I observe. "I'm cold."

"Well," says Stratton, "when you think about it, lots of performers keep going past when they ought to retire."

Paladino says, "Exactly. I'm sixty-six years old. Money's tight."

I find that hilarious, but I also know rich people can go broke just as easily as anyone else.

Paladino brings me up short when he says, "I'm scared." He turns and looks to the river, flowing there behind the stage, white ice chunks bobbing along in the chop. "I don't know what's gonna happen next."

What would Celeste LaPorte say? "You need," I go, "a third act that's as good or better than music. And it would help if you got your expenses under control."

"I was worried about you," says Stratton.

This needs to conclude. Sternly, I get their attention. "Men!"

I pause. "Men. It is way too cold to keep talking here. I know a café. Here, Mr. Vic. You help me down from here, OK?"

He moves to the edge of the stage. Hops down, offers me his hand.

"Ah, thank you. We go now."

On the way to a soul food café just up Jefferson, Paladino starts to come back to himself. We don't talk, but I sense him relaxing. In the restaurant Stratton's and my glasses fog up. We cram into a booth, and I order hot chocolate for everybody, plus a plate of warm biscuits.

The place is welcoming and smells like heaven. I remembered it from years ago. Good soul food cafés never go out of business. You can count on the hot biscuits.

"Huge plate of them," I specify, "like ten. Lots of butter."

"Sure thing," says the waiter, who wears big black glasses same as Stratton's. Before turning to the kitchen, he pushes them up, and I push mine up.

Our trio sits quietly until the steaming mugs of delicious cocoa arrive. Most of these places only serve pop, coffee, and beer, but I remembered the owner here had a thing for chocolate.

"Now," I say to Paladino, "you tell me all about it."

Between sips, he says, "I'm OK, as you can see. This isn't like the other time."

"When you kinda went psycho." Stratton remembers it, whatever it was.

"Yeah, when I kinda went psycho."

I break a biscuit open, butter a piece, and hand it to Paladino like I would a toddler. The biscuits are almost as big as my fist. Hot, flaky, smelling like some theoretical grandma's kitchen.

"Sandy told me about her work with her father on the new drugs." He munches the biscuit, elbows on the table. He's too tired and sad for manners. "I'm against drugs except when it's me that needs them." He barks a laugh and looks at me. "I know I'm not fooling anybody anymore. I told her I'd be a subject for her experiment—for her thesis on performance anxiety and new medical compounds. I was anxious to do it!"

"I thought that might be the case," I go.

"I helped her, and she was so bright and lovely. She was attracted to me—devil knows why. We both knew if we got involved, that would ... mix things up. Well." He considers. "If she'd never met up with Joe Myers—I mean that Kullen bastard—she would probably ..." Paladino stops. Not looking at anything, he nods to himself and chews slowly.

After a bit, Stratton says, "You know you need to get clean."

"Yeah." Long pause. "Will you help me arrange something?"

"'Course."

"I'll tell you, man," I chip in, "for sure you need to get into a program. But after. Boy howdy, after. That's when I can help you."

Paladino is quiet.

But not terrified.

I'm pleased to see that. Good sign. Being an addict, even a well-managed one like Paladino, is a knife-edge existence. When you're young, you can convince yourself it's fun, living like that. My heart feels a surge of warmth towards Paladino right now. Like a real physical flow of comfy heat.

I comment, "Life's short."

Nobody disagrees. There's definitely a feeling of understanding among the three of us. It feels good, it feels almost like family, somehow.

Chapter 54

Major, Major Rush of Shame Here

eople kept delaying my escape from Detroit. When I get back to Gordy's house, I decide to take just five more minutes to search for my flashlight. I'm on my hands and knees peering under the stove when the door pounds.

Alvarez. He takes off his fedora. I wash my hands and make tea.

It randomly occurs to me that ever since I got to Detroit, I've learned a lot of stuff while drinking beverages with people.

"I'm glad to see you," I tell him as I pour water into the kettle. A jolt of guilt hits me. He's helped me, detective Alvarez has, for days and days now. He's helped me and Laura and Gordy, all because I threatened to tell his wife about our affair if he didn't. Ages ago that affair was, granted, but time never matters to a betrayed mate. Danger abounds.

"Ted, I've barely thanked you. You put your neck on the line for Gordy, I know you did, reaching around in the department, no doubt cashing in any number of favors."

Slight smile from him. He's watching me make tea.

I go on, "You didn't have to do that much. In fact, I realize right now you didn't have to do a thing. You could have lied to me about working behind the scenes but not getting anywhere because of whatever obstacles, and I wouldn't have known any different. It was only because I was mean enough and well, desperate enough, to blackmail you by threatening to—"

"Never mind. You're welcome."

"I forget, do you like sugar in your tea? I don't have any milk."

"Plain's good."

We take our tea cups to the dining room, where we'd sat together before on cushions on the floor. We hunker there, our cups on the rug. Even though the bloody couch is gone, I still don't like to be in the living room.

"Well," I go, "you have something more to tell me about Gordy or Kullen?"

"No. But I am wondering, like you, probably, about that cheerleader up north."

"Yeah, that's a puzzle, still. And maybe a potential danger to Gordy."

"I wouldn't worry much about that aspect. But if that girl's dead and justice hasn't been done—"

I break in, "Then it should be!"

"Yeah."

"Somehow."

That's worth thinking about.

The planes of Ted's face are *composed*—is that the right word? Like without tension. He clears his throat. "Look, Bambi. I know you're not interested in me right now, despite our former—"

Oh, Lordy. OK. Gotta nip this right now, hard. "I'm not interested in anybody right now or ever."

"I know. But—"

"But nothing. But your wife. Darlene."

"Darlene died two years ago."

"What?" If my cup hadn't already been sitting safely on the rug, I'd have dropped it.

"Yes, Bambi. She got stomach cancer, and it took her fast."

"Oh, my God."

"Yeah."

"I—I'm so—Oh, my God. I'm so sorry, Ted. If I—if I'd only ... Oh, my God."

Major, major rush of shame here.

He adjusts his legs, in his nice charcoal-colored wool suit pants, to sit cross-legged. He'd wiped his shoes carefully at the door. I sit cross-legged too, and now we're face to face, there in that disintegrating rented house where a woman died violently for no good reason. Shadows on the ceiling.

Alvarez laces his fingers together and leans forward a little. He watches me thinking.

I go, "So ... when I said ..."

"When you said 'Darlene,' when we first talked, you thought you were holding a gun to my head."

"Yeah."

"But as you see, it was loaded with blanks."

"Blanks."

All I can think is *wow.*

Eventually, I go, "Wow."

We just sit for a while.

At last I ask, "Why?"

A smile from him, easy smile. "I don't know, Bambi. I never thought much of Gordy, from what I knew of him. Besides the murder victim, a truly innocent party here was you guys' daughter."

"Laura."

"Laura. Nice girl. Turned out pretty well, it seems, despite ... everything."

"She has. She has."

"I like her. And I like you."

I give him a warning glare, but he goes on, "But not in the old way I did."

"No?"

"I don't know. I see you differently now, Bambi."

"Huh. Me too."

He eyes me quizzically.

I say, "I mean, I see myself different too. It's like I'm not scrambling for pieces of me anymore. I'm whole. I'm mine."

"You stopped Wade Kullen."

Silently, suddenly, I'm now OK with being Bambi. King of the woods. Can a doe be a king? Why not? It's just a feeling. *I am Bambi Pentecost. Don't call me BB. Consider hard before you mess with me. You don't know what I might do.*

Ted goes, "Do you think you might want to stay in Detroit?"

I blink. "As in ...?"

"As in move here from the UP."

"Uhhh ..."

"Yeah. Laura's probably going to be here for a few more years, what with college, right?"

"I can't, Ted."

"We could be real friends, you and I."

I don't tell him how tempted I was to grab a drink or a pill here and there, since getting to town. I barely acknowledged it to myself, every time it happened. A filmy cloud, like, would pass over me, or maybe through me, and I'd know what I wanted. I wouldn't let the thought get solid, though. It shouldn't make that much of a difference, but back in Balsam Ridge I felt safer, even though that's where I first took a sip of cherry brandy and swallowed my first Valium. Something about the woods, something about the air. The lack of masses of people.

You can't explain everything just so.

CHAPTER 55

AGAINST A GUSTING WIND

Head down against a gusting wind, Laura Walsh makes her way along Cass Avenue toward State Hall for her afternoon class. Today, Wednesday, there'll be a lecture about the effects of collective agriculture on the domestic production of the Soviet Union. Good stuff. She likes getting into the weeds on political science. She'd stayed up late last night catching up on her reading. "Getting into the weeds" was a term she'd picked up from Sandy O'Rourke.

"Laura Pentecost." A woman's voice beside her, clear and startling. Pentecost. She's Walsh, except for that time when she introduced herself to Professor Emily Peltz-Sprague.

The professor falls into step with her, and together they navigate the salt-stained walkway, around and against the stream of people during class change.

Neither woman is wearing a hat. Professor Peltz-Sprague's white, poufy hair flips about in the wind. Gonna look interesting when she gets indoors.

The bare sycamores on Cass toss spasmodically in the gusts.

"Did you get what you wanted from that laptop?" inquires the professor. Definite edge to her tone, there.

"What laptop?"

314

"We really should have coffee again."

"Uh."

"I think I understand what you were doing. You could have just asked."

"No, no."

"When you feel like it, look me up, all right?"

Laura is relieved when the professor peels off at the corner of Kirby.

Sandy.

Sandy, who had helped Laura in all sorts of ways. Basically given her information on being a real grown-up woman. Like it's shabby to hog a table in a café and study there for too long, if the place is full. Most students are either oblivious or feel entitled, Laura observed. Like little things mean a lot, a thank-you gift or a card in your own writing. How to refuse a beer without people thinking you're uptight. "I'm good for now, thanks." She'd used that line just last night at Becka's.

She wonders whether she'll ever feel like meeting the professor for coffee.

Might should.

How come?

Don't know.

CHAPTER 56

SCARY MOVIES WITH POPCORN

I think we can agree that popcorn made fresh in your biggest pot on the stovetop is better than microwave. You have to use enough oil so it doesn't burn, and then of course you have to melt plenty, and I mean pah-lenty, of butter to toss it with, plus then your salt. If you can't afford to buy enough butter, then you can't afford to have decent popcorn. Eat some crackers. I'm sorry.

I divide the first batch into my two large food bowls and bring them out because the amazing has happened. Laura is in my apartment, sitting on my couch. It's three weeks since I left Detroit.

The movie is cued up and ready to go.

"Mmm," says my daughter, nestling her bowl into her lap. "Smells great." She pops a few kernels into her mouth. Munches. Savors. "Yeah."

A dim memory comes into focus. A little girl eating popcorn in toddler fashion, where you grab a bunch, lift it to your face, and then chomp forward as you gradually open your fist. I note Laura has moved on from that to the standard grown-up fingertip method of two or three kernels at a time. The single-kernel eating method is only for compulsive-type people.

We are alone together. My girl came to see me for the weekend. She got on an Indian Trails bus in Detroit early this morning, a Friday in March, it is, and I picked her up at the depot in St. Ignace at ten at night. Super long travel day for her, with layovers in Flint and Bay City. It's after eleven now, black dark and cold outside. She insists she's not tired. An early-March storm is coming up, I can hear it. The blinds are down.

Laura told me what she wanted when we met up at the café at Wayne State. She wanted to sit together and watch scary movies with popcorn. We each have a cold bottle of Faygo Rock & Rye and plenty of napkins. We have our feet up on the coffee table. I gave her a pair of the same kind of thick socks I wear.

I start the movie.

The Birds. Alfred Hitchcock.

It's a good one, right?

I invited her to come, and she did.

I think she doesn't hate me anymore. Not that she ever said she hated me, come to think of it. It was just a vacuum where love might be. Rightly should be. If I'd been a respectable mom, there wouldn't have been such an empty space there in her heart.

What there is of *us* is so much in the distant past. She did text me a thank you for getting her dad out of jail, after I went back home.

Laura doesn't know a whole lot about the UP. She was so young when we reloed to Detroit, she considers herself a Detroiter. My goal is to get her to like the north. I felt such relief when I pointed my car that way on I-75. North.

North.

As I expected, Jimmy took me back at the religious-supplies warehouse, and I resumed operations with Jaunty Taxi. Yesterday I had three fares from St. Ignace to the Soo. Good money. My philodendron, Alan, was in excellent health after his stay with Connie. He's now back in his place on a little table next to the window.

We watch the movie, we eat and drink. My TV's on the small side, but the picture quality's decent. I have only one lamp turned on, low, for atmosphere. The storm outside gets going as the opening scenes roll. We hear wet sleet, then ice crystals, spattering on the windows, behind the shades. The weather report said we'd get maybe three inches of wind-driven snow.

I didn't want one large bowl of popcorn between us, in case Laura needed to squeeze tighter to me, like reflexive, if she got scared. That's why the two bowls for our laps.

We haven't talked much since the night Wade Kullen kidnapped me and pumped bullets in my direction.

During the early banter between Tippi Hedren and Rod Taylor, I imagine myself as the gorgeous, bold-as-brass Melanie Daniels, and Stratton as the masculine, witty Mitch Brennan. In reality, Stratton's much closer to a tough movie hero than I am to a striking leading lady. Boy howdy. I would need so much makeup, for a start. And those clothes of hers. Can you buy replicas of movie clothes? I bet you can, somewhere. Melanie's the wild child, only perfectly chic.

When the birds start to gather, then when they attack the kids at the party—well, I'd seen the picture before, a few times, but incredibly to me Laura hadn't. I think she doubted an old movie could get into her brain that much.

But yeah. She starts to squirm, physically squirm, when those birds are checking out the party from the sky.

"You OK, honey?"

"*Yes.*" Indignant-like. Makes me smile to myself.

Suddenly, when Melanie's waiting outside the school, smoking a cigarette with the birds massing on the monkey bars while the kids sing that creepy song—that part's so good, eh?—the TV goes out. The lights go out at the same instant, and we're in the dark. Power failure. The wind howls louder.

"Oh, my," I go.

Laura makes a sound of distress, like a small animal. I know the sound. She collects herself right away, though, taking a deep breath. I reach for her hand, which grips onto mine pretty strong.

"It's OK, honey." But a power outage in winter here is a serious matter. Within seconds, the temperature in the pitch-black apartment feels cooler.

First things first. "I have candles." I start groping my way towards the kitchen. "Because I never did find my—" A burst of light stops me. My giant shadow on the wall. Silently Laura lights my way to the kitchen cupboard where the candles and matches are. "Laura, honey, that's great, you having a flashlight on your phone. I don't have one on mine." Too cheap for anything but the basics. Plus I don't even know exactly how phone lights work. There's a real lightbulb or something on the back, right, or is it an app on the front? I don't know.

I get a couple of candles out and strike a match. But before I can touch it to a wick, the power comes back on. "Oh, that's lucky." I flip the kitchen light on and turn to Laura, who quickly hides something behind her back. She looks away, as if noticing how interesting my poster of vegetables is. Gift from Connie Blue Smoke when I moved in.

"What's that, honey?" I notice her phone on the counter near her purse, so she wasn't holding it.

"Nothing."

I'm confused, but whatever. "Let's get back to the movie, hey?"

"Yes."

I start to leave the kitchen, but foxily look back in time to see her slip a small, nicely machined black flashlight into her side pants pocket.

For a second, I'm stunned.

"Laura, honey." She meets my eyes, and her expression firms up. I inquire, "Is that my flashlight?"

"No, it's mine."

"Well, mine has a scratch halfway around the butt end, plus a notch in the front rim from when I dropped it on a rock." I stand blocking the kitchen doorway. My kitchen is white with yellow painted cupboards. One window, overlooking the parking lot. Fairly pleasant.

Laura sighs and hands it over.

"I looked all over for this before I left town, you know. When did you get ahold of it?"

Solid and strong, she folds her arms and leans against the counter. "I came to the house once or twice while you were out. I needed a couple things from my room." Her cheeks stretch with a little smile. Young little smile, winning smile. "I looked through your things."

"Of course you would."

"*You* looked through *my* things."

"Of course I did."

"Fair enough, then."

"Except I didn't steal anything of yours. I borrowed that Seneca book, but I put it back before I left."

"Bam, I like that flashlight. I wanted it."

"Well, you have good taste." I heard a clerk say that to a customer in a 7-Eleven once.

In another second I realize something. "You've been carrying it in your pocket ever since?"

No answer.

I hold the light out to her. "Here, keep it. I'll get another one."

"Now I feel bad."

Well, that's something.

"You shouldn't. Seriously. Take it."

"OK."

She shrugs the whole thing off in an instant. The flashlight's back in her pocket.

There are things I'd wish to know about my daughter: primarily, how did she survive as intact as she did? What did she learn, outside of school? How much *street*, you know, did she learn? Were there kind people in her life? Must have been. Smart people? If so, what did she learn from them? Maybe we can talk more about the Stoics and in particular that guy Seneca, who I suspect has been some sort of agent in this conversation. Sounds funny, I know, but that's the best I can explain it.

We return to our popcorn and scary movie, with its pecked eyes, gasoline fires, and splintering doors, and I feel increasingly certain there'll be time in the coming months—years?—for us to talk about all those things, and many more besides.

———————

SPECIAL NOTE

You may know this already, but the simple act of recommending a book strengthens the mind, elevates cheerfulness, and helps de-stress the cardiovascular system. Further studies have confirmed that people who recommend a good book to others experience a higher likelihood of their favorite sports team winning the championship. This is all true.

If you liked this book, please consider posting a review and letting your friends know about it on social media. Fellow readers, and I, will thank you. Because ratings and reviews—even just a word or two—help draw new readers to a possibly valuable experience. If you feel at a loss, here are sample one-sentence reviews, which you are welcome to use verbatim:

"This is one of the most compelling crime novels I've ever read!"

"I wish I could take the charming Bambi Pentecost out to dinner at a fancy restaurant!"

"I loved how the author wove the plot and the characters together into an absolutely dynamite story!"

More good reviews and word-of-mouth mean I can spend more time writing new stuff! With thanks and love,

Elizabeth

ABOUT ELIZABETH

Elizabeth Sims is the author of the Rita Farmer Mysteries, the Lambda and GCLS Goldie Award-winning Lillian Byrd Crime Series, and other fiction, including the standalone novel *Crimes in a Second Language*, which won a Florida Book Award. Her work has been published by a major press (Macmillan) as well as several smaller houses, and she's written short works for numerous collections and magazines. She publishes independently under her personal imprint, Spruce Park Press.

In addition, Elizabeth is an internationally recognized authority on writing, having written scores of feature articles on the craft of writing for *Writer's Digest* magazine. Her instructional title, *You've Got a Book in You: A Stress-Free Guide to Writing the Book of Your Dreams* (Writer's Digest Books) has been specially recognized by National Novel Writing Month and hundreds of other web sites and bloggers. She has taught creative writing at Ringling College of Art and Design in Sarasota, Florida, and at conferences and workshops around the United States.

Elizabeth earned degrees in literature from Michigan State University and Wayne State University, where she won the Tompkins Award for graduate fiction. She's worked as a reporter, photographer, technical writer, bookseller, street busker, ranch hand, corporate executive, certified lifeguard, and symphonic percussionist. Elizabeth belongs to several literary societies as well as American Mensa.

Website: www.ElizabethSims.com

Amazon author page: https://www.amazon.com/author/elizabethsims

BOOKS BY ELIZABETH SIMS

Nonfiction

You've Got a Book in You: A Stress-Free Guide to Writing the Book of Your Dreams
Writing a book is easy and fun—yes, *EASY AND FUN*—but it may not always feel that way. How do you find the time to write? How do you keep momentum? How do you deal with the horror of showing anyone a single sentence of your work-in-progress? The answers remain *fun and easy*, and author Elizabeth Sims will take your hand, dispel your worries, and show you how it's done in this stress-free guide to accomplishing your dream of writing your book.

Shop here: https://www.amazon.com/Youve-Got-Book-You-Stress-Free-ebook/dp/B00CJJWURQ

Fiction

It's not necessary to read either series in order.

The Rita Farmer Mysteries

The Actress [#1]

Aspiring actress and single mother Rita Farmer has gone from struggling to find work to downright desperate. If she doesn't land a paying job soon—horror movie, soap commercial, anything—she's afraid her ex-husband will use her dire financial straits to take away Petey, her cherished four-year-old son. While she's charming the crowd at storytime at the L.A. public library, a celebrity defense attorney approaches her with an unusual job offer: So long as she's discreet, Rita can rake in a thousand dollars a day preparing his client for her appearance in court.

Easy money? Hardly. His client, Eileen Tenaway, is not only a wealthy heiress and a queen of the tabloids but she's been charged with the murder of her own child. The attorney needs Rita to coach Eileen secretly to help her seem more sympathetic, more human. He needs the jury to believe not only her words but the subtle cues of body language, facial expressions, even vocal style. Rita knows she can do it, but what she doesn't know is how determined she'll become to find out what really happened to Eileen's family—once her own life and Petey's life depend on it.

Shop here: http://www.amazon.com/Actress-Rita-Farmer-Mysteries-ebook/dp/B00BQKZX6Y

The Extra [#2]

Rita Farmer knows what it feels like to be flat broke. Even now, when studying to be a lawyer, Rita is so far in debt that she has to scrounge for acting jobs to keep herself and her son afloat. Decked out in police uniform as an extra on a low-budget movie shoot, she wanders into a rough part of town and is pulled into a vicious assault. Rita chases off the assailants but doesn't escape unscathed, and the boy they attacked isn't out of danger yet. His injuries could last the rest of his life.

Rita's heart goes out to him and his grandmother, Amaryllis B. Cubitt, the director of an urban mission that Rita had turned to for help years ago. But the mission has changed from its unassuming past and is now flush with secret donations and gruff guards posted at the doors. Rita can't but wonder if now Amaryllis is too proud to ask for the help she needs.

Shop here: https://www.amazon.com/Extra-Rita-Farmer-Mysteries-Book-ebook/dp/B00CMEW8SY

On Location [#3]

Rita Farmer knows exactly how hard it is to break into the movie business. Acting was the big dream that brought her out to L.A. in the first place. And while she never made the red carpet, that big dream did turn into a modest profession that kept her and her son afloat. So from time to time she'll lend her talents as a favor.

Kenner and Lance de Sauvenard, heirs to a timber fortune, don't really need a favor to make their art film, but since Lance is dating Rita's sister, Gina, there's no way for Rita to worm her way out of a read-through. Gina is all for the project—or at least her new boyfriend—and she goes with Lance to scout locations on his family's land holdings in the Northwest. When they don't return as planned and flood waters start to rise, Rita can't help dashing into the wilds to bring her sister home, and when foul play becomes more and more likely, her sometime lover, George Rowe, is right on her heels.

Shop here: https://www.amazon.com/Location-Rita-Farmer-Mysteries-Book-ebook/dp/B00F0XD5Q8

The Lillian Byrd Crime Series

Holy Hell [#1]

Lillian Byrd is a small-time reporter with a flair for making big-time mistakes—like getting fired for fending off the boss's son with an X-Acto knife and breaking up with her girlfriend for no good reason—so her investigation into the disappearances of women in the Detroit area might not be the best idea. But when one of the missing women turns up dead and Lillian recognizes the bizarrely mutilated corpse, she's in too deep to get out. Of course, it doesn't help that she's still fighting off the boss's son and ducking the intensely aggressive amorous overtures of the roughest dyke in town. Now, after simultaneously blowing the case for the police and revealing herself to the off-kilter killers, she's completely on her own. Can she catch the murderers before they catch up with her?

Shop here: https://www.amazon.com/Holy-Hell-Lillian-Byrd-Crime-ebook /dp/B0052BDMW0

Damn Straight [#2]

- Lambda Literary Award Winner -

After her narrow brush with death in *Holy Hell*, you'd think Lillian Byrd would have learned to keep her head down, but when a friend in crisis calls from California, Lillian jumps on a plane and wings her way from Detroit to Palm Springs—and danger. It's the weekend of the Dinah Shore golf tournament, the wildest women's sporting event in the world, when thousands of lesbians descend on the desert community and take over.

At a pre-championship party, Lillian leaps into a slippery romance with a top LPGA star. But her superstar athlete has a secret: Someone is quietly terrorizing her. Lillian, eager to help, goes undercover as a high-profile reporter, an unhinged nun, and a professional caddie while uncovering layer after disturbing layer of the golfer's past. Finally, with violence erupting at every turn, Lillian discovers her lover's ultimate horrifying secret—and it is not at all what she had guessed. *Damn Straight* sizzles and zings and will have you laughing through your shivers.

Shop here: http://www.amazon.com/Straight-Lillian-Crime-Series-ebook/d p/B005515ANG

Lucky Stiff [#3]

Once again Lillian Byrd is down on her luck, strumming her mandolin for spare quarters alongside Blind Lonnie, Detroit's resident blues guitarist. But a chance encounter with her childhood friend Duane is about to completely turn her life upside-down. One summer night when Lillian was twelve, flames ripped through the Polka Dot, her parents' beloved tavern. Three bodies were found in the ashes: those of her mother, her father, and the barmaid, Trix Hawley. Or so Lillian has always thought. But when Lillian and Duane put their stories together, the past erupts into a wild enigma.

As the two friends travel—accompanied by the tenacious crime writer Minerva LeBlanc—to the underbelly of Las Vegas to find the truth about their parents, Lillian must face the demons of the past in ways she never dreamed possible.

Shop here: http://www.amazon.com/Lucky-Stiff-Lillian-Series-ebook/dp/B0058KBVZA

Easy Street [#4]

Lillian Byrd's battered Caprice is convulsing through the last of its death throes; her pet rabbit, Todd, ails; and as usual she's single—and flat broke. For a few extra bucks she signs on to help an old friend, retired police detective Erma Porrocks, renovate her house, but of course nothing ever goes smoothly in the life of Lillian Byrd. The end of her first day on the job yields a partially demolished wall, a mysterious stash of cash, and a fresh corpse. And Lillian's attentions are diverted by the appearance of a drop-dead gorgeous neighbor.

Nonetheless, Lillian throws herself into chasing down every complex thread, especially after Porrocks is injured in a suspicious accident. The action ranges from Porrocks's Detroit riverfront neighborhood to a nursing home in Cleveland, where Lillian and Todd pose as animal therapy workers to shamelessly coax information from an elderly resident. From there Lillian goes undercover to Boise, Ft. Lauderdale, and points beyond, facing deception and danger the whole way—as well as the bewildering emergence of her own dark side.

Shop here: http://www.amazon.com/Street-Lillian-Crime-Series-ebook/dp/B005D9DS4S

Left Field [#5]

Lillian Byrd has been searching her soul after the gut-wrenching experience of killing someone in self-defense. Scrabbling to make ends meet, she takes a job as a quasi detective, solving life's little mysteries for a pair of eccentric women in one of Detroit's last prestigious neighborhoods. When she spots a corpse on the next-door lawn, she jumps back into honest work as an investigative journalist.

Her friend Mercedes reveals that the dead woman, Abby Rawson, played on a women's softball team she manages and pressures Lillian into taking her spot. Softball turns to hardball when Lillian not only plunges into a love affair with the team's sought-after pitcher but also goes undercover as an exterminator, a squatter, and a charity worker to investigate Abby's death and the corrupt medical organization she worked for. No one on the team is above suspicion, and as they get closer to snagging the coveted championship title—and Lillian gets closer to discovering the dark truth behind Abby's murder—she fights to keep her new love in her life and literally save her own.

Shop here: https://www.amazon.com/Left-Field-Lillian-Byrd-Crime-ebook /dp/B00RHDD6YU

Tight Race [#6]

For once, life is good for Lillian Byrd: She's working as the media liaison for Detroit mayoral candidate Leon Sorrel, and getting paid for it, too! But she's courting danger by conducting a torrid affair with the married campaign manager, Marie Chamberlain. After discovering Marie and her husband dead in a catastrophic double murder, Lillian lands in a soup of suspicion, and Sorrel's in trouble too.

Sorrel's opponent, the incumbent mayor Andromeda Jacobs, isn't above using dirty tricks to win, aided by a crooked cop and a venomous gossip columnist. When the lead detective on the murder investigation tightens the vise on Lillian, she has no choice but to square off against powerful enemies, seen and unseen, to clear herself and get Sorrel's campaign over the finish line.

Lillian's old pal Flora Pomeroy uses her connections among the city's A-listers to outmaneuver their enemies, while the dashing DPD Lieutenant of Internal Affairs, Anna Hughes, employs hardball strategies to advance the murder investigation.

But when Mayor Jacobs surprises Lillian by asking her help in locating her missing daughter, the threads start to come together. And as Lillian and Anna grow closer, their challenges mount, and suddenly their lives are on the line. Can they confront the killer, rescue the mayor's daughter, and stop the chaos before the election?

Shop here: https://www.amazon.com/Tight-Race-Lillian-Byrd-Crime/dp/B09Q4DXV5J

More Fiction

Crimes in a Second Language

Elnice Coker and her husband Arthur, retired schoolteachers, move from Indiana to the Hollywood Hills in a last-ditch attempt at novelty and happiness. California alone can't do the trick, but when Elnice befriends her housecleaner, Solita, her life opens up to friendship and intrigue. Elnice teaches Solita English, although Solita's common-law husband, Luis, is against it. The women build a secret, tentative friendship.

Meanwhile, wannabe novelist Jason M is busy writing faulty information into tech manuals for airplane-making machines at a factory in the Valley. One of a swarm of corporate saboteurs scattered around Los Angeles, he's bossed by a nameless, exacting mentor. But when he begins to have ethical doubts, he discovers it's harder to get out than it was to get in.

The lure of easy money casts its spell over everybody, and as Elnice and Solita grow closer, they encounter treachery and danger where they least expect it. The saboteurs intertwine, innocent lives hang in the balance, and as Elnice risks everything to dig deeper, she learns the value of rejecting safety—and living life to the max.

Shop here: https://www.amazon.com/Crimes-Second-Language-Elizabeth-Sims-ebook/dp/B01N7V0EQB

I am Calico Jones
Four Short Stories

These four short stories are close to Elizabeth's heart. Love stories? Happy endings? Tough breaks? We got 'em. If you're a fan of the Lillian Byrd crime novels, you'll be delighted to finally know what Calico Jones thinks about when she's tied up, awaiting execution at the hands of geopolitical terrorists. Regrets? She's had a few. The three other stories explore a range of lesbian experience from wacky to warm, from heartbreak to hilarity. Says a reviewer: "You'll laugh, you'll cry, you'll want to go camping." We might add, you'll never feel the same standing in front of a bank teller again.

Shop here: http://amzn.to/1HIOjDn

Go-Go Day

Four Literary Tales with a Dash of DARK

If a story by Flannery O'Connor and a story by Chuck Palahniuk got together and had kids, they would be these intense, bitingly sharp tales. Elizabeth Sims digs into the heart of humanity, with characters who start out knowing what they want, and end up knowing what they need. Their paths are rutted and dangerous. In "Dixon Amiss," a lithograph pressman gets a visit from a couple of guys with a life-changing message for him. Regina, a routinely shamed student in "The Cashmere Club" has a crummy life, but seizes a chance for a strange yet comforting makeover. The manchild at the center of "West Forkton Days" teaches himself a searing lesson about chance, love, and art. And the heroine of "Go-Go Day" yearns to be doted on, yet seeks ultimate liberation on her own terms. These are stories for readers who love to think—and who love life.

Shop here: https://www.amazon.com/Go-Go-Day-Four-Literary-Tales-ebook/dp/B07FWBBBH9

For up-to-date information about everything Elizabeth:

www.elizabethsims.com

Free Starter Pack

Three E-Books by Elizabeth

I love connecting with my readers! Occasionally I send out email newschats about forthcoming work, events, and other this-n-that. If you sign up, I'll send you this free e-book collection as a special thank-you:

- *Deep Trouble,* a novelette featuring Lillian Byrd, my alter ego and heroine of the Lillian Byrd Crime Series.

- *Nine Fast Character Hacks,* a brief for writers on how to efficiently write compelling characters. Even if you're more a reader than a writer, you might find this piece an enriching behind-the-scenes glimpse.

- *The Lake Effect,* a personal essay about being a writer from the Midwest.

Here's an easy sign-up link:

http://eepurl.com/zvM1j

You can also get to it on the front page of my secure website:

https://www.ElizabethSims.com

You'll never be spammed. And every email has an easy unsubscribe link.

THANKS

I'm indebted in the writing of this book to my friends and family, as usual. To my readers, warm gratitude, as always.

My profound appreciation goes to these faithful beta readers for their generous story analysis and advice: Joan Verizzo, Kathleen Cristman, Kendra Pecci, Marcia Burrows, Marjorie Scott, and Ryan Van Cleave.

I'm obliged to the Office of the Mayor of the City of Detroit, the Detroit Police Department, and the Wayne County Road Commission.

Special thanks for expert advice and assistance to Capt. Joan Verizzo, ret., Sarasota County Sheriff's Office.

My deepest gratitude goes, as always, to my beloved Marcia.

Made in United States
North Haven, CT
10 April 2025

67794088R00207